THE KING'S OWN VIRGINIANS

D1528807

COVER

Oil painting by Jim Hofley

Also by Lenny Bernstein

The Great Rebellion:
Book One of The Autobiography of William Watson

The King's Own Virginians

BOOK TWO OF
THE AUTOBIOGRAPHY
OF WILLIAM WATSON

LENNY BERNSTEIN

KIMBERLY CREST BOOKS • ASHEVILLE, NC

Kimberly Crest Books

This is a work of fiction. Apart from well-known people, places and events that figure in the narrative, all names, characters, places, and incidents are products of the author's imagination or are used fictitiously. Any resemblance to current events or locales, or to living persons, is purely coincidental.

THE KING'S OWN VIRGINIANS

Book Two of The Autobiography of William Watson
Copyright © 2017 by Lenny Bernstein

Copyeditor: Nicole Ayers (www.ayersedits.com)
Cover art: Jim Hefley and Double Exposure Art
             (www.doubleexposureart.com)
Interior design: Doug Gibson
             (www.douggibsonbookdesign.com)
Author photo © 2016 Michael Mauney

Kimberly Crest Books, Asheville, NC
Contact us at www.kimberlycrestbooks.com

ISBN: 978-0-9861932-3-1

Printed in USA

Dedicated to the British riflemen who served in the Peninsular War—
arguably the best soldiers of their time. The King's Own Virginians could
not have been created without their example.

THE KING'S OWN VIRGINIANS

In my introduction to the first book of eighty-year-old William Watson's autobiography, I described how I found his manuscript in a chest in a derelict barn in Wellington County, Tennessee, and transcribed it into modern North American English. The document was so long that I divided it into three books, each of which I gave a title. The only changes I intentionally made were to break Watson's tale into chapters and split his page-long paragraphs and hundred-word-long sentences into more readable lengths. This book is the second third of his saga. Since this part of Watson's story mentions many locations that many readers will not recognize, I have also included four maps to clarify the geography.

In the first book, Watson told how the Great Rebellion of 1775 and 1776 left him an orphan—how as a thirteen-year-old schoolboy from Graves End, a small village ten miles from New York City, he joined the rebels rather than live with his grandparents—and how he was captured with the rest of George Washington's army after they were defeated at the Battle of Trenton. Watson was protected by Donald Mackenzie, a backwoodsman, who took him along when he escaped captivity. The two worked in Philadelphia for two years, then made their way to Salisbury, North Carolina, where Daniel Boone taught Watson fur trading and deer hunting. Watson fell in love with Jenny Cartwright and would have married her had he not gone on one last fur trading expedition and ended up a prisoner of the Spanish for four years. He lived with the Cherokee for two years after that, married Awinita, and was happily looking forward to family becoming a father. Awinita died giving birth to their first child, a son that Watson could not raise. He returned to Salisbury to find that he had fathered another son whom he never expected to see.

Watson spent the next eighteen years as a shopkeeper in Davidson's Fort, the westernmost settlement in North Carolina. He developed a gambling addiction, fell into debt as a result of being cheated, and embezzled money from his employer. Book One ends with Watson joining the British Army to escape the consequences of his crime.

The events Watson writes about occurred over two centuries ago and have faded into the historical background. I remember studying them briefly in school, where the Great Rebellion was dismissed as a regrettable incident in an otherwise amicable relationship between Britain and her North American colonies, but not giving any thought to them afterwards. However, since finding Watson's manuscript I have become fascinated by the times in which he lived. I have read widely and found nothing that contradicts Watson's story. The candour with which he reports his occasionally less than admirable behaviour leads me to believe that he is truthful about his personal life. But read his story and draw your own conclusions.

Watson's formal education ended when he was thirteen, but he is a surprisingly literate author with an excellent vocabulary. Like many men of his era, he was self-educated. When books were available, he read voraciously. Since he wrote his autobiography when he was eighty, he had a lifetime of reading to draw upon.

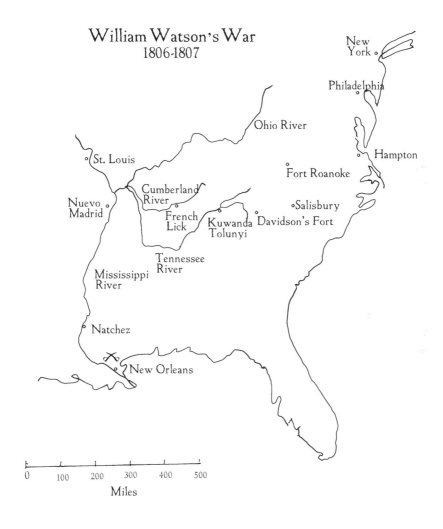

William Watson's War
1806-1807

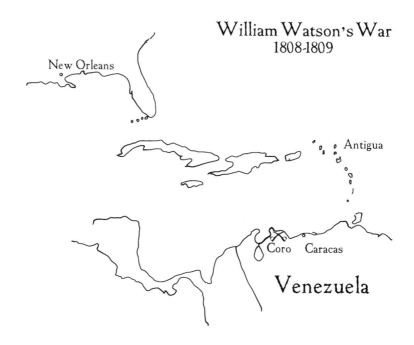

William Watson's War
1808-1809

New Orleans

Antigua

Coro   Caracas

Venezuela

0   250   500   750   1000

Miles

William Watson's War
1810-1812

Spain

Portugal

River
Huebra   ✗ Salamanca
Almeida   ✗
          ✗
Coa   ✗
Bridge   Ciudad
✗ Bussaco Rodrigo
° Coimbra
                              to
                          Madrid →

Lines of Torres Vedras
✗✗ ✗✗✗✗
° Lisbon   ✗ Badajoz

0   50   100
Miles

William Watson's War
1813-1814

CHAPTER 1

On Friday, 11th October 1806, I presented myself to the recruiting sergeant at Davidson's Fort. I took the King's shilling and a five-pound enlistment bonus, swore to serve faithfully, and became a private in the King's Own Virginians, a regiment of riflemen, usually referred to as the Virginians. We were fencibles, whose enlistment contracts obligated us to serve in North America until the French were defeated—not regular army recruits, who served for life and could be sent wherever they were needed, India, Australia, or some equally remote part of the world. I wasn't certain that this distinction meant anything. Britain had been at war with France since 1793, and it seemed like the war would go on forever. I might well have to serve for the rest of my life.

There should've been no need for the British Army to form the Virginians—there should have been no French presence in North America. Britain had ejected the French from the continent in 1763, after winning what has become known as the Seven Years War. A year earlier, anticipating their loss, the French gave their huge colony of Louisiana, the watershed of the Mississippi River, stretching from the Appalachian Mountains to the Rockies, to their ally, Spain. As the victor, Britain could've taken all of Louisiana, but it took only the eastern part, from the Appalachians to the Mississippi. Pitt the

Elder, who was Prime Minister at the time, argued that the western part with its huge distances and hostile Indian tribes would cost far more to govern than it could generate in revenues. Britain left the Spanish in control of the western part of Louisiana and the colony's only town of any size, Nouvelle Orleans. The Spanish renamed the town Nuevo Orleans, but did little else. In 1800, a much stronger France took back the western part of Louisiana, and threatened to use Nouvelle Orleans, as it was again called, as a base to attack Britain's North American colonies. Officially, the Virginians were to protect against a French attack, but everyone believed that their real mission was to again oust the French from North America.

The Monday after I enlisted, five other recruits from Davidson's Fort and I began a thirteen-day journey to Fort Roanoke in Virginia. Since there was no direct road to the fort, we travelled east to Salisbury, then north on the Great Wagon Road. There hadn't been rifles or uniforms at Davidson's Fort to outfit us. I carried a British Army Brown Bess musket and wore my own clothes—a linen shirt, buckskin jacket and pants, and a broad-brimmed Quaker hat, which I only put on when it rained or I needed shade from the sun. The few extra clothes and other items I still owned fit easily into the wicker basket I carried on my back. Mr Henderson had taken my rifle and everything else as partial repayment of the money I'd embezzled from him.

Sergeant Pew, who commanded our little expedition, wore a uniform, the red coat of a British infantryman, not the green of a rifleman. Pew wasn't a martinet. He allowed us to walk and talk rather than marching and maintaining silence. "You'll march enough once we get to Fort Roanoke," he said. I had no doubts about the truth of that statement.

Army Regulations called for us to rest for fifteen minutes after each three miles of our journey. Since we weren't marching and carried far less than fully equipped soldiers, we stopped when convenient—usually by a stream. It was as gentle an introduction to army life as one could imagine, and did nothing to prepare me for the rigours I'd face once we got to Fort Roanoke.

We found quarters each night at a farmhouse or inn. Our hosts were not pleased to see us, since they had to accept the British Army's payment of four pence a head for our food, drink, and lodging, much less than they received from their civilian customers.

I should've been melancholy. Anyone looking at my situation would've said that I'd ruined my life. Instead I was cheerful. I'd embezzled money from my employer, Leonard Henderson, a serious crime, but my punishment—banishment from Davidson's Fort—was almost a relief. Truth be told, it'd been a long time since I'd been happy there. Much had changed during my eighteen years of residence. Davidson's Fort was still the westernmost village in North Carolina, and would remain so as long as white settlement was limited to the eastern slope of the Appalachian Mountains. The other side of the mountains was reserved for the Cherokee and other Indian tribes. Whilst Mr Henderson still called his enterprise a trading post, it had become a general store. Decades of hunting and trapping had killed all the buffalo, elk, beaver, and otter on both sides of the mountains. Only a few deer remained and their skins were usually poor quality.

There was still some ginseng in the woods near Davidson's Fort, but diggers had to spend days collecting the four pounds of roots needed for one pound of dried 'seng. Everyone believed that there was much more 'seng west of the Proclamation Line. But the few brave souls who crossed into Cherokee land had no more success than the diggers who stayed east of the line.

Whilst hunters and ginseng diggers suffered, the farms around the village prospered. Britain needed to import more grain from America. The war with France had greatly reduced her trade with Europe. The price of grain rose, and farmers and their wives had more money to spend. They asked for, and I'd stocked, finer grades of woollen and linen cloth, ribbon with silver or gold trimming, and all manner of luxury items that previously wouldn't have been seen in the shop. In the early days, when the trading post still had fur traders and hunters amongst its customers, I'd enjoyed listening to their tales. There was no such pleasure listening to farm wives complaining about their husbands and children.

Sergeant Pew had been in the army for thirty years. He was grey-haired and limped from a musket ball that had grazed his left hip during the Great Rebellion. "An inch to the right, and I'd have been a cripple," he told us more than once.

"Why'd you join the army?" I asked Pew over a supper of pork stew and cornbread on our first night on the road.

"'Twas simple. My family was starving and I poached a rabbit. The judge could've had me hanged, but he was lenient. He gave me the choice of being transported to America, as one of His Majesty's seven-year passengers, or enlisting in the army for life. I chose the army, and what's the first thing the army did? It transported me to America to fight in your Great Rebellion."

"What's a seven-year passenger?" I asked.

"A prisoner who's been sentenced to seven years' servitude, though few survive to the end of their terms."

Pew told us that whilst he'd not been at Trenton when the rebels surrendered to end the Great Rebellion, he'd been part of General Howe's triumphal march into Philadelphia a week later. I decided not to tell him about my service in the rebel army, though in all like-lihood, he would've laughed at the coincidence.

"Why'd you stay in the army once you got here?"

"I'm regular army, not a fencible like you lads. You'll be discharged after we beat the French. I'm in for the rest of my life or until some officer decides I'm too old and ships me off to Chelsea Hospital. I'd rather die from a French musket ball than face that fate. The hospital is just a warehouse. They keep you there until you die."

We walked all day but had plenty of time to relax in the evenings. As men will do, we took the measure of each other. Gideon Long was easily the strongest, something he proved our third night on the road by quickly winning arm wrestling matches with the rest of us. He forced my arm down in less than ten seconds. Randolph Culpepper was the most argumentative—it didn't take long for the rest of us to start ignoring his acid comments. Manfred Zellenbach was the youngest and looked like he'd only started shaving a few months earlier. At forty-two I was the oldest recruit, and he started asking me questions about army life, even though I knew no more on the subject than he did. Morgan Trotter was an enigma. Tall and taciturn, he looked like he might have Indian blood. He would sit staring into the fire whilst the others of us bantered. Harry Judkins, the last member of our expedition, was a troubled man. He'd lost his wife in childbirth, an experience with which I was all too familiar.

With her gone, he seemed to have lost his will to live. I wondered how he'd survive.

"You six will probably end up as messmates," Pew told us. "You'll fight together, eat together, and sleep together. You'll be closer than brothers, so you'd better get to like each other."

I knew about messmates—most of the men in the rebel army had joined small groups that ate together, but they didn't sleep or fight together. I could easily see having Gideon Long as a brother, and Zellenbach and Trotter seemed sound, but the idea of having to be close to either Culpepper or Judkins was far from appealing. Not that I'd have any choice in the matter.

One evening during the second week of our journey, whilst we were relaxing, Pew surprised us with, "You Johnny Newcombes think you'll be rich, what with your five-guinea enlistment bonus and your pay of a shilling a day. The recruiting sergeant didn't tell you about stoppages, did he?"

"What stoppages?" Randolph Culpepper asked in a querulous tone of voice. He was a skinny twenty-year-old redhead from a farm near Davidson's Fort. I wasn't surprised that he'd asked the question that was on my mind and must have been on the minds of the other recruits. He'd been a rebellious boy and hadn't become any less contrary as he grew to manhood.

"You have to pay for the rifles you'll get, uniform, kit, and meals," Pew answered. "You'll be left with only a shilling a week, if you're lucky and don't have to pay for breaking a rifle or losing a knapsack. And you'll get your money only if your company commander and the paymaster are honest."

"Doesn't the army give you everything you need?" Culpepper asked.

"They don't give you enough rum to ease the pain, or a woman now and then, and a man needs both to survive."

"How do you live on so little money?" I asked.

"There are ways, but you'll have to discover them for yourself. Still it's better than when I first joined the army. We were paid only eight pence a day, and the stoppages could be more than that." Pew paused for a few moments whilst each of us pondered this news. "But cheer up, lads. Some of you'll figure out how to enjoy army life. I have. And who knows, there may be a chance for a bit of plunder after we beat the French. A silver crucifix or a few gold coins can buy you more than one woman and more rum or gin than you can drink."

"You look like a fighter," Pew said to Gideon Long during a rest break the next day. "Think you can best me?"

Long's stature belied his name. Short and solidly built, he looked as if he could absorb the first blow and keep fighting.

"I ain't been in the army long, but I know better than to hit a sergeant," Long responded.

"I'll take off my coat with my sergeant's stripes, then I'll be just another soldier. Surely a strong young lad like you can get the better of a gimpy old man."

Long looked at the rest of us recruits. We smiled in anticipation of seeing a good fight. "No punishment if I beat you?"

"God as my witness, no punishment."

Long put his fists up in the classic boxer's pose. Pew took off his jacket and approached Long, his hands dangling loosely at his sides. Long took a swing, but Pew grabbed his arm and threw him to the ground. Then, in a motion too fast for me to follow, Pew pulled a knife and held it at Long's throat. The fight, such as it was, was over in less than fifteen seconds.

Pew put his knife back in the sheath he had hidden at the small of his back. He pulled Long up and began brushing the dust off him.

"How'd you do that?" Long said, more in amazement than anger.

"That's another thing you'll have to learn for yourself if you're going to survive," Pew replied. "I can't teach you."

"How'd you learn?" I asked.

Pew pointed to his face. "See this scar? Big bugger in my first company give it to me no more than two weeks after I enlisted. Said I was sitting in his place at the mess table. I caught him behind the barracks a few weeks later and cut him up so badly he had to be invalided out of the army. I was sentenced to three hundred lashes for that, but my colonel stopped the punishment after fifty. No one has ever challenged me again." He pulled off his shirt and showed us his back, which was covered with scars from the flogging.

Pew's story hadn't answered my question, but I couldn't ask it again. I felt ill thinking about some brute attacking me, or being flogged for defending myself. No one said anything, so I think I was successful in not showing what I felt. I hadn't thought about these realities of army life when I decided to enlist.

CHAPTER 2

Fort Roanoke had been a simple wooden stockade when I'd first seen it in 1778. Even in 1796 it had only one stone wall. Now it was a classic British fortress, a stone square with diamond-shaped bastions at each corner. There must have been forty gun ports, each with the nose of a twelve-pounder protruding. I wondered why the British Army needed to build such an imposing fortification at the edge of the North American wilderness. Even if the French managed to land an army at Nouvelle Orleans, as they threatened to do, they'd be over a thousand miles away.

The inside of the fort looked as if it was covered in canvas. It normally housed two companies of infantry, two squadrons of cavalry, and gunners for the cannon—fewer than five hundred men—who lived in barracks built into the fort's walls. They were still present, though some of them had been displaced to make room for The King's Own Virginians' officers. In addition, room had to be made for the thousand soldiers and non-commissioned officers who made up the regiment. Tents were packed tightly together, but even so, not all of the Virginians could be housed inside the fort's walls. Since our small party from Davidson's Fort was amongst the last to arrive, we had to find accommodations in the tent village that had sprung up in a field east of the fort.

"Thank God we're going to have cabins," Sergeant Pew said, looking at the construction under way beyond the tents. "It'd be damn cold in them tents once winter comes."

I hadn't thought about the coming winter, but I was rapidly learning that an old soldier like Pew always had an eye out for what few comforts army life provided.

Despite the crowd, Fort Roanoke was orderly. Tents stood in neat lines with narrow streets between them. Small logs or gravel covered the muddy spots. Latrines had been dug and woe betided the man who didn't use one and cover over his droppings afterwards.

I couldn't help but contrast this scene with the encampments I'd lived in during my brief time in the rebel army. They had tents scattered hither and yon and, because so little care was taken to build proper latrines or streets, the look and smell of pigsties. I knew I would have to put aside what I learned in the rebel army, but until I saw Fort Roanoke, I didn't fully comprehend how different life in the British Army would be.

With Sergeant Pew and the other recruits from Davidson's Fort, I was assigned to Captain Meriwether Lewis' Fifth Company. After we signed the company roster, Pew marched us to the quartermasters. Our days of relaxed walking were over.

"Right, you Johnny Newcombes, hand me those muskets," the sergeant behind the counter said without greeting us or identifying himself.

"I signed for this musket at Davidson's Fort," Culpepper said. "I want a receipt to show that I returned it to the army."

"Well, well, well," the quartermaster sergeant said. "What've we here? A barracks-room barrister? Give me any more of your lip and I'll have a receipt written on your back with a cat-o'-nine-tails."

We turned in our muskets without further complaint.

"This is a Baker rifle," the sergeant said, handing one to each of us. "You will be charged a stoppage of two pounds, five shillings for it. Lose it or break it and you will be charged the same amount for a replacement. Now sign here to show that you've received your rifle."

My uniform and the rest of my kit brought the stoppages to four pounds, eight shillings, six pence. That left me with only eleven shillings, six pence from my enlistment bonus, and the quartermaster sergeant said he didn't know when it would be paid. I wondered what other items I would have to pay for out of that money.

The Baker rifle was shorter and lighter than the one I'd given Mr Henderson in partial payment of my debt. I loaded my old rifle, which reached two inches shy of my nose, with a powder from a measure. The Baker only reached my chest and used paper cartridges. After priming the pan with a small amount of powder from a horn, I tore open the small paper envelope with my teeth, poured the powder it contained down the barrel, wrapped the ball in a patch that had already been cut to size, and rammed it home. No more measuring out powder or cutting a cloth patch, and the shorter barrel made ramming easier.

Firing a Baker rifle created as much smoke as firing any other gun. After a few rounds, my face was black. I could clean it with a good scrub, but the rifle marked me in another way. It was impossible to tear open a cartridge with your teeth without some of the gunpowder colouring your lips black. No amount of scrubbing would remove that stain. I had a rifleman's black lips for the duration of my service in the British Army and for many months afterwards.

After a few days, I could load my Baker rifle twice as fast as I'd been able to load my old rifle. I thought these changes would reduce the Baker's accuracy, but I was wrong. I could hit a target at a 150 yards just as often with the Baker as with my old rifle. Some of the Virginians' marksmen could hit a target at 250 yards, a feat I could never match. Even with arms as short as mine, I could load and fire the Baker whilst lying on my stomach, instead of having to stand and present a target to the enemy.

The rifleman's uniform I wore had a short, dark green jacket. Everything else was black, the tight fitting pants, the leather shako hat with a cockade, and the leather belts that crossed my chest and went round my waist. I must've cut a dashing figure, but it took some weeks to get used to the tighter clothes and wearing a hat all the time. Wearing buckskins and going bareheaded had been far more comfortable.

Sergeant Pew, who'd traded his infantryman's red for a rifleman's green, instructed us on keeping our uniforms clean. He said we were lucky not to have white belts like the infantry that needed to be kept clean with constant applications of pipe clay. I didn't pay sufficient attention to Pew. A week later I failed his inspection and earned two hours' punishment detail cleaning latrines. I was more careful after that.

I carried a knapsack on my back and a cartridge box, powder horn, and bayonet strapped to my waist. The bayonet was eighteen inches long and locked onto my rifle. Bayonet charges were an important part of many battles, but the Virginians were used as skirmishers and long-range marksmen and took part in only a few of them. The charges I took part in were sufficiently fearsome that the French broke and ran before I reached them. This was fortuitous, since I doubt that I would've had the courage to stick a bayonet into a French soldier. But maybe I could've done it. When a man's blood is up, as it always is in battle, he can do many things he thinks impossible.

Despite never using it directly against the enemy, my bayonet was very useful for sundry tasks such as cutting firewood or holding a candle upright. A tent, which provided some shelter against the elements, could be made using two blankets, two rifles for poles, and four bayonets for stakes. I made certain that my bayonet was always clean and sharp —sharpening its tip so frequently that I wore it away in four years. I had to replace it, incurring a stoppage of ten shillings. After that I was less zealous with the whetstone.

On my second day at Fort Roanoke, I saw a familiar face.

"Captain Smith?" I asked. He'd lost most of his hair and what was left was gunmetal grey. He'd remained lean, but no longer had the taut body of a young man. Still I was certain it was him.

"It's Private Smith, and who might you be?" He was wearing the single chevron of a chosen man. This marked him as more than an ordinary private—chosen men were usually given special duties, such as being company clerk, and sometimes given command of a few other men—even if the army didn't pay him any better.

"William Watson, sir. I was your messenger for a few days before the Battle of Brooklyn."

"William! I never would've recognised you. You were only a boy then." He looked me up and down, and I remembered how I'd been subjected to a similar inspection thirty years earlier when I told him that I wanted to join his company. "We're both privates, so call me Samuel."

"I was thirteen, you weren't much older."

"I was twenty. There weren't many officers in the rebel army younger than me." He smiled a little when he said that, as if remembering happier days.

"Captain Jackson told me you'd joined the regiment when he passed through Davidson's Fort on a recruiting mission last summer," I said, "but not why."

"It was debtors' prison or the army. Food's better in the army."

Samuel Smith didn't seem like the foolhardy type who would've ended up in debt. "Debtors' prison? What happened?"

"After the Great Rebellion, Mordechai and I formed a trading company."

"Major Gist? I was his messenger, too."

"Yes, it was the major. He told me how you became an orderly for General Washington." Smith paused for a few seconds. "You'll have to give me a moment or two. Telling what happened is still painful."

I waited patiently until Samuel began. "Mordechai and I had a successful business, until he died five years ago." I mumbled my regrets, which he acknowledged with a small nod.

"Two years after he died, I entered a partnership with Abner Nichols. He came highly recommended, but turned out to be a thief. A year ago last fall, just after we'd sold a cargo of fine woods from Brazil, he absconded with all our cash—money we needed to repay the debts we'd incurred procuring the wood. After paying everything I could, I still owed thirty pounds." His shoulders slumped as if he had thirty pounds of weight on them.

"Suddenly the army looked like a good alternative. Captain Lewis snapped me up as his clerk, and I got a chosen man's chevron. What about you? You're a bit old to be joining the army."

I told him about my life since the Great Rebellion and my eighteen years as a shopkeeper at Leonard Henderson's trading post. I didn't tell him about my gambling and the theft that it had led to. I claimed that I'd joined the army out of boredom.

"You always did have an adventurous streak. You could've stayed with your mother and gone to New York City, rather than coming back to your father and the rebels."

I felt pleased when he said that, even if he was talking about the impetuous act of a boy.

We began drilling the Monday after our arrival at Fort Roanoke. Sergeant Pew, who had been so relaxed and friendly during our journey from Davidson's Fort, now became a stern taskmaster. We spent at least four hours each day marching in formation across an empty field just beyond the fort's walls, moving from column to line and line to column, and forming and un-forming the squares we would need to repel a cavalry attack. We learned the difference between loose files, where we were in line formation six inches apart, open order, where we were two feet apart, and extended order, where we were six feet apart. Keeping in a straight line was easy when I was only six inches from the man next to me, but seemed impossible when we were six feet apart.

Once drill was over we worked on building cabins. Since this was work that would directly benefit us, we attacked it with gusto. I'd chopped firewood for my own use in Davidson's Fort, but usually for only a short while. Cutting trees, trimming logs, and hauling stone for the fireplace and chimney for hours at a time left my hands raw and my shoulders aching. Tired as I was at the end of the day, I had difficulty finding a comfortable position for sleeping. I often tossed and turned for what seemed like hours before finally falling asleep, only to be woken by the bugler after a brief rest. My fellow recruits, all far younger men, seemed to have no similar difficulties. Their snores started immediately after they retired. After three weeks my body became accustomed to the hard labour and I, too, was able to sleep without difficulty.

We moved from tents to cabins in early December. The Fifth Company had eight cabins, arrayed in two rows of four. Captain Lewis' smaller cabin was set between these two rows. Each cabin was supposed to house a dozen men — two groups of messmates, including a corporal, who would be the cabin's commander. The Virginians didn't have any corporals—we were told that there'd be promotions from the ranks in due course, but not given any hint of how long that might be.

The six of us from Davidson's Fort became messmates. We had no choice. All of the Virginians who'd arrived earlier had formed groups, and since the quartermasters would only issue rations to groups of six, it was either band together or go hungry. I was wary of Judkins and Culpepper, but neither caused any difficulty during those first months at Fort Roanoke.

Judkins did everything he was told to do, whether by an officer, a sergeant, or one of us messmates. He could've easily been the butt of many a joke, but his sorrowful face prevented most from trying to take advantage of him. The rest of us from Fort Davidson protected him against the few who didn't sense that he was suffering enough without their adding to his burden. Protecting Judkins was the first thing that bound us together.

A few punishment details and the threat of flogging convinced Culpepper to curb his tongue whenever even a sergeant was in earshot. This didn't spare us, his messmates, from his grousing, but we'd already learned to ignore most of what he said.

As the oldest recruit, I was appointed brevet, or acting, cabin commander, responsible for seeing that the cabin was kept clean, that the men stored their kits properly, and that we chopped enough wood for our own fireplace plus a contribution for the captain's fire. I was worried when I was given these duties, but everyone, including Culpepper, cooperated. Had we not, the whole cabin would have been given a punishment detail, and no one wanted to be responsible for having his mates punished.

The cabins were bare. We'd been promised cots, but these didn't appear during that winter. We slept on pine boughs spread on the ground. It took a while to find and chink all of the gaps we'd left in the cabin's walls, but after a few days we were able to keep the cabin warm through the night. Sergeant Pew had to admit that even without cots, we slept in comfort.

An army company should have a captain and two lieutenants. As is still the case in the British Army, officers' commissions are sold first by the army, then by whoever owned them. I remembered discussing, whilst I was an orderly on General Washington's staff, whether the sale of commissions was better than the rebel army's practice of electing its officers. Both systems produced some excellent officers and some truly incompetent ones. But at least the rebel army didn't have twelve-year-old boys as officers, as some British regiments had.

When the Virginians were formed, the army planned to sell only the captains' commissions and transfer lieutenants from other regiments to provide the Virginians with some experienced officers. But only two lieutenants were willing to join our regiment. Both were old soldiers who had been promoted from the ranks for valour during the Great Rebellion. Since they weren't gentlemen, they were never accorded the respect officers should receive. Colonel Whiteside, our commander, kept them as his staff rather than assigning them to companies. Someone had to tell him how a British Army regiment should operate.

We were better supplied with sergeants. Each company had at least one old soldiers like Pew, who'd been transferred from a regular army regiment. Some had two or three, but none had the five that a company should have. In a normal regiment, the shortage of both junior officers and sergeants would've led to disaster, but the dedication of the Virginians was such that we didn't need someone looking over our shoulders at all times.

After six weeks the Fifth Company attained some level of precision at drill. We could march as a company, split to form platoons, split again into half-platoons, move from column to line or squares, then back again. We could load and fire *en masse*, then reload and fire again in much less than a minute. Since we were arrayed in three lines, which fired one after the other, we were able to fill the air with enough lead to keep attackers at bay. Having mastered these basic skills, we felt that a more relaxed drill schedule would have been appropriate, but Captain Lewis kept us at it. He told us that his goal was to have the best company in the Virginians, and that Sergeant McMillan was drilling Captain Jackson's First Company even harder than Pew was drilling us.

"We're riflemen. We're supposed to fight Indian-style, not in a line. All this drill is a waste of time," Culpepper complained one evening as we smoked and relaxed after supper. He received a chorus of yeses and you're rights in support.

"You there, Culpepper," Sergeant Pew began the next morning when we were formed up for the day's drill. "You think that all riflemen have to do is fight Indian-style?"

Culpepper was wise enough not to answer.

"Let me tell all of you. Fighting Indian-style is fine when you're on a scouting mission, or in a skirmish line ahead of the main body of infantry, but it doesn't work if you're up against a column of Frenchmen." Pew looked around to make certain we were all paying attention.

"The crapauds can fire their muskets twice as fast as you can fire your rifles. Sure you'll get off your first round before they're close enough to do you any harm, but whilst you're reloading, they'll close to musket range, then to bayonet range. Your only hope is to form files and fire steadily enough to keep them at a safe distance."

What Pew said reminded me of what Daniel Boone had taught me about fighting Indians. You only had one shot, then you had to fight with a rifle butt or tomahawk. Other men in the company must have come to the same conclusion because I saw nods of agreement. Culpepper was not one of them, but he didn't challenge Sergeant Pew.

We drilled hard that day and won some mild praise from Captain Lewis.

Two days later we were held in formation at morning parade for longer than usual. After fifteen minutes of standing at attention I began to feel the morning's cold. I knew from the coughing and muttering I could hear from some of the soldiers around me that I wasn't the only one suffering. Our uniforms were too thin for a North American winter. I wondered what I'd feel like in February.

Finally, Colonel Whiteside mounted a small platform and addressed us. He was a fleshy man with a florid complexion, a small, bristly moustache under his nose, and a limp in his left leg. He was said to have made a large amount of money as a ship-owner, but each version of the story had a different source for his wealth: slaves, rum, silk from China. The colonel was no orator and some of the more disrespectful Virginians mocked his speaking style.

"Virginians!" the colonel started. "We now, uh, have our orders. We are to march overland, capture St Louis then proceed down river to capture Nouvelle Orleans. When we do that, we will, uh, complete our conquest of Louisiana and add a vast new area to the king's dominion. Three cheers for King George! Hip, hip."

I shouted huzzah as long and loud as anyone. The rumours were true. We were embarked on a historic mission.

General Delancy, commander of the British Army in North America and the author of our orders to conquer Louisiana, couldn't have realised the obstacles we'd face in carrying them out. Fort Roanoke to St Louis is more than six hundred miles, as the crow flies. In 1806, that distance was trackless wilderness, without a single road or white settlement. We'd have to build a road as we went to ensure a steady flow of supplies—we couldn't live off the land the way armies normally did. The few Cherokee or Shawnee villages we'd pass grew only as much food as they needed for themselves. The Indians had no need to grow extra for trade. The British Army bribed them with muskets, cloth, and iron tools to keep the peace. If the Virginians bought or commandeered food, the Indians would go hungry, and if they were hungry, they were likely to attack us. Getting to St. Louis would be difficult enough without having to fight Indians as we went. The army planned to placate the Indians with even more lavish gifts than usual.

St Louis to Nouvelle Orleans is over seven hundred miles, but that trip would be easier. We could build rafts and float down the Mississippi. There were also a few white villages along the river, where small amounts of food might be obtained.

In early January, Captain Lewis called me to his cabin and told me to report to Captain Jackson, who needed a clerk to keep the First Company's records. My many years as a shopkeeper made me the ideal choice. I was promoted to chosen man, but would be paid no more than an ordinary private. I still had to attend parade and drill for two hours each morning, but I was relieved of all other rifleman's duties. Jackson had no difficulty filling the rest of my day.

Part of my responsibility as a clerk would be keeping the company's accounts. I worried that if Jackson ever found out that I'd embezzled money from Mr Henderson, he'd strip me of my chosen man's chevron and send me back to being a rifleman. I didn't know whether I could bear that disgrace. I wasn't given a choice about becoming a clerk, but even if I had been, there would've been no way I could've turned down the position.

My immediate problem was finding some messmates, and I had no idea how to do this. I missed dinner at noon on my first day as Jackson's clerk and was looking forward to missing supper that evening when Sergeant McMillan took pity on me.

"Talk to Private Dixon," he told me. "His mess group has only five members. They can take you in."

"Where will I find Dixon?"

"Do you know where our company's cabins are?

"Yes."

"Dixon should be in the second cabin on the right."

"Thank you, Sergeant. I'll look him up."

I found Harry Dixon in a few minutes. He was a broad-shouldered, fair-skinned man of about twenty-five, who seemed none too pleased to have me join his mess group, which had been together for more than six months. But there wasn't any way that he could say no, since six was the normal number for a mess group and Dixon's was one man short.

I joined my new messmates for supper. The others in the group were Ed Farrell, John Price, Stuart Fox, and Adam McNair. Their welcome to me was no more warm than Dixon's—especially when they found out that I would be a chosen man, and have at least a slightly higher rank than them. I faced the usual interrogation about why I joined the army, and answered with the same lie I'd been telling for the last six months—that I was bored of being a shopkeeper and wanted some adventure.

I moved into the cabin that housed my messmates. Since the cabin had no corporal, Dixon was cabin commander. I could've used my rank as chosen man to usurp that position, but decided that would be a very unwise move. I cut my share of firewood and did my share of keeping the cabin clean without comment. Dixon appeared very desirous of even the small privileges that being in charge of the cabin afforded.

Over the next few weeks, I learned that my other messmates were a varied lot. Ed Farrell had been a farm labourer in the Shenandoah

Valley, and had the powerful arms and legs that such work produced. He was a jovial type who always seemed to have a quip or jest to amuse the rest of us. He wouldn't give a serious answer when I asked why he joined the army.

John Price had been a clerk for a timber factor who'd gone bankrupt. Price was left without a job—his reason for joining the army was obvious. Price had more education than any of my other messmates, and I was surprised that Jackson hadn't chosen him as company clerk.

Stuart Fox was the youngest of my messmates—probably no more than eighteen— and had the tall thin frame of a growing boy. He'd been rejected by the girl he asked to marry him and joined the army in a fit of despair. He'd long since repented his ill-conceived action, but was stuck in the army until the war was over.

Adam McNair, the last of my messmates, was a typical Scots-man—fair-skinned, sandy-coloured hair, and not an ounce of fat on his body. His brogue was thick enough that it took several weeks before I understood everything he said. He was dour and taciturn. I eventually found out that he'd been the victim of a swindle that left him penniless. He joined the army rather than risk starvation.

CHAPTER 3

"Dammit, Watson, we've got to find a way to get the Virginians to St Louis without taking three years to build a road," Captain Jackson shouted out of frustration.

I stood erect, not quite at attention, in front of a map-strewn desk in the one-room cabin that served as Jackson's quarters and office. I'd been his clerk for a month, but was still unsure about what liberties I could take.

"Our orders are to capture St Louis from the French this year, then proceed as rapidly as possible to capture Nouvelle Orleans."

"Wouldn't it be easier to have the navy transport the Virginians to Nouvelle Orleans then march upriver?" I asked. I was taking a chance. Jackson had an explosive temper and I'd already experienced a tongue-lashing from him for speaking out of turn.

Jackson looked at me as if I'd said something as obvious as the sun rises in the east. "Of course, it would be easier to do it that way. But the navy can't spare the ships. The French are building a fleet to invade England. So far the navy's kept them from leaving harbour, but if they get loose, the French'll be marching on London in a fortnight."

"Didn't Admiral Nelson's victory at Trafalgar change that?" I asked. During the past week we'd heard that the previous October, the Royal Navy under Admiral Nelson had destroyed the French and

Spanish fleets at the Battle of Trafalgar. "Shouldn't the Navy have ships to transport us to Nouvelle Orleans?"

"They should," Jackson replied, "but our orders remain the same. Travel overland."

Jackson stared yet again at the maps, such as they were, of Kentucky, Tennessee, and the Ohio Territory. He'd been studying them for the past month. They showed many rivers flowing to the Mississippi, a few Indian villages, and large blank areas. He and the other users of these maps knew they weren't accurate. The rivers existed and would eventually lead to the Mississippi, but they could be full of shoals not indicated on the maps, and the Indian villages might, or might not, be where they were shown.

"Beggin' your pardon, sir, but isn't it Colonel Whiteside's problem to figure out how to get us to St Louis?"

"That pompous old fool couldn't find his way to the jakes without a guide. The only reason he's commander of the Virginians is that he had enough money to buy the commission."

Jackson paced the room. His anger appeared to subside. At more than six feet he towered over my five foot six. Narrow-shouldered and lean to the point of gauntness, he couldn't have weighed more than ten stone. I wasn't fat, but with my broader shoulders, I must've weighed more than he did. He had a long narrow face with sharp features, deep blue eyes, and a mane of sandy-brown hair. Jackson never added any weight to his frame. I wish I could say the same. In the years I knew him I developed a respectable, some might say disrespectable, paunch.

Some of the Virginians said that Andy Jackson, as he'd been known as a young man, had earned quite a reputation as a carouser and a dueller. By the time I knew him, those days were long gone. He was stern, rarely smiled, and seemed to belong in the uniform he now wore, even though he'd never before been in the army—he was too young to have taken part in the Great Rebellion. He'd been a successful solicitor in South Carolina, but gave up his legal practice and bought the first captain's commission in the Virginians. What impressed me the most about him was his great fortitude. He shrugged off difficult marches as if they were mere strolls and never seemed troubled by heat or cold.

"No Watson, if the Virginians are to get to St Louis this year, I'm going to have to figure out how, then convince our good colonel that it was his idea," Jackson said when he finally stopped pacing.

"Have you thought about asking Daniel Boone? He's hunted and trapped all over Kentucky and Tennessee and knows all the Indian trails. Once he's been to a place, he never forgets its location."

"Boone? The stories I've heard about him couldn't possibly be true."

"Some of 'em have grown a bit in the retelling, but there's more than enough truth in them to make him worth talking to. I'll swear to that."

"You know him?"

"Since I was a boy, almost thirty years ago. I went deer hunting and fur trading with him, and he recommended me for the shop-keeper's job in Davidson's Fort you found me in last summer."

"Can you find Boone?"

I relaxed a little, but remained standing. I didn't want to chance annoying Jackson by moving around or sitting. "He's got a homestead near the Yadkin River. It's winter, so he's almost certain to be there. He won't leave until the maple sugaring is over and that's not for another two months."

Jackson smiled for the first time in days. He'd told me more than once how he ached for a chance to win glory fighting the French. Now I'd offered him a way to make that happen.

"Take a horse and get him. Ask him to come see me, and tell him that he'll be well paid for his time and trouble. If he won't come, arrest him in the name of the Crown and bring him here in chains."

"I'm sure that won't be necessary. He swore an oath of allegiance to the King after the Great Rebellion, and Daniel Boone is a man of his word."

"Bring him here as quickly as you can, Watson."

"Yes, sir," I said, before saluting and turning on my heel to leave Jackson's office.

To get to Boone's homestead I rode south on the Great Wagon Road over the mountains into North Carolina, through the Moravian settlements in Wachovia, then west to the Yadkin River. Since it was early February, the trip, which would have taken five days in summer, took seven. Higher up the road was frozen, lower down it was muddy. I was able to find an ordinary, a farmhouse that offered food and lodging to travellers each night and didn't have to sleep rough. Even though they had no other customers, my hosts were not pleased to see me and to have to accept the British Army's meagre payment. I found their food as dreadful as ever, but at least I didn't have to share a bed with other travellers.

I reached Boone's two-room cabin at mid-afternoon. It was set next to a small stream and surrounded by a barn, chicken coops, corncrib, and a smoke house. A gravelled pathway led to the front door. Everything was well tended and prosperous looking.

"Who goes there?" a young boy on the porch said as I dismounted. He pointed a stick at me as if it was a rifle.

I saluted him as if he was my superior. "Private William Watson of the King's Own Virginians on a mission to see Mr Daniel Boone."

"Grandpa, a soldier's here to see you," the boy shouted.

"Thank you, Gabriel. You're a good sentry," Boone said as he came out onto the porch. He was seventy-two. I'd seen him less than two years earlier and knew that the only change the years had brought was that his once black hair was now silver.

"Hello, William," Boone said. "Looks like what I've heard is true. You've joined the army."

"I enlisted four months ago."

"You here on army business?"

"I'm afraid so, Daniel."

"Well, come in and tell me about it," Boone said, waving me into the cabin. His wife Rebecca sat in front of the fire, knitting. I hadn't seen her since I was last at their cabin, eighteen years earlier. Then she'd been a tall, buxom, beautiful woman, even though grey-haired and tired-looking from decades of housework and raising children. Now age had taken its toll. She was white-haired and shrunken. She gave no sign of recognition when I told her my name. Tears formed in my eyes as Daniel slowly explained who I was. It took her a few moments to understand, but when she did, she smiled, welcomed me to their home, then returned to her knitting.

Boone's cabin looked in much better repair than when I had last seen it. The puncheon floor had been replaced and no longer had gaps in which rubbish could collect, the chairs had new caning, and the trenchers and other kitchen utensils stacked on the table were clean. The room smelled of fresh pine boughs. I knew that Boone had a large family and that they all lived nearby. I thought his daughters and daughters-in-law must've been helping with the housework, which seemed beyond Rebecca's capability.

"Have a seat, William," Boone said. "Cup of tea?"

"No thanks," I said, sitting on a stool facing him.

"Why'd you leave that job at Leonard Henderson's trading post I helped you get?"

"It was a good job, and I thank you again for the good character you gave me, but eighteen years is a long time to be doing the same thing." I was telling the truth, but far from the whole truth, and that pained me. Daniel thought highly of almost everyone and I didn't want to diminish his regard for me.

"That's true," Boone said. He paused and scratched his head. "You said you were on army business. What do they want?"

"The Virginians need help figuring out a way to get to St Louis. I told Captain Jackson that you were the best man for the job. Please come to Fort Roanoke with me."

"I'm glad to help, but why can't Andy Jackson come here instead of asking an old man like me to travel over the mountains in the middle of winter?"

"He's got a company to command. He can't just up and leave."

"Well, I've got a wife and family to tend. I can't just up and leave either."

That was not the way I'd hoped our conversation would go. I moved my stool closer to Boone. "Daniel, I'm asking you as a friend."

"And if I say I no?"

"Then I'm to arrest you in the name of the Crown and bring you to Fort Roanoke."

"That ain't what a friend would do."

"I don't want to arrest you. That's why I'm asking you to do this as a friend. Captain Jackson said you'll be well paid for your time and trouble."

The mention of money changed Boone's demeanour. He'd been frowning, but now he had a wry smile. "You know me. I can always use some extra money. I'm still paying off the £60 the court levied against me three years ago."

Boone was one of the most trusting men I'd ever met. He had a long history of co-signing loans or entering business deals with un-scrupulous partners. They would abscond, leaving him with a court judgement requiring him to pay their debts. He could've ended up in debtor's prison, but his reputation for always repaying money he owed kept him from that fate.

Rebecca had said nothing whilst we were talking and seemed to have forgotten that I was in the room. Boone made no attempt to include her in our conversation, but I was concerned. "Who'll take care of Rebecca whilst you're gone?"

"Nathan can see to his mother and the rest of our children live nearby."

As if bidden by the mention of his name, Boone's youngest child appeared. I'd last seen him as a five-year-old boy playing on the cabin floor. Now that he was fully-grown, he looked like Daniel had when I first saw him all those years earlier, about five foot eight and eleven stone, with a large head, blue eyes, and black hair.

"Nathan, I'm ordered to appear at Fort Roanoke," Daniel said. A troubled look crossed Nathan's face.

"Not to worry, son. The army wants me to tell them how to get to St Louis and they're willing to pay. Can't make money any other way during the winter, so I might as well go and earn a few shillings."

The look Nathan gave me wasn't at all friendly, but I decided not to say anything.

"It's too late to start this afternoon," Daniel said. "Will you stay and break bread with us?"

The return trip to Fort Roanoke took another week. Daniel had lost none of his skill as a storyteller and I spent many hours listening to him tell of his encounters with bears, Indians, and white thieves.

"William, you remember the time we went deer hunting in Kentucky?"

"How could I ever forget? Those thieving Cherokee stole our rifles, packhorses, and deerskins." I could feel my face going red with anger as I thought about the incident.

A small smile crossed Boone's face. "I told you then and I'm telling you now. The Cherokee didn't see it that way. They exchanged their British Army muskets for our rifles and gave each of us a blanket for our horses and deerskins. They would claim to this day that all they did was get the better of us in a trade."

"It's not exactly a fair trade when you've got a dozen muskets pointed at you."

"True, but I suspect they leave that detail out when they tell the story."

"Captain Jackson, this is Daniel Boone," I said as soon as we both were in Jackson's cabin.

"Thank you, William. Please remain. I may need your help."

"Mr Boone, it's a pleasure to meet at long last. I've been hearing stories about you for as long as I can remember." Jackson walked from behind his desk, which had been cleared of the maps and papers that usually resided there, and stuck out his hand to shake Boone's.

Boone clasped Jackson's hand briefly, then drew back, as if he hadn't really wanted to shake hands. Jackson left his hand out for a moment before withdrawing it, then returned to his desk.

"Don't believe all the stories you've heard about me. Most of 'em ain't true," Boone said. "But you didn't order me here to talk about stories."

I was surprised that Boone had turned testy and expected an explosion of Jackson's famous temper. Jackson took a breath before continuing calmly.

"I'd hoped that we could have a friendly chat."

"If you wanted a friendly chat, you should've come to my cabin instead of dragging me over the mountains in the middle of winter."

"I'm sorry I couldn't do that. My duties here wouldn't permit me being gone for two weeks."

Boone was silent for a minute, apparently considering whether to be Jackson's friend or adversary. The captain remained standing and patiently waited for Boone to make the next move.

"Call me Daniel," Boone said at last. "The only time I get called Mr Boone is when I'm in court and that always ends up costing me money." He paused to give Captain Jackson a chance to respond, but when no response was forthcoming he continued. "Young William here tells me that you need help figuring out how to get to St Louis. I've been pondering that question for the past week. Got a map of Tennessee? I've been to St Louis twice and can show you two ways to get there."

"William, get the map of Tennessee from the cupboard," Captain Jackson ordered. It took me only a few seconds to find the map. I spread it on the desk, then backed off.

"You need to get to the place where the Holston and French Broad meet to form the Tennessee River," Boone said, pointing to a river junction in north-eastern Tennessee. "The Cherokee call it Kuwanda-talunyi, because of the mulberries that grow there. Always thought it would be a nice place to live, but I guess it floods too often for the Cherokee to build a village."

Boone paused to let Jackson study the map.

I moved closer and joined Jackson staring at the map. I'd been to Kuwanda-talunyi twice on hunting trips during the two years I lived with the Cherokee, but until Boone mentioned it, I'd never given any thought as to why it didn't have a village.

"Pray proceed, Daniel," Jackson said after a half minute.

"From the river junction you have two choices. You can build rafts and float down the Tennessee, but you'll have to portage around the huge shoals at Daguno-hi." Boone pointed to a spot on the long loop the river made through the Yazoo country of western Georgia before returning to Tennessee. I'd never been to the shoals, but had heard many descriptions of how dangerous they were.

"Or you can use the Cherokee trail to French Lick, then float down the Cumberland River," he continued.

"Either way," Boone said, "you'll end up on the Ohio River not far upstream from the Mississippi. When you get to the Mississippi, cross over, and you'll be between Nuevo Madrid and Cape Girardeau, about a hundred fifty miles downriver from St Louis."

"That's not a very direct route," Jackson said.

"No, it isn't. But the straight line is across Kentucky and the Ohio Territory. Can't show you because it's off this map. I've hunted and fur traded all over that area and I don't know of any trails that go the way you want to. Everyone, white man and Indian, uses the rivers whenever they can."

"What do you think, William?" Jackson asked.

"Daniel's right. Rafting down a river is much easier than traveling overland."

Jackson pondered this information for a while, then started measuring the length of the Tennessee River on the map using the tip of his thumb as a ruler. "That river must be six hundred miles long," he muttered when he finished.

"At least that, maybe longer," Boone said. "This map is as good as any I've seen, but the river's never been surveyed. Seemed like it had more twists and turns when I went down it."

"And we'd have to build rafts twice. We can haul our supplies around the shoals, but not the rafts. We won't have Indian canoes we can carry."

"You're right." Boone seemed surprised. He was used to travelling in small groups with packhorses and perhaps a wagon or two. I don't think he'd given any thought to what it would take to move a thousand Virginians and their supplies.

Jackson studied the map for a few moments. "If we follow the Cherokee trail across Tennessee, we'd have to build two hundred miles of road, but it'd be only about a hundred miles on the Cumberland."

"Right again."

"Is there a road to St Louis once we get across the Mississippi?"

"Not a very good one," Boone replied. "The Spanish travelled downriver by boat, but they couldn't pole or row their way upstream, so they built a wagon road on the west side. They called it *El Camino Real*, the Royal Road, but it was full of potholes and washouts when I saw it seven years ago. I haven't been back since the French took over. Maybe they've repaired it."

Jackson asked me to get the map that showed the Mississippi River, and studied it before continuing. "This map shows two towns, Cape Girardeau and Ste. Genevieve, between the Ohio River and St Louis. We'll have to capture them along the way, and there'll be no chance of surprising the French in St Louis."

"You're not going to surprise the French," Boone said in a voice that precluded questions. "The Cherokee or the Shawnee or one of the other tribes will tell them you're coming long before you get to the Ohio. The Frenchies will have plenty of time to prepare a welcome."

"And there's Nuevo Madrid south of the Ohio. Any Frenchmen there will be behind us."

"Unless you start at the Gulf of Mexico, you're always going to have Frenchmen behind you."

Jackson rubbed his right temple as he did when he was thinking through a problem. "You haven't given me any easy choices."

"There's no easy way to St Louis, unless you know how to fly," Boone said, smiling a bit, in what appeared to be an attempt to lighten the mood.

"How do we get to the beginning of the Tennessee River?" Jackson asked, his finger tracing a line on the map from Fort Roanoke into Tennessee.

"That's simple," Boone replied. "There's a good path from Fort Roanoke to Cumberland Gap and the beginning of the road to Kentucky that I built in 1775." He pointed to blank space on the map to indicate where the road junction would be. "My road's overgrown, but you should still be able to find the junction. When you get there, you'll find a Cherokee trail heading south to Kuwanda-talunyi. Should only be about a hundred miles."

"Another hundred miles of road to build?"

"'Fraid so."

"Which way would you go, Daniel?" Jackson asked after another pause.

"I'd go overland," Boone replied without any hesitation, as if he had expected the question. "I like to have my feet firmly on the ground."

"A little while ago you told me that everyone uses the rivers whenever they can."

"Most times that's the best choice, but too many bad things can happen when you're on a wild river like the Tennessee. The Cumberland's pretty gentle. You shouldn't have much trouble with it. Same with the little stretch of the Ohio you'll need to float down."

Jackson straightened up and flexed his shoulders. He'd been bent over maps for the last half hour. "Daniel, William, walk with me for a few minutes. I need to think."

We followed Jackson out of Fort Roanoke and along a path through the nearby woods. He said nothing for about ten minutes until we came to a small clearing, where he sat on a tree stump. Daniel and I remained standing.

"You've told me there's good road from Fort Roanoke to the junction of your road to Kentucky," Jackson said, challenging Boone to disagree.

"That's right, Cap'n."

"From there we would have to build a hundred miles of road to Kuwanda-talunyi and two hundred more to French Lick."

"Right again."

"And from French Lick we can float down the Cumberland and Ohio Rivers to the Mississippi, then take the Spanish road to St Louis."

"Yes, sir."

"And you think this is the best route."

"That's the way I'd go."

"Good," Jackson said as he stood up. "Now all we have to do is convince Colonel Whiteside that going overland is his idea." He rubbed his right temple once more. "Daniel, I'd like you to be our guide. You know the country better than anyone else. We'll pay you well."

"Can't do that, Cap'n Jackson. You'll be away for at least a year and my wife is failing. Plenty of fur traders and Cherokee know the route. You don't need me."

"I could arrest you and make you serve as our guide," Jackson said, dropping his genial manner for the first time.

"You could do that," Boone replied, in a surprisingly mild tone, "but it wouldn't be a good idea. You need to trust your guide. How well could you trust me if all I was thinking about was how fast I could get home?"

Jackson thought for a few moments. I knew he didn't like being opposed, but the truth of Boone's statement must have been as evident to him as it was to me. He took his loss with good grace.

"Well said. Two guineas fair wages for your time and trouble?"

"More than fair."

"Come have supper with us," Jackson said. "You can start back home in the morning."

"Young William going to join us?" Boone asked.

"If you wish." Jackson treated me as a confidant and told me many things that only officers should hear, but he normally drew the line at my being present in the officers' mess or other places off limits to ordinary soldiers.

The Virginians' other company commanders joined us at supper. None of them raised an eyebrow at my presence. They had some of the democratic spirit that pervaded the rebel army during the Great Rebellion.

Colonel Whiteside and his deputy, Major Seabury, were in Philadelphia, consulting with General Delancy, which allowed the company commanders to speak freely. After Boone told them about the route he'd suggested—overland to French Lick, then down the Cumberland and Ohio Rivers to the Mississippi, then along the Spanish road to St Louis— they peppered him with questions about the fortifications and number of French soldiers in the towns we'd have to take. Boone said that the last time he'd been there St Louis had about a thousand people. Ste. Genevieve was a little smaller and the other towns were just villages. There had been only two hundred Spanish soldiers in the area and St Louis was the only town with any fortifications. Since the French would have plenty of warning about our coming, they would have a chance to build stockades and other defences before we arrived, and might even be able to send more soldiers.

"What kind of people live there?" Jackson asked after the military questions had been answered.

"Mostly French, some Spanish, some Germans, and a fair number of English," Boone replied.

"Are they likely to be friendly?"

"The French won't be. Most of them are from families that left Canada after we conquered it in 1759. They support the French revolutionaries. I was in St Louis on 23rd September 1798, the revolutionaries' New Year's Day. The French had a big celebration, even though the Spanish had banned any show of support for the revolution."

"What about the English? Will they help us?"

Boone shook his head. "Don't think so. They're in Nuevo Madrid, the town George Morgan started about fifteen years ago. He was a colonel in Washington's army during the Great Rebellion and never could reconcile himself to being a subject of the King. He collected a group of settlers who felt the same way. The Spanish were happy to have them and gave them free land once they swore allegiance to the King of Spain. They don't pay taxes, but they have to tithe to the Catholic Church. I'm sure that's changed now that the French are in charge, but my guess is that Morgan and his settlers would rather live under a French dictator than King George."

"And the others, the Spanish and Germans?"

"The Spanish won't help. By now they must know that we declared war on Spain over a year ago. Can't tell you about the Germans. The French've conquered most of Germany, but I don't know whether the settlers care. Anyway, there're too few of them to matter."

Jackson had no doubt been hoping we'd have some local allies when we attacked St Louis. Boone's assessment, which we had no reason to question, left him in a gloomy state. He left the table once the discussion ended. The other officers were in no hurry to leave. A jug of whisky appeared. Boone stayed for more than an hour, regaling them with some of his more famous stories.

We said goodbye to Boone the next morning. "Do you want some-one to ride with you?" Jackson asked.

Boone laughed. "Cap'n Jackson, I've been travelling these moun-tains for sixty years. I don't guess I need one of your soldier boys to help me find my way home."

CHAPTER 4

A week after Boone's visit, Captain Jackson summoned me to his cabin. "Colonel Whiteside returned last night and I've been able to show him the wisdom of the overland route," he said, smiling broadly. "We'll start work on improving the path to Boone's Road as soon as the weather warms up a bit. But we need to find a guide for the rest of the route."

"Wouldn't the officers who lead the patrols through Cherokee lands know the trails?" I asked.

"They might, but they're all regular army and regular army officers haven't been helping the Virginians. You'd think we were planning another rebellion rather than trying to fight the French. I want this to be our victory, and I don't want some regular army officer saying that we couldn't have done it without him. You know any fur traders who could guide us?"

I knew there was animosity between the regular British Army officers, who served at the King's pleasure or until they sold their commissions, and the Virginians, who as fencibles served only for the duration of the war and only in North America. But until Jackson said that he didn't want to accept help from a British officer, I hadn't realised the depth of that feeling. I wondered whether the regiment's other officers felt as strongly as he did.

"There hasn't been much fur trade for the last twenty years since the army started giving the Cherokee all the supplies they need," I said. "The only thing left to sell the Cherokee is whisky and I wouldn't trust any of the whisky sellers."

"I should've asked Boone for a recommendation whilst he was here." That was one of the few times I heard Jackson acknowledge an error.

"The only fur trader I still know is Geoff Carlyle in Salisbury."

"Go to Salisbury. Find Carlyle and bring him here. Tell him he'll be well paid for his time and trouble, but arrest him if he doesn't come freely."

"Yes, sir," I said before saluting and leaving Jackson's office. He hadn't heeded Boone's warning about needing to trust your guide, but I wasn't going to remind him.

Geoff Carlyle had been the third member of the fur-trading expedition Josiah Terrill and I undertook in February 1780. We'd planned to trade with the Cherokee, then sell our furs to the Spanish in Nuevo Orleans, as New Orleans was then called. We'd be breaking the law that said all furs gotten in trade with Indians in British territory were subject to a one-fur-in-ten duty and had to be sold to British merchants, but there was very little risk of us being caught. Not having to pay the customs duty, and the higher price we'd get for our furs in Nuevo Orleans, would make our venture far more profitable.

After we had a full load of furs, Carlyle had a change of heart and turned back to Salisbury. Terrill and I continued on, but as we approached Nuevo Orleans, we were warned not to enter the town because of a fever epidemic. Despite my misgivings, I agreed to Terrill's suggestion that we go to Nacogdoches, the nearest village in Spanish Texas, to sell our furs. By the time we got to Texas, Spain and England were at war and we were held prisoner for four years, until the war was over. I spent another two years living with the Cherokee in Tennessee before returning to North Carolina.

I found Carlyle at his farm a few miles west of town. He was still a friendly looking man with a quick smile, but now his hair was turning grey. Geoff was easy to talk to, and I'd found him better company than Terrill. We'd last seen each other for only a few moments eighteen years earlier. He didn't recognise me, but after I explained who I was and that the army wanted to hire him as a guide, he welcomed me to his house.

Most fur traders were poor farmers. They liked the freedom of the woods far more than the discipline of ploughing, planting, tending, and harvesting crops, and took every opportunity to escape what they considered drudgery. Carlyle was no exception. His house and its furnishings were in need of repair. His wife offered me an infusion made from local herbs, rather than the imported tea or coffee a guest would have received in a richer household. We didn't get down to business immediately.

"I guess I was right to turn back to Salisbury rather than continuing with you and Terrill," Carlyle said, as we sipped our drinks.

"You did a wise thing, Geoff. Continuing with Terrill was the worst mistake of my life." That was a lie—stealing from Mr Henderson was the worst mistake of my life, but I wasn't going to tell Carlyle about that.

"Is what I heard true? Did you just leave Terrill's body in the woods?"

"Yes. When the Cherokee found us, Terrill was dead and I was too sick to do anything. I was lucky they didn't leave me there to die."

"That's a hard fate, being left for the buzzards and wolves."

"I know. No man deserves that."

We were both silent for a while. I didn't know whether Carlyle was judging me or just contemplating the injustices of the world. I hadn't thought about Terrill's fate in years, but now the whole story came rushing back: Captain Ortiz releasing us after he found out that England and Spain were again at peace, but giving us only enough supplies to reach Nuevo Orleans . . . leaving Nuevo Orleans without sufficient supplies to get back to North Carolina . . . being in too much of a hurry to get back to Salisbury to hunt . . . deciding that we could eat the dead deer we found on the trail . . . becoming ill . . . falling unconscious and waking to find Terrill dead and four Cherokee standing over me . . . the Cherokee leaving Terrill's body and taking me to their village.

"Tell me what the army wants," Carlyle said. I was so deep in thought that his voice came as a surprise. It took me a moment to answer.

"The Virginians have been ordered to take Louisiana from the French. We're to march to St Louis, take the town, then capture Nouvelle Orleans."

"So the rumours are right."

"They are. Daniel Boone told us the best way to get to St Louis is to take Cherokee trails to French Lick, float down the Cumberland to the Ohio, then down the Ohio to the Mississippi. We need a guide who knows the trails to French Lick."

"I've been on those trails, but it was a dozen years ago," Carlyle said quietly. Then, to counteract any doubt he may have planted, he continued more firmly. "If I can talk to Boone and get some landmarks, I'm sure I'll be able find the way to French Lick."

"We could stop at his homestead on the way to Fort Roanoke," I said, realising that Carlyle was eager to take the job.

"Good. Can't make any money fur trading nowadays, and I haven't made much money from this farm for years. It'd be nice to have a few pounds to fix it up," Carlyle said, looking around his shabby cabin. "How much is the army willing to pay me?"

"I don't know, but Captain Jackson said that you would be well paid." The Virginians had never before hired a guide. I was sure that Jackson would want to bargain with Carlyle.

"Would I have to join the army?"

"No, you wouldn't have to enlist. You'll be free to go after you get us to French Lick."

"Can I take a day or two to get my affairs in order and say goodbye to my wife?"

"That won't be a problem."

Two days later Carlyle and I headed for Daniel Boone's homestead. He and Boone spent three hours talking. When they were done, Carlyle was smiling broadly.

"I can find the way," he said as we mounted our horses and waved goodbye to Boone.

Carlyle quickly charmed Captain Jackson and Colonel Whiteside, who hired him as the Virginians' guide at two shillings a day, twice what I was being paid. He could eat at the officers' mess if he paid the subsistence stoppage. He didn't get the five-guinea enlistment bonus that riflemen received, but he didn't have to buy an army rifle, uniform, and kit. As a civilian, he dressed in buckskin and used his own rifle.

Now that we had a guide, the Virginians were in high spirits and anxious to get underway. Nevertheless, I was troubled and had to ask the question that had been worrying me since I first learned that the Virginians were to conquer Louisiana—how would we get back from Nouvelle Orleans? I couldn't ask Captain Jackson. I knew how he yearned to fight the French and feared that raising any concerns about our enterprise might be viewed as cowardice. I turned to Samuel Smith, the only person I was certain wouldn't think ill of me for such a query.

"How will we return home after we beat the French?" I asked.

"Retrace our steps, I presume."

"We can do that using the Spanish road along the Mississippi, but what happens when we get to the Ohio?"

"We'll have to build a road, just as we'll have to build a road to get to French Lick."

Samuel seemed unperturbed by the prospect of having to build nearly two hundred miles of additional road, and I didn't question him further. A voice in my head kept chiding, "Why are you worried about getting back to Virginia? You've no place to return to and no one to care about you."

CHAPTER 5

On Monday, 24th March, a week after Geoff Carlyle had been hired, the Virginians left Fort Roanoke. Carlyle, Captain William Clark, and the Virginians' Third Company left at dawn to scout the way to French Lick. They were to map and blaze the route, then return. Clark was the best mapmaker amongst the Virginians' officers and an experienced backwoodsman. The rest of the regiment departed at mid-morning. We were to follow Carlyle's route as quickly as we could, building a wagon road as we went.

The good path that Boone had described existed only as far as Christiansburg, about twenty-five miles southwest of Fort Roanoke. After that, it was overgrown with bushes and small trees. Greenbrier and other vines turned them into an impenetrable barrier, harder to clear than full-grown trees, which could be chopped down. In some places the path's route was through flat ground and we could relocate it to a less densely wooded area. But in most places the path was on a shelf cut into the side of the mountain. There we had no choice but to clear the old path bush by bush. It was slow, tedious work and we cleared only ten miles in our first week. Once we got to the junction with Boone's road we would have only Indian trails to follow and the going would be even slower.

About five miles west of Christiansburg, we crossed a small gap between two low hills. It wasn't obvious then, but after a day we noticed that the streams were flowing west towards the Mississippi and the Gulf of Mexico, not east towards the Atlantic. That gap was on the Proclamation Line and we were now on land promised to the Cherokee. Most of the Virginians were wary and kept their rifles close at hand. Jackson and the other officers tried to explain that this was an unnecessary precaution. The Cherokee were not going to attack a regiment of British soldiers. These assurances did nothing to calm the Virginians, most of whom had never seen an Indian.

Being Captain Jackson's clerk meant that I was spared the back-breaking labour of road-building. I had the far easier tasks of keeping the company's records and allocating its rations. Although I wasn't Jackson's personal servant, I also set up and dismantled his tent and did similar chores.

"You're turning into quite the skulker," Adam McNair said to me over our evening meal during our second week on the road. This was a serious accusation. One of Sergeant Pew's first lessons was that skulking, not carrying your share of the load, whether in battle or in camp, was one of the worst crimes a soldier could commit. He'd be letting down his messmates and his company, who soon would want to have nothing to do with him.

Harry Dixon came to my defence. "A man's not a skulker if he does the duties given to him. Watson's smart enough to keep the company's records. Could you do that?"

I was surprised to hear Dixon come to my defence. I still wasn't certain that he accepted me, or that he'd stopped worrying about my taking his position as leader of the mess group away from him.

"What do the rest of you think?" McNair asked, looking at our other three messmates for support. "We bust our backs chopping out a road, whilst Watson pushes a pen. That sounds like skulking to me."

"Watson's following orders, just the same as we are," John Price said. "He's lucky enough to have light duty. I'm not going to begrudge him that." Farrell nodded in agreement. Fox said nothing. McNair had lost, and he knew it. He looked down and began eating his rations.

Colonel Whiteside soon realised that at the pace the regiment was building road, it wouldn't get to St Louis that year. I was showing Captain Jackson the company's daily report when the colonel entered his tent.

"Captain Jackson, the men have to, uh, work harder," Colonel Whiteside said after returning our salutes.

"Sir, the Virginians are riflemen, not nigger slaves or Indian navvies."

This response must have angered the colonel because his face turned red. "You were the one who suggested this route. You told me that if we used it we would be in St Louis this summer."

"I suggested the route," Jackson said, "but I never said we would reach St Louis this summer."

"You question my memory? I could have you brought up on, uh, charges of insubordination."

"No disrespect Colonel, but I don't remember saying that."

The colonel didn't answer immediately. I wondered whether anyone else had heard the exchange, and if so, what they made of it. Captain Jackson had kept his temper in check, but he was hardly being respectful.

Whiteside glared at Jackson for a few moments. "Since we're committed to this route, what do you suggest to speed our progress?"

"Sir, if we only had to clear a path wide enough for a pack train, the work would go much faster."

"True, but if we are to bring artillery, uh, to support our attack, we need a wider road," Colonel Whiteside said. His demeanour was now calm. This was the first time I'd heard mention of cannon. That would require the help of the regular army. The Virginians had only their rifles and bayonets, a few pistols, and the swords their officers carried. None of them were gunners who knew how to load, aim, and fire cannon.

"Artillery?" Jackson asked. He must have been as surprised as I was.

"Nouvelle Orleans and St Louis are fortified. I've told General Delancy the Virginians need artillery if he expects us to capture them."

"And what did the general say?"

"He said he'd talk to General Lawrence who commands the artillery batteries."

Jackson winced. I could almost hear the wheels turning in his brain as he tried to figure out a way to take the towns without cannon, and more importantly, without help from the regular army. "Sir, Boone told us that St Louis' defences are crumbling. We don't need artillery to take the town."

"Yes, but reports are that, uh, Nouvelle Orleans' walls are in good repair. The French will have plenty of time, uh, to strengthen St Louis' defences once they hear we're on the way."

For the first time that I'd known him, Jackson was at a loss for words. Far from being a pompous old fool, Colonel Whiteside had shown he understood the problems the Virginians faced and quickly had seen the flaw in Jackson's suggestion for a narrow packhorse path.

"Sir, let me think about this for a day."

"Very well, Jackson. Carry on."

Captain Jackson didn't come up with a solution in a day, or in a week. The Virginians built only nine miles of road that second week, and there were the inevitable injuries. One rifleman was killed when a tree fell on him. Another nearly bled to death when his axe slipped and cut a large gash in his leg. The men were beginning to complain. They'd joined the Virginians to fight the French, not to work with pick and shovel building a road. Jackson was a strict disciplinarian who had no tolerance for grumbling. If his men were ordered to build a road, they'd build a road.

Other officers in the Virginians were less authoritarian and behaved more like the officers in the rebel army during the Great Rebellion. They listened to their men and relayed their concerns to Colonel Whiteside. The colonel took no action for a few days, then met with his company commanders. Captain Jackson later told me that after two hours they all agreed on the need for a wagon road, difficult as it was to build. The only suggestion for making the task easier was to use slaves from farther east, but that would require army funds to pay their owners. Colonel Whiteside said he would ask, but doubted the money would be forthcoming.

There were few secrets in the Virginians and when word got out that Colonel Whiteside was going to try to hire slaves to build the road, work slowed to a crawl. Jackson and the other company commanders exhorted, cajoled, and threatened, but to no avail. We completed only three miles of road in our third week.

"I don't like being dependent on the commissary officers at Fort Roanoke," Sergeant McMillan groused. He was an old soldier, who'd been in the army for over twenty years— not long enough to have served in the Great Rebellion, like Sergeant Pew. He'd served in North America for over a dozen years, and was one of the veterans transferred to the Virginians to train us in army ways.

"Why not?" I asked. We were getting our full rations, a pound of meat, a pound of biscuit, and a quarter pint of rum each day, and even some tea and sugar. "I'm eating well."

"But what if the quartermaster decides to stop sending us our full rations, or a wagon master decides to sell part of his load? No way to get any food out here in the wilderness. We'd starve."

I didn't want to provoke McMillan. I chose not to tell him that many in the Virginians knew how to live off the land and that there was no reason for us to starve. Even though he'd been in North America for many years, I doubted he would believe me. The British soldiers I'd met at Fort Davidson showed no interest in learning frontier skills. That would've been seen as going native and losing status. Whether they were English, Scots, or Irish, they saw themselves as superior to the Cherokee and other tribes. They scoffed at men like Boone, calling them white Indians in a derogatory fashion. Frontiersmen used the same term, but as one of high praise.

On Monday of our fourth week of road-building, as I was standing near Captain Jackson's tent, Private Morrison from the Second Company sidled up to me. I knew him slightly. He was an unpleasant fellow, about forty-years-old, skinny, and none too clean in his personal habits. His eyes always seemed to dart about as if he was afraid that someone might sneak up on him.

"A word in confidence, Watson?" he said.

"If you wish," I replied, trying to fathom his intent.

"They say that you've Captain Jackson's ear and that the captain 'as Colonel Whiteside's ear. I can tell you something that will make you look like an 'ero in their eyes."

"Captain Jackson doesn't suffer fools lightly, but if you have something important to say, he'll listen. Tell him yourself."

Morrison didn't respond immediately and I started to walk away.

He took hold of my arm to stop me from leaving. "Can't tell 'im, cause of the way I learned it."

"I don't understand what you're saying," I said, removing his hand from my arm.

"You'll understand, once I explain, but you've got to swear you'll tell Captain Jackson you won't tell 'im where you 'eard it."

"And if I don't swear?"

"Then I'll find someone else to tell an officer and 'e'll get the glory."

Unsavoury as Morrison was, he seemed to be telling the truth, so I agreed to his terms.

"We don't need to work ourselves to death building a road for cannon," Morrison said. "We can use rockets that can be carried by packhorses."

"Rockets? Like fireworks?" I was incredulous. Fireworks could burn you, but they couldn't knock down even the flimsiest wall.

"I guess you could call 'em giant fireworks, but Tippoo Sultan's army caused us more than a little grief with 'em."

"You were in the Indian Army?"

"I was. That's why I can't talk to any officer. It was the King's pleasure for me to serve for longer than I wished to."

"If you deserted why'd you join the Virginians?

"Seems like army life is the only life I'm suited for. I reckoned I was safe in the Virginians, that nobody'd recognise me from India."

I decided not to question Morrison further about his desertion from the British Army. "What did the Indian rockets look like?"

"'Em rockets was iron tubes packed with gunpowder. They was mounted on a long bamboo pole. That rocket would come flying through the air like a giant spear and go right through two, maybe three, men. Some of 'em 'ad iron blades that 'ould spin around like scythes. Some of 'em was just an iron tube that'd cut through a company like a cannon ball. They did us fearful damage."

"Why are you telling me this now? You could've told someone whilst we were still at Fort Roanoke."

"Yes, but they probably won't 'ave listened to me. Now that they know 'ow 'ard it is to build a road, they'll listen."

It didn't take any great thought to see that Morrison was right. "But how would we get rockets?" I asked.

"That's the beauty of it. Back at Fort Roanoke I 'eard one of the sergeants saying that they're making 'em at Woolwich Arsenal, back in England."

I waited until I could be alone with Captain Jackson to tell him what Morrison had said about rockets and the damage they had caused the army in India.

"Watson, this is the solution to our problems. If all we have to build is a packhorse path, we can be in St Louis by fall and without the help of the regulars." He was so enthusiastic that he didn't ask me how I had learned about rockets.

"Will Colonel Whiteside agree?"

"Of course he'll agree. There's no glory for him unless we get to St Louis this year. Let's see him now."

We found the colonel in his tent writing a report. He looked up as we entered the tent and saluted.

"What is it, Jackson?" he asked.

"Sir, my clerk Watson has some information that might interest you."

The colonel looked at me for a moment as if he was having trouble placing who I was. "Very well, Watson. What've you, uh, got to tell me?"

I quickly relayed what Morrison had told me.

"Very interesting. How did you learn this?"

"One of the soldiers told me."

"His name?"

"I'm not at liberty to say, sir."

"I could have you flogged." That prospect was frightening and I thought for a moment about naming Morrison, but as a deserter, he would be executed by firing squad, and I didn't want that on my head.

"But I won't," the colonel continued after a few tense moments. "It's the information that's important, uh, not its source. You know, I read someplace about the difficulties the army had in India because of rockets. Can we take your fellow's word that Woolwich Arsenal is producing them?"

"I don't know, sir. You could send a messenger back to Fort Roanoke to ask."

"I could. Would you like that task, Watson?"

"If it's the colonel's wish, I'd be pleased to."

"Done. Ride back to Fort Roanoke. Find out what you can about rockets. Captain Jackson will give you your orders. Until you return we'll keep this talk private. The men will continue building the road."

"Yes, sir," Jackson and I said in unison.

I left early the next morning and was in Fort Roanoke before nightfall. I presented my orders to Lieutenant Abelson, the officer of the day, who immediately deduced that Artillery Sergeant Guthrie was the source of Morrison's information. It took only a few minutes to find him at his station by the cannon on the fort's west wall.

"Sergeant," the lieutenant began, "this man has been sent to find out about rockets. Tell him what you know."

"Be happy to, sir," the sergeant said saluting. "I was at Woolwich Arsenal when Colonel Sir William Cosgreve started working on rockets."

"How big are they?" I asked.

"They come in three sizes. The largest is a thirty-two-pounder." Guthrie spread his hands about two feet apart to show me the size of the rocket. "There's a twenty-four- pounder and a twelve-pounder."

"So a packhorse could carry five or six of the heavy ones."

"Easily."

"How good are these rockets?"

"The heavy rocket strikes with the force of a twelve-pound cannon ball, but it doesn't bounce like a cannon ball. Still it can cut through infantry or knock down a wall."

"If they are so good, how come we don't have them here?"

Guthrie lowered his voice as if he were letting me in on a secret. "A rocket ain't like a cannon. They don't fly true. You have to fire off a score or more to be sure that one of them'll hit your target. Colonel Cosgreve, he tried to make a virtue out of this, saying that rockets would scare the enemy more than cannon. But no one believed him. Me, I like to know that when I fire a gun, the shot will go where I aimed it." He smiled and patted the cannon we were standing next to.

"Thank you, sergeant," the lieutenant said, indicating that the interview was over.

Whilst I was at Fort Roanoke I heard about the victory that the French revolutionaries had won over the combined armies of Austria, Prussia, and Russia. Dumouriez was now master of all Europe. Only the Royal Navy stood between us and France's all-conquering army.

I was full of trepidation as I rode back to the Virginians. I was the bearer of bad news and wondered how I'd be treated when I delivered it. Rockets were too inaccurate to be a replacement for cannon. We would have to continue building a wagon road. And the French victory would make it possible for them to send an army to Nouvelle Orleans that would overwhelm the Virginians when we got there.

Captain Jackson and I went to see Colonel Whiteside as soon as I returned. The colonel's reaction to my report astounded me. He was excited about the rockets and dismissed their inaccuracies. He seemed unperturbed by the news that the French now ruled all of Europe.

"The French have beaten the Austrians and Prussians before, but they come back to fight again," he told us. "Russia will do the same. None of those countries is willing, uh, to be ruled by the revolutionaries."

It seemed to me that the colonel was building a fantasy that allowed him to believe that the Virginians could capture Nouvelle Orleans. For the Virginians to succeed, rockets had to be accurate and the French unable to send an army to America. If that was what he had to think, that was what he thought. He was not the first, or the last, officer to deceive himself with a vision of victory.

"Jackson," the colonel said after we finished discussing what I had learned at Fort Roanoke, "convey my compliments to Major Seabury and tell him to prepare for a trip to Philadelphia tomorrow. We need to confer with General Delancy. You'll be in charge here until we return. Tell the men, uh, they can start building a packhorse path. If we're wrong, they'll have to come back and widen it into a wagon road."

"Three cheers for Watson," Ed Farrell shouted after parade the next morning. "He's saved us from being worked to death." Three ragged cheers and many words of congratulations followed. I was embarrassed and could only mumble my thanks and say that I didn't deserve the praise. All I had done was ride to Fort Roanoke and back. Morrison caught my eye and smiled, but said nothing. He'd been right. His information had made me a hero.

The Virginians attacked their work with renewed vigour. We completed twenty miles in the next five days, but then the pace slowed to what it had been. Two weeks later, Carlyle, Captain Clark, and the Third Company returned with a map of the route to French Lick. Carlyle said that they had found the Cherokee trail and clearly marked it. Building a packhorse path would be hard work, but we should face no unusual difficulties. Some of the Virginians began to wager on when we would reach St Louis. Most felt it would be no later than September. I had my doubts. As the old adage goes, "There's many a slip 'twixt cup and lip."

The first of those slips occurred the next week. The pack train arrived with our rations and a letter from Major Michaels, the quartermaster at Fort Roanoke, saying that there were shortages of salt meat and dried cod at Fort Roanoke and he could no longer supply them to us. He promised to supply us with additional peas, beans, and maize to make up the shortage and suggested that we hunt for fresh meat. He closed by assuring us that our rum ration wouldn't be cut, the only good news in his letter.

"That misbegotten son of a pox-ridden whore," Jackson swore when he read the letter. "Watson, don't let the pack train return to Fort Roanoke until I have a chance to write a reply. How do they expect the Virginians to both hunt and build a road?"

I didn't see Jackson's reply to Major Michaels, but from the oaths I heard emanating from his tent it must have been a masterpiece of invective, certainly not likely to make the quartermaster more amenable to providing us with meat.

Jackson cut our meat ration, normally a pound a day, in half.

"You were right to worry," I told Sergeant McMillan, the next time I saw him.

"Won't be the first time I've had to go without meat," he relied. "Just as long as they don't cut the rum ration. Can't expect the men to work without their rum ration each day."

Sending out hunting parties wasn't a problem. The hunters were overjoyed at a respite from road building, but every man out hunting was one less advancing us towards St Louis. Jackson ordered the other company commanders to choose hunting parties and gave each company a direction in which to hunt. All of the officers claimed they had chosen their best hunters, but those left to work on the road saw favouritism in the selections, and grumbled about it—the first serious discord amongst the Virginians.

For a few days there was enough game for all hunting parties to bring home a kill—bear, deer, or turkey. Every one of the Virginians had meat with his evening meal, but not always the full half pound he was supposed to receive. Some hunting parties, including the First Company's, were more successful than others, which meant that their companies ate better. Jackson was accused of taking the best hunting area for his company, adding to the regiment's discontent.

All of this intense hunting scared away the game, and by the end of a week, some hunting parties returned empty handed. No one went hungry—Major Michaels had sent extra supplies of maize and dried pea soup—but discontent rose to such a level that Jackson had to order that all meat the hunters brought back be shared amongst the whole regiment. Any hunter found withholding meat from the common pot would be flogged.

"Damn your eyes, Watson," Private Edwards hissed as we stood in morning parade, "couldn't you have kept Captain Jackson from talking about flogging? Now the other officers'll have the same idea."

"I'm just a private like you are," I replied. "What do you expect of me?"

"They say you have his ear and he listens to your advice on everything."

"They're wrong. Captain Jackson's his own man. He makes up his own mind."

"Then tell him that the First Company will mutiny if he tries to flog any of us."

I repeated what Edwards had told me to Captain Jackson without mentioning his name and got the expected reply. "You tell any man who mentions mutiny that mutineers are shot, and that I'll be more than happy to give the order to fire if he rebels."

Being a courier between Captain Jackson and the men of the company wasn't a happy position for me. I decided that Edwards and the others already knew the punishment for mutiny, and that harmony would be better served if I didn't convey Jackson's message. In the end, none of the hunters were accused of withholding meat—it's hard to hide a deer or turkey carcass—and talk of flogging and mutiny died down. But a distance had been created between me and the men of First Company. They stopped talking and joking when I approached, as if I were an officer, even though I was only a chosen man. I was not happy with this state of affairs, but could see no way to change it.

Men began deserting a week after some of them went meatless. They disappeared in twos and threes, not in scores or even hundreds as had been the case in the rebel army. Private Edwards was amongst the first to leave. Randolph Culpepper, who'd been part of my first mess group and complained about the army from the day he enlisted, left on the third day. Jackson took no action for five days, until company reports showed that more than a dozen men had deserted.

"Soldiers, you took an oath to serve King and country until the French are beaten," he told the Virginians at morning parade. "I expect you to honour that oath, no matter what the hardships. And I remind you that desertion is a capital offence. Desert and we'll hunt you down and hang you, no matter how long it takes. Now return to your duties."

Jackson's speech did nothing to assuage the Virginians' unhappiness, and the desertions continued for another ten days until some fifty of the most discontented had left. The rest, even some of the grumblers, stayed—some, like me, out of a sense of duty— others because of Jackson's threat—but most because, difficult as life in the Virginians had become, their prospects outside the army were even bleaker.

Despite his threat, Jackson did nothing to pursue the deserters. Trying to track them through the forest was a hopeless task. He listed their names in a report he had me prepare to be sent back to Fort Roanoke, but I don't think he expected the army to search for them.

"Good riddance to those bloody whingers," he told me after a week with no further desertions. "The regiment is better without them."

I agreed with him, but couldn't say so.

Colonel Whiteside returned three weeks after Jackson's speech. He looked disheartened and Major Seabury was not with him. Jackson's report did nothing to cheer him up. In his seven-week absence we'd progressed only a hundred miles and still hadn't reached the North Carolina border. The colonel had stopped at Fort Roanoke and knew that we were no longer being supplied with meat. He'd argued with the quartermaster but to no avail.

After listening to Jackson's report on what had happened in his absence, the colonel assembled the regiment.

"Virginians, it is not, uh, usual practice for officers to share their discussions with their superiors with the men they command. But

since I am certain that all of you know that Major Seabury and I
went to Philadelphia to request rockets for our assaults on St Louis
and Nouvelle Orleans, I will break with protocol and tell you what
General Delancy told me."

I was as stunned as any of the other Virginians. The colonel had
never talked this way before. There was absolute silence as we waited
for him to continue.

"General, uh, Delancy is familiar with rockets. When he decided to send our regiment to conquer Louisiana, he requested rockets
for our use. Woolwich Arsenal told him that their whole production
was to be used in Europe, but they sent plans for the rockets and
told General Delancy to arrange to have them manufactured here
in British North America. Rockets are simple devices. They need
an iron tube and high quality gunpowder. Before the major and I
arrived in Philadelphia, General Delancy's staff had determined that
the ironworks at Andover Forge in New Jersey could make the rocket
tubes, and that the gunpowder could be supplied by a French *émigré*
named DuPont from his plant on Brandywine Creek in Delaware.
These two enterprises will work together to manufacture the rockets
we need before we reached St Louis. Major Seabury stayed behind
to make the necessary arrangements."

"Three cheers for Colonel Whiteside," someone shouted. It was
immediately followed by three loud huzzahs. The colonel, who'd
never before been cheered by the Virginians, seemed embarrassed.
He coughed a few time, then retreated to his tent.

The simple way in which the problem of procuring rockets had
been solved seemed too good to be true, and the Colonel's demeanour over the next few days confirmed that he was worried about
something.

"Why does the colonel seem so unhappy?" I asked Captain
Jackson. I expected him to tell me that it was none of my business,
but he was surprisingly forthcoming.

"The colonel knows that rockets are highly inaccurate," Jackson
said, "and he is worried that the ones that will be manufactured here
will be even less accurate than the ones Woolwich Arsenal makes."

"Why should that be? Our craftsmen are as good as those in
England," I responded.

"Probably true, but that doesn't stop the colonel from worrying. He
knows that if we are successful, he'll be a hero, probably be knighted.

But if we fail, he'll be considered incompetent and a laughingstock. Can you blame the man for worrying?"

CHAPTER 6

Two weeks later we reached the ruins of the station that Joseph Martin built in 1775 as a resting place for travellers on their way to Kentucky. Since it was west of the Proclamation Line the British Army burnt it in 1777. The stonework of five fireplaces and chimneys protruded through the trees and undergrowth, and bits of glass and pottery could be found on the ground. We camped there for a night. Some of the Virginians were intrigued by the ruins and spent the available hours of daylight scouring the ground near the chimneys for thirty-year-old artefacts. But others, like Captain Lewis, were dismayed.

"So much work for naught," he said to no one in particular. "Didn't Martin and his band know that they were breaking the law and would be punished?" He sat down on a rock near one of the chimneys and held his head as if he were in pain. After a few minutes Samuel Smith shook his shoulder and suggested that he retire to his tent. Lewis complied, like a small child being told to go to bed.

The Virginians reached Cumberland Gap and the junction with Boone's road a week after that. After three months of road and path building we were stronger and more fit for the work than when we'd started, but it was now late June and the days were much hotter. We advanced only five miles that next week. A dozen men collapsed from the heat. Since we were eating fresh meat instead of the salted meat that normally would have been in our rations, we needed more salt to deal with the weather. I knew where to get it.

"Captain Jackson, sir. There's a salt lick in Kentucky about three days' ride from here. I was there with Daniel Boone twenty-five years ago. I think I can find it."

"That's the best news I've had in a while. What would you need to bring back enough salt to get us to French Lick?"

"I'd like Geoff Carlyle, five other men, and four packhorses. We'll need shovels to dig the salt, kettles to boil it, sacks to bring it back, and two weeks' rations."

"Done. Take your messmates. You can leave tomorrow morning. Meantime, I'll see what I can do about convincing the colonel to give the men a few days' rest."

As soon as we were away from the Virginians' camp, Carlyle started questioning me. "How we going to find this salt lick?"

"We'll go back to Boone's road, follow it for a while, then ride west for a day to a cave at the base of a limestone cliff. The salt lick is about a mile from there." I was taking a chance. My memory for places was not as good as Boone's, but I thought if I got anywhere near the lick, the paths made by deer and bear would lead me to it.

"You sound very sure of yourself."

"We set up camp there when I went deer hunting with Boone."

"My going to be blamed if we come back empty handed?"

"Don't worry, Geoff. If anyone gets blamed, it'll be me. I asked for you because you know the forest."

If I failed to find the salt lick, my reputation with Captain Jackson would be tarnished, but I thought that would be the worst of it.

We backtracked to the junction with Boone's road, which was completely overgrown and impassable. But you could tell where it had been because the trees that grew on it were shorter than the surrounding forest. If we stayed in the woods a bit to the side of where the road had been, we could slowly follow its path. The difficulty lay in deciding where to turn west. Boone had followed his road for a day on our expedition, whilst it was still passable. I decided that since we were going much slower, we'd follow it for two days. It was a good decision. The day after we turned west, we came to the limestone cliff near the salt lick. It took two hours of searching to find the cave that Boone had used as a campsite, but only a short while after that to find the salt lick, a large area of salty soil.

To get pure salt, we shovelled the salty soil into a kettle and filled it with water to dissolve the salt. Then we poured the salty water into another kettle and boiled off the water.

On our third day of work, John Price, who'd been cutting firewood a few dozen yards from camp, shouted, "Indians." The rest of us grabbed our rifles and ran to join him.

Four Cherokee were riding slowly towards us. I recognised Us-ti-waya, their leader, a man of about sixty, who had a scar on his left cheek and wore the markings of the Blue Clan. He had been the leader of the hunting party that found me near death after eating tainted deer meat. The other Cherokee wanted to leave me to die, but he convinced them to take me back to Tuskeegee, their village. I owed my life to him. He was also the uncle of my Cherokee wife, Awinita. Since Awinita had no older brothers, Cherokee custom made him responsible for teaching my son Onacona the skills men need. I owed him a debt of gratitude I had no way of repaying.

"Greetings, Usti-waya," I said when he was about fifty yards away.

"Dalonige-ugithi? I am afraid that my eyesight is not as sharp as it once was," he said.

"Yes, it is me, Yellow Hair. I've never thanked you for teaching my son."

"It was my duty."

"How goes your hunt?" I asked.

"We have found nothing. You British soldiers have killed all the animals near the road you are building to fight the French, and now you have scared them away from the salt lick. We have nothing to eat but the dried meat the army gives us. It keeps our bodies alive, but a man has to hunt and kill his meat to be a man. It has been that way since the days of Kanati, the first man."

His face was impassive and he made no gestures, as is Cherokee custom. They depend on the eloquence of their words to convey their emotions. The other three Cherokee remained silent, showing their deference to Usti-waya.

I dipped my head. I was not as eloquent as the Cherokee and had to show my feelings in other ways. "I am sorry. Our King has ordered us to conquer the French and we must build a road to do that. We cannot slip through the forest the way the Cherokee do."

"Yes, the army told us that and gave us more presents to make us happy, but it does not make me happy. These gifts make our young men lazy. All they do is drink whisky and boast. Your son Onacona is one of the few who knows how to hunt properly, but even he is not skilled in the ways of a Cherokee warrior."

"And how is your sister, Ahawee?"

"She died last winter. She was an old woman, greatly respected. I am sure I will soon follow her to the land of the spirits."

"You must stay alive to teach the young men of Tuskeegee how to be Cherokee warriors."

"My life is in the hands of the spirits. They will decide when it is time for me to join them."

When I had known him twenty years earlier, Usti-waya had been a cheerful man. I was dismayed to hear him talk this way. The years since I'd last seen him must have been hard on the older Cherokee, who still remembered their ancestral ways. I looked down and remained silent for a half minute, the Cherokee way of showing that I was thinking about what he said, before replying.

"Perhaps there are deer in the Great Meadow." I could think of nothing to say that would ease the sorrow he felt.

"Yes, deer may still be there. That is the way we were going. I wish you good hunting, Yellow Hair." He turned his horse and rode west. The three other Cherokee followed.

My conversation with Usti-waya had been in Cherokee. Carlyle was the only one of our party who understood what had been said. He knew that I'd lived with the Cherokee for two years and that I'd had a wife and son, but the others didn't. Yet again I recalled how many in the colonies looked down on white men who took Indian wives and fathered children with them. I didn't want to have to endure the insults I might have received if it became known that I had done this. It was easier to keep those events secret—an act of cowardice. But Awinita was dead and Onacona didn't consider me his father.

Geoff must have sensed my discomfort because as soon as the Cherokee left, he walked towards me. "I won't say anything about your son," he said in a low voice.

"Thanks," I whispered.

When I'd lived with them, the Cherokee were warriors, as they had been for centuries. Smallpox and other diseases had greatly diminished their numbers, but they still fought other tribes and attacked white settlers. It was their way of life, but it was not one that we white men could tolerate. We fought several wars against the Cherokee, killing a few of them and burning their villages. Had this continued we would've destroyed them, but the British Army took a different approach. It bribed the Cherokee with guns, food, and tools to keep them from attacking settlers and other tribes. This, and the whisky we sold them, destroyed their pride and their way of life. They lived, but not as the men they wanted to be. I'd known this for many years, but until I saw how disheartened Us-ti-waya was, I didn't understand the consequences of the army's bribes. Seeing him a shadow of the proud warrior he'd once been made me heartsick.

It took a week to prepare two hundred pounds of salt. We cut so many trees for firewood and left so much ash that no one would have a problem finding this salt lick again. Three days later we were back at the Virginians' camp.

Colonel Whiteside was overjoyed. He'd been giving the Virginians every third day off from path-building. Even with the rest, men had been collapsing from the heat. Now with an adequate supply of salt, we could resume building the path at a faster pace.

"Watson, the colonel has promoted you to corporal," Captain Jackson told me the day after we returned. "You get a second chevron and three pence a day more in pay. At this rate you'll be an officer before long."

"Thank you, sir, but I doubt I'll ever be an officer. I don't have the money to buy a commission."

"Some men get promoted from the ranks."

"I've heard that, but haven't seen it."

"You'll see it when we get into battle and some of us officers are killed."

I said nothing more. Officers getting killed in battle didn't seem like the best topic of conversation with Captain Jackson. I was happy with my new rank and extra pay. I could now accumulate a little money after the stoppages. There was nothing to spend it on in the middle of the wilderness. The Virginians hadn't collected the usual train of camp followers who sold soldiers everything from replacement clothing to whisky and women. We were too far from civilisation for that. Still, the idea of having a bit of extra cash was comforting. But my promotion to corporal further distanced me from my messmates. Dixon had to relinquish his formal position as head of the group to me, but my messmates still looked to him for leadership. I had no choice but to continue taking my meals with them, but there was little of the camaraderie that should have existed between us. I sucked in my gut and sadly accepted it. Luckily the rest of the Virginians didn't feel that way.

"Corporal Watson, join a friendly game of French Ruff? We need a fourth," Albert Sams called out as I passed him and two other men from the Second Company preparing to play on a warm summer evening a week later. "Ha'penny a point. Surely you can afford that."

I didn't know how to reply and was speechless for a few moments. This was the first time since I'd joined the army that I'd had to face the temptation to gamble. I stammered for a few moments before saying, "No thanks."

I didn't know whether Sams or the others noticed my reaction to his invitation and I decided not to call attention to it with an explanation. I realised I needed a response to similar invitations in the future. I couldn't tell the truth about the problems that gambling had caused me, and it would seem ridiculous if I, a forty-four-year-old man, said that I wouldn't gamble because my parents had forbidden me to. After a few days, I decided on a version of the truth. I would say that I no longer gambled because I was a poor card player, that I had once lost more money than I could afford, and didn't want to repeat the experience.

Just after dawn on a Sunday morning in late July, I heard a pistol shot from the direction of the Fifth Company's tents. I pulled on my trousers and boots, then rushed out to see what had happened. By the time I got there, it seemed as if half the Virginians were milling about. Several officers, including Captain Clark, stood in front of Captain Lewis' tent, dour looks on their faces.

"What happened?" I asked.

"You'll find out when the colonel arrives," Clark replied.

Colonel Whiteside and Captain Jackson arrived a short while later and spent about a minute in the tent. "Captain Lewis is dead," the colonel announced after a short conference with his officers. "He shot himself. Captain Jackson will take temporary, uh, command of the Fifth Company in addition to his own First Company. Return to your duties."

I later learned that Jackson had been the first officer to see Lewis' dead body and had gone to find the colonel. I wondered whether that had any influence on the colonel's decision to give Jackson command of Lewis' company. Jackson seemed to be the colonel's favourite, and had been given temporary command of the regiment when both the colonel and Major Seabury left.

"Watson, find Sergeant Pew and Private Smith and bring them to my tent," Jackson ordered.

Ten minutes later the three of us crowded into Jackson's tent. He sat at his campaign desk, rubbing his right temple as did whenever he was perplexed by a problem. "Pew, Smith, any idea why Captain Lewis shot himself? He seemed cheerful enough in the mess and happy to be in the Virginians. He didn't have to buy his commission. He raised a company from amongst his neighbours in Albemarle County and was made its captain. His men seemed to like him."

Sergeant Pew followed the old soldier's code of never telling an officer anything more than you had to. "I haven't a clue, sir."

Samuel Smith was silent for a while and looked as if he was struggling to find the right words for what he had to say. Jackson waited.

"Captain Lewis suffered from melancholia," Smith started. Pew glared at him, but if Samuel noticed, he paid no attention. "He'd be cheerful for a few days, sometimes for a week, then a black cloud would descend over him for a day or two, then he'd be cheerful again. It wasn't too bad last winter at Fort Roanoke, but once we began building the road, he started muttering about never getting out of this accursed forest. The black cloud descended when we were at Martin's Station a month ago, but this time it didn't lift."

"It hasn't been pleasant for any of us, but did he give any sign of wanting to kill himself?" Jackson asked.

"A week ago Tuesday morning, when I came to his tent, I saw him holding his pistol to his head. He must've seen me, because he quickly turned it to a position where he could look down its barrel, as you would if you were checking whether it was clean. It wasn't my place to say anything, but it was strange behaviour."

"No one will fault you, Smith. Once a man decides to kill himself, no one can stop him." Jackson looked at him, but Samuel had nothing further to say. "Now are there any problems in the company that I should be aware of?" Both Pew and Smith shook their heads no. "Then have the men carry on with their duties. Dismissed."

We buried Captain Lewis that afternoon. Indeed, he never left the forest he'd cursed.

Lewis' suicide had one great benefit for me. Since we now both reported to Captain Jackson, Samuel Smith and I worked together on a daily basis and soon became fast friends. Samuel joked that since I was a corporal and he was only a chosen man, I was his superior officer. That was true, but I never gave him an order.

I hadn't had a friend since I was a boy in Graves End, someone I could talk to honestly without fear of being ridiculed or seeming weak. Donald Mackenzie would've been my friend had we been closer in age, but he was too much like a father for me to treat him as an equal. Josiah Terrill could've been my friend, but he was a taciturn man who didn't make friends. I should've made friends amongst the scores of men that I knew in Davidson's Fort, but I never sought any of them out or responded strongly enough to their overtures. That was my failing. Had I made a friend or two in Davidson's Fort, I might've had an alternative to the gambling that had led me to steal from Mr Henderson.

I told Samuel many things that I hadn't told anyone before . . . about leaving Jenny pregnant and my son David Stahlworth, who I thought I'd never see . . . about marrying Awinita and my second son, Onacona . . . about my five-year affair with Judy Slater and her rejecting my marriage proposal . . . but I stopped short of telling him why I joined the army. I wasn't ready to share that secret with anyone. I told him the same lie I had been telling everyone else: that I joined the Virginians because I was bored with life in Davidson's Fort.

He told me about the sorrows in his life . . . how he'd been married and had been blessed with a wonderful wife, two sons and two daughters, all of whom were now dead as the result of illness and misfortune

. . . how difficult it was to face the men who had trusted him and tell them he could not repay the debts Abner Nichols had saddled him with when he absconded with the proceeds of their trading venture.

We agreed that by joining the army we were running away from our problems, but neither of us could see any alternative. Samuel hoped that by being frugal with his salary and the possibility of some plunder if the Virginians were successful in battle, he might be able to pay off his debts and return to Williamsburg. I envied his having a place he wanted to return to. I couldn't return to Davidson's Fort.

Reaching Kuwanda-talunyi and the beginning of the Tennessee River had been the Virginians' goals since leaving Fort Roanoke, but when we got there in mid-August, we didn't stop to rest. We continued building the pack-train path towards French Lick and soon left the mountains. Whilst the valley was still covered with forest, its gentler terrain should've allowed faster progress. But with the Virginians' losses due to injury, illness, and desertion, and the need to have many men out hunting, only about half the regiment actually worked on the path, and they were downhearted. The cool dark green forest, alive with red bee balm and purple spiderwort, should've been inviting, but neither I, nor any of the Virginians, cared. We weren't as dispirited as Captain Lewis had been, but each of us, in his own way, cursed the forest.

"We're not going to get to St Louis this year," Captain Jackson said to me one morning in mid-September. Nothing had prompted this remark, but its truth was obvious. It had taken us six weeks to build the last hundred miles of path and we had no reason to believe that the remaining hundred miles to French Lick would go any faster. Then we would have to build rafts, float down the Cumberland and Ohio Rivers to the Mississippi, and march a hundred fifty miles upstream to St Louis. And somehow we'd have to get the supplies we needed for the trip. We wouldn't be able to hunt once we started floating down the rivers.

Spending the winter in the wilds of Tennessee didn't seem like a good idea. We could build cabins, but how could we get enough food? We'd been successful hunting these past few months, but that was because it was summer and game was plentiful. And even if the quartermaster at Fort Roanoke was no longer supplying us with dried meat or fish, he still sent a pack train with dried vegetables, hard tack, and rum each week. That would all change in the winter. If we stayed in one place, we'd quickly overhunt the area and lose our meat supply. Snow and ice would make the trail from Fort Roanoke difficult, if not impassable. We could starve before spring.

"We can't just stay here in the forest," I said timidly, since I had no idea how Jackson would respond.

"You're right. I guess we'll continue for as long as is prudent, then march back to Fort Roanoke and start again next year."

"Has the colonel agreed to this?"

"Not yet, but what alternative does he have?"

Jackson's prediction came true two days later. Colonel Whiteside announced that the Virginians would build path only as far as French Lick, then return to Fort Roanoke for the winter. We would start out again for St Louis in the spring. The news was a tonic for the regiment. We built the remaining hundred miles of path in four weeks.

The colonel gave the regiment two days' rest at French Lick. He needed fresh information about St Louis' fortifications and he wanted it now. As Captain Jackson explained to me, the French knew we were coming and would have ample time to strengthen their lines. Waiting till spring, when the regiment would again be on its way, to find out what defences we would have to overcome might be too late. We would have no chance to get reinforcements or to change our plans.

The colonel asked Geoff Carlyle to lead a small scouting party to St Louis. Geoff said that he hadn't been there and didn't know the route. When Colonel Whiteside couldn't convince him to undertake the task, he didn't threaten to clap him in irons, as Captain Jackson would have. Instead he ordered Captain Clark to choose four men from his Third Company to join him in making the reconnaissance. It would be a dangerous mission. Clark and his men would be in uniform and wouldn't be hanged as spies. But if the French caught them, they would be held prisoner until rescued or the end of the war. We left Clark and his men building canoes when we started our nearly five-hundred-mile march back to Fort Roanoke.

CHAPTER 7

Tired, but jubilant, the Virginians reached Fort Roanoke at the end of November. The cabins we built the previous year were waiting for us, still without cots. As a corporal, I was in full command of my cabin, but I chose not to take advantage of my rank. I cut my share of firewood and did my share of keeping the cabin clean.

Captain Alexander Pettit took command of the Fifth Company a day after our arrival. Samuel Smith and I no longer worked together as closely as we had, but by this time a strong bond had formed between us.

The regiment also received three more lieutenants and a dozen sergeants. The lieutenants had bought their commissions—there were still no officers from other regiments willing to join the Virginians—but the sergeants were all old soldiers. And I hadn't been the only soldier promoted to corporal. There was at least one in each company. We were beginning to look like a normal regiment.

Colonel Whiteside paid Geoff Carlyle his wages and dismissed him without any thanks. He was still peeved that Carlyle hadn't been willing to undertake the reconnaissance of St Louis, but Geoff showed no signs of being troubled by the colonel's displeasure.

"Thank you again, William, for remembering me," he told me before leaving Fort Roanoke. "It will be good to get back to my wife and buy her a few fripperies. It's been a long time since we had any extra money to spend. Good luck to you and come visit if you're ever in Salisbury again."

"I'll do that, Geoff. Godspeed to you."

Since there was no place to spend money in the wilds of Tennessee and Carlyle was not a gambler, he left the Virginians with many more than the few pounds he'd hoped to earn. I envied him having a wife and home to return to.

Fort Roanoke provided many relaxations, but none was greater than being able to change out of my grime-encrusted uniform, which I'd worn for eight months. I'd been able to wash in streams, and I shaved regularly, unlike many of the Virginians who'd grown beards down to their chests. I'd even had my hair cut by Private Ardsley, who'd been a barber before he joined the Virginians. But I could do nothing more than brush the dust off my uniform. Even so, I was better dressed than many of the Virginians, whose uniforms were in tatters. By the time we returned, our regiment wouldn't have looked out of place in the rag-tag rebel army in the last days before Washington surrendered.

The colonel told the commissary officers to issue new uniforms to the Virginians immediately. Of course we had to pay for them with the usual stoppages, but having new clothes and boots was a luxury. In a week the Virginians were transformed from their bedraggled state into a normal British Army regiment. We may not have had the spit-and-polish look of the guards, but we were easily as well turned out as the regulars at Fort Roanoke.

Colonel Whiteside gave Captain Jackson the task of determining what supplies the Virginians would need to capture St Louis and how to get them to French Lick.

"Watson, how many days do you think it will take the Virginians to march to French Lick?" Jackson said as we started our calculations.

"Will the path we built be open or covered with blow downs?" I asked.

Jackson rubbed his right temple, as he did when he was troubled. "How in God's name should I know?"

"We could do two sets of calculations, one assuming that the path is clear and the other assuming it isn't," I said. Jackson nodded in agreement and I continued. "If the path is clear, the Virginians ought to be able to march twenty miles a day and get to French Lick in three weeks."

"Twenty miles every day might be too fast," Jackson said. "Add a week."

"Yes, sir. Four weeks."

"And if the path is blocked?"

"Clearing downed trees shouldn't be as difficult as building the path. Perhaps another ten days."

There were many things we wished we knew. Besides the question of whether the road we built would still be open or clogged with downed trees, we had to guess how fast our rafts would float down the rivers, and whether the road to St Louis would be usable. After the first day we gave up trying to make two sets of calculations. If we were unlucky and everything worked against us, we'd be unable to get to St Louis before winter, which was not an answer that Captain Jackson would accept.

Jackson and I laboriously cyphered out how many days each leg of the trip— marching to French Lick, building rafts, floating down the Cumberland and Ohio Rivers, then marching to St Louis—would take. Then we calculated how many rations and what quantities of other supplies the Virginians would need. When this was done, we determined how many packhorses would be required to carry everything.

We made our best guesses and prayed that we were right. If we were wrong the Virginians would run out of rations in the middle of Tennessee and have to live off the land. We'd survive, but we'd soon be very hungry and have no choice but to abandon our mission. I felt a heavy responsibility and woke in the middle of the night worrying about the decisions we'd made that day. Should I suggest to Jackson that we redo our figures? If I did, what better numbers could I suggest? I lay awake until dawn listening to the snores of my companions and tried to reassure myself that our estimates were correct.

By the end of a week, we had our totals. Captain Jackson arranged for us to present our results the next morning to Colonel Whiteside and Major Seabury, who'd been waiting for us when we returned to Fort Roanoke.

"Captain Jackson, these numbers can't be correct. The tons of supplies and number of horses you say we need are immense," Colonel Whiteside responded, after Jackson presented our calculations.

"Would the colonel like me to show him how we arrived at our estimates?"

The colonel nodded and Jackson proceeded to spend the next two hours carefully explaining what we'd done.

"I have no choice but to agree with your numbers for rations and supplies," the colonel said, "but you haven't taken into account the horses we'll need to transport the rockets Major Seabury assures me we will have before we leave."

"And how many will that be?" Jackson asked, looking at the major.

"We have been promised two hundred rockets. They weight thirty-two pounds each," the major replied. "A horse should be able to carry seven of them."

"Thirty more horses," Jackson said quickly.

"Jackson," the colonel said after a few moments, "have you thought about how the Virginians will procure the food and horses you say we'll need?"

"No, sir."

"Kindly give some thought to that problem."

"Yes, sir."

"Dismissed, Captain Jackson, Corporal Watson."

We left the colonel and the major in deep discussion.

Captain Clark returned from his reconnaissance in mid-January bringing good news. The French had only a wooden stockade for protection at St Louis. The only soldiers in the area were a company of militia recruited from local residents. Clark didn't think much of their military ability. They had no cannon, and were armed with a variety of rifles and muskets, probably their own weapons before they enlisted. And they weren't alert. He'd been able to sneak up to the base of their stockade one night without being detected. Clark saw no reason for the whole regiment to attack the town. He thought two companies could take it, whilst the other eight floated down the Mississippi and captured Nouvelle Orleans.

Colonel Whiteside agreed with Clark and decided that it was within his authority to make this change in the regiment's orders. Once we reached the Mississippi, Clark would take his Third Company and Captain Joyner's Second Company, proceed north to capture Cape Girardeau and Ste. Genevieve, then complete his mission by capturing St Louis. He would then become military governor of Louisiana north of the junction of the Mississippi and Ohio Rivers and stay until the King appointed a royal governor.

It would be a risky mission. If the French decided to resist, Clark and his men could face hundreds of armed civilians in addition to the company of militia in St Louis. I remembered what Boone had told us about not expecting any help from the settlers. None of the other Virginians seemed to be worried about this possibility, but some of the company commanders seemed jealous of the favour shown to Clark. They gave him his due as a skilled backwoodsman, but questioned his ability to govern such a large province.

Captain Jackson and I went back to our calculations.

A week later Major Seabury assembled the Virginians to watch a demonstration of the rockets he'd procured in New Jersey. The six rockets looked exactly as Private Morrison had described them, iron tubes full of gunpowder mounted on long wooden poles. A long fuse extended from the back of each rocket. The poles were rammed into the ground at a forty-five-degree angle. At Major Seabury's command, the fuses were lit and the rockets launched. Only one of them flew straight. The others flew erratically, veering left and right like a drunk trying to find his way. One of them landed in a latrine, creating a great shower of excrement. Luckily none of them flew backwards towards us. Who knows how many Virginians would have been killed if they had.

The regiment laughed and joked until Colonel Whiteside cast a stern eye towards us.

"It's like trying to shoot an unfletched arrow," Captain Clark said.

"Explain what you mean, Clark," the colonel said in an angry tone.

"Sir, if you try to shoot an arrow without feathers around its end, it won't fly straight."

"I know that, but what's that got to do with rockets? We can't, uh, very well put feathers on them."

"But might it be possible to put on something else that would serve the same purpose?"

"If Woolwich Arsenal can't figure out how to make a rocket fly straight, what makes you think you can?"

"Nothing, sir. Just an idle thought."

Colonel Whiteside walked away and the conversation was forgotten until a month later when we were again assembled to watch a rocket demonstration. Captain Clark had three rockets ready to be fired, but they were not the straight tubes we'd seen before. Each had three short strips of iron affixed along the rear of its tube, as similar to feathers on an arrow as could be created out of metal. All three rockets flew straight and true.

I watched Colonel Whiteside's reaction to the rocket flights. His jaw dropped as they flew in graceful arcs, but he recovered his poise by the time they landed some five hundred yards away. "Congratulations, Captain Clark. You've made the rocket a useful weapon."

"It wasn't my doing. John Aiken, the blacksmith, had the idea, and he was the one who soldered the strips in place."

"But he wouldn't have thought about it if you hadn't talked about arrow fletching. I shall, uh, write to General Delancy in Philadelphia to tell him about your invention. I'm certain that both you and Aiken will receive the rewards you deserve."

John Aiken's new rocket design worked better than Colonel Cosgreve's original one. But converting the two hundred rockets Major Seabury had brought from New Jersey was a slow process. The gunpowder had to be removed from each rocket tube. The three fins—as they came to be known after Sergeant Pew said that they looked more like fish fins than bird feathers—had to be soldered in place, then the gunpowder repacked. It took many hours of work for each rocket, and Aiken still had his normal duties making and repairing ironmongery. Colonel Whiteside put out an urgent call for more blacksmiths. Two weeks passed before the first one arrived, but by the end of March we had four blacksmiths who were able to convert all two hundred rockets before we left Fort Roanoke.

John Aiken and Captain Clark never received the rewards Colonel Whiteside had promised, even though the British Army quickly adopted and improved on their design by adding a fourth fin. Rumour had it that Colonel Cosgreve was embarrassed that a backwoods officer and a blacksmith could solve a problem he couldn't and used his connexions at Horse Guards, the British Army's Headquarters, to quash any recognition of their contribution. It was not the first time the British Army failed to reward Americans for their efforts.

The Virginians needed replacements for the men who'd deserted or been killed or injured during the past year. They weren't hard to find. Word spread that we were going to conquer Louisiana for the King and recruits came to Fort Roanoke eager to join. David Stahlworth from Charleston was one of them. As soon as I heard his name, I knew that he was the son I'd fathered with Jenny Cartwright. But I didn't know whether he knew that I was his father, and if he did, what Jenny had told him about me. I watched him surreptitiously. He had her round face, light brown hair, and blue eyes.

David was assigned to Captain Pettit's Fifth Company. I didn't come into contact with him, but Samuel Smith, who was the company's clerk, did. I'd already told Samuel that I had a son named David Stahlworth, so my questions about him came as no surprise.

"You'll have to talk to him," Samuel said.

"What can I say? That I left his mother for what was supposed to be two months, but was gone for more than six years, and then promised his grandfather that I wouldn't bother either of them. Do I just walk up and say, 'Hello, I'm your father'?"

"No, that wouldn't be right. Let me find out what I can."

"Thank you, Samuel. You're a true friend."

Over the next weeks Samuel told me that both Jenny and her husband Adam were still alive and that they had a large family, three boys and two girls in addition to David. Adam had been a merchant, but lost his business after a series of poor decisions. The family had fallen on hard times, which is why David joined the Virginians. He appeared to know nothing about me.

Samuel's news left me in a quandary. Part of me longed to know this son better, to tell him that his mother had kept her promise and named him after my father, then to tell him about the grandfather he never knew. But I feared being rebuffed. My Cherokee son Onacona had sought me out, but after satisfying his curiosity, told me that I was not his father because I'd abandoned him when he was only three days old. Would David feel the same way? I'd abandoned him before he was born, and I didn't know what he thought of Adam, the man he knew as his father. Was David a loyal son who was willing to stand by him, even though his mistakes had brought the family low?

That was the honourable thing to do and I wanted it to be true, even though it would make my course more difficult.

In the end I kept the promise I'd made to Amos Cartwright. I didn't approach David or identify myself as his father. He seemed like a fine young man, and my resolve to keep my distance became stronger.

Whilst I was occupied during December and January, many of the Virginians were not, and the devil does indeed find work for idle hands. With eight months' back pay in their pockets, and access to as much rum and gin as they cared to buy, some of them went on a rampage. Eight men from the Sixth Company badly damaged Mr Ingles' tavern when he refused to serve them more gin because they were already drunk. The men were arrested and clapped in irons whilst Colonel Whiteside and his officers decided what to do with them. The normal punishment would have been a hundred lashes or more, but no Virginian had yet been flogged.

The next day Captain Pettit came to Captain Jackson's cabin. I started to leave, but both captains motioned me to stay.

"I don't want to see any of the men who damaged Mr Ingles' tavern flogged," Pettit said after they'd exchanged pleasantries.

"Surely they richly deserve punishment," Jackson replied.

"That they do, but once we start using flogging it will be easy to use that punishment for the most minor of infractions. We'll be no better than the regular army, where soldiers do what they are ordered to only because they fear the lash. We need soldiers who can think and act for themselves in battle." Pettit took a deep breath, as if he was surprised at the vehemence of his statement.

"Some of our soldiers are like children," Jackson replied, "and they need to be treated like children. As Proverbs say: 'He that spareth his rod, hateth his son; but he that loveth him, chasteneth him betimes.'"

Pettit smiled. "Are you the devil who can quote Scripture for his own ends?"

"I hope not, but what do the other company commanders say."

"You're the last one. The others all agree with me."

"Let me think on this matter," Jackson said. Then, turning to me, added, "You'll keep this conversation confidential." I nodded.

I remembered Private Edwards' threat of mutiny if the lash was used, but I still was surprised that anyone questioned whether the men from the Sixth Company should be flogged. They had to be punished for the damage they'd done. Colonel Whiteside deliberated for a full week before reaching his verdict.

"I have decided that the eight prisoners are guilty, uh, of causing grievous damage to Mr Ingles' tavern," the Colonel announced to the full regiment at morning parade. "They shall be fined twice the cost of repairing the damage, the excess to be given to Mr Ingles in consideration of his lost custom. In addition, they shall be dishonourably discharged from the army."

The men from the Sixth Company were standing in front of him in irons, no doubt expecting to hear how many lashes they would receive. They looked stunned when they heard they were not to be flogged. Two of them wept. A cheer rose from the ranks.

The colonel waited until order had been restored. "I have been, uh, convinced not to impose a more severe punishment because the prisoners caused no injury to Mr Ingles or to the other customers in the tavern." He didn't specify what punishment he would've meted out had there been injuries. We found that out three weeks later when a soldier from the Fourth Company was hanged after a court martial found him guilty of ravishing a farmer's wife.

Fort Roanoke offered few diversions that winter other than drinking, gambling, or a few minutes with one of the whores in the rooms above Mr Ingles' tavern. Drinking didn't interest me and gambling scared me. As for the whores, I considered joining the line waiting to be serviced each evening until word circulated that the surgeon was treating several men with mercury for diseases they had no doubt received along with any satisfaction of their lust. These prostitutes quickly disappeared to be replaced in short order by a new crop. I couldn't help but remember Sergeant Roidan educating me about syphilis and warning me to stay away from "hoors" during my days in the rebel army, thirty years earlier. I hadn't always followed his advice, but this time it seemed like the prudent thing to do.

The few unmarried women in the village were constantly surrounded by crowds of officers and men. I joined those crowds twice, but getting the attention of any of the women proved to be a hopeless task. Reading was my favourite diversion, but by the end of January I'd read what few books were available. I filled some of my empty hours talking to Samuel Smith and slept more than I had since I was a child, but there were still many hours of idleness and boredom. I looked forward to restarting our expedition to Nouvelle Orleans.

In mid-March Sergeant Pew and I watched as a company of sappers marched into an already overcrowded Fort Roanoke. They brought with them five hundred prisoners chained together in mess groups of six.

"That could've been me thirty years ago if I hadn't joined the army," Pew said. "Look at those wretches. They've been starved for months. Wonder why they're here. They'll drop from exhaustion by the scores if the army forces them to do any hard work."

I felt ill looking at the prisoners and willed myself not to show it. I realised I could've been one of them had Mr Henderson sworn out a warrant for my arrest after he discovered that I'd stolen money from him. I knew that prisoners were treated harshly, but seeing their rag-clad, emaciated bodies was still a shock. It reinforced my conviction that I had to keep my crime a secret at all costs.

"Doesn't the army need to keep them fit to work?" I asked.

Pew shrugged his shoulders. "The army doesn't care. Judges in England and here in the colonies are only too happy to keep a steady supply of replacements available. The only people who might complain are the plantation owners back east. If the army works all the prisoners to death, there'll be none left for them."

Pew looked at the prisoners and at the train of wagons that followed them for a few moments longer. "Surprised there're no bed-warmers, unless they're hidden in those wagons," he said.

"Bed-warmers?"

"Most times each officer finds a wench or two from amongst the prisoners to keep his bed warm at night," Pew answered. "Sometimes, if there're enough trollops to go round, they'll let sergeants like me, and even corporals like you, pick one out. But that causes discontent in the ranks. The men accept that officers get special privileges, but they don't think the likes of you and me should have them. Besides, the women who are left after the officers take their pick are usually ugly and mean-spirited." From the wistful look on his face, I guessed that he'd had a bed-warmer sometime in the past and wouldn't mind having another if there were any women in this batch of prisoners.

"Virginians," Colonel Whiteside began in his unpleasant voice at morning parade the next day. "Some of you may have wondered how we will get back from Nouvelle Orleans after we have captured it. The sappers and prisoners you saw yesterday will widen our pack train path to French Lick into a road, then build a road from French Lick to Nouvelle Orleans. We will, uh, wait in Nouvelle Orleans until the road is built, then march triumphantly back to Fort Roanoke. Three cheers for King George! Hip, hip."

The cheers that followed were much weaker than usual. The Virginians knew how hard road-building was, and only the most foolish believed that five hundred emaciated prisoners would be able to build the many hundreds of miles we needed.

I sought out Samuel Smith later that day. He was relaxing outside Captain Pettit's cabin in the late afternoon sun. He greeted me with, "William, you look troubled."

"I am," I replied. "It took the regiment a month to build twenty-five miles of road last year. It's another four hundred miles to French Lick, five hundred miles from French Lick to Natchez, and almost two hundred miles from Natchez to Nouvelle Orleans. Does the army really think that these prisoners can build all those miles of road?" I was surprised that Samuel didn't share my concerns.

"It's not as bad as you make it sound," he replied, standing and looking directly at me. "Our pack train path is a good start on a road to French Lick. And it's five hundred miles from French Lick to Natchez if you follow the Choctaw trail you told me that you and Terrill took. But it's only two hundred miles from French Lick to the Mississippi. The sappers will have to build new road for that distance, but once they get to the Mississippi, there'll be the road the Spanish built from Nouvelle Orleans to St Louis. It's easier to improve an existing road than build a new one."

"There's still more than a thousand miles of road to either build or improve. Those five hundred prisoners can never finish the job, especially if they start dying as quickly as Pew thinks they will."

"The army will have to send more men."

"More prisoners?"

"Perhaps," Samuel replied, with a shrug "but it would make more sense to send men willing to do the work."

"They'd have to be well paid," I said. "It's hard work."

"True, but war isn't cheap. If England wants to control Louisiana, it has to have an easy way to get soldiers there. That means roads."

"And will the roads be completed in our lifetimes?" I asked. I didn't expect the answer to be yes.

"They will, if the army sends more men to build the road."

"Then let's hope the army appreciates your excellent logic." Samuel hadn't done anything to dispel my fears, but being able to talk to him was a small comfort.

The sappers and their prisoners left Fort Roanoke two days after their arrival.

CHAPTER 8

The Virginians were supposed to depart for Louisiana at dawn on 1st April 1807. We were awakened an hour earlier, grabbed our kits and formed up by companies. We'd been told we'd have no breakfast, but would stop for a meal at mid-morning. Dawn came and went. We weren't given the order to march. We could hear men cursing and horses bellowing in the stable, but had no idea why. Finally, about an hour after dawn, a red-faced Colonel Whiteside appeared. After a hurried conference with his company commanders, we were called to attention. The colonel explained that there was some difficulty loading the rockets onto packhorses and that we would leave without them. He assured us that the packhorse train would catch up to us by the next day. The sun was well above the horizon by the time we left.

Major Seabury was not with us when we marched through Fort Roanoke's gate. A week earlier he had fallen to the ground unconscious in a fit of apoplexy. We thought he'd died, but he regained consciousness after a few minutes. The fit had left his speech slurred and his right side paralysed. Colonel Whiteside didn't have time to find a replacement from outside the regiment. Normally, a vacancy such as this would have been filled by promoting one of the regiment's captains to brevet, or acting, major and, given the colonel's past preferences, I'd assumed that Captain Jackson would receive the honour. But the colonel didn't promote Jackson or any of the other captains. It was a precarious situation. Should anything happen to the colonel we had no second-in-command.

After the past summer's difficulties, most of the Virginians would've been just as happy to spend the rest of the war at Fort Roanoke. We couldn't believe we were actually on our way to Nouvelle Orleans.

"This is just an April Fool's Day prank," someone in the ranks muttered. "We'll turn around in an hour and march back to the fort."

"I wager we'll wait until the road's built," another answered.

But it was no prank and we didn't turn back to Fort Roanoke. We marched twenty-five miles to Christiansburg that first day, then another twenty-five the next day to where the Virginians had stopped building road the previous year. On our third day, we started on the road the prisoners had built. It was wide enough for wagons, but stumps and other obstacles protruded from its roadway. It had no drainage ditches and looked as if it would wash out in even a middling storm. I was surprised. I'd assumed that British Army sappers would've built a better road. There hadn't been much rain in the three weeks since the prisoners started their work. We made good progress, covering the forty-five miles of new road in two-and-a-half days.

"My God, look at that," a voice behind me exclaimed. It was an unnecessary instruction. All eyes were fixed on the same sight. One of the prisoners held a stout pole, atop which a fly-encrusted head was mounted.

"Where's Captain Bates?" Captain Pettit, who was at the head of our column, asked.

"At the front of the work party," a sergeant, whose arm was in a sling, answered.

Pettit stormed off to find the sapper commander. The rest of the column followed. Sappers and their prisoners moved aside to make way for us.

"Captain Bates, what is the meaning of this ghastly display?" Pettit asked, his anger obvious in the tone of his voice.

"I don't believe we've been introduced, Captain," Bates answered, in a no less angry tone of voice. "I like to know the name of my interrogator."

"I'm Alexander Pettit, commander of the Fifth Company of the Kings Own Virginians. We were introduced at Fort Roanoke, but you've obviously forgotten."

Bates was shorter than Pettit and had to look up at him, but this did nothing to diminish the sense of superiority he conveyed. "Well, Captain Pettit," he said, "since you've poked your nose into something which is none of your affair, you might as well know the whole story. The head on the pole belonged to John Trusdale, who'd been transported for life for assaulting a gentleman. Three days ago he attacked my sergeant with a broad axe. I had to shoot him with my pistol to protect the sergeant's life. Unfortunately, I killed him and he escaped the punishment he'd earned. His head on that staff serves as a warning to the other prisoners. Now if you'll excuse me, I have a road to build." Bates turned back to his work, leaving Pettit with no opportunity to reply.

It was about an hour before sundown. Normally, we would have stopped and set up camp. I had no desire to spend any more time amongst the prisoners and neither did our officers. Colonel Whiteside came up to Pettit and after a brief parley ordered the column forward. We marched until it was too dark to see clearly, putting at least three miles between us and the prisoners, then set up camp.

"You know he wanted to die," Samuel Smith said to me the next day at our noon break.

"Who wanted to die?"

"Trusdale, the prisoner whose head was on the pole."

"How do you know that?"

"I heard it from one of the prisoners. He said Trusdale told him that being flogged to death or some other punishment was better than being worked to death. His only hope was that he could kill Bates' sergeant first. Seems like the sergeant was harder on prisoners than any of the other sappers."

"I guess getting shot was an easy way out. Hate to think of what Bates would have done to him had he been taken alive."

We reached French Lick at the end of April and immediately began building rafts for the next stage of our journey. Captain McIntyre, commander of the Seventh Company, and his clerk had spent the winter drawing up plans for this activity. We needed fifty rafts, each forty feet long, capable of carrying twenty men and a share of the supplies. The rafts were to be built from ten logs, about a foot in diameter, lashed together with stout cordage. Logs that big are too heavy to be lifted—they had to be trimmed, then rolled into the river.

Felling and trimming trees for the rafts was hard work, but there were few complaints. Whingers, like Private Edwards, had deserted the previous summer and been replaced with men who were proud to be part of the regiment.

The Eighth Company was assigned to dig two sawpits to cut boards for tillers and posts to hold them. The pits had to be deep enough for a man to stand well below the log being sawn. A second man stood above the log and the two of them used a six-foot-long saw for their task. The regiment's companies took turns supplying four men to work a day in the sawpits. I heard that some company commanders—which ones depended on who was telling the story— wanted to use sawpit duty as a punishment, but that Captain Pettit convinced them that to do so would result in poor quality boards. He suggested that turns in the sawpit be chosen by lottery. Colonel Whiteside apparently didn't think much of this idea, but he allowed it to be used. It was successful. Those chosen for the sawpit could only blame their bad luck.

Whilst my status as Captain Jackson's clerk had saved me from road-building duty the previous summer, I had no such immunity this time. Corporals and sergeants had to work as hard as privates. I even spent a day in the sawpit. It was every bit as difficult and unpleasant as Donald Mackenzie had described. Only officers were exempt, but some of them, especially Captain Pettit, worked along-side their men. I watched him, jacketless with his sleeves rolled up, helping to move a log into place so that it could be lashed to others to form a raft. Seeing him reminded me of how Captain Alexander Hamilton had helped his men push their cannon along New Jersey's muddy roads during the Great Rebellion. I knew that the British

Army would never be as egalitarian as the rebel army had been, but perhaps some change was possible.

"Captain Pettit, uh, uh, what is the meaning of this display?" Colonel Whiteside fumed when he saw Pettit working with his men. The colonel's face was redder than usual and he looked apoplectic. "Remember your place, man. Roll down your sleeves and put your jacket on. Immediately."

"Yes, sir," was the only thing the captain could say.

"I'll see you in my tent as soon as you have washed and again look like a British officer," the colonel said as he walked off.

The men who had been working with Captain Pettit kept their faces blank, but the story sped around the regiment that night, redounding to the captain's credit. The colonel was held in such low esteem that one more story had no effect on his reputation.

We'd stayed in our own companies during the trip to French Lick. Since I was in the First Company and my son, David Stahlworth, was in the Fifth Company, there had been little opportunity for me to see him. That changed once we set up camp at French Lick, where there was a constant ebb and flow of men across the regiment's bivouac area. I saw David, either alone or with his mates, on a regular basis. He seemed more convivial than I would have been—smiling and jesting with his companions—traits he must have learned from his mother. Samuel Smith confirmed my observations.

"David's never a problem for Captain Pettit," Samuel told me. "More than once I've seen him head off a fight with a jest or a soft word." I was proud to be his father, and thought about approaching him, but I kept the promise I'd made to his grandfather not to bother him or his mother.

Pack trains with supplies arrived every few days. We had plenty to eat and the stockpile of provisions for our trip downriver grew appreciably, so much so that it attracted thefts by the local Cherokee. Colonel Whiteside was forced to mount a dusk-to-dawn guard.

"What progress are the sappers on the road?" I asked Tom Lincoln, one of the pack train drivers, in early June. He was a civilian hired by the army, so he could speak freely.

"Not much. They've driven the prisoners so hard that fully a quarter of them have either died or been sent back to Fort Roanoke as invalids. Bates keeps driving the rest of them, but most of those poor wretches can hardly swing an axe."

"Is he still parading Trusdale's head around on a pole?"

"No, that only lasted a fortnight," Lincoln said. "Bates said he couldn't afford to have a man not building road. But the other prisoners learned their lesson. None of them have attacked a sapper."

"Have you any good news?"

"If you believe the London papers, the Russians finally beat the French. Did it someplace in Poland. Can't remember the name."

"So the French aren't invincible," I said. "When did this happen?"

"Sometime in early February. The battle doesn't seem to have changed much. The French are in Warsaw and the Russians have retreated. Don't know why the papers are saying that the Russians won." He left to tend his horses.

Other pack train drivers told us that the rains of the past month had washed out some of the road the prisoners had built. Bates was forced to send a hundred of them back to do repair work. They claimed Bates was to be replaced by another sapper captain and that a new group of prisoners was on its way to relieve the ones who had been so poorly treated.

We finished the rafts and loaded them with supplies in mid-June. The colonel gave the regiment a day's rest before we boarded the rafts on our way to Nouvelle Orleans. The Cumberland had no shoals and, since it was well after the spring flood, the current was gentle. Our steersmen had no difficulty keeping us in the middle of the stream. The rest of us had little to do other than to watch the dark forest that bordered both sides of the river slowly pass by. This idleness seemed strange after the hard work of marching to French Lick and building rafts, but my tired body appreciated it. I slept many hours during those first days on the river.

"Reminds me, uh, of punting down the River Cam," Colonel Whiteside said after we had made camp on our first night. This remark was met by blank looks.

"The River Cam at Cambridge University." That brought some looks of comprehension.

"Beggin' your pardon, sir, but what is punting?" one of the officers asked.

"A punt is a long flat-bottomed boat, somewhat like a pirogue. It's poled along by a boatman, but it feels like you're floating. A favourite way, uh, to relax on a warm summer afternoon."

"Didn't know you'd spent any time in England."

"My father sent me there for a year when I was twenty to learn how to be a gentleman. Lived in rooms in Cambridge and even attended a lecture or two at the university. Best year of my life."

I couldn't see the connexion between punting at Cambridge and our rafting down the Cumberland, but I wasn't going to question the colonel.

We took twelve days to reach the Ohio River and another four to reach the Mississippi. I breathed a silent sigh of relief when we made our first camp on the western side of the river. Captain Jackson and I had allowed twenty days for this portion of the regiment's journey. We were four days ahead of schedule, which boded well for the rest of the expedition.

We spent a day in camp reloading supplies before Captain Clark could set off for St Louis. Even though there were now only eight companies and fewer supplies, we kept all fifty rafts. The Mississippi had a reputation for being a treacherous river. I could attest to the strength of its current from the time Terrill and I crossed it during the spring flood on our ill-fated trip to Texas. The colonel was being prudent keeping as many rafts as he could and dividing our supplies amongst them. Odds were that we'd lose more than one of them before we reached Nouvelle Orleans.

Clark's party left at dawn. The colonel had given Clark twenty rockets, a tenth of our supply. Clark chose the largest, strongest men in his command to carry them. Each of these men also carried his rifle and ammunition, his other kit, and as much food as he could manage. The men not hauling rockets transported more food. Most men were loaded with a hundredweight or more and could hardly stand straight. Clark's burden was only slightly less than that of his men. He wasn't as democratically-minded as Captain Pettit, but this was no time for him to stand on the privileges of his rank.

The food that Clark and his men took should've been sufficient for the 150-mile trip to St Louis. If not, they would have to depend on hunting and what food they could find at Cape Girardeau and Ste. Genevieve, the two towns they would have to capture along the way. Once they got to St Louis they'd live off the town's food supplies. Two hundred hungry men emptying the town's larders was not likely to endear them to the local inhabitants, some of whom might go hungry as a result.

I'd expected Colonel Whiteside to make a speech to Clark's men, but he spared us that ordeal. He had a few private words with Clark, after which Clark stepped back, saluted, then turned on his heel and ordered his command to walk easy along the Spanish road. We watched until they rounded a bend about a quarter mile away and were no longer visible.

I don't know why, but the departure of Clark and two companies of Virginians made me feel terribly isolated. We were hundreds of miles from the nearest friendly faces. Whilst we were on the pack trail, we could always turn around and return the way we came, as we had done last fall. But we'd floated nearly three hundred miles down two rivers. We couldn't turn the rafts in the opposite direction and go back. We could only go forward. If my raft hit a snag or overturned in a storm, I'd drown. I could swim, but not well enough to reach the bank from the centre of the river, or to overcome a storm's turbulence.

There was no time to muse on my possible fate. The colonel ordered us to board our rafts and we were soon underway. We'd noticed the previous night that the lighter water of the Ohio did not mix with the darker water of the Mississippi, but stayed in its own stream along the eastern side of the river. As we continued down river we were amazed at how long this separation persisted.

"Ah, the sweet, virginal Ohio, not about to yield to the crude Mississippi," one wag said.

"Yes, but that dirty old man of a river will get the best of that sweet young thing before too long—and she'll probably enjoy the experience," another responded. The conversation quickly became more ribald. If any of my raft-mates shared my concern about being so far from help, they didn't show it. I hadn't seen such high spirits since we left Fort Roanoke.

CHAPTER 9

Nuevo Madrid was only about seventy miles downriver from the Ohio, and the Mississippi moved much faster than either the Cumberland or Ohio. Most of the Virginians thought we'd make the trip in two days and began speculating on whether there would be a battle when we arrived. Wagers were made and spirits rose even higher. But at the end of our second day, we were still a dozen miles north of the town.

With ownership of Louisiana switching from France to Spain, then back to France again, names got confusing. When they took charge again in 1800, the French had changed the name of Nuevo Orleans to Nouvelle Orleans, but they didn't bother to rename Nuevo Madrid. It was probably too small for French mapmakers to worry about.

"We could be floating into a trap," Captain Jackson said as I set up his tent that evening. "The map shows Nuevo Madrid on a bluff above the river. Riflemen hidden on that bluff could cut us to pieces. We should send a scouting party to find out whether the people there are going to fight. I need to convince Colonel Whiteside to be prudent."

Jackson left to see the colonel. He didn't look happy when he returned.

"The colonel agreed to send a scouting party, but put Lieutenant Conroy in command."

Conroy was one of the three lieutenants added to the regiment last winter. No company commander wanted to take them. All were happy with the arrangements they'd worked out with their sergeants and corporals. This left Colonel Whiteside to find employment for the three junior officers. Conroy was a jovial, gormless man from Williamsburg. He had no frontier skills and was the butt of many practical jokes. He never seemed to take offence and laughed along with their perpetrators.

"I told the colonel that Conroy would need an experienced corporal to assist him and said that I was certain you'd be willing to volunteer." Whilst he wasn't ordering me to accompany Conroy, there seemed no way that I could refuse to go. "Find four more volunteers. You leave at dawn. The regiment will await your return. Don't let Conroy get you killed."

The first four men I approached all volunteered, and even though the scouting party was complete, more men came up to me asking to be included. Some were so persistent that I had to send them to Captain Jackson to be told that they could not be part of the scouting mission. He didn't suffer this intrusion on his time lightly and blistered the ears of the first man who approached him. That was sufficient to convince the others not to plead their case.

We took supplies for a four-day trip and headed overland towards Nuevo Madrid. The land close to the riverbank was swampy and overgrown with green briar, which would've been impossible to traverse. We found the Spanish road about a mile inland. It had been cut through dense forest, and even though it was poorly maintained, it would've provided easier travel than our off-road route. But Lieutenant Conroy decided against taking it. He told us he was worried we might run into a party of Frenchmen too large for us to fight. As a result, we had to detour an additional four miles inland to find terrain open enough for easy travel. We headed south through a cool, shaded forest of chestnut trees, but Conroy fretted that we would miss the village. I convinced him that we would see smoke from its chimneys. The lieutenant thanked me profusely for this advice.

I was wrong. We didn't see smoke, but at mid-morning on the second day of our expedition, we came to a rough path that seemed to lead inland from the river. We concluded that it had to be from

Nuevo Madrid, since there was no other place it could come from. We followed the path back towards the river and after an hour and half came to a field that'd been ploughed but not planted.

"Back into the woods men," Conroy ordered. "I don't want to announce our presence quite yet."

Something was wrong. It was nearly noon and the village should've been a bustle of activity. We should've heard normal farmyard noises—cocks crowing or cows mooing— but the only sound we heard was the buzzing flies circling our heads.

"Form a line, loose files, across the centre of the field and let's see what's happening," Conroy said after we'd spent about ten minutes watching and listening. After his cautious behaviour, he was taking a large risk. Six of us could not hope to prevail if the men of the village had set a trap.

We made our way across the first field, through a short section of woods, into a second field, and up to a hedgerow. From there it was less than fifty yards to a farmhouse, the nearest building. Other buildings, a score or more, were also visible.

Lieutenant Conroy put his hand up as a signal for us to halt. "I'm going forward alone. Watson, you're in charge here. Wait for my return."

We watched tensely as he marched up to the nearest farmhouse. No challenge or shots rang out. He opened the door, peered inside, left the building, and walked to another. He repeated his inspection, then disappeared from sight as he continued exploring the village.

"No one's in the village," Private Perkins said. "It's safe to follow the lieutenant."

"Our orders are to remain here, and that's what we're going to do." Whilst I could see that the other men agreed with Perkins, I had no choice but to hold them back.

Conroy returned a short while later. "The village is deserted," he said, stating what was obvious by this time. "I haven't investigated all of the houses, but the ones I looked into didn't have a stick of furniture or anything of value."

"Where'd they all go?" I asked.

"That, Watson, is a complete mystery. Perhaps a more thorough search will help solve it."

We walked into the village and began methodically searching the houses. They were neat, clean, and completely empty, as Lieutenant

Conroy had reported. We finally got to the church on the far side of the village. On its altar, held in place by a rock, was the following letter.

To the Officers and Men of the King's Own Virginians
Greetings:

We left King George III's domain twenty years ago to avoid having to live under his tyrannical rule. The Spanish treated us with courtesy and left us to our own ways. The French have also left us to live our lives as we wished. Now you have come to once again subject us to the British Crown. We have no desire to surrender our freedom, but are too few to resist you. We have chosen to cast our lot with Spain. We will travel to Texas and ask for asylum there. Any of you who are no longer willing to live under British subjugation are welcome to join us.

It was signed by George Morgan on behalf of the inhabitants of Nuevo Madrid.

"At least we know that we won't have a battle here," Conroy said after reading the letter. "That should please the colonel."

We quickly completed our search of the village, found nothing more of interest, and started our return to the regiment. There was now no reason not to take the Spanish road, which ran though the centre of the village. We were back to the Virginians' camp before nightfall.

Colonel Whiteside was pleased when Conroy told him that Nuevo Madrid was deserted. We could continue on to Nouvelle Orleans without delay.

Morgan's letter bothered me. Why did he see British rule as being so tyrannical? I knew he'd been a colonel in the rebel army, but so many other members of that army, myself included, had come to terms with being subjects of George III. We had to pay taxes, but so did everyone on Earth. We weren't represented in Parliament, but that no longer seemed as important as it had thirty years earlier during the Great Rebellion. The British restricted settlement to east of the Proclamation Line, but there was still much land available. The two grievances that still remained, at least to my mind, were that Parliament permitted slavery in the colonies even though it was prohibited in Britain, and that the British used the colonies as a dumping ground for their miscreants.

Whilst maps showed Nuevo Madrid first as part of the Spanish Empire, then as part of France's, neither country was strong enough to control the outer edges of its domain. What looked like a decision to allow Morgan and his companions to live in freedom was more likely a manifestation of this weakness.

Nacogdoches, Texas, where I was held prisoner for four years, was also at the outer edge of the Spanish Empire. Many of its residents chose to live there, to endure its isolation and poverty, because it was far from the seat of power and the demands of the Spanish aristocracy. Captain Ortiz and Padre Esteban, who represented Crown and Church, were reasonable men, who ruled with light hands. But had they been less reasonable, they could've set up their own little fiefdom and been as tyrannical as they wished. Their superiors in San Antonio and Mexico City were too far away and too weak to have stopped them. But Morgan and his band were moving closer to the centre of Spanish power in North America and risked feeling its arbitrary nature. I hoped they wouldn't regret their decision.

As the crow flies, it is about six hundred miles from Nuevo Madrid to Nouvelle Orleans, but we were travelling down a river full of twists and turns, most of which were not shown on our maps. Our route would be much longer.

The Mississippi was now over a mile wide. Our steersman tried to keep our raft at the river's centre to avoid sand bars and to take advantage of the best current. We were too far from shore to make out individual trees. It seemed like we were floating between two black walls. We had no shade. Any parts of our bodies that were exposed to the sun had long ago turned bright red, peeled, and were now burning again. The glare of the sun at midday was blinding. We were tormented by mosquitos and other biting, stinging insects. What had started as a pleasant float down the river was now hellish.

We had an hour of activity in the morning breaking camp and another hour in late afternoon setting up camp for the night, but the long hours on the water were filled with idleness. At first this inactivity was enjoyable, but soon finding a way to spend the hours became taxing. We talked, but after a week ran out of topics to gossip about or stories to tell. Some men, who were confident in their swimming ability, stripped off their clothes and swam alongside the raft for a while. The river was warm, almost tepid, but a dip in its waters was still refreshing. Others fashioned fishhooks out of whatever bits of metal they could scrounge then spent hours trolling. The fish they caught were a welcome diversion from the salt beef, dried pea soup, and hard tack that made up our supplies.

"This damn water is putrid," Private Perkins said, spitting out a mouthful of the river water we all drank. We'd set up camp and were eating our evening meal.

"And the hard tack has weevils," Private Dawson added.

"Consider them currants and make believe you're having a scone at a cream tea," Private Crowley said.

"Are you mocking me?" Dawson said springing to his feet.

"Easy now, just go back to your supper."

"I'll have an apology from you."

"Apology? For what?" Crowley was now on his feet facing Dawson.

"For mocking me."

"I'll not apologise for making harmless jest. Sit down and let me finish my supper."

Dawson emitted a low growl as he sprang at Crowley. But Crowley was ready and grabbed him in a bear hold. The two grappled on the ground, neither able to land a punch or do any serious damage to the other. They looked like two boys wrestling in a schoolyard. Other Virginians gathered around to watch the melee—the most exciting thing that had happened in the week since we'd left Nuevo Madrid—and started yelling advice to one or the other of the combatants.

The noise got Captain McIntyre's attention. He emerged from his tent about fifty yards away. "Stop that fighting," he ordered, after a quick survey of the scene. "Stand at attention. You, Dawson. Who started this fight?"

"Me and Private Crowley had a bit of a disagreement. Nothing to trouble you with, sir."

"Crowley?"

"Private Dawson is right. Just a bit of a disagreement."

"Corporal Watson, can you tell me what happened here?"

"No, sir. They were already fighting when I arrived." This was a lie. I'd heard the interchange between Dawson and Crowley, but I wasn't going to further distance myself from the men of my company.

"Can anyone else tell me what happened here?"

There was silence all around.

"Since no one will tell me the truth," McIntyre said, looking sternly at Dawson and Crowley, "I have no choice but to place both of you under arrest. Colonel Whiteside will determine your punishment."

They were led off and tied to separate trees. Fighting could be punished by as many as a hundred lashes, but in the two years since the regiment had been formed, no Virginian had been flogged. It was a record none of the men, and few of the officers, wanted to see broken.

Colonel Whiteside had the regiment form up for morning parade the next day, something we hadn't done since we started floating down the Cumberland a month earlier.

"It has come to my attention," the colonel said, "that Privates Dawson and Crowley were found fighting in the Seventh Company's area last night and that Captain, uh, McIntyre found it necessary to place them both under arrest."

We stood in silence waiting to hear the colonel pronounce sentence.

"Since this was the first infraction, I sentence both men to ten days' bread and water. But do not try my patience. Any further fighting will be punished by flogging."

The colonel's threat kept the peace for five days. Then Privates O'Malley and Hardwick from my company got into fisticuffs after Hardwick called O'Malley a bog-trotting paddy.

The next day the regiment assembled for morning parade around a punishment frame that had been erected during the night. We were made to watch as O'Malley, shirtless, was strapped to it and given a leather strap to bite on. Sergeant Major Potter then administered twenty-five lashes with a cat-o'-nine tails. Each drew blood and a grunt from O'Malley. By the time the punishment was completed, his back was dripping. One of his friends poured a pint of rum over the wounds to prevent infection. O'Malley groaned at the rum's sting, staggered a bit, but was able to walk away without assistance. Hardwick was then strapped to the frame and subjected to the same punishment. He bore it equally well. Both men were placed on light duty for three days.

Some members of the regiment bore the floggings less well than their recipients. Many gasped as each lash was applied, and one man broke rank, turned away, and vomited. The punishment, which was necessary and mild—they could've received sentences four times as severe—was a milestone for the Virginians. We were now the same as any other regiment in the British Army. We could be flogged for even minor misdeeds. Whilst there was no talk of mutiny, as there had been last summer when Captain Jackson threatened hunters who withheld meat from the common pot with the lash, the mood was sombre. No jests were made and voices were subdued as we broke camp and pushed the rafts into the river.

"I suppose this day had to come," Samuel Smith said to me that evening, referring to the flogging.

"Why? There were other punishments the colonel could have ordered."

"Yes, but he didn't have many choices. He couldn't put O'Malley and Hardwick in gaol. That left bread and water or hanging. He tried bread and water—it didn't work—and I don't think you'd want to see men hanged for brawling."

"He should have tried bread and water again."

"No. He told the regiment that further fighting would mean flogging and he had to make good on that threat. We're hundreds of miles into the wilderness. If the colonel can't enforce discipline, we'll soon have anarchy. I'm surprised we've gone this far without his having to resort to the lash."

Samuel had been a captain in the rebel army. He thought like an officer, and this time he was right. The flogging served its purpose. There were no more fights. When tempers flared, others quickly separated the combatants.

Our first cases of ague, which is now being called malaria, appeared three days later. Ague's recurring bouts of chills, fever, and joint ache are so well known I feel no need to describe them. The surgeons knew that we would be travelling in a hot, swampy area and were prepared to treat it with cochineal bark from Java. The bark usually worked in a day, making the disease an annoyance rather than a serious problem, but after the first cases appeared, as many as one in ten of the Virginians were too ill for regular duty. The surgeons used so much bark they feared they would run out.

We looked forward to reaching Natchez, even though we didn't know what we'd find there. When we left Fort Roanoke five months earlier, word was that it was still in British hands, but that information could've been months or even years out of date. Spanish soldiers had captured the trading post during Bonhomme's War, twenty-five years earlier. There was no reason to think that the French, who now ruled Nouvelle Orleans, wouldn't do the same.

Colonel Whiteside was cautious and had the regiment make camp well north of the trading post. He sent Captain McIntyre and the Seventh Company overland to Natchez with orders to capture it from the French if need be. Hunting parties were sent out to get fresh meat. The rest of us were put to work retying the ropes that held the rafts together and redistributing supplies, waiting for word that it was safe to continue.

Two days later a messenger from Captain McIntyre reported that they had found Natchez abandoned and in ashes. There were no signs of bodies or new graves. Whilst there was some speculation that the Choctaws may have been responsible, it was far easier to believe that the French had captured the post and taken its residents prisoner. We boarded our rafts and started downriver again.

Natchez sat atop a bluff on the east side of the river. We made landfall at the base of the bluff, then company-by-company climbed the well-established path to the top to view its burnt out remains. The King's Own Virginians had been in existence for two years. Our mission had been to fight the French, but this was our first evidence of the enemy. There were muttered curses and vows of vengeance from the men of the First Company. When we were all assembled again by our rafts, the colonel made a brief speech reminding us that our orders were to drive the French out of Louisiana. The speech was unnecessary. To a man, the Virginians knew our task. We cheered long and loud for the King before starting out again.

Our maps showed three French forts along the river between Natchez and Nouvelle Orleans. The first of these, Tunicas, more than a hundred miles downriver from Natchez, was said to be a small wooden stockade that could house a half company of men at most.

Still, we approached it with care, only to find it abandoned. Outside the fort, a small plot, shaded by apple and pear trees, was planted in vegetables and herbs. Other than the wild berries we'd found along the riverbanks, the Virginians hadn't seen fresh fruit or vegetables in months. The garden and orchard were soon picked clean—a swarm of locusts couldn't have been more thorough.

The French hadn't been as diligent in removing their belongings from Tunicas as the English at Nuevo Madrid. The barracks and houses were full of discarded items, most of which were worthless. The Virginians picked over them with great care, each man trying to find the right item to take as a souvenir. I found a pewter button decorated with a *fleur-de-lis* as my keepsake.

The next fort, Pointe Coupé, about fifty miles farther south, was more substantial and looked as if it could house a company or more. Its stockade was built of wood and had bastions at each of its four corners, mimicking the design of larger forts. Like Tunicas, it was abandoned, but in addition to gardens and fruit trees, we found nearly a hundredweight of maize in its storehouse. The grain was beginning to sprout, but that made no difference to us. We located several hand mills and in a few hours had fresh bread for the first time since leaving Fort Roanoke.

We expected the last fort, Côte des Allemands, about fifty miles north of Nouvelle Orleans, to be abandoned, but to our surprise we found a German family, Rolf Hauser, his son Wolfgang, daughter-in-law Greta, and five young children, living there. Hauser looked to be about fifty and reminded me of my father. He was a short man with the powerful arms and legs of a farmer and a face that had been tanned by many hours in the sun.

The Hausers were the first people we'd seen since starting our float down the Cumberland, nearly three months earlier. I was sure there'd been Indians observing us from the woods, but they remained well-hidden, and as I have related, all of the settlements we passed had been abandoned.

I heard Hauser call to his family in German when the first of our soldiers approached. My German, which I'd learned from my Dutch mother, was a little rusty—I'd last used it thirty years ago when I was an orderly on General Washington's staff during the Great Rebellion—but I understood that Hauser was telling his family to get in the house and stay out of sight. Without thinking, I translated

Hauser's words out loud. Captain Jackson heard me and told the colonel that I could act as a translator. My services weren't necessary because we soon discovered that Hauser spoke English. After a few pleasantries, the colonel got down to business, questioning Hauser about the French.

"Why were Tunicas and Pointe Coupé abandoned?"

"Three weeks ago," Hauser answered, "we were told to go to Nouvelle Orleans. Major DuChamps paid the Choctaw and other tribes to tell him where you were. He knows you'll soon be knocking at his door. He wants every man who can fire a musket ready to greet you."

"But you stayed?"

"*Ja*, I stayed. I'm not going to leave my farm just because a French sergeant comes riding up and tell me to."

"Won't that make you an enemy of the French?"

"I am already an enemy of the French. I am from Mainz. The French conquered my city in 1797. Their army raped every woman they could find and stole everything they could move. I came here as soon as I could because Louisiana was Spanish. I thought I'd be free of those damn revolutionaries. But Spain was too weak. All Dumouriez had to do was say, 'Give me Louisiana.' and they did."

"How many soldiers do the French have in Nouvelle Orleans?" Captain Jackson asked.

"About two hundred. There are a few Frenchman who might be willing to fight with DuChamps' soldiers, but most of the white men in town are Spanish."

"I'd heard that Nouvelle Orleans was half French, half Spanish."

"It was forty years ago, after France gave Louisiana to Spain, but the French didn't like living under the Spanish and most of them moved away. A few have moved back since Dumouriez took control."

"Will the Spanish fight for the French?" Captain McIntyre asked.

"I think so. Spain and France have been allies for many years."

"What about the black men? Would DuChamps give them guns?"

"*Nein*, give the *swartzers* guns and they'll start murdering white men like they did in Sainte-Domingue. DuChamps knows this."

"No reason for them to help us either," Captain Pettit mused. "We're not going to free them." There was silence for a few moments whilst each officer tried to understand what we were likely to face in Nouvelle Orleans.

"Herr Hauser," the colonel said at last. "We can't continue floating down the river if the French know we are coming and are prepared for us. We need to travel overland. Will you lead a scouting party to Nouvelle Orleans to make sure the road is safe? We'll pay you generously for your services."

"Let me talk to my son." After a hurried conference in German, Hauser asked, "How much will you pay me?"

"Two shillings a day plus meals at the officers' mess." Geoff Carlyle had been paid the same amount, but had to pay for his meals.

"Half a Spanish dollar each day, and in Spanish coins, not English ones," Hauser replied. He was asking for nearly four shillings a day.

"Done," said the colonel, shaking Hauser's hand. From the look on Whiteside's face, it was clear that he wasn't happy having to pay this higher price, but he had little choice—Hauser and his son, who didn't speak English, were the only men who could serve as our guides.

But Hauser wasn't done. "You will order your men to leave my farm alone?"

"I will. I'll issue orders that any man who molests your family or steals your property will be hanged." After the flogging the previous month, no one questioned that the colonel would carry out his threat.

Herr Hauser smiled broadly and said that he had honey and fruit preserves for sale, an offer that we enthusiastically accepted. He led us to a small cavern, which had been dug in the side of the riverbank. He pushed aside the vines and briars that hid its entrance and was soon conducting a brisk business.

I was one of the lucky few who was able to buy a small flask of honey. Hauser charged five shillings for it, double the normal price, but I probably would have paid several times that amount. Like the rest of the Virginians, I'd had nothing sweet to eat since leaving Fort Roanoke. I shared my bounty with Samuel Smith. The two of us finished the flask in one sitting, which left me happy, but slightly nauseated.

The next morning Hauser led a six-man scouting party commanded by Captain Pettit to reconnoitre the road. Captain Jackson and I divided up the Virginians' stores and rockets into equal weight loads. With our rifles, ammunition, and personal belongings, each of us would carry about a hundred pounds.

After two-and-a-half months of floating down rivers, not having to carry anything heavy, I'd gone soft. I could barely move under my load. Looking around, it was obvious that I wasn't the only one suffering. To my surprise, none of the Virginians complained, though more than one man said he wished he'd been part of the scouting party. We all realised that if we remained on the rafts, we'd be sitting ducks if the French decided to attack us.

Late on the afternoon of our first day's march, we encountered a ten-foot-long reptile, which one of the men promptly shot. It was a huge animal, weighing hundreds of pounds, with teeth that looked like they would have no problem severing an arm or leg. I recognised it as an alligator. I'd seen one in Nuevo Orleans, twenty years earlier. Private Andrews from the Fourth Company, who'd been to Florida, told us that its meat was good eating, and since it was time to set up camp anyway, the alligator was quickly skinned and large strips of its meat were set out to roast. All of the Virginians wanted a taste, but most concluded after a bite or two that eating reptile was disgusting. I ate a small piece and found the meat vaguely reminiscent of chicken. But I agreed with those who had no desire to eat such a repulsive-looking creature.

We arrived at the gates of Nouvelle Orleans in three days.

CHAPTER 10

Nouvelle Orleans' defences were stronger than when I'd last seen them more than twenty years earlier. An impressive looking stone wall now shielded the river side of the town. Since the Virginians had no way of attacking from the river, that defence didn't concern us. Eight-foot-high earthen walls protected the three land-ward sides of the town. All trees within about a half-mile of the walls had been cut to provide the defenders a clear field of fire, but beyond that lay thick, swampy forest. Judging by the amount of manure in the cleared area, it was also used as pasture land.

The town's walls were not protected by an abatis, ditch, or moat, but they had bastions at each corner and in the centre of the wall opposite the river, next to the gate that provided a landward entrance to the city. The cannon on the landward side were mounted atop these bastions to provide overlapping fields of fire. The guns we could see appeared to be twelve-pounders with a range of about three-quarters of a mile.

We set up our tents in the trees, just outside the range of DuChamps' cannon and any rifles the French might've had, then established a picquet line at the edge of the trees. DuChamps' gunners fired a few shots at them, but soon gave up. Trying to kill our picquets with cannon fire was like trying to kill a flea with a sledgehammer. It would take a very lucky—or perhaps I should say unlucky—shot to do that. None of our sentries was killed, but several suffered minor injuries from tree limbs sent flying by French cannon balls.

Once the French realised that we couldn't attack from the river, they moved more cannon to the landward side, but they never had enough to give them the rapid rate of fire needed to fill the air with a wall of shot and obliterate an attacking army. Nouvelle Orleans' defences had been designed to protect against attack by Indians or pirates. The French never expected to be attacked by a regiment of riflemen.

The next morning, the colonel and Captain McIntyre, who spoke French, walked towards the city gate under a white flag. They were soon met in the middle of the cleared area by two French officers in full dress uniform.

"I am Theodore Whiteside, uh, colonel in command of the King's Own Virginians," the colonel said loud enough for us to hear. "I call upon you to surrender and spare your town the ravages of a siege." Captain McIntyre translated this into French, then translated the French officer's reply.

"And I am Major Armand DuChamps, commander of Nouvelle Orleans. It is you who should be surrendering. We are well supplied and safe behind our walls. You have only a few weeks' supplies and nothing to protect yourself from my cannon and sharpshooters. The land around here will not sustain your army."

"We found our trading post at Natchez in ashes," the colonel said, changing the subject. "Was that your doing?"

"Yes, my soldiers captured your fort."

"Natchez was a peaceful trading post, not, uh, a military fort. What happened to the men and their families who lived there?"

"I do not know. My men reported that the fort was abandoned when they arrived. They burnt it so that it would not be available for your use."

"Major, if I find that you are lying, I will hold you responsible for any harm done to the residents of the Natchez trading post."

"Colonel, I have no reason to lie to you. Most likely the men in the fort took their families and travelled up the Indian trail to French Lick."

The colonel and DuChamps traded a few more jibes before returning to their respective forces.

I knew as well as anyone that DuChamps was correct about our supplies. By my reckoning, the Virginians had enough food for twenty-six days at full rations. Hauser had told us that all food had been removed from the plantations in the area and that our hunters would find less game in the nearby swamps than they had in the middle of Tennessee. Our siege would fail if we ran out of food. The colonel must have known the same thing because he gave orders to immediately start building scaling ladders and making preparations for an attack.

To my surprise, the colonel planned a night attack. The regiment was to sneak as close as it could to the walls. Our rockets would be aimed and ready to fire, but the barrage would not begin until we were discovered. The colonel wanted to give the French as little time as possible to organise their defence.

It was an audacious plan. Firing rockets over the heads of the attacking Virginians would be dangerous. To determine how best to aim the rockets, the colonel ordered twenty of them fired over Nouvelle Orleans' walls. All but one of them landed in the town. We could see smoke from several fires but couldn't tell whether they had done any other damage. The rocket that failed flew long, sailing into the Mississippi. That gave the regiment more confidence that we wouldn't be killed by our own weapons.

As soon as the first scaling ladders were ready we practised mounting them whilst carrying our rifles, bayonets, ammunition, and the few other things we'd need in battle. Since we didn't have walls to practice with, we leaned the ladders against tall trees and climbed them as quickly as possible, then, once we had reached the top, made our way slowly down to allow the next man to practice.

Nearly a thousand Virginians were ready to attack on 10th September, a week after our arrival at Nouvelle Orleans. Once it was fully dark, we formed up in three lines by companies. I was in the second line, about ten yards behind the first members of my company, in command of a squad of eleven—my messmates and another mess group—who were to mount the wall on three ladders.

"You'll be the last one up your ladder," Sergeant McMillan told me.

"Shouldn't I be first?"

"You're to see that there are no skulkers . . . that every man mounts the ladders as he should."

I didn't know what I would do if one of the men skulked—prod him with my bayonet? Shoot him?

The colonel had us wait for several hours whilst the French settled in for the night and went to sleep. Our officers kept us from talking in any voice louder than a whisper. A loud voice or any other noise might alert the French. We couldn't engage in the normal banter that soldiers use to hide their fear.

I couldn't see him, but I knew that my son David was out there. I was more afraid that he might be harmed than I was about being killed or injured myself. Samuel Smith was the only one I could've shared these thoughts with, but he was with Fifth Company.

I wondered how my father felt when he saw me line up with Smallwood's Regiment, preparing to attack the Old Stone House during the Battle of Brooklyn, before Major Gist told me that I was just a boy and to leave the formation. Was father proud of me or worried that I might be harmed? David was far too old be to be considered a boy. He'd be part of the attack, and all I could do was pray that he'd be safe.

Finally, a little before midnight, the colonel gave the order to attack. The moon was just past full, but clouds scudded across its face, obscuring much of its light. Since we were trying to surprise the French, no bugles sounded and orders were whispered not shouted. We began crawling towards Nouvelle Orleans' wall, which was still some fifty yards away when our attack was discovered. A French sentry fired his musket and rang a loud bell to rouse the rest of the defenders.

The Virginians froze in place, waiting for our rockets to be fired. They soon passed over our heads with an ear-shattering roar. The smoke that trailed behind them blinded and choked us.

We were supposed to spring up once the rockets had passed and rush towards the wall. I got up as quickly as I could, but spent the next minutes coughing and gasping for breath, trying to clear my lungs of the smoke I'd inhaled. I couldn't see much, but could hear shouts of "forward" and other exhortations to continue the attack. I heard shouts in French from the wall, but couldn't see the defenders or understand what was being said.

The delay was devastating. From the shouts in French, I knew that more crapauds were coming to oppose us. By the time the smoke had cleared enough for me to see, several scaling ladders had been pushed back, throwing the Virginians who'd been on them to the ground.

Then it was my squad's turn. The ladders that we were supposed to climb were slammed against the wall. I waited a few seconds whilst Dixon, Price, and Fox climbed ahead of me. I'd just put my foot on the first rung when the ladder was pushed away. I jumped clear and landed on the ground without injury. My messmates were not as lucky. Harry Dixon made it to the top of the wall, where he was wounded and taken prisoner. John Price, who was high up the ladder, fell and was knocked senseless. Stuart Fox also fell and must have injured his left arm because it hung at a strange angle as he staggered away. In the confusion I lost track of Ed Farrell and Adam McNair.

The attack had failed. There were now too many French on the wall, either fighting the Virginians who had made it to the top or pushing away the remaining scaling ladders. We had no choice but to retreat. French gunners were in place, but couldn't depress their cannon barrels enough to fire on those of us close to the wall. Their shots sailed over our heads. The Virginians fired a few shots at the mass of men atop the wall, but it was impossible to distinguish friend from foe. With the help of another man who I didn't recognise in the dark, I dragged Price back to our lines. By the time we got two hundred yards from the wall, the French gunners realised that we were retreating and in range of their cannon. But they had shot, not canister, and only a few of our soldiers were killed.

Price recovered consciousness shortly after we reached our lines and seemed no worse for the wear. He told us that he'd always known he had a hard head, but now he had proof. Fox had a dislocated shoulder. The surgeon wrenched it back into place—causing him great pain—put the arm in a sling, and told Fox he'd be unfit for duty for at least a month, but should suffer no long-term consequences.

The regiment was a sad sight when we assembled for parade at dawn the next morning. Almost half of our number was absent—killed in the attack, taken prisoner, too seriously injured to be fit for duty, or ill with ague. My two remaining messmates, Farrell and McNair, were amongst the missing.

Those of us who were present were filthy, covered with the mud we had crawled through and smoke from the rockets. After survey-ing his command Colonel Whiteside ordered a day of rest with only essential duties carried out. We would be allowed to go to the river one company at a time to wash as best we could.

I looked for my son David in the Fifth Company's ranks, but couldn't find him. I told myself that he was there, but so covered with mud and smoke that I couldn't recognise him, or that he was lightly wounded and excused from parade. I couldn't make myself believe either of these stories. I feared that David was either dead or seriously wounded.

As soon as parade was dismissed, Samuel came up to me. "David's not amongst the wounded," he said. "He was in the first line and was probably taken prisoner."

There was hope. David could be alive inside Nouvelle Orleans' walls. I mumbled a thank you to Samuel and returned to my post at Captain Jackson's tent.

An hour later, Major DuChamps appeared at Nouvelle Orleans' gate under a flag of truce. He was immaculate in a blue French Army uniform. Colonel Whiteside had not crawled through the mud, nor had he been covered in rocket smoke, so his uniform was presentable, if a little tattered from nearly a half year of use. Captain McIntyre had been slightly injured in the attack and had not had the chance to clean the blood off his uniform. He looked worn and haggard as he accompanied the colonel to translate.

The two commanders met halfway between Nouvelle Orleans walls and our lines. "Good to see you Colonel Whiteside," DuChamps began. "I have one hundred ten of your men and two of your officers as my prisoners. I assure you that they will be treated honourably. Our surgeons are tending to the wounded."

"Thank you for that kindness," Colonel Whiteside replied. "I propose a two-hour truce to allow us to collect our dead and any wounded who have survived."

"I will order my men to observe a truce as soon as I return," DuChamps said. "I will also send wagons with the bodies of those of your soldiers who died on our walls. I am sure you will want to bury them."

Colonel Whiteside started to leave but DuChamps took his arm.

"*Mon Colonel*, now that you see the futility of attacking us, surrender and spare your men further hardship. Your captain here,"

DuChamps said, nodding slightly towards McIntyre, "survived last night, but I cannot promise he will be so lucky if you attack again."

"My orders are to capture Nouvelle Orleans and I intend to do so. Good day, Major." The Frenchman shrugged and returned to the fort.

The truce went into effect fifteen minutes later, and the regiment quickly moved forward to retrieve the casualties. We found only a score of wounded, but over a hundred dead either on the ground or in DuChamps' wagons. Farrell and McNair were amongst them. I grieved for them. They hadn't been as friendly as I might've wished, but I'd shared my meals with them for almost two years and they were as close to family as I was likely to have.

"You'd better come," Samuel said, pointing to a stack of dead bodies fifty yards away at the edge of the woods. "We found David's body lying at the base of the wall. He'd been in the first rank and must have made it to the top. A musket ball hit him in the chest. That would have knocked him down. I'm sure he died quickly."

I followed Samuel to the bodies and quickly recognised my son's corpse. His face had the ashen pallor of death and his chest was covered with dried blood. Flies swarmed around him. I swatted at them in a vain attempt to keep them from landing and feeding. After looking at the body for a minute, I turned away. I felt tears in my eyes, but I willed myself not to weep. I remembered my father's dictum that men don't weep.

I took one more look at David's body, squared my shoulders, and pulled in my belly, then, as resolutely as I could, walked back to the First Company's area. I needed to find someplace to be alone. No one paid any attention to me as I headed into the swamp behind our tents. After five minutes I found a log to sit on.

I knew I should mourn David, but no tears came. I didn't know him. I'd never spoken to him or identified myself as his father. I'd seen him numerous times and had no difficulty picturing him—a brown-haired, round-faced private laughing and jesting with his fellow soldiers—but I knew nothing about what he'd thought or felt. He must've been brave because he'd advanced as far as any of the Virginians. Samuel had told me that he had been loyal to Adam Stahlworth, the man he knew as his father. David spoke highly of Adam, despite Adam's poor business decisions that had reduced the family to poverty. He was a good man, and I wished I could've announced to the world that he was my son.

After about an hour the discomfort of sitting on that log overcame my other feelings. I had to stand and stretch. When I did, I realised that I needed to return to my company before I was missed. I didn't want to have to explain what I'd been doing. David's death became part of my personal sorrow, along with Awinita's death, Judy Slater's rejection of my marriage proposal, and my Cherokee son Onacona's denial of me as his father. In the gloom that followed the Virginians' defeat, no one noticed my grief. There were many other sad faces around.

One hundred seventeen men and three officers, all company commanders, had died in the attack. Almost two hundred more were too seriously wounded to carry out even light duties. DuChamps had told us another one hundred ten men and two officers were prisoners.

The heat made it imperative that we bury the dead as soon as possible. Colonel Whiteside had to rescind his order for a day of rest and put us to work digging graves. We had all of the men in the ground by sunset. When the regiment assembled for evening parade, the colonel said a prayer for the souls of the dead, then announced we would have our day of rest the next day.

Colonel Whiteside moved quickly to fill the vacancies in company commands. Lieutenant Conroy took command of the Fourth Company. The other two lieutenants who were waiting for commands were given the Sixth and Tenth Companies. Sergeants were placed in temporary command of the Eighth and Ninth Companies. Their captains had been taken prisoner. Despite what Captain Jackson had told me about men being promoted from the ranks when officers were killed in battle, there were no such promotions.

We settled into the grim business of siege. We had no assurance we would be successful. Two days after the attack, Captain Jackson and I recalculated our supplies. With our losses, they were now sufficient for twenty-five days at full rations. We reported this to the colonel who ordered the regiment onto half rations, to be supplemented by whatever game our hunters could kill. Each company was to send out a hunting party. As Captain Jackson had done the year before, the colonel ordered that all meat the hunters brought back be shared by the whole regiment. He also encouraged fishing in the streams near our camp. Any fish caught were also to go into the common pot, but that was a harder rule to enforce.

The swamps around Nouvelle Orleans offered little meat other than alligator and an occasional turtle. Faced with eating alligator or going hungry, most of the Virginians soon developed a taste for the previously despised reptiles. Our hunters began collecting the long eye teeth from the alligators they killed and wearing chains of these fangs around their necks. Captain Jackson ordered the First Company not to wear alligator teeth since they were not part of the Virginians' uniform. He had to relent when other company commanders not only allowed their men to wear these ornaments, but took to wearing the fangs themselves. Some of the hunters tried to fashion belts and other articles out of alligator hide, but since they had no way to tan the leather, these articles quickly stretched out of shape and became useless.

Usually I brought my worries about the Virginians to Samuel Smith, but this time he came to me.

"William, when the hunting parties are out each day, how many men do you think we have on our lines?"

"Probably about four hundred," I replied.

"And how many men do you think DuChamps has?"

"Probably three or four hundred."

"What would happen if all those men rushed out the gate and attacked us?"

"We'd be overwhelmed," I said. "There are probably no more than a hundred fifty men opposite the gate."

"DuChamps must think he's got more food than we do," Samuel continued, "so he can wait us out, but if he starts running out of food, he'll attack. We can hunt. He can't."

"I hadn't thought of that. I reckoned we were in the weaker position because we can't attack again. We fired almost all of our rockets in last week's attack. There can't be more than two dozen left."

"We'll be in the weaker position once DuChamps figures out he can overwhelm us any time he chooses."

"Do you think his soldiers would be willing to make such an attack? The first ones out of the gate will be easy targets for us."

"If the choice is attack or starve, they'll attack."

I was silent for a few minutes thinking about the possibilities that Samuel had just laid out, then he took his leave. I was troubled by what he'd said, but I couldn't argue with his logic. His fears became my fears as well.

CHAPTER 11

Even though it was late September there was no relief from the oppressive weather that had plagued us for the past two months. Each day was a copy of the day before—clear and relatively cool in the early morning, temperature rising as the sun climbed to its zenith, clouds beginning to form at midday, and, if we were lucky, a thunderstorm in the late afternoon that provided a brief cooler interlude before the heat and humidity returned. It remained sultry until midnight or later, when it finally became cool enough to sleep without being drenched in sweat.

The morning of Friday, 24th September, seemed like every other morning we'd experienced since arriving at Nouvelle Orleans. It was a bit hotter and there was even less wind than usual, but no hint of danger. In early afternoon flocks of black terns began arriving from the south. Some roosted in the trees around our tents, whilst others continued north. This was strange behaviour. Migrating birds should have been flying south at this time of year.

I was in Captain Jackson's tent, again reckoning how long our supplies would last, when Herr Hauser approached. He and Jackson had become friends over the past weeks.

"You look troubled, Herr Hauser," Jackson said. He knew enough about German customs not to address the man by his first name.

That was reserved for family. Even men who had been close friends for many years addressed each other formally.

"Captain Jackson, you must warn your colonel that a hurricane is on the way and that you have to find shelter," a clearly agitated Hauser said. "I tried to tell him, but he looked at the sky and said that there was nothing to worry about. He didn't believe me when I told him that the terns were a warning. They are called hurricane birds. They live at the coast and only fly inland when a big storm is coming."

"How much time do we have?"

"A day, two at the most."

"Then there's not much we can do," Jackson said. "The remaining rockets and food are under canvas and well protected."

"You must move everything away from the river. It will rise ten feet in the middle of the storm, and surely there is something more you can do to protect your men."

"I've lived through hurricanes in South Carolina and know how dangerous they can be. I'll try to convince the colonel to move our stores away from the river, but in a day or two we can't build anything strong enough to protect ourselves. The only thing we can do is strike our tents once the wind and rain begin. At least we can keep them from blowing away."

Jackson's reply did not ease Hauser's concern and he went off to find someone else who might give him the answer he wanted.

I'd heard about hurricanes, but had never experienced one. Amos Cartwright told me about one that'd hit Salisbury. Even though its force was diminished, it still damaged his house. None had reached Salisbury whilst I lived there, and Davidson's Fort was too far inland for ocean storms to be a concern. But Nouvelle Orleans must have experienced them often enough for Hauser to recognise the signs that one was on its way. I paid careful attention to the weather after his warning. The rest of the day and that night passed with no change other than more shorebirds flying north.

Dawn was gloomy. High, smooth clouds hid the sun and there were occasional gusts of wind to the northeast. Now no one questioned that a storm was on its way. The Virginians scurried around collecting clothes that had been left to dry and other unattached items. By mid-morning the wind had freshened to near gale force and we were pelted by brief, but intense, rain showers.

After a tent tore loose from its pegs, Colonel Whiteside ordered all tents struck, and any food or rockets close to the river moved to higher ground. The Seventh Company shifted its stores only a short distance from the shore. Hauser berated them and there was an ugly exchange of words until Captain McIntyre stepped in and ordered his men to move the stores to still higher ground.

The storm continued to intensify. Even though it was noon, the sky was almost as dark as night. Tree limbs flew through the air as if tossed about by giants. I found a tree I thought would withstand the maelstrom and huddled as close to its trunk as I could. Three other Virginians joined me, but with the wind howling like an army of banshees, conversation was impossible. Torrential rains had long since soaked me, but I rejected any thought of putting on oilskins. They'd be too hot to bear.

Then, after being assaulted for three hours, all was quiet. The rain stopped and the wind dropped to a light breeze. Sunlight filtered through high thin clouds. Slowly, the Virginians left whatever shelter they had taken and gathered to marvel at the sight. We were in the fabled eye of the hurricane, surrounded by a circular wall of black cloud so high that we couldn't see its top. The air was hard to breathe, but I couldn't fathom why. It seemed unnatural.

We could now see that the river had risen a half dozen feet or more, sweeping away everything but the largest trees. Herr Hauser had been correct in his warning about the river flooding. I wondered what had happened to the rafts we left at Côte des Allemands. Whilst we wouldn't need them again, they'd served us well, and it seemed like they deserved a better fate than to be washed away in the torrent.

Our respite lasted for less than a half hour, then we were again battered by the storm. Initially the wind and rain were as intense as what we had experienced earlier, but they soon began to diminish. After three more hours the storm was over and the sun reappeared low in the sky. The hurricane had taken the whole afternoon to pass.

Colonel Whiteside had us form up for parade and roll was taken. A dozen men were missing and two dozen more had injuries that required the surgeon's attention. A search was mounted for the missing men. We found them before nightfall. Seven were dead, the other five too seriously injured to walk, a further depletion of our ranks. Herr Hauser said that we were lucky that it was only a small hurricane and that we'd escaped so lightly. Unfortunately, the storm didn't do any damage to Nouvelle Orleans' fortifications. They looked as strong as ever.

The next day I started shaking with chills. At first I thought it was the result of having been soaked during the hurricane, but when the chills were followed by fever, I knew I had the ague. I reported to the surgeon, who gave me a dose of the tincture of bark that he used to treat the illness. It tasted foul, but I drank it down eagerly. I'd seen it work for other men and was anxious to be cured. I felt weak the next day, but other than that my symptoms were gone. I had another bout a week later and received more of the medicine. After that I was cured. Many others were not as lucky. They had recurring bouts of ague for months or even years after their initial illness.

Two days after I recovered from my second bout of ague, our foragers returned from a plantation whose owner, a Monsieur Piccard, hadn't followed Major DuChamps' orders to evacuate to Nouvelle Orleans. They captured him and his family, as well as two dozen slaves, and most importantly, two hogsheads of rum and three wagonloads of ham, bacon, smoked beef, maize, squash, and other vegetables. The food added to our dwindling supplies. The colonel declared a double rum ration and a full meat ration for the next day. We feasted on the contents of Piccard's larder.

Colonel Whiteside signalled that he wanted a truce. When Major DuChamps obliged, Piccard and his family were escorted through the gate to Nouvelle Orleans—the Virginians had no way to hold civilian prisoners. The slaves were put to work—the men chopping firewood, the women cooking, and the older children doing whatever tasks they were capable of. Other than Greta Hauser, the six slave women commandeered from Piccard's plantation were the first women we'd seen in six months.

"Sure would be nice to have a woman again, no matter what the colour of her skin," Private Hardwick said at evening mess that night, as he sipped his rum ration and stared lustfully at the young mulatto woman who was dishing out slices of ham. She spoke only French and some unintelligible dialect the slaves used amongst themselves.

She showed no indication that she understood what Hardwick had said, even if his intent should have been clear from the look on his face.

"It's been so long you've probably forgotten what to do with a woman," Private O'Malley joked.

"Just give me a chance. You'll see what I can do, you bog-trotter." After the two of them had been flogged for fighting, they'd formed a bond, and were now closer than brothers. They insulted each other freely.

Hardwick and O'Malley were not the only men eyeing the slave women. The colonel had them sleep in a tent near his. This dissuaded any of the regiment from trying to satisfy his lust that first night. At morning parade, Colonel Whiteside issued orders that no man was to molest the slave women. I didn't think he was worried about their virtue—it was obvious from the skin colour of slave children that Piccard or some other white man had fathered most of them. More likely the colonel realised that six slave women couldn't satisfy the lust of the entire regiment, and that some men having the privilege whilst others didn't could only lead to problems.

From the grumbling in the ranks that morning, it seemed that most of the men thought Whiteside was reserving the slave women for himself and the other officers. Captain Jackson assured the First Company that this was not the case, but that did little to stop the grousing. Discontent rose to such a level that after three days the colonel decided to return part of Monsieur Piccard's property to him. A truce was arranged and the slave women and their children were sent to Nouvelle Orleans.

A week later I heard sustained rifle fire from the south side of Nouvelle Orleans. It sounded like a skirmish of some sort, but I couldn't figure out why there should be fighting. Since our ill-fated attack, the siege had proceeded with only a random shot or two, when one of our riflemen thought he could hit a crapaud on the wall, or when a French marksman thought one of our soldiers had wandered into range. No one, Virginian or French, was injured by these futile attempts.

"Watson, find out what's happening," Captain Jackson ordered.

I trotted off and a few minutes later I was amongst the Ninth Company's riflemen who were firing at a small ship being towed upriver by sailors in rowboats. They'd killed or wounded some of the sailors, but the *Madeleine*, whose name was clearly visible on her bow, was able to make it safely to the dock below the riverfront wall.

"Damnation, couldn't your men have stopped that ship?" Colonel Whiteside, who arrived after I had, fumed at Sergeant Sommerville, acting commander of the Ninth. "It's probably carrying supplies for the town." It was not a question to be answered, and the colonel didn't wait for one. The men of the Ninth Company had done the best they could. I returned to Captain Jackson and reported what I'd seen.

"If that ship could get in, it'll have an easier time getting out when the wind and tide are right," Jackson said. "The French will know our situation and send reinforcements from Martinique. We have six weeks at most."

"Our food won't last that long, even at half rations," I said. The captain knew our supply situation as well as I did, so he couldn't accuse me of being faint-hearted.

"I wonder if some of our men could swim to the ship and take her, pirate-style, with knives and swords?" Jackson mused.

"If they did, what would they do next? They can't just sail off."

"Right," Jackson agreed. "DuChamps' men would recapture the ship and kill or take prisoner all of our men."

Jackson had no further thoughts and shortly afterwards dismissed me.

I was on picquet duty three nights later, opposite Nouvelle Orleans' main gate, when I heard a rustling in the trees to my right. It was nearly midnight and no one should have been about. The sound was too loud to be any of the small animals that still inhabited the woods.

"Who goes there?" I shouted.

"Don't shoot," a voice called in French, then repeated the appeal in Spanish.

"Advance and be recognised," I called, pointing my rifle in the direction the voice had come from. A man in a French Army uniform came slowly out of the woods, his hand held up as a gesture of surrender. Perkins and Connors, two privates who were also on picquet duty, had heard the exchange and were now at my side pointing their rifles at the French soldier.

"I wish to surrender," the soldier said, first in French, then in Spanish.

"Perkins, make sure he doesn't have any weapons."

The soldier submitted to Perkins' rough search.

"What is your name?" I asked in the Spanish I'd learned during my four years as a prisoner in Texas.

"I am Sergeant Antonio Montoya. I am happy that you speak Spanish. I don't want to speak French any longer than I have to. Please take me to your commanding officer. I come with an offer of help."

I decided to take the prisoner to Captain Jackson first. I didn't want to risk the colonel's displeasure in case our prisoner's offer was worthless.

"Connors, remain on picquet duty. Perkins, bring the prisoner along."

Jackson was still awake, rereading one of the books he'd brought with him.

"Beggin' you pardon, sir," I said when he looked up at the three of us. "This French soldier has just surrendered. He says he can help us. He's a Spaniard and would rather speak Spanish. I can translate."

"Right then," Jackson said after looking the solider up and down for a few moments. "How can you help us?"

"*Capitaine*, most of the soldiers you have been fighting are Spanish. Only the officers and a few young soldiers who arrived in the past five years are French. We were in the Spanish Army when Spain ruled Louisiana. We stayed after the French took command in 1802. We thought that France and Spain were allies against England, as they have been for so long."

Montoya paused whilst Jackson considered this news. After a few moments, the captain nodded to show he understood what he'd been told and Montoya continued.

"Three days ago, when the *Madeleine* arrived, we found out that the past February, France invaded Spain and forced King Carlos IV to abdicate. His son Ferdinand VII became king, but the French forced him to flee after less than three months. Marshal Masséna is now dictator of Spain."

"How did you learn this?" I asked.

"The French sailors bragged about it. They said that France would now have the riches of Peru and Mexico. They also told us that the people of Spain have been attacking French soldiers, but that the French Army slaughtered hundreds of them, that Masséna had been merciless."

Jackson cleared his throat as a signal that he wanted to speak and Montoya stopped his narrative.

"Spain has been a willing ally of France for many years," the captain said, eyeing Montoya suspiciously. "Why should they invade your country?"

"Who knows what goes on in the mind of that madman Dumouriez? When we heard how his army was killing innocent men and women in Spain, we soldiers decided that we could do no longer serve the French. We are not strong enough to overcome the French, but last night we decided that we can help you defeat them. But you must promise to treat the citizens of Nouvelle Orleans with respect and not molest their women or steal their property."

"How can you help us?" Jackson asked. He seemed intrigued with Montoya.

"We can open the city gates for you."

"When?"

"Tomorrow night, if you wish. I must sneak back into the city and alert my companions. We will have only one chance."

"The colonel needs to hear this story. Watson, bring the prisoner. Perkins, return to picquet duty."

We woke the colonel and, after hearing Montoya's story, he called all of his officers into conference. Montoya repeated his story a third time. When he was finished there was a long discussion of how to work with the Spanish inside the city. By this time it was dawn, too late for Montoya to return that night. After still more discussion, the colonel agreed that Montoya would sneak back into Nouvelle Orleans that night, and that our assault would be the following midnight. Montoya and the other Spanish soldiers would attack their French officers and open the main gate. The Virginians would be ready outside the city and would rush forward as soon as the gates were open.

All had been agreed and the meeting seemed ready to disband, when Captain McIntyre spoke up. "Sergeant Montoya, you are placing yourself at great risk. You'll have to hide in Nouvelle Orleans for more than twenty-four hours. If the French discover you, they will shoot for deserting your post."

"*Si, Capitan*, but the people of Spain, my people, are being slaughtered by the French. I cannot fight the French alone. If I help you, we can reclaim Nuevo Orleans for Spain."

"And how do we know this is not a ruse?" Captain McIntyre asked. "How do we know that you will not return to Nouvelle Orleans, not as a deserter, but as a hero who has tricked the British into making an attack that is doomed to fail? We will hear the sounds of fighting. The gates will be opened, and we will rush in to face French and Spanish soldiers waiting to slaughter us."

Montoya was speechless for a few moments. He hadn't thought about how his offer might be seen differently. "I swear by the Virgin Mary and the soul of my mother that what I have told you is true," he finally stammered.

Captain McIntyre seemed mollified, but I could see from the looks on the faces of some of the other officers at the table that he'd raised a possibility that none of them had considered.

"We have no choice but to put our trust in Sergeant Montoya," Colonel Whiteside said. "If we do not attack, our supplies will run out and our siege will fail. We are not strong enough to assault Nouvelle Orleans walls again. We need help from within the city, and that is what we are being offered. Gentlemen, my mind is made up. We attack at midnight the night after tomorrow."

Two nights later we were again arrayed outside Nouvelle Orleans' walls. Promptly at midnight we heard the sound of musketry. A few minutes later the gates of Nouvelle Orleans swung open. The Virginians sprang up and rushed through the opening. Inside a confused melee was underway with men in French uniforms fighting each other. Several of the Virginians fired their rifles in the air to gain attention. Montoya called out and the Spaniards assembled to our right. This left about thirty men milling around in the street, the officers and soldiers who actually were French. With over a hundred rifles pointed at them they quickly surrendered. Montoya had told the truth. In less than ten minutes we had become masters of New Orleans, as we began calling it.

We disarmed the French as quickly as we could and herded them into a large stable. The colonel posted a strong guard to ensure that they stayed there.

Colonel Whiteside's next thought was for the Virginians who had been taken prisoner in our first attack. I went with Montoya and Captain Jackson to where they were being held, a low set of buildings built into the riverfront wall. The gaoler was only too happy to unlock the rooms that held our men. A ragged cheer went up when the colonel arrived and told those who could to form a column and to march back to our lines. A quick count showed that twenty-seven prisoners had died in captivity and that a quarter of the living, including Harry Dixon, whose leg had been amputated by a French surgeon, were too severely injured to march. The colonel ordered Captain Jackson to commandeer transport to carry these men back to the regiment. The citizens of New Orleans, apparently eager to curry favour with their new masters, quickly volunteered wagons, teams, and drivers for this task.

Whilst the colonel was worrying about freeing our prisoners, the French and Spanish who had been wounded in the fighting were taken to New Orleans' hospital, and the dead collected in the city square. Major DuChamps was one of the dead.

It was now dawn and Montoya suggested that the colonel tour the city. The colonel was still unsure that all the city's residents knew that they were now under British control. Captain Jackson and the First Company provided a guard for him.

It felt strange walking through New Orleans without having fought another battle. The streets were empty and silent, except for the sounds of dogs barking and roosters crowing. I knew that we were being watched from behind the shuttered windows of the town's buildings. When we mounted the riverfront wall to continue our exploration, we discovered that the *Madeleine* had been scuttled. Only the tops of her masts were visible above the murky water.

"Who sank this ship?" Colonel Whiteside asked.

"The French sailors," Montoya answered. "They didn't want her to fall into your hands." It wouldn't have mattered if we had taken the *Madeleine*. None of the Virginians knew how to sail her, and the French wouldn't have helped us. We probably would've scuttled her ourselves to prevent the French from attempting to escape.

After his tour was complete, Colonel Whiteside decided that he would make his headquarters in the same house that DuChamps had been using. I quickly recognised it as the house that Major Mendoza, then the Spanish *commandante* of Nuevo Orleans, had used twenty-four years earlier when Terrill and I passed through the town after being released from captivity. I wondered whether Mendoza's fine china and cutlery were still in the dining room. The other officers moved into the best houses in town, and the Virginians were installed in the barracks.

Colonel Whiteside called a meeting of his officers the next day. Captain Jackson later told me that the colonel had been so focused on capturing New Orleans that he hadn't given any thought to how he would govern the town. Jackson said during a short recess after two hours of fruitless debate, he and Captain Pettit, both former lawyers, proposed that the colonel declare martial law, and be guided by the precepts of British common law in enforcing it. The colonel quickly adopted this recommendation.

We'd achieved our goal—we'd captured New Orleans—but we were more than a thousand miles from Fort Roanoke with no way to tell anyone what we'd accomplished, and, despite what Samuel Smith had said about building a road, with no way home. None of the other Virginians seemed to care. They were too happy to have access to New Orleans' ample supplies of rum and whores, and to no longer have to eat alligator or sleep in tents.

The only source of unhappiness was that the Virginians weren't allowed to plunder the town as some thought they should've been under the accepted rules of war. A besieged city had to be given a chance to surrender. Colonel Whiteside did this in his first meeting with Major DuChamps. If the offer was accepted, the city was to be spared. If it was refused, and the besieging army took the city by force, they were permitted to sack the place. New Orleans was a special situation. It hadn't surrendered when first given the chance, but neither had the Virginians taken it by force. Our attack had failed. It was only because the Spaniards in the French Army rebelled that we were masters of the city.

Arguments raged over meals whether we should've been given the right to pillage New Orleans because the French hadn't surrendered when first given the chance, or whether their belated surrender protected them. Then one wag—I never found out who— pointed out that it was the Spanish soldiers who should have the right to sack the town. By rebelling against their French officers and fighting the few French soldiers in the city, they were the ones who had actually conquered New Orleans. No one was able to counter this gambit, but dreams of the riches that might've been theirs stayed in the minds of more than a few of the Virginians.

None of this debate made any difference to Colonel Whiteside. He'd made a promise and, as he soon proved, he intended to keep it. Private Edmunds received a hundred lashes when he was caught breaking into a merchant's house, and Private Donaldson received the same number when a lady from one of the town's finer families complained that he'd made an indecent remark to her. These examples convinced the rest of the regiment to be on best behaviour.

With all that was happening in the aftermath of New Orleans' surrender, little thought was given to re-establishing mess groups. We were issued rations on an individual basis, much to the disgust of the soldiers assigned to commissary duty—they had to work harder. Fox took his meals with the other walking wounded. This left Price and me as the only remaining members of our mess group. We stayed together at meal times, but there was even less camaraderie between us than there'd been before. I think he may've been embarrassed to be beholden to me for pulling him back to our lines after he'd been knocked unconscious. I never mentioned the event, and certainly had no thought of collecting on whatever debt he might've thought he owed me. If, as Sergeant Pew had taught me, messmates were supposed to be closer than brothers, then I only did what a brother would do.

CHAPTER 12

At mid-morning a week later, Captain Jackson came looking for me in the company clerks' room in Colonel Whiteside's head-quarters.

"Watson, report to the colonel," he ordered.

"May I ask why?"

"No, you may not. The colonel will explain."

I was surprised at Jackson's demeanour. He was usually more forthcoming. I went upstairs to the colonel's office and was immediately admitted. I found him with Captain Pettit.

"Watson," the colonel said as soon as I entered. "I understand that, uh, you have travelled the Indian trail from Natchez to French Lick."

"I have, sir, but it was over twenty years ago."

"No matter. You know more about the trail than anyone else in the regiment. I need to send my report back to Fort Roanoke. Captain Pettit will carry it. You'll be his guide. The two of you will leave at dawn tomorrow. Go to your quarters and prepare for your journey."

I saluted and left, but didn't return immediately to my quarters. Instead I went to Captain Jackson's office. He wasn't there, and it took me an hour to find him. He was sitting in one of New Orleans' taverns with a beaker of rum in front of him. This was unusual. I'd never seen Jackson leave his post or drink before noon.

"You've seen the colonel and received his orders," he said without any preamble.

"Yes, sir."

"I tried to convince the colonel that it was too late in the year to send you back to Fort Roanoke, that you couldn't complete the journey before snow and ice made travel impossible." He took a long sip of rum and coughed a little.

"But that bootlicker Pettit volunteered for the mission and dismissed my concerns. Then I tried to convince Whiteside that you were needed here to translate Spanish and that someone else could accompany Pettit. For an instant the colonel agreed with me. Then Pettit said there were other men who could speak Spanish, but that you were the only one who had any knowledge of the trail. I hope you're not being sent to your death."

I didn't know what to say. I hadn't thought about the dangers I would face, but Jackson's words brought visions of freezing to death in the wilds of Tennessee. There was nothing I could do. If I refused a direct order from the colonel I'd be flogged or hanged for insubordination.

"Get the warmest clothes you can find," Jackson said after I'd been silent for a few moments. "Don't let me detain you."

"Thank you, sir," I saluted and turned on my heel to leave.

"Good luck to you, William," Jackson said as I walked out. His voice was low enough that I could pretend not to hear him. I made no reply. I should've said more than a simple thank you, but I couldn't think of the appropriate words.

Word that Captain Pettit and I were going to carry news of the Virginians' victory back to Fort Roanoke quickly spread through the regiment. That afternoon scores of men came up to me to wish me luck. A few pressed hastily written letters and a few coins for postage into my hands. I promised I'd do what I could to have them delivered.

Captain Pettit was brave, but he was no fool. He, too, realised that we would need protection from the cold. When we left the next morning, we each had a French Army greatcoat, woollen cap and gloves, and three thick wool blankets. We led a string of four pack-horses to carry supplies for what he thought would be a three-month journey. *In extremis*, we could eat the horses. From the dour looks on the faces of the Virginians who'd assembled to see us off, most must have thought we were on a fool's mission and wouldn't survive. I prayed they were wrong.

Pettit was not a man you'd pick out of a crowd. He was average height and weight with brown hair. He was clean-shaven with no scars or other identifying marks. It was only when he smiled, which he did often, that he became memorable—he had a grin that seemed to fill his whole face with joy. I knew he was a kind man, who abhorred flogging and had been horrified by the way Captain Bates had displayed the head of the prisoner he'd shot. As I got to know him better, I realised that his smile was the mirror of his soul—he was a happy man with a wry, self-deprecating sense of humour.

We were ferried across the Mississippi and rode north on the Spanish road. We needed to travel slowly so as to not wear out our horses, and to give them plenty of time to graze on the sparse autumn grass. It took us a week to reach a point opposite Natchez. We swam our horses back across the river, spent a night amidst the ashes of the trading post, then started up the trail to French Lick. It was early November. Most of the trees were bare. The weather was still pleasant, brisk in the morning, but warming to comfortable temperatures during the day. A few late-season asters dotted the sides of the path.

"I assume that you were given letters to post by men from the regiment," Pettit said after we had crossed the Mississippi and were headed north.

"I was," I said. "About two dozen, and money to pay the postage."

"I have a similar packet from the officers. Why don't you give me the letters you have and I'll take responsibility for all of them?"

"Happy to do that, sir."

Captain Pettit was an erudite man who had read widely. I knew some of the books he mentioned and was happy to find that his opinions were usually similar to mine. When I felt comfortable enough, I asked him the question I'd asked, or wanted to ask, of every man in the regiment.

"Why'd you join the Virginians?"

"For the worst possible reason," he answered. "I woke up one morning and realised that I was thirty-two years old and never had done anything adventurous. I didn't have a family or other responsibilities, so buying a commission in the Virginians seemed the easiest way to change that."

"And you, William, why did you enlist?" he said, with a quizzical look on his face.

"I'd been a shopkeeper for eighteen years and was bored with that life," I said, telling the same lie I'd told everyone else, even my friend Samuel Smith.

"So you and I are soldiers for the same bad reason."

"I guess so."

We experienced our first winter weather a month into our journey, when we were still ten days' travel from French Lick. We'd had frost every night for the past week, and that morning we awoke to find the ground covered with three inches of wet snow, which was still falling. Captain Pettit decided that both we and our horses needed a rest. I was restless and knew that the snow, which abated by mid-morning, would make it easy to track any game that might be nearby. When I asked the captain for permission to go hunting, he agreed, saying that he was tired of seeing me pace in front of our tent. I took my rifle, mounted my horse, and rode slowly north along the trail, watching for signs of deer or turkey. Bears should've already gone into hibernation.

I came across tracks an hour later, but not ones I wanted to see. In the two hours since the snow had stopped, six riders on unshod horses headed westbound had crossed the path I was on. Whilst it was possible that the riders were white thieves, it was far more likely that they were Indians, Choctaw or Cherokee. We were too far south for Shawnee. Our horses, rifles, and other belongings would have made a tempting target for six armed men, white or Indian. I abandoned all thoughts of hunting and quickly returned to Captain Pettit.

"I'm sure there's nothing to worry about," he said after I reported what I had seen. "You said the riders were headed west. We're headed northeast. It seems unlikely that they will see us."

"But if they turn around, they'll see our tracks, unless it snows again."

"You're right," he said after a moment's thought, "but I don't know what we can do about it other than to proceed as quickly as we can without wearing out our horses."

Rather than spending the whole day resting as Pettit had originally planned, we broke camp and by nightfall had put ten miles between us and the riders' tracks. For the next two nights, we shared watch responsibilities—two hours on, two hours off—but then we realised that keeping watch was so exhausting we wouldn't be able to continue our trip. We took a rest day before continuing on, then slept nights as we had been doing. We saw no new horse tracks, shod or unshod.

We arrived at French Lick at midday on 12th December. There was no reason for us to linger. After a brief stop for dinner, we continued on towards Kuwanda-talunyi on the packhorse track the Virginians had built the previous year. We reached that milestone on Christmas Day. Even though we still had 250 miles or more to travel, Captain Pettit's optimism had begun to infect me. I no longer feared dying in the wilderness. We were almost out of Tennessee. For some unfathomable reason I felt we would be safer in Virginia.

We reached the junction with Boone's road to Kentucky on New Years Day, 1808. By this time we were like horses returning to the stable and wanted to pick up speed. Normally, New Years Day would have been a holiday and a day of rest, but neither of us felt like stopping. We wanted our trip to be over as quickly as possible, and to be able to enjoy whatever comforts Fort Roanoke could offer. We continued on, reaching the ruins of Martin's Station less than a day later.

"I hope that Captain Lewis has found some peace," I said, remembering how melancholy he'd been when the Virginians stopped there two summers earlier. We'd passed the site of his suicide two days earlier, but hadn't stopped to pay our respects. Martin's Station seemed more of a memorial to him than his actual gravesite.

"Meriwether was a troubled man," Captain Pettit replied. "I tried to understand why, but to no avail. All he would say, God rest his soul, was that he had demons tormenting him."

Two days later and still more than a hundred miles from Fort Roanoke, we came to the end of the wagon road the prisoners had built. It was in an even poorer state than it had been when we'd used it last spring. Even though it was covered with snow, we could see that it wouldn't drain properly. We slowed to a walk and let our horses pick their way forward. A mile later we passed the first of the prisoner graves that lined the route, silent testimony to the price that'd been paid to build it, inferior as it might be. I could only imagine the suffering that Bates and his sappers had inflicted and again was thankful that I'd escaped a similar fate.

Even a poor quality road is easier to travel than a packhorse trail or an Indian path. We covered more than thirty miles that first day, probably our fastest rate of travel since leaving New Orleans. At this speed we would be at Fort Roanoke in another two days.

Captain Pettit was in front the next morning. I was about twenty yards behind, leading our packhorses, when he screamed. I watched in horror as his horse slid off the road and down a steep incline. I halted, dismounted, and ran as fast as I dared to the site of the accident, stopping just short of where Pettit's gelding had slipped. The road had washed out, creating an ice-covered incline that fed horse and rider down the cliff.

"Captain Pettit," I shouted.

He didn't answer. I worked my way down to where he lay trapped under the gelding. As soon as I could see him clearly, it was obvious from the angle of his head that his neck had been broken. A few moments later I was next to him. He wasn't breathing. There could be no question. He was dead.

The horse was still alive. Its right foreleg had been broken, and it was bawling piteously. I knew I had to put it down, so I climbed up the cliff, got my rifle, returned, and put a bullet into its skull. It bawled once more, then was silent.

I had to get the gelding off Pettit's body, but couldn't do it by myself. I climbed back up to the packhorses and found the rope that the captain had brought along. When I'd asked him why, he said we would find a use for it before we reached Fort Roanoke. He couldn't possibly have foreseen this use.

I was able to wind enough of the rope around the gelding's neck and saddle to have a secure grip on its body. I tied the other end to the saddle of my horse, and slowly backed the animal off. My horse was strong enough to lift Pettit's horse off his body and drag it to one side. Once I was sure that the gelding was clear of Pettit's body, I untied the rope and let my horse graze whilst I sat down to rest. I had much more to do, but I was exhausted.

Finally, after at least a half hour, I roused myself, climbed down, and removed the saddlebags from Pettit's horse. They contained Colonel Whiteside's report, which still had to be delivered. Next, I attended to Captain Pettit, searching his pockets. They were empty. I wanted to bury him, but didn't have a shovel and mattock with which to dig a grave, so I settled for piling a mound of stones over his body, which should've been sufficient to keep crows and other scavengers away. When this was done, I climbed back to the road. I wanted to rest, but by this time there were only two hours to sundown. I needed to find a place to camp for the night.

After securing Captain Pettit's saddlebags to the first packhorse, I wearily led the horses around the icy spot that had claimed his life. Then I mounted my horse and slowly proceeded along the road towards Fort Roanoke. It would have been safer to walk to ensure that there were no more icy slides, but that would've taken too long. I settled for keeping the horses at a slow walk and staring as intently as I could at the road before me.

An hour later I found a flat area, set up camp, and cooked my dinner—a stew of dried beef and maize—the first food I'd had since breakfast. I didn't think I'd be interested in eating, but once I started, I found that I was ravenous. A full belly made me drowsy. I crawled into my tent and was soon asleep. I didn't dream or wake until daylight the next morning.

After eating a cold breakfast of hard tack and jerky, I searched through Captain Pettit's saddlebags. Colonel Whiteside's report was there, wrapped in oilcloth and sealed with wax. A second oilcloth-wrapped packet contained the letters we'd been given to post by members of the regiment, and the money—nearly a pound—for postage. I considered taking both the letters and the money, but decided that it would be best to leave them in the saddlebags and trust that whichever officer at Fort Roanoke took charge of them would feel obligated to post them.

I also found a purse with five gold guineas and a number of other coins. The total was seven pounds, three shillings, four pence—a veritable fortune to me—as much money as I could make in three years after stoppages. My first thought was that the money belonged to Captain Pettit's next of kin. Although he'd said he had no family, I felt certain that he had a cousin or other relative someplace. A search of his kit turned up clothes, the comb and razor I'd seen him use, and a Bible, but no letters, or anything else that would indicate relatives or friends. Maybe he truly was alone in the world.

I thought briefly about turning over the money to the commanding officer at Fort Roanoke when I handed him Colonel Whiteside's report, but quickly rejected that idea. I knew that if I did, the money would end up in that officer's pocket.

I began to think about keeping the money for myself. Had I found it on the body of an enemy soldier, I'd have every right to keep it as spoils of war. But Captain Pettit was not an enemy soldier. He was a Virginian officer, one who had always treated me fairly. We were as close to being friends as any soldier can be with an officer. With the captain's money, I could repay the pound plus interest I still owed Leonard Henderson. I could send him a pound and five shillings. That was a reasonable amount for me to have saved. I'd still have nearly £6.

I didn't solve the problem of what to do with Captain Pettit's money that morning. Instead I put his purse amongst my belongings and told myself that the correct course of action would come to me in the fullness of time.

I maintained my slow pace and arrived at Christiansburg two days later. Much as I would've liked to have spent the night at the village inn, I knew that to do so would've invited questions about what I, a mere corporal, was doing travelling alone in the middle of winter. I didn't have good answers for those questions. I camped a safe distance from the village and arrived at Fort Roanoke in the early afternoon the next day. After explaining to the officer of the day that I was carrying Colonel Whiteside's report on the capture of New Orleans, I was told I'd have to see Major Madison, an aide to Brigadier Bradshaw, the fort's commander. The major was unavailable. I was ordered to spend the night in the barracks and to return the next morning.

The major's name was new to me. He hadn't been at Fort Roanoke the previous spring. I could only hope that he was competent and would respect the Virginians' achievements. I didn't question any of the soldiers in the barracks about him. I'd decided the less I knew about him when I first reported, the better.

CHAPTER 13

The next morning I was ushered in to see Major Madison, a big, ruddy-faced man who sat behind a desk curiously empty of papers or writing implements. He toyed with an unusual-looking knife. Its blade had a series of curves, giving it the appearance of a wiggling snake. I assumed he used it as a letter opener. He acknowledged my salute by raising the tip of the knife to his brow. I stood at attention as I told him that I was delivering Colonel Whiteside's report on the capture of New Orleans.

"Did Colonel Whiteside send you on this mission alone?" he asked, his raised eyebrow clearly indicating that he didn't believe me.

"No, sir. Captain Pettit was the messenger. I was his guide."

"And where is Captain Pettit?"

"Dead, sir. His horse slipped off the trail and down a cliff four days ago. The fall broke the captain's neck. I couldn't bury him, so I piled stones over his body."

"You're prepared to show me where you left his body?" the major said, pointing the knife at me.

"Yes, sir, if you wish."

"And what have you done with the captain's personal belongings?"

"They're on one of the packhorses." I was still standing at attention. The major hadn't allowed me to stand easy.

"Including his money and other valuables?" the major asked.

"Captain Pettit had no valuables—just his clothes, toilet articles, and a Bible."

"You're telling me that he travelled from New Orleans with no money?"

"Yes, sir. There isn't any place to spend money between here and New Orleans."

"And you are similarly penniless?" the major said, clearly not believing my story.

"No, sir," I replied. "I have some money. I carried it because there was no place to leave it. And I hope to get paid if I can find the right pay sergeant."

"Did Captain Pettit say anything about getting paid?"

"No, sir. It wasn't something we discussed."

I might've told the truth to a more sympathetic officer, but I knew that if I gave the major Captain Pettit's money, it would end up in his pocket. Far better in my pocket than his, I told myself. But I'd created a web of lies and was now trapped in them. There was nothing I could do but persevere. I would have to tell the same story to anyone else who asked.

"I don't believe you, Corporal, ah . . ."

"Watson, sir."

"Yes, Watson . . . I don't believe you. I have no way of proving you're lying, but if I ever catch you in a lie, you'll rue the day you were born. Now, where is Colonel Whiteside's report?"

"Here, sir," I said, laying the oilcloth-covered packet on his desk.

Madison looked at the report as if it were a bomb about to explode. "I suppose I shall have to read this," he said. When I didn't reply, he told me to return in two days' time.

"One other matter, sir," I said.

"And what might that be?" the major said, clearly annoyed at having to spend more time on me.

"Before Captain Pettit and I left New Orleans we were given letters to post and money for postage by members of the regiment. The letters and money are still in Captain Pettit's saddlebags. I'd like to get them so that I can post the letters."

"You shall have them when you return in two days. Dismissed, Corporal Watson."

I saluted, turned on my heel, and left.

I was angry when I left Major Madison's office. The Virginians had spent seven months getting to New Orleans and capturing it. Captain Pettit and I had spent two-and-a-half months traversing the wilds of Georgia and Tennessee to deliver the report of its capture. The captain had lost his life on our mission. I thought the report should receive immediate attention. The more I thought about how Major Madison had treated me the angrier I got, overwhelming any feelings of remorse I might've had about taking Captain Pettit's money.

Major Madison may not have been interested in the capture of New Orleans, but the soldiers in the barracks hung on my every word as I told and retold the story of our float down the Mississippi . . . finding first Nuevo Madrid then Natchez abandoned . . . and finally how the Virginians became masters of New Orleans. I was treated as a hero, as if I'd captured the city single-handedly, even though I told everyone who would listen that I had only a minor role in the enterprise.

A corporal told me that word had arrived in October that St Louis had surrendered to Captain Clark's men without a fight. The Virginians had accomplished their seemingly impossible mission— we'd conquered all of Louisiana. The French had again been ejected from North America.

Whilst at Fort Roanoke I met Zachariah Paulson, one of the Natchez's fur traders. He said that there were only three men left at the post when the Choctaws warned them French soldiers were on their way. They decided to take their families back to Fort Roanoke rather than risk becoming prisoners. They'd heard stories about the French army's rape and pillage in Europe, and didn't want to chance that the same would happen to them. Major DuChamps had told the truth when he said that his men found Natchez abandoned and had been correct in surmising that its residents had headed back to British territory.

"Brigadier Bradshaw has some questions for you," Major Madison told me when I reported to him. "We're to see him in an hour. Wait outside."

"Yes, sir," I replied. "When can I retrieve the letters that were in Captain Pettit's saddlebags?"

"Oh, those. See Sergeant Keeling at the stables. He'll give them to you."

"Thank you, sir," I said, before saluting and turning to leave the major's office.

At the appointed time we entered the brigadier's office.

"Major Madison and Corporal Watson, reporting as ordered," the major said as we both saluted. The brigadier returned our salute and told us to stand easy.

"It is unusual for me to have to depend on a corporal to answer my questions," the Brigadier complained, "but since you are the only man who can add to what Colonel Whiteside has written, I shall have to trust what you tell me. I am counting on your complete veracity. Do you understand?"

"I do, sir."

"Colonel Whiteside reports that three officers and one hundred forty-four men died in the two attacks on New Orleans, forty-five men later died of their wounds, and that one hundred twenty-seven men are seriously wounded and unfit for duty. He also reports that five men died and seven were seriously wounded in the hurricane, and that on any given day a hundred more are sick with ague. Are these numbers correct?"

"They are, sir. I kept account of rations for the regiment. They were the numbers I used."

"Your colonel says that he believes that the Spanish soldiers who rebelled against the French and opened New Orleans' gates for the Virginians would be willing to fight for Britain. How many are there?"

"Since we weren't supplying rations to the Spanish, we didn't make a count, but there were approximately three hundred, sir."

"So the Spaniards could make up most of the losses the Virginians have suffered."

"Yes, sir. In numbers." I wanted to say that the Virginians were riflemen and skilled woodsmen, and that the Spanish looked like lazy, poorly trained soldiers who could barely fire their muskets in a volley, but it was not my place to speak.

"Major, I think we have a solution to our problem. Philadelphia wants a full regiment. That would seriously weaken my command. But now we find we have the regiment we need in New Orleans."

I wondered why the army needed a regiment, but knew better than to ask.

"Right, sir," the major responded.

"I wish you to carry that message to General Delancy in Philadelphia. Take Watson with you in case there are questions that aren't answered in Whiteside's report."

"As the brigadier wishes. But will General Delancy listen to a corporal, especially one as shabbily dressed as this one? We can't promote him to lieutenant. Perhaps a clean uniform with sergeant's stripes would help."

"Quite right. Watson, you're promoted to sergeant. My clerk will issue orders for the paymaster to give you three months' back pay—you'll need a few pence in your pocket in Philadelphia—and the quartermaster to issue you a new uniform. We'll sort out the stoppages later. Dismissed."

I had been promoted to sergeant, had more than £2 in my purse—not counting Captain Pettit's money. I should have been happy, but the way in which the Virginians and I were being treated made me burn. The Virginians had travelled a thousand miles—overcome heat, a hurricane, and possible starvation—lost nearly a third of our number in battle—and now, without a word of praise, were treated as pawns in some plan the British Army had hatched. I'd travelled back that thousand miles, on a mission that cost Captain Pettit his life, to report our success, and the only comment I got was on how shabby my uniform was. I wondered whether the major or the brigadier ever had to face the choice of eating alligator or starving. True, the Virginians had been successful only because the Spanish soldiers in New Orleans had risen up against their French officers, but that uprising would've been in vain had not the Virginians been present to help them. And now I was to travel four hundred miles in the company of an officer who clearly thought I was unworthy of his consideration.

Once I was free of the brigadier and the major, I made my way to the stables to find Sergeant Keeling. He was an old soldier who, though they didn't look alike, immediately reminded me of Sergeant Pew. Perhaps it was his demeanour, which, like Pew's, told the world he was not a man to be trifled with.

"I'm William Watson. Major Madison said that you would give me the letters from my regiment so that I could post them."

"Right, here they are," the sergeant said, handing me the oilcloth packet.

"Where's the money that was with the letters?"

"What money? All I found were these letters."

"Thank you, Sergeant," I said, realising that it would be useless to argue with him. Any doubt I'd had about keeping Captain Pettit's money disappeared. I'd use some of it to post the letters once we got to Philadelphia. Perhaps I'd find some equally valuable way to use the rest of it. I probably shouldn't have left the money for postage with the letters, but I didn't fret over that decision.

We left for Philadelphia the next day. I'd assumed that we'd ride horses, but the major had use of an army coach driven by a grey-haired, gimpy old private whose surname was Rose. He must have been at least sixty. I wondered how he'd escaped being invalided out to Chelsea Hospital, the fate that Sergeant Pew so feared.

Rose and I were ready to leave shortly after dawn, but Major Madison was not an early riser. We had to wait until mid-morning before he appeared. Seeing Rose, he sniffed the air and said, "I hope you'd smell a little sweeter with some other name."

Rose said nothing, but I could see him grimace. Whilst I was tempted to make my own jest, I didn't. Rose had suffered enough.

The route to Philadelphia was via the Great Wagon Road. I'd last travelled that route thirteen years earlier to visit my sister and brother in New York. Whilst the road was little improved south of Fort Roanoke, where it was maintained by county officials, it was a fine highway north of the fort, where the army was in charge. I saw no prisoner graves along the way and assumed the army had hired slaves or indentured servants to do the work.

The trip to Philadelphia took ten days. I rode with Rose on the coach driver's bench. Except for a few hours in mid-afternoon, the temperature was below freezing. I was chilled to the bone most of the time, but the major never invited me to share the coach. We stayed at inns each night. Rose and I shared a room, and usually a bed. The major had his own accommodations and appeared to be studiously ignoring my presence, which was probably the best I could hope for.

Our first stop on arriving in Philadelphia was in Chestnut Street at British Army Headquarters, in a building that'd been the State House of the Province of Pennsylvania. In 1776 the rebels' Continental Congress had used this building when they met to write, then sign, their Declaration of Independence. Afterward they remained in session in the building, only leaving in December, when the British Army, having completed its occupation of New Jersey, set up camp across the Delaware River. Whilst most public buildings in America had been returned to their former uses after the General Amnesty of 1777, this one was deemed too closely associated with the rebellion to be given back.

Major Madison was to see a Colonel Lancaster, one of General Delancy's aides. I was not surprised when he took Colonel Whiteside's report and told me to stay outside by the coach with Rose.

"I'm to meet with General Delancy tomorrow at eleven," he informed us when he returned a half hour later. "You are to accompany me, Watson, but you will speak only when directed to. I made you a sergeant. I can just as quickly make you a private."

"Yes, sir."

Our next stop was at the visiting officers' quarters in a fine brick house that had belonged to Benjamin Franklin, one of the leaders of the rebellion. He'd represented Pennsylvania in London for many years before the rebellion. Once the rebellion started, he was appointed the rebels' ambassador to France. Despite being granted amnesty, he chose to remain in France. Rumour had it that he enjoyed the luxuries of aristocratic life he'd learned during his many years in Europe, and was willing to forgo his democratic ideals for them. When it occupied Philadelphia, the British Army commandeered Franklin's house. Franklin was hardly in a position to contest this action or to request compensation.

A young lieutenant rushed up to the major as he got out of the coach in front of the house.

"At your service, major," he said, after saluting. "I'm responsible for these quarters and for ensuring that you are provided with every

comfort. We assemble in the bar at seven each evening and supper is
served at eight. It'll be my pleasure to show you to your room."

"Most kind of you, lieutenant . . ." the major said, his voice rising
to indicate that he was asking the lieutenant for his name.

"Tarleton, sir."

"Very good, Lieutenant Tarleton. Lead the way."

"You two," the lieutenant barked. "Bring the major's kit and follow us. Then take the coach to the mews. You can spend the night at
the Man Full O'Trouble in Spruce Street. They'll give you a bed and
supper, but you'll have to pay for your own drink."

"Watson, report to me at ten o'clock tomorrow," Major Madison
added, and then turned to Rose. "Watson will tell you what my plans
are when he returns. Make sure that you're not too drunk to drive
the coach."

"Yes, sir," Rose and I answered in unison.

The name Tarleton intrigued me. A Major Sir Banastre Tarleton
had led the squadron of cavalry that captured Charles Lee, a rebel
general, in the last days of the Great Rebellion. After Rose and I had
placed Major Madison's luggage in his room and attended to the
coach and horses, I asked the lieutenant whether he was related.

"My father," he said with a broad smile. "How do you come to
know of him?"

"I've always been intrigued by the Great Rebellion and have studied its history," I lied. "I know that your father captured Charles Lee
and deprived the rebels of their most capable officer." I saw no value
in telling the lieutenant that I'd been on Washington's staff, and that
at the time my fellow orderlies and I thought his father's capture of
Lee helped Washington.

"Yes, Father was always proud of that deed," the lieutenant said,
clearly happy to be able to tell the story, "but he never claimed that
it was heroic. A loyalist told Father that Lee was spending the night
at an inn run by a widow named White and that he had only a few
guards to protect him. Father's men quickly overpowered the rebel
guards and threatened to burn the inn down around Lee if he didn't
surrender. Lee had been in bed with the widow, but he managed to
put on a dressing gown before surrendering. Father always got a big
laugh when he told how his sergeant offered to take Lee's place in
the widow's bed."

Listening to Lieutenant Tarleton, the memories of those trying days at the end of 1776 came back flooding back to me. In November 1776, after being defeated by the British at White Plains, Washington split his army. He gave seven thousand men to General Charles Lee, who had been a British Army officer before joining the rebels, and ordered them to protect the Hudson River crossings that were vital to the rebel cause. Washington took two thousand men and marched into New Jersey, where he expected to be reinforced with thousands more. Those reinforcements never materialised and the British chased Washington's rapidly diminishing force across New Jersey into Pennsylvania.

Washington needed more men and repeatedly asked Lee to march his army south to join him. Lee was insubordinate and refused to do so. After Lee's capture, General Sullivan marched his remaining soldiers—twenty-five hundred men, only half of whom were fit for duty—into Pennsylvania and placed them under Washington's command. This addition gave the rebels a force large enough to attack Trenton. That attack led to the rebels' final defeat and the end of the Great Rebellion.

I can only speculate as to what might have happened if Tarleton had not captured Lee. Having resisted Washington's pleas for so many weeks, it is unlikely that Lee would've had a change of heart and joined Washington in Pennsylvania. Without Lee's soldiers, it is equally unlikely that Washington would've attacked Trenton. Whilst most of the rebel army would have gone home on New Year's Day when their enlistments were up, the few hundred who'd enlisted for the duration of the war, and at least some new recruits who'd joined the rebels in December, would've remained through the winter.

General Howe had dispersed his army in winter quarters across New Jersey and had no plan to cross the Delaware to attack Washington before April or May. Similarly, he seemed content to allow Lee's forces to remain in northern New Jersey.

Howe's soldiers had been told to live off the land and were raping and pillaging with abandon. The men of New Jersey, most of whom had remained neutral until their homes and families were threatened, responded by attacking small groups of British and Hessian soldiers wherever they could find them. Howe's harsh treatment of New

Jersey's residents would have brought more support to the rebel cause and succoured both Washington and Lee through the winter.

Had Lee not been captured, the British Army would have had two rebel forces to contend with in the spring, Washington's and Lee's. Whilst there is no doubt that the British Army would've prevailed, the rebellion would have dragged on well into 1777. I believe that Tarleton's capture of Lee shortened the rebellion, possibly by six months or more.

The Man Full O' Troubles was a fine tavern, better than any we'd stayed in on the Great Wagon Road. Rose and I were able to claim a bed with a feather tick that normally slept four. No one else showed up to take the space, so we were far more comfortable than we'd been on our trip to Philadelphia. The bar was all brass and polished wood, and the ale was served in pewter mugs, not wooden tankards. I expected the place to be filled with officers, but none were present. As a sergeant, I was one of the highest-ranking men in the place and was treated accordingly. I started to order a pint of ale, but Rose signalled me to remain silent.

"Who'd like to hear how a gallant band of Americans marched to New Orleans and captured it for King George?" he announced in a loud voice. That got the attention of most in the room.

"The truth, or a pack of lies?" a voice asked.

"The Gospel truth, I swear it."

"Well then let's hear it."

"My sergeant here will tell the story, but he's a bit parched. He needs a pint to lubricate his throat, and I wouldn't mind one too."

Two mugs of ale appeared so quickly you'd think they'd sprung out of the table. Rose took a long draught and whispered to me that a little embellishment of the facts never hurt. I looked around the room at the eager faces and began recounting the Virginians' odyssey. I'd never before, even in the barracks at Fort Roanoke, told the story completely and was surprised at how dramatic it was, even without the embellishments that Rose recommended. I'd drained my mug by the time I got to the part about Captain Clark leaving for St Louis, but it didn't remain empty for long.

I must've talked for more than an hour without interruption. When I finally paused, I was bombarded with questions, everything from what alligator tasted like to what the Virginians would do next. Rose made sure that we got a meal and rum to drink with it. It was nearly midnight when Mr Dougherty, the innkeeper, who'd been listening as intently as any of the soldiers, announced last call.

I woke the next morning with a pounding headache and queasy stomach. I'd not felt the effects of too much drink as severely since Al Neely and the other fur traders encouraged me to down more whisky than I should have on my first expedition with Daniel Boone, thirty years earlier. I pulled on my trousers and boots, and staggered down to the bar looking for something to eat. Mr Dougherty was polishing the brass when I entered.

"Ah, our gallant sergeant," he said. I grunted something that I hoped would be taken for good morning, before asking, "What time is it?"

"Nearly nine."

"Damnation. I've got to report to Major Madison in an hour. Have you anything that will settle my stomach?"

"You look like you need some willow tea. Let me get a cup for you." He hurried off to do that chore. I didn't understand why an innkeeper was being so solicitous.

"Sergeant Watson," he said whilst I sipped the hot tea, "a friend of mine is a gentleman of the press. I'm sure he'd like to hear the story you told last night. Might even be willing to pay a pound or two for the privilege of publishing it in his newspaper. I'll be happy to introduce you to him at supper tonight."

"As you wish," I said.

"Meet me here at half seven this evening."

"I'll be here unless Major Madison detains me."

"We should keep this quiet. I'll ensure that Rose is entertained."

I didn't know what Dougherty was planning, but I had to make myself presentable and get to the visiting officers quarters in the next forty-five minutes or risk the major's wrath, which I judged could be considerable.

CHAPTER 14

I reported to Major Madison promptly at ten. I'd managed to shave and get my uniform on correctly, but my head was still pounding, and I hadn't eaten.

"Had a good night, Watson?" he asked after looking me up and down. He obviously knew that I was suffering the effects of too much ale and rum.

"Yes, sir," I said in as firm a voice as I could manage.

"Don't make a fool of yourself in front of the general."

"I won't, sir."

"And speak only when either the general or I direct you to."

"Yes, sir."

"Now wait outside until we're ready to go."

The major appeared a half hour later. We walked the short distance to headquarters in silence and were immediately admitted to General Delancy's office by the lieutenant who served as his clerk. It was a large, well-lit room with windows on two sides. The general sat behind a large rosewood desk with an intricate design of light and dark woods inlaid into its top. The general had brown hair and the ruddy complexion of a healthy man who spends a good deal of time outdoors. He looked to be in his early forties, a younger man than I would've expected. Colonel Lancaster and another officer, who wore a uniform I didn't recognise, sat on a small couch to his right.

"Major Madison and Sergeant Watson reporting as ordered, sir," the major said, saluting.

"Stand easy, Major, Sergeant," the general said, returning the salute, but remaining seated. "You've met Colonel Lancaster. Allow me to introduce Generalissimo Francisco de Miranda of the Independent Venezuelan Army."

The generalissimo stood, gave us a small bow, then returned to his seat. He was about my height, five foot six, and had the trim body of a man accustomed to vigorous activity. His white hair suggested that he was sixty or more, but his face was curiously unlined. He was dressed in a gaudy blue uniform, like none I'd ever seen. Its jacket was festooned with gold-coloured epaulettes and braid at its shoulders, and a gold strip ran down the trouser legs.

"I read Colonel Whiteside's report last night," Delancy continued. "The Virginians are to be congratulated for capturing New Orleans and all of Louisiana for the King."

I said nothing, but was immensely pleased. The general was the first British officer to say a kind word about the Virginians and to give them credit for their accomplishment. I realised that Captain Jackson had been right when he told me that he didn't want any help from British officers. Had there been one with the Virginians, I'm certain that he would've claimed credit for our victory.

"Tell me more about the Spanish soldiers who overcame the French and opened New Orleans' gates for you," the general said, looking directly at me.

Since the enquiry was directed at me, I could answer. "What would the general like to know?"

"How many are there?"

"About three hundred."

"Could they hold the city without the Virginians' help?"

"I'm certain they could defend it against an attack by Indians or pirates."

Major Madison started to say something, but since the general was addressing me, he choked off his words. I was looking forward and couldn't see either Colonel Lancaster or the generalissimo, but I heard some rustling from their direction.

"What if the French mounted an expedition to retake the city?" the general continued, his gaze focused on me. I realised that, as a newly minted sergeant, I shouldn't be making such judgements, but having gone this far, there was no retreat. Out of the side of my eye I could see that Major Madison's face had turned red and that he was struggling to control himself.

"They repelled our attack, sir," I answered.

"And they have no officers."

The general had made a statement, but I responded as if he'd asked a question.

"No, sir. The officers were all French."

"Then we'll have to supply officers," the general said quietly. "We can't have three hundred men commanded by a sergeant." I had the irreverent thought that Sergeant Montoya could probably do a far better job in command of New Orleans than many of the British officers I'd seen, but had enough presence of mind not to blurt that out.

"Yes, but the officers will have to speak Spanish. None of the Spanish soldiers speak English, and they detest French."

"Thank you for your advice, Watson," the general said dryly. Major Madison glared at me. I might've been able to justify my prior statements as only answering the general's question, but this last comment clearly overstepped the bounds. The general looked expectantly at Colonel Lancaster and the generalissimo, but neither said a word.

"Colonel Whiteside reports," the general continued, "that on most days he has only five hundred men fit for duty. That's half the regiment you seek, but I have no other soldiers to offer you, Generalissimo." The general didn't seem sorry as he delivered this judgement.

"General Delancy," de Miranda replied, "may I question your sergeant?" He remained seated and spoke in a conversational tone of voice, as if we were in a tavern, chatting over a beaker of rum.

"Certainly."

"Sergeant Watson, what kind of soldiers are the Virginians?" the generalissimo asked.

I glanced at Major Madison. His face was still red, but provided no clue as to how I should answer.

"Riflemen, sir," I said, "all from the colonies. We volunteered to fight the French after Dumouriez was elected Dictator-for-Life."

"I haven't read your colonel's report. Tell me how you managed to march across a thousand miles of wilderness."

I gave him a short summary of the Virginians' expedition, including my roles in finding the salt lick in Kentucky, acting as Colonel Whiteside's Spanish translator, and bringing his report to Fort Roanoke.

"Most impressive," he said when I finished. "And your officers . . . they too are from the colonies?"

"Yes, sir."

The generalissimo stood and adopted the posture of a man making a speech at a public meeting.

"General Delancy, in England I was promised eight regiments, but those soldiers are now fighting the French in Spain. Then I was promised a regiment of regulars from North America, which you now tell me you cannot provide." He paused for a moment, looked at Delancy for a response, but when the general remained silent, de Miranda continued.

"The people of South America yearn to be free. All they need to see is that England supports me and they will flock to my side. You know what happened in New Orleans. As soon as British soldiers appeared, the Spanish overthrew their French oppressors. The same thing will happen in the Captaincy-General of Venezuela, then in the Viceroyalty of New Granada, then in the rest of Spain's colonies. Give me this half regiment of Virginians and I will first take Venezuela, then all of Spain's empire."

De Miranda was a polished orator who spoke flawless English, though with a noticeable accent. My head spun at what I'd heard. The Captaincy-General of Venezuela—it was a Spanish colony, but where? I'd never heard of the place, but the generalissimo was asking to take the Virginians there.

"Generalissimo de Miranda," the general replied, tapping his fingers lightly on his desk, "let me choose my words carefully. We are at war with France. I can order my soldiers to fight the French. Until a year ago, Spain was our enemy, and I could have ordered my soldiers to fight the Spanish. But now Spain is our ally. I can no longer order my soldiers to fight the Spanish. You may have the Virginians for your expedition to Venezuela, but only to ensure that it is not under French control. King George III would not look kindly upon me if I encouraged a colony to rebel against its lawful monarch."

If de Miranda was troubled by this response, he didn't show it. "Thank you, General Delancy. You are right. Our mission must be to defeat the French. All other goals must be set aside until that one is accomplished."

"Major Madison," the general said, turning to him for the first time, "thank you for conveying Colonel Whiteside's report. You may return to Fort Roanoke. Sergeant Watson, you will place yourself under Colonel Lancaster's command and accompany him and Generalissimo de Miranda to New Orleans. Wait outside. You are both dismissed."

The major and I snapped to attention, saluted, then turned on our heels and left.

"Watson, if I could, I'd have you flogged for disobeying my orders," the major said in a low, angry voice. We were alone in the anteroom outside General Delancy's office—the lieutenant who normally sat there was not at his desk. Livid as Madison was, he didn't want to chance being overheard by his superiors.

"Sir, I only answered the general's questions, as you told me to," I replied.

"You did more than that, and didn't give me a chance to speak. Now go find Rose and tell him to bring the coach around."

"I can't do that, sir. The general told me to wait here."

Madison emitted a strangled growl, then left to find Rose. I'd made an enemy, but one I hoped wouldn't have the chance to do me any harm.

Colonel Lancaster and the generalissimo emerged ten minutes later. De Miranda questioned me in Spanish for five minutes on the details of what I'd said earlier. It was obviously a test, so I replied in his language.

"You speak the language of peasants," was his verdict.

"I learned your language from Mexican soldiers."

"Make certain that you use only English in the presence of Venezuelans."

"Yes, sir."

Colonel Lancaster told me that the plans for an attack on Venezuela were secret, and that I'd be hanged for treason if I disclosed them. It would take several weeks for him to arrange for ships to take us to New Orleans and then transport the Virginians to South America. I was to remain at the Man Full O'Troubles and report back to him in two weeks. If he needed me before that, he would get word to the innkeeper. "Enjoy yourself, but stay out of mischief," were his parting words.

I entered the bar at the Man Full O' Troubles that evening at half seven to find Mr Dougherty at the bar standing beside a short man whose face and demeanour reminded me of a rabbit. He had a small mouth with large upper front teeth, and looked around nervously, like he would bolt at any loud sound.

"This is Mr Cooper, the gentleman of the press I told you about. I know he'd like to hear your story."

"Pleasure to meet you, sir," I said.

"Supper's on you, Cooper," Dougherty said. "Shall we go around the corner to the Huntsman? I'm likely to be interrupted if we stay here."

"Our hero, Sergeant Watson, deserves better," Cooper said. "Let's go to the Grove."

We walked two blocks to an attached row house with a doorman in fine livery in front. Cooper whispered something to the man, who immediately admitted us into a marble-floored entry hall, where a servant took our coats. We were greeted by the maître d', who escorted us to a table covered with a fine linen cloth. A moment later, a waiter brought a bottle of wine and three crystal glasses. Cooper examined the bottle and nodded his approval to the waiter, who opened it, then decanted it into a silver ewer. Once the wine had settled, he poured a small amount into Cooper's glass. Cooper tasted the wine, looked contemplatively at the ceiling, then indicated his approval. The waiter then filled our glasses.

Cooper had obviously organised this display to impress me. It brought back memories of the disastrous dinner I'd endured at my brother's house more than a dozen years earlier. I knew the wine in the glass in front of me would be excellent and that a fine meal would follow, but after the previous night's excess, I was in no condition to enjoy them. My head still hurt and I wasn't sure of the state of my stomach. I took a small sip of wine—it was indeed excellent—complimented Cooper on his choice, then put my glass down. Cooper looked disappointed. I think he expected me to down the wine like a tankard of ale and stick my glass out for more.

"I've already ordered supper," Cooper said. "I trust you like roast lamb with mustard and caper sauce. It's a specialty of the house."

"Sounds capital," I said.

There were a few moments of silence. Cooper may have been waiting for me to say something, but when I didn't, he started.

"Dougherty told me of your exploits and of the capture of New Orleans by the King's Own Virginians," he said, nodding at the pub owner across the table. "It's a thrilling story, and I'd like to publish it in my newspaper, *The Philadelphia Chronicle*. I'll pay you two pounds for exclusive rights."

I must have looked confused because Cooper followed with, "By exclusive rights I mean that you cannot talk to any other newspaper or magazine. When your report becomes public, they'll seek you out like buzzards attracted to a corpse."

"You'll publish my words without embellishment?"

"Yes. From what Dougherty tells me, there's no need for embellishment."

Doherty nodded in agreement, but remained silent. I began to realise that he'd been instructed not to interrupt Cooper.

"And you won't identify me by name."

"As you wish."

"Done," I said, extending my hand to seal the deal. Suddenly my financial problem was solved. I could pay my debt to Leonard Henderson with substantial interest and still have money left over.

"Shall we enjoy our supper?" Cooper said as he shook my hand.

The meal was indeed excellent, and I discovered, after my first tentative bites, that I was hungry. After eating I started my tale. It was slow going. Cooper took copious notes. I had only finished the story of the Virginians' first year's expedition when the maître d' came up and whispered something in Cooper's ear.

"I'm afraid that we shall have to continue tomorrow," he said, an embarrassed look on his face. "We need to let them close up. It's nearly midnight." A servant appeared with our coats. Cooper thanked the maître d' profusely and we left. Once outside we agreed that I would appear at his office in Walnut Street at ten the next morning.

I was elated. The story of the Virginians' exploits would now be public. Mr Dougherty also looked happy. I guessed that he'd also be receiving payment from Cooper.

I met Mr Cooper the next morning and spent three hours completing the saga of the Virginians' expedition to New Orleans and my return to Fort Roanoke. Cooper seemed particularly interested in the story of the prisoners. He agreed not to identify Captain Bates by name but said that he'd publish the details of the sappers' cruel treatment of prisoners —that he'd often written about similar excesses.

"What's next for you, William?" he asked, when I'd finished. He'd taken to calling me by my given name earlier that morning, but I never learned his.

"I have two weeks' leave, then I am to report back for further orders." I'd no intention of risking being charged with treason by mentioning de Miranda and his expedition to Venezuela.

"And what of the Virginians? When will they be returning?"

"You'll have to ask General Delancy. He doesn't share his plans with sergeants."

"Well said. I'll do that once your story is published in my next issue," he said, handing me two pounds. "Will you join me for dinner?"

"My pleasure." We ate at the Huntsman, which was a simple tavern, much like the Man Full O' Troubles.

Now that I had the money to repay Mr Henderson, my next question was how to get it to him. My leave was not long enough for me to ride to Guilford Courthouse and repay him in person. I'd heard about bank drafts as a way to transport money, but didn't know how they worked.

"It's simple," Mr Cooper said, after I explained my situation to him—omitting Mr Henderson's name or the reason I owed him money. "Go to a bank—I suggest the Bank of Pennsylvania—and say you want a draft payable to the gentleman you owe money to. They'll take the money, write out a draft, and affix their seal to it so that people know it's legitimate. You can then mail the draft as repayment of your debt. The bank will charge you two shillings for their service, but that's a reasonable fee."

I thanked him and went to the bank, where I purchased a draft for one pound, ten shillings. I hoped this would be adequate to discharge my debt. After posting the draft to Guilford Courthouse, I returned to the Man Full O' Troubles to await my story becoming public.

The next issue of *The Philadelphia Chronicle* appeared on a Monday, three days later. My account of the Virginians' capture of New Orleans spread over most of four pages. I could hear people talking about it as I walked around the centre of Philadelphia. I wanted to announce that I was William Watson and that it was my story, but I thought it better to remain unknown and hear what people honestly thought. Most comments treated me and the Virginians as heroes, but more than one dismissed the story as a fabrication. I could understand that scepticism. When I read the story, it seemed so fantastical that I would've questioned its veracity myself had I not lived it.

Mr Dougherty met me when I returned to the Man Full O'Troubles. "Colonel Lancaster sent a messenger," he told me. "You are to report to him at nine tomorrow morning."

Good feeling drained from me like water out of a leaking bucket. The colonel ordering me to report this quickly couldn't be good news. I hadn't thought about what he or General Delancy would think about my making the Virginians' story public. I'd already told the story at Fort Roanoke and on that first night at the Man Full O' Troubles without any censure. Telling it to a newspaper wasn't that much different—or was it?

I reported to Colonel Lancaster as ordered the next morning.

"Watson, are you the source of this story?" the colonel asked, waving a copy of *The Philadelphia Chronicle* at me.

"Yes, sir. I am."

"Who gave you permission to talk to a newspaper?"

"No one, sir. It was never discussed, and I'd already told the story both at Fort Roanoke and here in Philadelphia."

"The story redounds credit on everyone except Bates, the sapper captain, and he isn't named. You've made yourself a hero, so I can't very well punish you. But take this as a warning. A sergeant does not talk to newspapermen without specific permission from his commanding officer."

"Yes, sir."

"Report back to me in ten days. Dismissed." I saluted, turned on my heel, and left. Once outside his office, I breathed a sigh of relief. I'd transgressed an unwritten rule, but had avoided the consequences. I didn't know what the punishment for talking out of turn was and didn't want to find out. Colonel Lancaster would be my commanding officer for many more months, and I hoped that he wouldn't hold this incident against me.

CHAPTER 15

I was unable to keep my identity secret. By noon I was known as the source of the story in the *Chronicle*. A steady stream of people came up to me on the street to congratulate me or to ask about the fate of some man they knew in the Virginians. I was unable to answer most of their questions, which made me feel that I was failing to fulfil my moral duty. By the end of the day, I was tired of Philadelphia and the notoriety I'd achieved.

Since I had both the time and the money, I decided to make a quick trip by coach to New York to see my sister and brother. I'd last seen them in 1796, but had continued to correspond with my sister. Richard couldn't be bothered to write, but Charlotte kept me informed as to his doings. I'd last written to her more than two years ago, after my theft from Mr Henderson had been discovered and I'd decided that joining the Virginians was my only alternative. I told her the same lie I told everyone else—that I was joining the Virginians because I was bored with life in Davidson's Fort. She couldn't respond to that letter. I hadn't given her a new address.

Having decided to travel to New York, I had to move quickly. The trip would take two days each way, leaving me only four days for my visit. I didn't write—the letter would probably arrive after I did. I told Mr Dougherty of my plans—someone should know where I was.

The morning after seeing the colonel, I boarded a New York-bound coach. I had five travelling companions: two merchants, a minister, and an elderly couple on a visit to their son. Seeing me in my rifleman's green, the conversation quickly turned to the story of the Virginians' capture of New Orleans. One of the merchants, a rotund man of about forty who said he traded in leather goods, guessed that I was the source of the account. When he asked, I didn't deny my role.

"You're quite a hero, sergeant," he said in a voice that held more than a hint of awe.

"A soldier follows orders."

"But you volunteered to lead a party to the salt lick in Kentucky…to be part of the reconnaissance of Nuevo Madrid . . . and the trip back to Fort Roanoke couldn't have been pleasant."

I was amazed that he had read the newspaper article so closely and remembered it in such detail.

"True," I said, "but those were hardly heroic actions."

"No matter," the merchant said, "they were instrumental in your regiment's success and made it possible for us to know of their exploits."

"Many others contributed to the regiment's success."

"A modest hero. Refreshing in these days with so many blowhards."

I wanted this conversation to end but the rest of my coach-mates kept it going for many hours with their questions and praise. Finally, at mid-afternoon, the topic changed to the latest rumours about King George's health and I was able to retreat into a cocoon of silence.

We arrived in New York too late the next evening for me to make my way to my sister's home. I spent the night at the coaching inn where I discovered that Mr Cooper's article about the Virginians' capture of New Orleans had been reprinted in its entirety three days earlier in the *New York Gazette*. I would have no anonymity in this city either.

I arrived at Charlotte and Phillip's house, three miles to the north at mid-morning. Phillip was serving another customer when I entered his apothecary shop, which occupied the building's ground floor. He motioned me to a bench by the fireplace. I sat quietly until he was done.

"How may I be of service, sergeant?" he asked politely. Not surprisingly, he didn't recognise me, given that he hadn't seen me in a dozen years.

"Have you anything to ease the pain in an old soldier's joints?" I said, trying to disguise my voice.

"I have several remedies that might help, but tell me more about your . . ." He stopped in mid-sentence and stared intently at my face before saying, "William?" in an uncertain voice.

"Yes, it's me."

He came around the counter and we shook hands. He remembered that I'd avoided his embrace the first time we met.

"What are you doing here? Charlotte told me that you'd joined the King's Own Virginians. The papers say they're in New Orleans." Then a smile of recognition crossed his face. "You were the messenger who carried the Virginians' report to Fort Roanoke, then to Philadelphia."

"I was."

"But I still ask, what are you doing here? Shouldn't you be in Philadelphia?"

"I have ten days' leave and decided to visit you and Charlotte. I wanted to see my nieces and nephews."

"I'm so glad you've come, but none of the family is at home. Charlotte is visiting Mrs Maddox, an old woman from our church, who is ailing."

Phillip beamed as he gave me a quick summary of their children. My nephew David, now almost twenty, was reading law in the offices of Fitch and Bryson. Phillip assured me they were amongst the most prestigious barristers in New York. My niece Jacoba, now almost eighteen, had married seven months earlier and had just announced to Charlotte and Phillip that they were to be grandparents. The youngest three, Samuel, Warren, and Patricia, were in school and all excellent students.

"Go upstairs and make yourself at home," Phillip said when he concluded. "You do remember the way?"

I thanked him and headed up the stairs. Charlotte returned an hour later. I could hear her in the shop as she reported to Phillip on Mrs Maddox's health.

"There's a small surprise waiting for you upstairs," Phillip said when she had finished.

"Oh, and what might that be?"

"Your brother William is paying us a visit."

"William? He's with the Virginians . . . was he the one who carried word from New Orleans?"

Phillip must have nodded yes because the next sounds I heard were her steps rushing up the stairs. I went to meet her.

"William," she shouted. "What a wonderful surprise." She advanced to embrace me, but unlike a dozen years earlier, I opened my arms to welcome her.

"When I read in the newspapers," she said once she had released me and taken a step back, "about how many of the Virginians had died, I thought I'd never see you again. Can you stay a while?"

"I have to report to my colonel in seven days, but if you'll have me, I can spend four of them with you."

"Of course we'll have you . . . has Phillip told you that Jacoba is married?"

"Yes, and that you are soon to be a grandmother."

"They live only a half mile from here. I'll go by and tell her and Micah to come to supper tonight. Do you want to see our brother Richard and his wife Amanda?"

"I suppose I must."

"He's been in poor health this winter. I'll send him a note saying that you're here and ask if we can visit."

I was the centre of attraction at supper that night. I told the story of the Virginians' odyssey to New Orleans and my harrowing return to Fort Roanoke yet again—I was getting quite practised at relating these tales—then faced an interrogation from Samuel and Warren, my two younger nephews. They were eleven and nine, and, like most boys that age, intrigued by all things military. David, as befitted his status as a student of the law, asked a few questions, which I couldn't answer, about how Louisiana would be governed. I assured him that Captains Jackson and McIntyre had probably sorted out the answers to all the questions he'd asked.

But I was most taken by Jacoba. She was beautiful—blonde and blue-eyed—a picture of her mother and grandmother. Her belly was just beginning to press against her dress revealing that she was pregnant. She glowed, as women in her state often do. Even though they looked nothing alike, seeing her brought back memories of Awinita in the same condition and how happy I had been in the expectation of becoming a father. My memories of Awinita, which came often, were usually of the pain I felt when she died. It took a conscious effort to recall the many happy moments I'd had in our brief married life. I wanted to tell someone about these feelings, but didn't think I could. Even my loving sister might be repelled by the idea that I'd had a Cherokee wife and son.

Richard responded to Charlotte's note the next day saying that we were welcome to visit Amanda and him at three in the afternoon on Monday, two days hence, and apologised for being unable to invite us to supper. Phillip declined the invitation, because he had to keep the shop open. I wished I had as convenient an excuse.

Richard and I had separated the day our father joined the rebel army. Father had ordered the two of us, my mother, and my sister to take the ferry to New York and go to our grandfather's house. Mother and Charlotte obeyed his orders, but neither Richard nor I did. Richard went to Queens County. I went back to the rebel army and joined father. I went to my grandfather's house a week later, after father was killed in the Battle of Brooklyn. When I got there, mother told me that Richard had joined a loyalist militia. I felt he had betrayed father, which made him my enemy.

I didn't see Richard for another twenty years, until my last visit to New York. By that time he was a rich man, living elegantly, whilst I was a frontier shopkeeper in North Carolina. Richard taunted me, which did nothing to soften the enmity I felt towards him for joining the loyalists.

On the appointed day I drove Phillip's carriage to Richard's town-house in the centre of New York. Having been there once before, I was less awed by its opulence. The same Negro butler who had greeted us twelve years earlier admitted Charlotte and me to the drawing room, where Amanda sat waiting.

"Richard's unable to get out of bed today," she told us. "Please come upstairs."

We followed her up to Richard's bedroom. He lay in an ornate four-poster bed covered with a thick duvet and wearing a bedcap. His face was even more florid than it had been on my last visit, but this time I felt it really was due to a fever. Small bottles of medicine and a silver water pitcher sat on the table next to the bed.

"Welcome to my humble abode," he greeted us. Charlotte went up and kissed him on the forehead. I stood back.

"Come closer, William," he said. "My doctors assure me that pleurisy is not contagious."

"Do they say when you'll recover?" I asked, taking a step closer.

"No, and I wouldn't believe them if they did. They're all a bunch of quacks, but in my condition, I'm at their mercy." He coughed a bit, as if to emphasise his illness. Amanda moved to his side and wiped his brow with a damp cloth.

"She's an angel," Richard said, squeezing her hand a bit. It seemed like genuine affection, something I hadn't seen on my previous visit. Then he'd treated her like a prized possession.

"So, you're the hero of the moment," Richard continued, turning his attention back to me. "The unnamed soldier who carried word of the Virginians' victory across a thousand miles of winter wilderness, carrying on after his officer's death. A modern Phidippides, though you didn't drop dead from the effort."

"Sorry to disappoint you."

"And they made you a sergeant as your reward."

"I guess so." I wasn't going to share the insulting details of my promotion with him.

"I should have thought that after eighteen years as a shopkeeper you would have amassed a sufficient fortune to have bought at least a lieutenant's commission, or did you have some secret vice on which you spent all your money?"

I realised that Richard was just taunting me, but he had landed a lucky shot. His next coughing fit saved me from having to answer this sally. Amanda poured an elixir onto a spoon and fed it to Richard, then poured a glass of water, which he drank.

"I think we'd better let Richard rest," she said, after she had finished ministering to him. We wished Richard well and returned to the drawing room.

"I fear for his life," Amanda said after we were seated. "He's never been this bad before. The medicines seem to calm his coughing, but they do nothing for the congestion in his lungs. But I'm being a poor hostess. Would you care for some tea?" She rang a small bell to summon the butler.

Charlotte carried the conversation whilst we had tea, telling Amanda about her children and going into great detail about Jacoba's pregnancy.

"My great sadness is that Richard and I never had any children. If he dies, there will be no one to carry on his name. I know that he's been hard on you, William, but he's really a good man. He just can't picture any life other than the one he's built for us. And he works very hard—not the way you work hard, William—but keeping the powerful men who run this city as friends is difficult work. I fear that his current illness is the result of that hard work."

I listened attentively as Amanda poured out her woes, but, uncharitable as it was, I couldn't help but think that Richard's illness was far more the result of gluttony than hard work. Charlotte and I excused ourselves after another half hour, and I drove us back to the apothecary shop.

I'd done my duty. I had visited Richard on his sickbed. Now I would put him out of my mind and think only about the members of my family whose company I enjoyed. Only I couldn't. I kept thinking about Amanda and the devotion she was showing to Richard. What would become of her if he died, which seemed likely, given what I had seen earlier that day? As a woman, she couldn't control whatever property Richard left her. Charlotte had told me when we first started corresponding that Amanda had come from a wealthy family. Perhaps they would take her back, with her father or a brother taking charge of Richard's estate.

I had to take the coach back to Philadelphia the next morning. By this time the Virginians' conquest of Louisiana was old news and I could travel in peace—and worry about what awaited me when I returned.

CHAPTER 16

When I reported to Colonel Lancaster, he told me that two ships had been secured and that we would leave for New Orleans in three weeks. He ordered me to make myself available to Lieutenant McAdams at the docks to help in loading supplies on those ships.

The port was full of ships but only one, *HMS Calcutta*, a huge, three-masted East Indiaman, had a mountain of crates, barrels, and bales on the dock beside it. Two marines guarded the entrance to the pier. After identifying myself to the sentries, I was allowed to proceed. Halfway down the pier, hidden by part of the cargo, I found the lieutenant, a young, fair-complexioned, blond-haired man, who probably would have looked gallant on parade or leading a company into battle. But when I first saw him, he was sitting behind a large crate that he was using as a desk, looking completely befuddled.

"Sergeant Watson, reporting as ordered," I said when he looked up from the papers before him.

"Whose orders?"

"Colonel Lancaster told me to place myself under your command."

"Oh? He didn't say anything about that to me. Who are you?" McAdam's voice croaked a little, like a boy whose voice was changing.

I explained that I was the soldier who'd carried the report of the

Virginians' victory at New Orleans back to Fort Roanoke and that I would be returning to the regiment, probably on this ship.

"Know anything about ships' bills of lading?" he asked.

"A bit." I didn't tell him about my years as a shopkeeper or keeping track of rations for the Virginians.

"Well that bit is probably more than I know," he said, smiling to show that we were still on friendly terms. "I have all these lists of the supplies we are supposed to have and there are all these containers on the dock, but I don't know how to verify that the lists are correct and the supercargo won't let me load anything until I do."

"What's a supercargo?" I asked.

"He's the officer responsible for the cargo once is placed aboard ship. Ensign Walton is the *Calcutta's* supercargo, and he says he isn't going to take responsibility for any of this," McAdams said, waving his hand over the array on the dock, "until I give him a correct list."

"Isn't everything labelled?"

"Yes, but the names on the crates," he said, looking back at the pile of cargo behind him, "aren't the same as the ones on the list."

"Do any of the crates or barrels have the same labels?"

"Some do."

It seemed obvious that the packages with the same labels would have the same contents and that if we opened one we would know what the rest contained. We needed to separate everything into groups by label, then open one of each type. I suggested this to the lieutenant as politely as I could. When he finally understood, a big smile crossed his face.

"That's it, Watson," he said. "That's what we will do."

"Have you got men to do the work?"

"I've been given a team of niggers. They're in the shed waiting for orders. You get them working. I'll check things off the list as you identify them."

I would have preferred things the other way around, that I was the one checking off the list. I'd long before decided that slavery was wrong, an immoral practice. I'd been around slaves before, but had never told one what to do. I didn't want to start now, but there seemed no way to avoid it.

As I approached the shed, I heard voices and laughter, which stopped as soon as I opened the door. I was met by a score of blank-looking black faces.

"Who's in charge here?" I asked.

"I guess I is, suh," a grey-haired black man with a scar on the right side of his face answered.

"What's your name?"

"Cicero, suh."

"Well, Cicero, we have all those supplies on the dock to sort out. Can you read?"

"No, suh. None of us can."

"Right, then. We'll start by separating everything by size."

It took Cicero and the rest of the slaves the remainder of the day to sort the supplies by size and shape. Identifying the contents of half the containers was easy. The large barrels contained rum, the small barrels, gunpowder. The large crates contained hard tack, the small ones, dried pea soup. Lieutenant McAdams dutifully checked these off his list. An hour before sunset he decided that we'd finished work for the day and we would identify the contents of the remaining containers the next day. He said good night to me and left. He hadn't said a word to any of the slaves since I arrived.

Cicero told me that the slaves were to return to their masters for the night but would be back, ready to work, at dawn the next morning. I said good night and thanked him for his help. He looked at me quizzically. He seemed ready to say something, but held his tongue. Later it occurred to me that in all probability, he'd never before been thanked for his work.

We finished identifying the remaining packages the next morning. Small amounts were missing, but less than I would've expected. After an extended parley with Ensign Walton, Lieutenant McAdams received permission to stow the supplies in the ship's hold. Nothing was to be loaded on our second ship, a brig named *The Pride of Yarmouth*. This seemed foolhardy, putting all our eggs in one basket, but Walton was adamant. He was responsible for our supplies once they were loaded aboard ship and he wasn't going to allow any of them out of his sight.

Loading the supplies was slow and laborious. Cranes were erected to lift the heavier parcels on board then lower them in the hold. Each parcel, large or small, had to be tied down so that it wouldn't roll or break loose when the ship was underway. It took the slaves eight days to finish this work. The *Calcutta*'s sailors stayed as far away as they could. None of them wanted to risk being drafted to help.

When all the supplies had been loaded, Walton gave Lieutenant McAdams a signed receipt for the stores. McAdams thanked him profusely, told me to send the slaves back to their masters, then promptly disappeared.

"We should clean this place up, suh," Cicero said, when I told him that the work was over and that he and the other slaves could return to their masters. "Don't like leaving this mess." He had a point. There were bits of bale wrapping and other debris strewn around the dock.

"Right then. Clean it up before you leave."

The slaves started picking up the rubbish and carefully depositing it in a bin. They handled each small piece of trash as if it were some fragile, precious relic. I started to reprimand them, but decided to watch instead to see how this charade played out. They started at mid-morning and were able to stretch the work out until mid-afternoon, by which time the dock was as clean as my mother's kitchen floor. Apparently judging that it was late enough in the day for them to return to their masters without risking being given another task, Cicero slowly inspected the area, before announcing that it was complete and that they could leave. I'd seen one of the tactics that slaves used to keep their lives bearable. None of them could be faulted, and they'd managed to spend the better part of a day without having to work hard. I could only admire Cicero's ingenuity.

I'd learned the names of most of the slaves and personally thanked as many as I could as they left. By now they were used to me doing this, but none of them knew how to respond. Some smiled, but most kept their faces blank.

I was now alone on the pier and, in a strange way, in the same position that the slaves had been when the heavy work of loading the ship was complete. I'd been ordered to report to Lieutenant McAdams to help with loading the ship. I could say that it was his responsibility to give me further orders, which clearly he wouldn't do, or I could say that now that the ship was loaded, it was my responsibility to report back to Colonel Lancaster. An old soldier like Sergeant Pew would've made the first choice, but the prospect of enforced idleness didn't appeal to me.

The next morning I made my way to British Army Headquarters in Chestnut Street. Colonel Lancaster now had an aide, a Captain Gwynne, a huge redheaded Welshman, who spoke in a lilting soft voice that belied his stern demeanour. He intercepted me at the entrance to the colonel's office and told me I was now under his command.

"I've been told that you're quite a hero," he said, "but that you have a loose tongue and an inclination to talk to gentlemen of the press. I see nothing heroic in being a message carrier, and I'll have you flogged if you disclose anything about our mission to the newspapers."

"Yes, sir," was the only possible response to his lecture.

"I've also been told that you are useful as a clerk. The expedition's accounts need tending. I expect them to be ready for inspection at all times."

"Yes, sir."

"Take these account books," he said, pointing to a stack of ledgers on his desk. "Find a desk in the orderlies' room, and get to work. Report to me at nine o'clock each morning for orders. Dismissed, Sergeant."

I saluted, picked up the ledgers, turned on my heel, and left. My first thought was that I should've idled at the dock, but I quickly realised that, had I done that, the captain could've legitimately found me guilty of shirking. Unpleasant as he might be, I'd made the right choice in returning for additional orders.

CHAPTER 17

We finally boarded the *Calcutta* at mid-morning on the 15th April 1808, a month later than originally planned. We stood on deck not knowing what to do whilst Colonel Lancaster conferred with Commodore Brady, the ship's captain. There were a score of us, Captain Gwynne, six more officers—three captains and three lieutenants—and the generalissimo. De Miranda had an entourage of a dozen Spaniards, who seemed more like gentlemen of leisure than army officers. I was the only enlisted man in the lot.

The colonel returned after a few minutes. We snapped to attention.

"Stand easy, gentlemen. We sail with the turn of the tide in four hours. You'll be assigned cabins on deck. Our first stop will be the mouth of the Chesapeake to pick up new recruits for the Virginians. From there we'll sail for New Orleans. You'll have no duties whilst on board, but Commodore Brady requests that you do your best to stay out of the way of his sailors. We'll take our meals in the portside petty officers' mess, which has been vacated for our use. I'll see you there promptly at one o'clock. Are there any questions?"

None of the officers spoke. I had many questions, but lacked the temerity to voice them. I'd have to find answers by myself.

As if by signal, three ensigns appeared to escort the officers to their cabins. I had a fleeting vision of spending the voyage in relative luxury, but was quickly disabused of that folly when a petty officer appeared, handed me a hammock, and pointed to an open hatch through which I could see a ladder to the hold.

"You'll sleep down there with the common sailors," he told me.

I made my way below deck. Since the *Calcutta* was still tied to the dock, she didn't rock and I could walk normally. I stopped at the bottom of the ladder whilst my eyes adjusted to the dim light filtering through the gun ports that lined both sides of the hull. I was in a large enclosed area, but without the hallways, doors, or rooms that a building would have. I didn't know what to do next. My confusion must've been obvious because after a few moments an old sailor sidled up to me.

"You look down in the jib, mate," he said.

I had no idea what he was talking about, and my face must've shown it.

"Down in the jib, unhappy."

"Right you are. What am I supposed to do with this?" I said, holding out the hammock."

"String it up, you lubber."

"Where?" I could hear the exasperation in my voice, but this fellow was being no help at all.

"Any place it fits, but you'd best choose someplace amidships, and as high up as you can reach."

I didn't ask why that advice but started looking around. The sailor grabbed my shoulder and pushed me to a nearby gun port. "These two posts'll do," he said. "Reach up and tie the end of your hammock around this one and I'll tie the other end around that one."

He didn't approve of the knot I tied and retied it with what he called a double reef. "There we are, all ship-shape and Bristol fashion," he proclaimed when he finished.

"Thank you, Mr . . . what's your name anyway?"

"I'm Will Robinson, but me mates call me Jack, or Jack Nastyface, on account of me scar."

I hadn't paid any attention to his face, but now I could see that he had a scar running down the left side of his face from his scalp to his chin. "How'd you get that?" I asked.

"From a Barbary pirate that was trying to board the *Duke of Cumberland* about twenty-five year ago. The big heathen come at me with one of those curved swords they use. I stuck him in the belly with my cutlass, but as he fell his blade raked my face. We tossed him overboard for the sharks to eat. The surgeon sewed me up, ad I've carried this scar ever since. Doesn't seem to bother the ladies. They all want to hear how I got it."

"Well thanks, Jack. Any other advice?"

"Go topside and watch the land disappear, and pray that you'll soon see it again. Too many who set sail never return. Storms, pirates, French raiders . . . there's so many ways the sea can kill a man."

I didn't need any encouragement to go back to the main deck. The air inside the hold was rank and the dim light made it gloomy. I had no choice about sleeping there, but I could spend the rest of the day on deck.

Having found a place to sleep, the next question was where would I take my meals? At one o'clock I made my way to the portside petty officers' mess, where Colonel Lancaster had told us to report for dinner. Colonel Lancaster looked at me, thought for a moment, then said nothing. Captain Gwynne was less restrained.

"With respect, Colonel, we can't have a mere sergeant eating in our mess."

"Normally I would agree with you, but under the circumstances I think we can make an exception." Turning to me, the colonel added, "Watson, I am sure that you will mind your manners and speak only when spoken to."

"Yes, sir. Thank you, sir," I replied.

The meal was excellent. Roast pork and maize, with wine and ale to wash it down. I followed the colonel's instructions and said nothing, but I listened intently. Some of the new officers questioned Generalissimo de Miranda about what we could expect to find in Venezuela. He assured them, as he'd assured General Bradshaw, that the people of Venezuela and all of Spanish America would rise up and overthrow the French as soon as they saw him with British Army support. Most of the officers accepted this. Captain Gwynne did not. He started to question de Miranda, but Colonel Lancaster cut him off.

"Our orders are to support Generalissimo de Miranda and it is not an officer's place to question his orders," he said.

I would've liked to ask Captain Gwynne about his misgivings, but given his reaction to me, that was not possible. I had my own questions. Were there French soldiers in Venezuela? Would the people there be willing to rise up against the French knowing that it would mean returning to the Spanish monarchy? I could only hope that Colonel Lancaster or one of his commanders had answers to these questions. If not, the Virginians were embarked on a fools' mission, and fools didn't live long in time of war.

Shortly after dinner there was a flurry of activity on deck. The ropes tying the *Calcutta* to the dock were loosened and tied to three rowboats, each manned by a score of slaves. They proceeded to tow the *Calcutta* to midstream, after which they cast off and returned to shore. The outgoing tide carried the ship downriver. *The Pride of Yarmouth*, our companion for the voyage, followed a short distance behind. Philadelphia is an ocean port, but it's a long way from the open sea. It took us a full day under short sail to reach the broader waters of Delaware Bay. Even though we could still see land, the bay was wide enough for the *Calcutta* to unfurl her full complement of sail and move us along at a brisker clip.

It was my first sea voyage and I was awed by it all. I'd been warned by all and sundry about seasickness, but I didn't suffer that malady, at least not in the gentle waves we encountered off Delaware. But even in those calm seas, I found myself clutching the nearest firm support, much to the amusement of the *Calcutta*'s sailors, who walked the deck without difficulty and scrambled up and down the rigging like so many monkeys. They planted themselves on the ropes and proceeded with whatever task was at hand, furling and unfurling the ship's huge sails as if they were mere rags.

I quickly learned the rituals aboard ship. Time was counted not by hours and minutes but by watches and bells. The day was divided into six watches, each four hours long. Each watch was divided into eight half-hour periods, which were marked by the ringing of the ship's bell, once at the end of the first half hour of the watch, twice at the end of the first hour, and on to the full eight bells at the end of the watch.

Sailors were issued rum rations twice a day. The first time was at noon, but the ritual leading up to it began an hour earlier at six bells in the forenoon watch. A bosun's mate began the process by piping "Up Spirits." At that signal the petty officer of the day climbed to the quarterdeck and obtained the keys to the rum locker from the officer of the watch. With the ship's cooper, and guarded by a pair of Royal Marines, he ceremonially opened the rum storage compartment, located next to the captain's cabin. The cooper then pumped one-eighth of a pint of rum for each petty officer and sailor on board into a keg. The marines lifted the keg to the deck, where cooks from the petty officers' mess waited with pitchers. Petty officers could drink their rum ration straight. The rest was poured into a tub and mixed with four times as much water, a bit of lime, and some Demerara sugar to make grog, the drink that was served to common sailors. Their serving was more than a half pint, which could be made to last for much longer than the mouthful petty officers got.

At eight bells, the bosun's mate piped "Muster for Rum," and the sailors lined up with their mugs to receive their tot. Some drank it on the spot, but others had debts to pay. The usual wager amongst the sailors was so many rum rations. Winners could drink all of the loser's ration, but amongst friends it was customary to take only a small sip.

The whole ritual was repeated again in the early evening during the dog watch.

The sailors worked from dawn to dusk, then stood watch for part of the night. When they were not up in the rigging, adjusting sail or mending frayed rope, they were on their hands and knees holystoning the deck. This close to the American coast, we had little to fear from French raiders, but the captain held drill anyway. The gunners fired a practice broadside, which shook the ship, and the sailors, armed with cutlasses and pistols, practised repelling boarders. The idea of armed Frenchmen swarming over our decks seemed more like an adventure story than reality, but the sailors regaled me with tales of exactly that happening to ships that didn't maintain a proper watch.

Most British Army regiments have two battalions, one fighting in the field, and a second at its home post to find and train new recruits. When the newbies had a reasonable level of training they were transferred to the First Battalion. Fencible regiments, such as the Virginians, which are recruited to serve only for the duration of a war, normally don't have a second battalion. Usually they stay close to home and can accept new recruits directly. But the Virginians, with our orders to travel a thousand miles to New Orleans, weren't an ordinary fencible regiment. Some high-ranking officer must have realised this, because a Second Battalion of the Kings' Own Virginians was established at Hampton Barracks, the army post adjacent to the large naval base that guarded the entrance to Chesapeake

Bay. It collected recruits and gave them a modicum of training in preparation for their joining the rest of the regiment.

We arrived at the mouth of the Chesapeake a day after leaving Delaware Bay. A launch was dispatched to Hampton Barracks to announce our arrival. The new recruits would be ferried out to us to save the time it would take for the *Calcutta* to be towed in and out of Hampton Harbour. The colonel hadn't said, and none of his officers had asked, how many new men there would be. The Virginians needed five hundred to return to full strength.

I was disappointed when I saw only seventy-three recruits come on board. Now that the Virginians had conquered Louisiana, and as far as anyone knew would spend the rest of war on garrison duty, joining the regiment was not an exciting prospect. Most of the new Johnny Newcombes looked undernourished—driven to join the army by poverty. A few looked unsavoury—as if their choice was the army or prison. And there were a few young boys who looked like they joined because they thought the army would offer them a taste of adventure. It was another sign that the Virginians were rapidly becoming just another regiment in the British Army.

Once the recruits were aboard, we set sail southeast to round Cape Hatteras. A mess was set up for the lower ranks. We ate the same fare the sailors did, hardtack and salt meat. My short stay in officer territory was over, and I was back in a more accustomed place.

"It's a fearsome place, Hatteras is," Jack Nastyface told me. "Navy put up a lighthouse a few years ago, but that don't help much. It's the graveyard of the Atlantic. So many ships sink, the people who live onshore . . . they call them Bankers . . . don't bother farming or fishing. They live off what they salvage. And when the weather is calm, they ride their little ponies up and down the shore carrying lanterns. Steersman thinks he's headed for Hatteras light and next thing he knows his ship is hard aground. The Bankers are real helpful. They're out to the ship in no time flat to rescue the crew . . . and help themselves to the cargo."

I didn't know how much of what Jack told me about Cape Hatteras and its inhabitants to believe. The part about the Bankers luring ships to their doom seemed a bit fanciful, especially since none of the navy officers seemed concerned about our route. We rounded the Cape in broad daylight and changed our course to south-southwest to follow the coast.

Our passage was uneventful and four weeks later we reached the mouth of the Mississippi, ready to be towed to New Orleans. By this time, I had found my sea legs and could walk the deck as comfortably as if I were on dry land. I'd even been up on the rigging as high as the lower cross spar, but that required having at least one hand on the ropes at all times. I wouldn't have been able to do any work from that position.

CHAPTER 18

We reached our mooring at New Orleans at noon after being towed for nearly two days. The Virginians, far fewer than the five hundred I expected, were arrayed on the dock to greet us. I could see Captain Jackson—his tall, lean frame was unmistakable—but Colonel Whiteside was not present. Neither was my friend Samuel Smith. The Spanish soldiers, whose uprising had led to our capture of the city, were clearly visible, but also in diminished numbers. They still wore French uniforms. We tied up to the pier and a gangplank was extended for Colonel Lancaster. As he reached its bottom, a sergeant—I couldn't see who—ordered attention.

"Colonel, it is my pleasure to relinquish command of Louisiana to you," Captain Jackson said, saluting.

"Thank you, Captain," Colonel Lancaster replied, "but it was my understanding that Colonel Whiteside was in command here."

"He was, sir, but he died of yellow fever three months ago. Since there was no second-in-command and I am senior captain, I took command of the regiment."

"Captain . . .?"

"Jackson, sir."

"Captain Jackson, I was told that the Virginians had five hundred men fit for duty and that the Spanish added another three hundred. I don't see that many men here. What is your strength?"

"314 Virginians and 167 Spanish. The rest died of their wounds or yellow fever. On any given day as many as a hundred of my men are ill with the ague."

"And your officers?"

"Besides me, three other captains have survived."

"Very well, Captain Jackson, dismiss your men. I shall meet with you and the other surviving officers at four this afternoon. Can you show me to my quarters and make arrangements for these other officers?"

"Yes, sir."

"What are my orders?" I asked Captain Gwynne as soon as the Virginians were dismissed.

"Return to your company. I shan't have further need of you."

"Thank you, sir," I said, saluting, relieved to be returning to friendlier circumstances.

The First Company was still housed in the same buildings it'd occupied more than six months earlier, when Captain Pettit and I left for Fort Roanoke. I had to wait almost an hour for Captain Jackson to return. During that time I heard the mournful news of all who had died of yellow fever. The company was a skeleton of itself. O'Malley, who was now a corporal and the company clerk, told me that only twenty-two men were fit for duty at parade that morning. He eyed me suspiciously, no doubt wondering whether I'd displace him from his current job.

"Where's Captain Pettit?" were Jackson's first words when he saw me.

"Dead, sir," I said, then recounted the accident that claimed his life.

"And you're a sergeant."

I told Jackson the humiliating story of my promotion. He was sympathetic, assuring me that I fully deserved to be a sergeant and to put the circumstances that led to my advancement behind me. "You're my company sergeant now. McMillan died of the fever."

"And what are my orders?"

"We'll be getting some of those new recruits you brought with you. Your task will be to make sure that they are well-trained and fit to be members of the First Company."

Jackson was ordering me to do an ordinary sergeant's job, but I hadn't drilled since the Virginians had left Fort Roanoke, over a year earlier. I wondered whether I was still proficient, and if I could inspire the feelings of fear and awe that a good drill sergeant must.

"Did Samuel Smith die of the fever?" I asked when I finally had a chance.

"No, but he's ill with the ague. The surgeons ran out of cochineal. I hope you've brought more. If you have, Smith should be fit for duty in a few days."

First Company received fifteen of the new recruits. They had been in the army long enough to have developed a healthy fear of sergeants. One of them, Private Stanton, had already been flogged. Whatever they thought, none of them challenged me. I remembered enough of the routine that Sergeant Pew had put me through to do a credible job of teaching them to march and deploy into files. Most of them had used guns before and quickly became proficient in the use of the Baker rifles they'd been issued.

I visited Samuel Smith in the regiment's hospital as soon as I could. The surgeon had already received a resupply of cochineal bark and administered doses to the ague victims, but Samuel was still racked by the chills and fever that accompany the disease. I could only wish him a speedy recovery and promise to return the next day.

I knew that the Virginians were headed for Venezuela, but couldn't tell anyone, not even Captain Jackson. I waited impatiently for the news to become public, whilst all the supplies the *Calcutta* had brought were unloaded. I wondered about this—shouldn't most of them have been left on-board for the trip to Venezuela? The days stretched into a week. The officers met with Colonel Lancaster and Generalissimo de Miranda almost daily, but no word filtered out of their meetings.

Finally, ten days after we had landed, Colonel Lancaster assembled the regiment, but not our Spanish allies. He climbed onto a platform that had been erected the day before. Generalissimo de Miranda, in his resplendent uniform, was at his side.

"Virginians," the colonel began, "your terms of enlistment were to serve in North America until the French were defeated. You've defeated the French in Louisiana, but the war is not over." He paused, surveying us from above. We were at attention, but even without any visible movement, there was a rustling in the ranks. None of us knew what was coming next.

"Those of you who are willing to amend your terms of enlistment, and serve wherever needed until the war is over," the colonel continued, "can wrest Venezuela, one of Spain's American colonies, from France. Those who are not willing shall stay here in New Orleans until we are completely victorious over the French. The King's Own Virginians, your proud regiment, will go to Venezuela. Those who stay will form the Louisiana Battalion and will serve with our Spanish allies to defend New Orleans. You have twenty-four hours to make your decision. Dismissed."

There was hubbub as the regiment dispersed. Everyone was full of questions, the first of which was, "Where's Venezuela?" I was able to answer that one and drew a crude map on the ground showing the Gulf of Mexico and Caribbean, then Venezuela on the northern coast of South America. The next question was, "Who's the Spaniard in the funny uniform?" I identified him as Generalissimo de Miranda and explained that he would be rallying the people of Venezuela to our cause.

Many of the Virginians were eager to join the expedition. They had been in New Orleans for almost a year and were bored. The prospect of going into battle seemed much more appealing than staying on garrison duty for who knew how many more years. Some men had found "wives" amongst the women of the town. Most of them decided to stay after they learned that they wouldn't be able to bring their women along when we sailed for Venezuela. There were also a few timid souls for whom the dangers of a sea voyage and an uncertain reception when we landed were more than they could countenance.

When we assembled the next day, I, my messmate Stuart Fox, and three hundred other members of the regiment volunteered to go to Venezuela. We signed new enlistment contracts obligating us to serve at the King's pleasure until the French were defeated. Eighty, including John Price, my last remaining messmate, who'd found a wife, opted to stay in New Orleans.

Captain Simmons, the only Virginian officer who had declined to volunteer for the expedition, was given command of the Virginians who decided to stay in New Orleans. Captain Gwynne was promoted to major and left in charge of the New Orleans garrison, which included the Spaniards who were now on our side.

The regiment was organised into six new half-strength companies. Captain Jackson was given command of the First Company; Captain McIntyre, command of the Second Company; and Captain Dey, who'd joined the regiment in 1807, command of the Third. Captains Squire, Craig, and Hopewell, British captains who'd travelled aboard the *Calcutta*, were to command the Fourth, Fifth, and Sixth Companies. The appointment of these British captains to command Virginian companies caused a wave of resentment within the regiment. Until then all of our officers had been from the colonies. But we were now fully a part of the British Army and would receive no special treatment. It was a bitter pill to swallow, but the sooner we realised our position the happier we would be.

I was pleased to learn that I was assigned to the First Company as Captain Jackson's sergeant. He later told me that much of the ten days it took to decide on the expedition to Venezuela were spent convincing Colonel Lancaster he could not simply order the Virginians to Venezuela. If he did, they would mutiny. Captain McIntyre came up with the suggestion to have the Virginians who were willing to go to Venezuela volunteer anew. Generalissimo de Miranda was present for all of these discussions and fumed about how the British Army had continually reneged on its promises to him. Finally, Colonel Lancaster silenced him by threatening to withdraw all support for the expedition.

Now that we knew how many men were going to Venezuela, work began on estimating the supplies that would be needed and reloading them on the *Calcutta* and *The Pride of Yarmouth*. We wouldn't be putting all our cargo on one ship this time. A third of them, along with a third of our men, would be on the smaller vessel.

Two days after the Virginians made their decisions, we were again assembled, this time to hear Generalissimo de Miranda.

"Men of the King's Own Virginians," he began. "I am honoured to serve with you on this holy mission. We are only three hundred, but with three hundred, the Spartans turned back the Persian horde." De Miranda didn't add that all but one of the Spartans died in the process, which I prayed wouldn't be our fate.

"The people of Venezuela," the generalissimo continued, "yearn to be free of French tyranny. All they need see is the British flag and they will flock to our side. Our three hundred will become three thousand, then thirty thousand. All of Spanish America, from

Texas to Argentina, will rise up and drive the French from our lands."

He continued on in this vein for another ten minutes. When he finished Colonel Lancaster rose, but didn't dismiss us as I would've expected.

"Virginians," the colonel said, "our orders are to support Generalissimo de Miranda to drive the French from Venezuela. I trust he is correct that the people of that colony will support us. We have no orders concerning the rest of Spain's colonies, and we will not leave Venezuela for any other destination until we do."

De Miranda sat looking at the ground as the colonel spoke. I knew he had much bigger plans than the British Army would support. I couldn't help but think that de Miranda's plans could get all the Virginians killed. I silently thanked Colonel Lancaster for restraining the generalissimo.

The King's Own Virginians set sail for Venezuela on 8th July 1808. We were towed a short distance from the dock into the Mississippi's steady current and a day later entered open water. We sailed for nearly six weeks, through the Gulf of Mexico, the Strait of Florida, then north of Cuba, Hispaniola, and Puerto Rico to the British island of Antigua, where we stopped for resupply. The weather was sultry, and enforced idleness did nothing to improve our tempers. The veteran Virginians, who had experienced similar conditions floating down the Mississippi, sought whatever shade they could find and dozed or gossiped. The new recruits were less resigned. They paced the deck like caged animals and several fights broke out. These were quickly stopped by bystanders, who didn't want to see the men involved flogged. The generalissimo and his entourage were rarely seen, emerging from their cabins only to take their meals.

We spent four days in port and the Virginians were given only a few hours ashore. The generalissimo and his entourage were under no such constraint. They left the *Calcutta* as soon as we docked and had to be brought back by marines after ignoring requests to return to the ship so that we could get underway. I was on deck when the Spaniards arrived. The generalissimo went directly to his cabin, but this was not the end of the affair.

"I resent being hauled back to this ship like a criminal," Captain Pimental, one of de Miranda's subordinates, yelled at Lieutenant Pharr, who was officer of the day.

"Sir, we have to sail with the tide," Pharr replied in a calmer voice than I would've used. "You would've been left behind if I didn't send the marines to find you. Didn't they treat you courteously?"

"They were polite, but I was attending to important matters and did not wish to be interrupted."

"And what were those matters? I didn't know that there was any business to be conducted on this island other than resupply."

"My activities are none of your affair, Lieutenant," Pimental said, before stalking off to his cabin.

I later learned that Pimental had been in bed with a whore when the marines found him and demanded that he return to the *Calcutta* immediately. It was easy to understand why he was upset, but he should've had the good grace to be silent.

Once underway, the Virginians assembled on the *Calcutta*'s deck each day for morning parade, when we were given our orders for the day by our company commanders. But on the first morning after we left Antigua, we were surprised to see Colonel Lancaster and Generalissimo de Miranda, both in full dress uniform, waiting to address us.

"Virginians," the colonel said, "our orders are to land at the port of La Vela de Coro, then march a dozen miles to the town of Coro, where Generalissimo de Miranda will establish his headquarters." These names meant nothing to me and I had no idea where they were.

De Miranda then spoke. "Coro is a place of great importance to Venezuelans. It is our oldest city and was our first capital. From Coro we will establish the new Venezuela." He signalled one of his men, who ran a tricoloured flag up the halyard.

"This will be the flag of our new country, yellow for the riches it contains, blue for the sea that laps at its shores, and red for the blood of its heroes."

Colonel Lancaster interrupted before de Miranda could continue.

"Generalissimo, I remind you that my orders speak only to ejecting the French from your country so that it can be returned to its rightful sovereign, King Ferdinand VII. I will not order my men to support a rebellion against Spain. Take down that flag immediately. If I see it again, I will order Commodore Brady to return to New Orleans."

De Miranda ordered his man to lower the flag. As soon as the flag was down, he folded it and took it back to his cabin. The rest of the Spaniards followed, sullen looks on their faces.

"Virginians," the colonel said, once de Miranda had left, "our enemy is France, not Spain."

CHAPTER 19

After leaving Antigua we made our way past the chain of islands that separate the Caribbean from the Atlantic, then turned west to follow the northern coast of South America. With two hundred Virginians filling the *Calcutta's* hold, not all of whom were fastidious in their personal habits, the air was almost unbreathable. A small sail had been positioned to divert wind below deck, but the *Calcutta's* progress was so slow that only a whisper of fresh air made its way to our quarters. I spent as much time as I could on deck, seeking whatever breeze and shade I could find. The heat affected the sailors too, who seemed to move in slow motion, despite constant haranguing from their petty officers.

The Virginians had suffered heat and idleness on our float down the Mississippi the previous year, but those difficulties were nothing compared to what we now faced. Whilst we were on our rafts, we landed each night and had two hours of activity, one setting up camp in the evening, and a second breaking camp the next morning. We could also enjoy walking on solid ground each evening. Aboard ship we had twenty-four hours a day of inactivity. We'd been just as idle during our sail from New Orleans to Antigua, but the cooler weather had made our lives more bearable. Now that we were fully in the tropics, nothing relieved our torpor.

And our food was poorer than on the trip to Antigua. The bananas and other fresh fruit we took on board in Antigua had to be consumed in a few days before they spoiled. All that was left were the limes, which we received daily to prevent scurvy. We didn't have the berries or wild herbs that were available to us whilst floating down the Mississippi. For most of this trip we had nothing but gruel, salt meat, and hardtack infested with weevils. At first we tried picking these noxious insects out, but soon gave up and ate them along with the bread.

There was too little fresh water to permit washing. I tried washing with salt water, as I had seen some of the sailors do, but it left my skin dry and itchy. I decided that uncleanliness was more desirable, even though I realised that I was contributing to the below deck stench.

Two weeks after leaving Antigua, my bowels rebelled against the diet and inactivity and stopped working. After a few days I had no choice but to go to the surgeon for a purgative, which he quickly supplied, along with the advice that I get as much exercise as possible by promenading the *Calcutta*'s deck. I did this each morning as soon as it was light enough to avoid the many obstructions that littered the way.

"Doing the missionary walk, I see," Jack Nastyface said when he saw me at my morning constitutional. "Trying to keep your bowels working?"

"Yes, but how did you know?"

"Many years ago, the navy took a boatload of missionaries to India to convert the 'eathens. Suffered mightily from constipation, they did, but they discovered that if they spent several hours pacing the deck they could keep their bowels working. Surprised someone didn't tell you that before you set sail."

"I only found out when the surgeon told me."

"'e's like all 'em quacks. Tells you how to cure your problems after you've got 'em, but not how to prevent 'em in the first place. Guess 'e just wants to keep 'is customers coming back."

We arrived offshore La Vela de Coro after nearly four weeks of sailing, and not a day too soon for the Virginians. We'd already been told that our ships would not dock. Commodore Brady had decided to keep them offshore where they would be easier to defend and he'd have less problem controlling his sailors.

A small fort defended the port, but when its commander saw two Royal Navy ships with their guns preparing to fire, he quickly raised a white flag. It would've been a very uneven contest had he decided to fight. Colonel Lancaster was rowed ashore to formally accept the fort's surrender. He paroled the Spaniards on their word that they wouldn't attack us. Once these formalities were concluded, the rest of the Virginians were rowed ashore. We camped that night at the edge of the jungle, about a mile from the port. The colonel had issued strict orders against looting. The best way to enforce his orders was to keep us away from the town. This, of course, did not keep the townspeople from approaching our camp with fresh bread, fruit, and rum. All were eagerly purchased. Some of the men grumbled that it would have been nice to have a woman, but La Vela seemed too small to support even one member of the world's oldest profession.

The colonel appointed Captain McIntyre quartermaster for our expedition and told him to procure carts and draught animals to carry our supplies to Coro. When the generalissimo asked for an oxcart for his books and papers, the colonel said that he would have to find these on his own. It took a full day for McIntyre to carry out his mission. He collected two of the sorriest-looking horses I'd ever seen and four old mules. De Miranda did far better, purchasing a sturdy cart and two oxen.

After morning parade the next day, twenty men and a sergeant from the Fourth Company were ordered to guard the fort. The rest of the Virginians formed a column and marched to Coro. The two horses the captain had obtained dragged the lightest of the fort's guns, a three-pounder. The mules pulled two wagons that carried our food and ammunition. De Miranda's ox-cart carried several large, heavy crates that seemed to weigh as much as all of our supplies. None of the Virginians felt comfortable leaving the ships, our only way home. Colonel Lancaster assured us that Commodore Brady had promised they would remain close by for as long as they were needed.

We could only move at the oxen's pace. It took most of the day to cover the dozen miles to Coro. We were on a good road, but the jungle was a solid wall on either side. It was as if we were in a long green trench. We heard the squawks of birds, and occasionally the sound of larger animals, but few were visible. The heat and a multitude of biting, stinging insects tormented us. The foliage had a fetid smell, but it was far less noxious than the *Calcutta*'s hold.

The jungle ended abruptly in cleared sugar cane fields a mile from Coro. We could see the town's buildings in the distance. A small group, the town's garrison, marched towards us. They fired one volley when they were still too far away for it to be effective. The colonel ordered the Virginians into line formation and had the cannon we'd brought moved into position. The Spaniards quickly surrendered when faced with our much larger force. They'd satisfied honour by firing at us, but had been careful not to anger us by inflicting any casualties. They, too, were paroled. There were no French to be seen.

Coro had a large church and some fine houses along the town square—all in need of repair and fresh paint. It was a sleepy place that had seen better days.

The morning after we arrived, Generalissimo de Miranda, in full uniform and standing on the church steps, read a long, flowery proclamation in Spanish about our coming to free Venezuela from the tyranny of French rule. His audience was limited to the priest, two altar boys, a dozen old women, Colonel Lancaster, and me. None of the Venezuelans were impressed. The colonel seemed unconcerned when I gave him a summary of de Miranda's speech. Perhaps the generalissimo had finally realised that he couldn't openly advocate revolution against Spain.

The town's men, young women, and children kept out of sight for the first two days after our arrival, apparently uncertain about our intentions. By the third day, when Coro's residents realised that we weren't going to loot the town or molest its women, they slowly emerged. A brisk trade soon developed for fresh food, rum, and the services of the town's two whores.

The generalissimo harangued every townsman he could find, but none was willing to join his cause. He grew more desperate as the days passed. His voice became shriller and his rhetoric more inflammatory. I was one of the few Virginians who understood his rants. He crossed the line Colonel Lancaster had drawn, and was now preaching rebellion against the Spanish King. Since he was having no success in attracting converts to his cause, I felt no need to inform the colonel.

A week into our stay, Colonel Lancaster called a meeting of his officers, to which he invited Lieutenant Hernandez, the commander of Coro's garrison. Generalissimo de Miranda and his officers were excluded, but I was invited to translate.

"Lieutenant, are there any French soldiers in Venezuela?" the colonel asked after an exchange of pleasantries.

"None that I know of."

"Are there any Venezuelans who'd support the French?"

"A few perhaps, but we've all heard of fighting in Spain and how the French have ravaged our country."

"If the generalissimo raised the flag of rebellion against the Spanish King, would he find followers?"

"Again, a few perhaps," the lieutenant answered, but with far less certainty than before.

The colonel thanked the lieutenant for his honesty and me for translating, then dismissed the two of us. Captain Jackson later told me that the colonel and his officers had discussed what to do for a half hour without coming to any conclusion. His orders were to fight the French, but there were no French to fight. The British Army would probably applaud if he captured all of Venezuela, but he could only do this by allowing Generalissimo de Miranda to start his rebellion, a move that wouldn't win the colonel any accolades. Jackson said that the colonel wanted to leave, but didn't feel that he could. He had only Lieutenant Hernandez's word that there were no French. He'd look like a fool or a coward if there were French in Venezuela and we left before finding them.

Two more weeks passed with no change in our situation. There were no French to fight and the generalissimo couldn't raise an army—or even a company. In his frustration, he'd taken to cornering individual Virginians and pouring out what he claimed to be his life story.

"I have been in exile from Venezuela for more than thirty years," he told me one morning, as I relaxed in the shade of Coro's church. "I was a captain in the Spanish Army and a loyal subject of His Most Catholic Majesty, Carlos III. For him I fought the Moors in Africa, but I was treated badly. I was a *criollo*, a colonial, not worthy of notice by the nobility of Spain," he said, anger creeping into his voice. "Worse yet, my father was born in the Canary Islands and suspected of not having pure Spanish blood. How can one be loyal to a King who permits such injustice? You British have a much fairer system."

I could have matched his story with my tale of the disdain the British Army felt for the Virginians, but decided that this would just inflame him further and I'd probably be trapped for a longer time.

"I left the service of the King in 1783," de Miranda continued, in a much calmer voice. "Since then I have been devoted to the cause of freedom for my people and the people of all Spanish America. I have travelled the Earth seeking help. In Russia I was presented to the Tsarina, the great Catherine." He paused for a moment contemplating what must have been a much happier memory. It could've been my opportunity to escape, but I wasn't quick enough, and the generalissimo continued.

"Catherine was much interested in Spanish America. Her fur traders had established their first post in Alaska, and she knew that Russia might eventually have to fight the Spanish in California or you English in Canada to keep that land. I tried to convince her that freed Spanish colonies would not be interested in a frozen wilderness like Alaska, even if it did contain a wealth of furs. The Tsarina offered no help, so I moved on.

"Gossips have spread a rumour that I was her lover. I wish that was true," he said almost wistfully, "but Catherine was an old woman when I knew her. She treated me as a mother would treat a son."

I found de Miranda's story about Tsarina Catherine too fantastical to believe. It beggared the imagination that this clown in a pompous uniform could've been a favourite of a monarch as powerful as Catherine. But this was only the first of his fabulous tales. He also claimed to have met the Kings of Poland and Sweden, the historian Edward Gibbon, and more famous men than I can remember, and to have been a general in the French Revolutionary Army.

"How were you able to convince the British Army to provide you with soldiers for this expedition?" I asked after listening to him for nearly an hour. It was the only part of his story of any interest to me.

"I have powerful friends in London," he answered with a conspiratorial smile. He clearly wanted me to ask who, so I did.

"Admiral Sir Home Riggs Popham has always supported my efforts."

I had to accept this part of de Miranda's story. The Virginians were in Venezuela. This could only have happened if he had a powerful friend in London.

Now that I've had the opportunity to read some of the histories of the long war against the French revolutionaries, the name Popham explains much. He's been largely forgotten, except by scholars of that war, but in his time he was a controversial figure. In 1806 he commanded the naval fleet that captured the Cape of Good Hope from the Dutch, adding that huge colony to Britain's empire. Had he stopped at that, he would have been a hero. But then, without orders, he sailed his ships and sixteen hundred men under the overall command of Brigadier William Carr, Viscount Beresford, across the South Atlantic. General Robert Craufurd was their field commander. They surprised the Spanish and captured Buenos Aires, but only temporarily. Once the citizens of Argentina realised how few soldiers we British had, they rebelled and took them prisoner.

But they were lucky. Spain was in the midst of changing from Britain's enemy to her ally. Instead of being held for a long period of time, they were packed onto ships and returned to Britain as a gesture of Spanish goodwill. Popham, Beresford, and Craufurd were greeted as heroes by London's merchants for their attempt to expand Britain's empire. The British Army and Royal Navy were less enthusiastic. The three were court-martialled and found guilty of acting without orders, but given their public support, that meant little. All were given new, more prestigious commands—Popham as commander of the fleet that attacked Copenhagen, Beresford as the commander of the Portuguese Army, and Craufurd as commander of Sir Arthur Wellesley's Light Brigade. Given his actions at Buenos Aires, it is not surprising that Popham would champion an adventurer like de Miranda.

I hadn't had much chance to talk to my friend Samuel Smith since we'd left New Orleans. His company was one of two that made the trip on *The Pride of Yarmouth*. But now, with little else to do, we spent hours talking.

"How long do you think we'll stay here?" I asked one afternoon after three weeks in Coro. We were sitting in a small tavern across Coro's square from the church, enjoying a punch made of rum and the juices of local fruit.

"Not much longer, I'll wager," Samuel answered. "By now the

Spanish commander in Caracas must know that we're here. He's
probably gathering his forces to evict us as we speak."

"Do you think we'll fight?"

"We'd be idiots if we did. I'm certain the Spanish know how few
of us there are and will come with many times our number."

"So we've been sent on a fools' mission," I said, taking a sip of punch.

"It would appear so. I hope that we can escape without harm,"
Samuel replied, tapping his beaker against mine.

Samuel's words were prophetic. Two mornings later, I saw an
agitated Generalissimo de Miranda and a man in the uniform of a
Spanish Army officer hurrying towards Colonel Lancaster's headquarters. A few minutes later a call went out for all officers to attend
the colonel, and a half hour after that we were formed up for parade.

"Virginians," the colonel began after we'd assembled, "word has
arrived that the Spanish are marching from Caracas with three
thousand men, ten times our number."

A groan rose from our ranks.

"Lieutenant Castro," the colonel continued, nodding towards the
Spanish officer at his right, "has brought a letter from the Spanish
governor in Caracas calling upon us to surrender. We will not yield,
but it would be prudent for us to return to La Vela and our ships. We
march at dawn. We will leave the cannon and wagons and carry only
the supplies needed for a day's march."

The Virginians hurried to the dozens of tasks that had to be done
to prepare us for leaving. No one groused or complained. All wanted
to quit Coro as quickly as possible. The Generalissimo had his crates
loaded on his ox-cart.

At dawn the next morning, we formed a column. The colonel told
me to stay by his side in case he needed Spanish translation. At his
command, we stepped off briskly to begin our march to La Vela. Our
pace was much faster than de Miranda's ox-cart. He and his entourage
soon fell several hundred yards behind. Seeing this, he rushed forward.
The colonel halted the column to allow de Miranda to catch up.

"Colonel Lancaster, I request that you slow your march to allow
my men and cart to keep pace with you," Miranda said.

"I cannot place my regiment at risk," the colonel replied. "You and your
men are welcome to join us, or to stay with your cart. The choice is yours."

"I understand completely," de Miranda replied angrily "The British Army is breaking yet another promise to me."

The colonel replied by ordering the column to resume its march. De Miranda returned to his cart, which was soon out of sight, behind us.

Two hours later, about halfway to the port, a half dozen Spanish cavalry cantered down the road towards us. As soon as they realised who we were, they beat a hasty retreat.

The colonel ordered us into a line formation, but the jungle was too dense and the road too narrow for three hundred of us to array in the normal two-line formation. Even in loose files, where we were only six inches apart, we had to form ten lines. It took us nearly fifteen minutes to achieve this unorthodox formation. Once we had, we slowly marched forward.

No more than five minutes later, we saw Spanish cavalry, far more than the half dozen we'd seen earlier. A Spanish captain rode forward, signalling that he wanted a parley. He was followed, two horse-lengths behind, by an ordinary cavalryman. Colonel Lancaster told me to follow him, three paces behind, as he stepped forward from our lines. We met the Spanish fifty yards in front of our formation.

"Good morning, Colonel," I translated. "I have been ordered to arrest Francisco de Miranda and the traitors who follow him for rebelling against His Most Catholic Majesty, Fernando VII. If you surrender them, I promise you and your men safe passage to your ships. I will also release the twenty men you left at La Vela de Coro, who are now my prisoners."

"Do you not know that Spain and Britain are now friends and allies?" the colonel asked. "Friends do not make such demands on each other." I waited a few moments before starting to translate the colonel's words. I didn't have to. The cavalryman who'd accompanied the Spanish captain began an excellent translation. I quickly realised why de Miranda had warned me against speaking my "peasant" Spanish in the presence of Venezuelans.

"Friends do not protect criminals from justice," the Spaniard replied angrily. His tone caused his horse to stir, but he quickly brought the animal under control.

"Generalissimo de Miranda and his party are under my protection," the colonel replied calmly. "We mean no harm to Spain. We came to fight the French, but now that we have learned that there are no French in Venezuela, we are leaving as quickly as we can."

I was surprised at the colonel's response. He clearly would've been happy to be rid of de Miranda and the other Venezuelans, and wouldn't have shed a tear if the Spanish had captured them. He could've told the captain that the generalissimo and his party were behind us, and let the cavalrymen through our lines to capture them, but I guess honour demanded that he not simply surrender them.

"Since you are protecting traitors, you leave me no choice but to destroy you and your soldiers. May God have mercy on your souls." The two Spaniards turned their horses and rode back to their troop. Colonel Lancaster and I returned to our lines to await the Spanish attack.

Colonel Lancaster ordered our first line to lie on their stomachs, the second line to kneel, and the third line to stand. "When I order fire," he said in a loud voice, "the first three lines are to fire at once, then make their way as quickly as possible through the trees, reload, and reform their lines in the rear. The next three lines will repeat this drill, then the next three."

Our riflemen quickly took their positions. I was in the second line, a little right of centre, nervously awaiting the colonel's order. The Spanish cantered towards us in a column of threes. When they got within about three hundred yards of us, a bugle sounded, and they spurred their horses into a gallop.

The colonel waited until they were within about a hundred fifty yards of us before ordering "Fire." Thirty rifles fired in unison. As I scrambled to the trees on right side, I could see that the front three horses had fallen, throwing their riders and blocking the road, the next three lines of Virginians taking position, and the Spanish reorganising their formation. After a few moments, their column charged. Again the front three horsemen were cut down by fire from thirty rifles. That was enough to convince the remaining Spanish to retreat.

Six downed horses blocked the road in front of us—four were dead, the other two were quickly dispatched. The men who had fired the second volley rushed forward for whatever plunder they could find. The colonel allowed this to proceed for a few minutes before ordering them back into formation. Two of the six cavalrymen were dead, and one had had his right leg crushed when his horse fell. The other three could walk. They were stripped of their weapons and anything of value, then their hands were tied behind their backs. One of our men was detailed to guard each of them. We made a crude litter for the man with the crushed leg and took turns carrying him. We couldn't afford the time to bury the two dead and left them there.

No more than ten minutes after the Spanish had retreated we were back in formation marching towards La Vela. We were in high spirits. We had won the Virginians' first true victory. We had prevailed at New Orleans, but only because the Spanish opened the city gates for us.

The road was clear for the next five miles. When we got to the edge of the fields around La Vela, we saw the troop of Spanish cavalry arrayed in a line in front of us, ready to attack. We hastily formed a square about fifty yards into the fields, fixed bayonets, and prepared to repulse their charge. I was again in the second rank, which this time was the rear rank, directly facing towards the enemy.

The Spanish captain again signalled for a parley. Colonel Lancaster, with me as his translator, met him a dozen yards in front of our square. Four riflemen carried the wounded Spaniard's litter, which they laid on the ground between the colonel and the horsemen. As soon as this task was over, the colonel ordered them back to their positions.

"Thank you colonel for returning this man. How many of my men do you hold prisoner?" the captain asked.

"Three."

"I can see that the traitor de Miranda is not with you," the captain said. "Release my men and accept my offer of safe passage and the return of your men. We will find de Miranda."

"My orders, Captain, are to protect Generalissimo de Miranda," the colonel replied. "I intend to defend the entry to this road until he can join us."

The captain said nothing more as he turned his horse and rode back to his troop. Six horsemen came forward to where we were standing. Four dismounted and took the litter with the wounded man. The other two led the rider-less horses back to the Spanish lines. Two minutes later, a Spanish bugle sounded and the troop began riding towards us, first at a canter, then at a gallop.

"Hold your fire until they're closer," the colonel ordered.

"Front rank, fire," he ordered a few seconds later, when the first of the Spanish were about 150 yards away. There was a deafening roar and through the smoke I could see a number of horses fall. "Second rank fire." More horses fell. The rest of the cavalrymen swept by our square, firing their carbines as they approached. Some of our men fell. I was too busy reloading my rifle, and the smoke was too thick, for me to be sure what had happened. None of the Spanish tried to penetrate the wall of bayonets they faced. When they reached the trees, they wheeled about and returned to their original position.

Three wounded men were pulled into the centre of the square, and we closed ranks to fill the gaps. We had withstood the first Spanish charge and were ready to repel another.

By now it was noon, and my throat was parched from both the heat and the smoke, but we weren't allowed to stand down. To get to our canteens, we would have to remove our packs and be unprepared to repulse an attack. I could hear the cries of some of the wounded Spanish, and am certain that their captain could hear them too. Had he asked for a truce to collect his dead and wounded, I'm certain Colonel Lancaster would have agreed.

Fifteen minutes later the Spanish charged again. Their line was not as straight this time, since their horses wouldn't ride over the downed horses that blocked their approach. We added to their casualties with two well-placed volleys, and suffered more of our own—two dead and two more wounded.

Stuart Fox, my last remaining messmate was one of the dead. In the months since leaving New Orleans, we'd become friends after a fashion—not the kind of friendship I had with Samuel Smith, but more of the "hale fellow well met" friendship that messmates should have. This was somewhat remarkable since he was only twenty and I was old enough to be his father, and I was a sergeant and he, a private. But I tried to treat him as an equal and he responded in kind. Somehow it worked and by the time we landed in Venezuela, we were bantering as if we'd been friends all our lives. But the field outside of La Vela was not the place or time for grieving. We still had to fight our way back to our ships. I told myself that I would mourn Fox at the appropriate time. That time never came.

The Spanish cavalry couldn't break our square and they didn't have the artillery that would normally be used against an infantry formation. The guns at La Vela must've been too immobile for them to use. But we couldn't advance to the port to board our ships, nor could we retreat to Coro without risking finding more Spanish there.

At one p.m., the generalissimo appeared with his entourage and his ox-cart full of heavy chests. The Spanish were not slow in noting his presence. Less than five minutes after his arrival, the captain signalled that he wanted yet another parley. The colonel shrugged his shoulders and walked forward. I trailed a respectable distance behind.

"Give up the traitor, and you're free to go," the Spaniard said.

"I have told you that I cannot do that," the colonel replied, "but I am willing to give you a thirty-minute truce to collect your dead and wounded."

"I accept your gracious offer. Let truce begin when I return to my men."

Colonel Lancaster told us that we could stand easy and remove our packs for twenty-five minutes. I gratefully found my canteen and took a long swallow of water, followed by a second. My thirst temporarily satisfied, I ate some of the hard tack and dried beef we had for rations for the day. The colonel allowed us to break ranks a line at a time to relieve ourselves and take advantage of the fruit trees that were no more than fifty yards from our square.

We were back in position five minutes before the end of the truce. Captain Jackson used the truce to determine that we'd downed forty-three Spanish horses, and presumably removed an equal number of Spaniards from the fight. Captain McIntyre reconnoitred Spanish lines and estimated that there were no more than a hundred Spanish fit for duty. It seemed too small a force to overcome our square, but ten minutes after the end of the truce, the Spanish charged a third time. De Miranda stood behind the second rank bravely observing the cavalry as they approached. He seemed every inch the soldier he claimed to have been as a young man. His entourage huddled in the centre of our square; his ox-cart a short distance behind us, where the road entered the jungle.

Our volleys downed at least a score of the Spanish before they retreated. We lost only two on this attack, one dead and one wounded.

I wondered how many more times the Spanish would attack, then remembered the bravery of Smallwood's Marylanders at the Old Stone House in the Battle of Brooklyn all those years ago. They charged six times into the hailstorm of British fire, losing more men each time, until there were too few to mount a charge. My father was killed on the third charge. Was there any reason to believe these Spanish cavalrymen would be less brave?

There was calm after the third charge for nearly an hour. Then, to our surprise, we heard a large explosion.

"What was that?" one of the men in the ranks asked loud enough to be heard by the colonel.

"I suspect that was La Vela's armoury," the colonel replied is a shocked voice. "The Spanish must be preparing to retreat, if they are willing to blow up the fort's ammunition."

Five minutes later the Spanish mounted their horses and formed up around two wagons that appeared to carry the wounded. The twenty Virginians the Spanish had taken prisoner marched alongside the wagon. They appeared to be unhurt. The procession withdrew to the east, the direction of Caracas.

Generalissimo de Miranda had come up to observe the happenings. "Could this be a ruse?" Colonel Lancaster asked him.

"I think not," the generalissimo answered in a calm voice. "If it was a ruse, they wouldn't have blown up the fort's ammunition. The Spanish captain has satisfied the demands of honour. He charged three times and lost a third or more of his men. He's taken prisoners. His superior officers will accept that he did the best he could."

The colonel ordered a score of men to dig graves at the edge of the field for the three Virginians who'd been killed. Once they were ready and the bodies placed in them, he read a short funeral service. The graves were covered and crude crosses erected. La Vela had a small church, but its padre would never let a non-Catholic be buried there. We could only hope that the farmers who tended this field would respect the graves of our comrades.

Despite the generalissimo's assurances, the colonel was wary. He sent a patrol led by Captain Craig to follow the Spanish, whilst the rest of us slowly proceeded to the port. The captain returned an hour later. He met us at the dock whilst we were boarding boats to take us to the *Calcutta* and *The Pride of Yarmouth* and reported that the Spanish cavalry were nowhere near.

I expected us to weigh anchor and immediately set sail for Trinidad, the nearest British naval base, but we didn't. We got underway the next morning, but for Antigua, which we had left two months earlier. No explanation was given for the choice of this more distant destination.

Once aboard, the generalissimo and his entourage retreated to their cabins. Relations between them and our officers were frigid, to say the least. Rumour had it that de Miranda was concocting a story that the expedition would have been successful except for Colonel Lancaster's cowardly behaviour in not staying in Coro. To a man the Virginians would've testified that this was nonsense, but the story would seem plausible to someone who knew nothing of the facts.

The air in the *Calcutta's* hold was as foul as ever, and the food, which was no better than on the outbound voyage, was in short supply. After two weeks, Commodore Brady put the Virginians on half rations to provide full rations for his sailors. The Virginians accepted these hardships with an air of resignation.

We were a dispirited group. We had been sent on a fools' mission. We had defeated the Spanish, but still felt that we'd failed. We'd lost one in ten of our men, twenty of whom were now prisoners of the Spanish. I heard more than one man grumble that the colonel should have traded de Miranda and his Venezuelans for the men of the Fourth Company being held prisoner. The sailors, who'd taken to referring to us as the "Conquerors of Venezuela" whenever no officers were within earshot, did nothing to help our mood. Several fistfights broke out between sailors and Virginians. After one of them, Private Samuels and a sailor I only knew as Bill were each given twenty-five lashes. This was enough to squelch the fighting, but did nothing to improve tempers on either side.

CHAPTER 20

We landed in Antigua on Thursday, 9th November 1808, a month after leaving Venezuela. We were temporarily attached to the island's garrison until orders for our disposition could be sent from Horse Guards, British Army Headquarters. One of the garrison's soldiers told me that it usually took about six months for a message to make the round trip.

We had regular quarters and food, and our duties weren't onerous. The garrison soon learned the details of our unsuccessful expedition to Venezuela. The mocking we'd received aboard the *Calcutta* intensified. Any acclaim the Virginians earned by capturing New Orleans was wiped out in a flood of jokes and snide comments about our being the Conquerors of Venezuela. Memories of Samuels being flogged aboard the *Calcutta* were enough to prevent us from responding. But then we had a change in heart.

Samuel Smith started it by proclaiming, "We have nothing to be ashamed of. We may not have conquered Venezuela, but we acted honourably and defeated the Spanish cavalry." Others soon agreed, and started responding to taunts with, "When was the last time you were in battle?" For many who were making jokes at our expense, the answer was never, and for most of the others, it was not for many years. Within a week of challenging our harassers, the teasing disappeared.

This made our lives much more pleasant, but, even though it was winter, the heat and humidity were a constant trial. Only the island's ample supply of rum made life bearable.

The first ship for England left two weeks after we arrived. Both Colonel Lancaster and Generalissimo de Miranda were on board, each intent on telling his very different version of what'd happened in Coro to whoever would listen. I prayed that the truth Colonel Lancaster would tell would prevail. No doubt he would face an army court of enquiry and be required to justify his actions. He took Captains Squire and Craig, two of the British captains who'd joined the Virginians in New Orleans, with him to support his story. This left the regiment short two company commanders. Lieutenants Castleton and Spenser, two of the junior officers who'd also joined the Virginians in New Orleans, were given brevet, or acting, captaincies and command of the companies. They could be replaced if an officer with a permanent rank of captain appeared.

We still had no major to take command in Colonel Lancaster's absence. As senior captain, Jackson filled that role, but very uneasily.

"Dammit, Watson," he exploded to me one day. "Why are these British officers so high-and-mighty? Some wet-behind-the ears captain who just bought his commission, or more likely whose father just bought it for him, asked me what club I belonged to. I knew he meant a London club, so I had to say none. 'Belong to Boodle's myself. Take you there some day,' the twit said."

I'd told him of the insulting behaviour the British officers at Fort Roanoke when I arrived with the report of the capture of New Orleans, and didn't want to fan his anger by repeating the story. I said nothing, and Jackson continued.

"The only way to get any respect from them will be to show valour in battle in Spain. By God, I hope we get that chance soon. If not, I'm going to punch one of those popinjays in the nose."

The Virginians didn't know it, but our future depended on the success of the British Army now fighting the French in Spain and Portugal.

Dumouriez had systematically defeated France's enemies on the continent of Europe; Austria in 1805, Prussia and Russia in 1806. He needed plunder to pay his army, to carry out the many civic projects he'd undertaken in France, and to maintain the lavish lifestyle he and his fellow revolutionaries had adopted. And he had to keep taxes low, or risk that the French people would rebel against him as they had against Louis XVI. Even though Spain was still France's ally, it was the richest target within his reach, and he decided to add it to the growing French Empire. He was aided by the turmoil within the Spanish Court, a story too long and convoluted for me to tell. If you wish to delve into the details, Sir Owen Madden's masterful *A History of Spain and Portugal, 1760-1814*, does a far better job than I could ever do.

Dumouriez's victories left Portugal as Britain's only ally on the European continent. He demanded that the Spanish allow the French Army to cross their country to attack the Portuguese—a demand he correctly judged Spain could not accept. When the Spanish dithered, Dumouriez sent the French Army into Spain, forcing the both King Carlos IV and his son Ferdinand VII to abdicate. In February 1807, Marshal Masséna was installed as the country's dictator. When some Spaniards resisted, the French took hostages, who they slaughtered by the hundreds. The Virginians knew of these events. They were what led Sergeant Montoya and the other Spanish soldiers in New Orleans to rebel against their French officers and open the city's gates to us.

In October 1807, the French started their campaign against Portugal. Britain evacuated the Portuguese Royal Family, its court, and most of its treasure to Brazil. The French captured Lisbon, the Portuguese capital, but it was a hollow victory.

As soon as it could, Britain sent an army to northern Portugal under the field command of Sir Arthur Wellesley. He aggressively pursued the French, defeated them at Vimeiro, and had them bottled up in and around Lisbon. But before he could administer a *coup de grâce*, he was ordered into a defensive position by the senior generals who'd taken overall command. These generals then allowed the French to evacuate Portugal, taking their weapons and everything else they could carry. The British Army marched into Lisbon, but Wellesley's victory had been wasted. He'd not been given the chance to destroy the French force. Wellesley was so angered by these events that he left the army and returned to his family estate in Ireland.

Whilst part of the French Army was engaged in Portugal, most of it was busy occupying Spain, which it did with little difficulty. But the French didn't take into account the spirit of the Spanish people. Small groups had been fighting the occupiers from the time they invaded Spain, but on 2nd May 1808, the citizens of Madrid, Spain's capital, rebelled. For three hours they killed every Frenchman they could find. When the French Army regained control, it massacred thousands of Spanish as a reprisal. This bloody incident was followed by a series of similar uprisings in other Spanish cities.

In early June a Spanish emissary arrived in London to request British aid in their fight against the French. Britain responded quickly. In October, fourteen thousand men landed at Corunna on Spain's northern coast and marched south to join forces with twenty thousand men marching north from Portugal. They were to be further reinforced by the Spanish Army, which had liberated Madrid. The French were on the defensive. News of these early successes reached Antigua in mid-December, and the general feeling was the war in Spain would soon be over.

On our arrival in Antigua, along with the Virginians' other sergeants, I joined the sergeants' mess. After some mandatory teasing about being one of the Conquerors of Venezuela, we were treated with courtesy, and offered a variety of advice about both our role as sergeants and life on the island.

"Take care where you do your drinking," Sergeant Dempsey, who'd been on Antigua for more than a year, warned me a few days after we arrived. "Some of the islanders will get you drunk and steal everything you own."

I didn't take his warning seriously until a week later when Corporal O'Malley woke up in an alley one morning with a very sore head and wearing only his smalls. He hobbled back to camp in his underwear and was placed under arrest for overstaying his leave. O'Malley was a handsome man with a headful of black, curly hair, bright blue eyes, and just the slightest hint of a brogue. Whilst he was clearly intelligent, he seemed to court trouble. It was hardly surprising that he'd found the wrong place to drink.

"Poor O'Malley," Captain Jackson said, when I reported to him later that day. "He'll be the laughing stock of the regiment until another dunce does something even more stupid." He looked like he was trying, but not quite succeeding, to suppress a smile. "I shall have to punish him, but I don't want to see him flogged."

At morning parade the next day, Jackson announced that O'Malley was sentenced to ten days in gaol on bread-and-water, a reduction in rank to private, and would have to pay the stoppages for his lost kit. I saw amazed looks on the faces of the Virginians around me. Captain Jackson had a well-deserved reputation for being a fair, but strict, disciplinarian. I think the Virginians would've liked to cheer after his announcement, but none dared risk it.

"I was in a tavern called The Parrot," O'Malley complained when he returned from gaol. "I'd had a beaker of rum, when this islander comes up and offers to buy me a second. He had an Irish brogue, so I thought I could trust him. We were talking about where in Ireland we came from when my head started swimming. The next thing I knew it was morning and I was lying half-naked in a pile of pig shit."

Several of us volunteered to return to the tavern with O'Malley to find his Irish "friend," an offer he quickly accepted. Late that afternoon, five of us followed him into The Parrot. It looked like any of the score of bars near Antigua's docks, dimly lit by a single ship's lantern and what little daylight penetrated its open door and filthy windows. A half dozen men sat at the bar. A few tables, one of which was occupied by two scantily-dressed whores, filled the rest of the room.

"You thieving bastard. What'd you put in my drink?" O'Malley shouted at the man he identified as the one with whom he'd been drinking.

"Who you calling a thieving bastard?" the man replied, reaching for the knife in his belt. Two of the other men at the bar grabbed him before he could get it free.

"Easy, Jack. Let's not be starting fights with soldiers," the bartender said. "It's bad for business. What's your name, soldier?"

"O'Malley."

"And what's your complaint?"

"I was in this bar two weeks ago. Jack here," O'Malley said, pointing to the man, "slipped something in my rum, stole my money and kit, then left me in a pile of pig shit."

"I never saw this soldier before in my life," Jack said, without the Irish brogue O'Malley claimed the thief had.

"Any of you see this soldier before?" the bartender said, looking at his customers.

There was a chorus of noes.

"I run a respectable tavern, Sergeant," the bartender said to me. "I can't help it if your corporal got drunk and was the victim of thieves."

"How'd you know he'd been a corporal?" I asked.

"Did I say corporal? It must've been a slip of the tongue."

"You bunch of bloody liars," Private Hardwick, O'Malley's closest friend, snarled, as he lowered his head and charged towards the Antiguan nearest him. The rest of us joined the melee. I grabbed one of the islanders, but he squirmed out of my grasp before I could do him any harm. Out of the corner of my eye I could see the bartender duck for cover and the whores scurry out the door.

After what could not have been more than a half minute, I heard the whistles of the Provost Marshal's patrol. Three of them entered the bar and began swinging their clubs, not concerned whether they hit the Antiguans or us. I caught a glancing blow on the shoulder that could've broken a bone had it hit me directly. The fight ended a few seconds later.

Since I was a sergeant, and the commander of the patrol was only a corporal, I was able to convince him that the fight was only a friendly scuffle, even though Hardwick was bleeding from a knife cut on his face and one of the Antiguans had been knocked unconscious.

"You men will return directly to the barracks?" the corporal asked.

"Most certainly," I replied.

"And you agree that this was a friendly scuffle?" he asked, staring at the bartender, who'd emerged from behind the bar.

The bartender started to complain, but the corporal silenced him with "My report will say that this was a friendly scuffle and ignore what I am sure are numerous infractions that I could find if I chose to look."

"As you say, Corporal, it was a friendly scuffle."

"Good, then let's all be on our way."

On our way back to the barracks, Dawson, another of O'Malley's friends, argued that we should go back to the bar and finish what we'd started. I told him that was not a good idea—that I'd been able to talk the Provost Marshal corporal out of arresting us once, but was unlikely to be able to do so a second time. Dawson said that we ought to wait a few days, then burn the place down. That was an even worse idea—we'd probably burn half the town if we tried that. We finally agreed to think about what we could do for a few days. By which time everyone's anger had cooled.

The next day, I talked to Sergeant Dempsey, who told me that O'Malley was not the first soldier to lose his possessions at The Parrot.

"Why didn't you tell me that when you warned me to be careful where I drank?" I asked, indignant that he'd withheld such important information.

"You didn't pay attention when I told you to be careful where you drank, did you? Most new arrivals on our fair island don't," he said in a resigned tone of voice.

I sheepishly admitted that I hadn't. He then gave me the names of a half dozen other bars that should be avoided. I spread their names amongst the Virginians and no others suffered O'Malley's fate.

December passed slowly. It was strange to celebrate New Year's Day 1809 in balmy weather, but so much else was different that I only thought about it when we were relieved of duty and had a festive meal. There was much jesting about where we would be on New Year's Day 1810. India and Australia were amongst the more outlandish suggestions, but the mood was such that they were taken seriously and reasons given for why such a posting might make sense.

"Watson," Captain Jackson said one day in mid-January, after I'd completed drilling the First Company, "what do you think our orders will be?" I'd gone to his office to make my daily report.

I'd thought about this question—all the Virginians had—but decided to answer cautiously. "It's not for a mere sergeant to speculate about such matters."

"But surely you've thought about it. You've a brain in your head."

Since Jackson seemed calm and reasonable, I decided to respond.

"I think there are three possibilities. We could be sent back to New Orleans, but that would be foolish since there are sufficient men to defend the town." Jackson nodded in agreement, so I felt comfortable continuing.

"We could be sent back to Fort Roanoke to help enforce the Proclamation Line. That would make sense. Many of the Virginians are skilled backwoodsmen." Jackson frowned at this suggestion.

"Or we could be sent to Spain."

"By God, I hope it's Spain," Jackson said, pounding his desk for emphasis. "There's no glory to be had chasing settlers back to where they belong or bribing Indian tribes to keep the peace. Spain is where the French are and where a man can show his true mettle—and show these arrogant Brits what we Americans can do."

Samuel Smith and I had discussed the same question and come to the opposite conclusion. We'd be just as happy to spend the war at Fort Roanoke, safe from any undue hardship. But I wasn't about to tell the captain this. "We'll know in a few months," I said. Jackson chose not to reply to this last comment and our conversation was at an end.

Captain Jackson wasn't the only Virginian who dreamed of going to Spain. Some sought adventure, whilst others were driven by the chance for plunder. The latter were certain that the rules against looting that had been enforced in New Orleans and Venezuela would be relaxed in Spain. As for myself, I'd had enough adventure on my journey from New Orleans to Fort Roanoke. I'd been in combat during the Great Rebellion, the Virginians' failed attack on New Orleans, and just recently outside La Vela. These were grim reminders of how fragile life was. I didn't think of myself as a coward, but saw no reason to court danger.

The first ship of the year from London arrived in Antigua in mid-April. It didn't bring orders for the Virginians, but did bring news of a stunning reversal of British fortunes in Spain.

Dumouriez responded to Britain's initial successes with a massive reinforcement of his army. The French quickly recaptured Madrid and defeated the Spanish Army. The twenty thousand men under the command of Sir John Moore who'd marched north from Lisbon were in central Spain, but threatened with starvation. It was the middle of winter and the countryside was barren. Snow blocked the passes from Portugal making resupply from Lisbon difficult, if not impossible. The fourteen thousand men under the command of Sir David Baird, who'd marched south from Corunna, were in northern Spain, unable to provide any assistance.

Moore could've been expected to retreat back into Portugal, but instead he decided to make a dash for Corunna, where he could join up with Baird's army before being evacuated by the Royal Navy. It was a harrowing ordeal under harsh winter conditions. Half of Moore's soldiers died or were captured before they could reach the coast. Moore was killed as he watched the last of his troops embark on ship. The only British soldiers left on the Iberian Peninsula were the forces that Moore had left behind in Lisbon. Any hope the Virginians had of joining a victorious army in Spain were dashed.

Our uncertainty finally ended in mid-June, when we received instructions to sail from Antigua to Hampton, Virginia, pick up another batch of recruits, then cross the Atlantic to Southampton. On 1st July, we boarded our old friends the *Calcutta* and *The Pride of Yarmouth* for our six-week journey to the mouth of Chesapeake Bay. Compared with our return from Venezuela, it was a pleasure cruise. We had full rations, and as we sailed northward, the weather became cooler. The breeze was brisk enough that we were able to get a little ventilation through the *Calcutta's* hold.

We spent two weeks ashore at Hampton Barracks whilst we were paid and issued new clothes and kit. Two hundred fifty new recruits joined us, bringing our six companies to nearly full strength. The regiment should've had ten companies, but that would've required another four hundred recruits and a dozen additional officers, more than we could possibly hope for.

"What do you think of the new recruits?" I asked Samuel Smith one afternoon as we relaxed over beakers of punch in one of Hampton's taverns.

"They're a better looking lot than the ones we got last year."

"Not surprising. Last year all a recruit could look forward to was spending the rest of the war on garrison duty in New Orleans—hardly an exciting prospect."

"Yes, but safer than fighting the French in Spain," Samuel replied, taking a sip of punch.

"You're talking like an old man," I chided him. "I've been listening to some of the new men. They look forward to giving the French a good whuppin' and to the plunder they'll take."

"Wouldn't mind some plunder myself," Samuel said quietly. "I could pay off the debts I owe in Williamsburg and re-establish myself as a merchant. I'll never be able to save enough from my pay to do that. But plunder'll do me no good if I'm dead." With that sober thought, we returned to our punch.

Two hundred fifty new recruits were nearly as many men as had returned from Venezuela. They hadn't known the elation we felt when we captured New Orleans, nor our dismay at being called Conquerors of Venezuela, when our expedition had to retreat with nothing to show for its efforts. These new men would change the regiment, but I had no way of knowing how.

CHAPTER 21

We made an uneventful crossing to Southampton in thirty-seven days. We expected to disembark, but were ordered to remain on board our ships. Bumboats came out to sell us gin and fresh food, both of which were eagerly purchased.

The operators of the boats also told us the latest war news. After driving Sir John Moore's troops out of Spain, the French occupied northern Portugal. In April 1809, twenty-three thousand British soldiers, under the command of Sir Arthur Wellesley, landed at Lisbon to join an equal number of British and Portuguese troops already there. Sir Arthur re-joined the army after he was assured that he would be senior general in Portugal, answerable only to Army Headquarters at Horse Guards. There would be no repeat of the previous year's debacle, when his victory was wasted. He quickly moved to drive the French out of Portugal, after which he left the Portuguese, supported by a large number of British troops, to protect their country. Then he marched the rest of his army into Spain to attack the French. The French marched to meet him, and the two armies collided in battle at Talavera, a small town about a hundred miles east of Madrid. Wellesley was victorious and rewarded with a peerage. He was now to be known as Viscount Wellington.

The British Army had a victory, but the French were far from defeated. They withdrew to Madrid and it was clear that there would be much more hard fighting before this war was over. Even Captain Jackson, who worried that there might not be time for the Virginians to get into battle, recognised this.

After three days in port, we set sail for Dover, a mere twenty miles from France. From there we marched west to the barracks at Shorncliffe, high above the English Channel. We were assigned bunks and told how to get our meals, but other than that we were left alone, as if we were unexpected guests.

Colonel Lancaster hadn't re-joined the regiment, so Captain Jackson was still in command. He ordered four hours of drill each morning for all companies to ensure that the new recruits could march, and load and fire their rifles as well as veteran Virginians. Afternoons were to be spent on other tasks that were assigned each morning. Jackson's goal seemed to be to ensure that the Virginians didn't have an idle moment from dawn to dusk, and sometimes into the night.

It was only mid-September, but the weather already had a taste of winter. There was heavy fog each morning, and it was cooler than anything I'd experienced for over a year. Our bunks had no blankets, nor was there any coal for the fireplace. I slept fully clothed, but still woke up cold and stiff in the morning.

"Captain Jackson, sir, is there any chance we could be issued blankets and greatcoats?" I asked after making my daily report.

"I've already asked the quartermaster that and was told that they will be issued when winter arrives."

"When will that be?"

"December at the earliest. Do your best to keep warm."

Colonel Lancaster returned two weeks after our arrival at Shorncliffe. He addressed us at morning parade the next day.

"Virginians," he started, "the court of enquiry that investigated our expedition to Venezuela found that we acted honourably and without fault. They commended our performance in the fighting near La Vela, and concluded that our retreat in face of a much larger enemy force was prudent. Three cheers for the Virginians!"

I cheered as long and loud as anyone.

"We will be sailing for Portugal to join the Light Brigade under the command of General Craufurd. However, before we do, you are to undergo three months' training as skirmishers, the role the army assigns to riflemen. I am certain that you will acquit yourselves well in that training and bring further pride to the Virginians. Dismissed."

I wondered why the army thought we needed more training—with the help of our veterans, our new recruits were rapidly becoming proficient at both drill and marksmanship.

After we'd been dismissed, Captain Jackson added to the colonel's report, saying that the court of enquiry had told Generalissimo de Miranda that he would not receive any further aid from the army. The generalissimo threatened the officers of the court with retribution from his powerful friends, but needless to say, it was an empty threat.

The next day, at morning parade, a large, fierce-looking sergeant ambled up to the First Company.

"So you're the Johnny Newcombes I'm supposed to teach how to keep yourselves from being killed," he said, an amused smile on his face. "I suppose I can do that — I've had worse-looking to deal with."

"Your name, Sergeant?" Captain Jackson said, clearly not happy with the man.

"Patrick Harper, sir. My orders are to act as Training Sergeant for the First Company, King's Own Virginians," he said, handing over an envelope.

"Sergeant Harper," Jackson said after reading the envelope's contents, "this is Sergeant William Watson, who's been a member of the Virginians for four years, and served meritoriously. He's not a Johnny Newcombe, nor are many of the members of this company."

"Beggin' your pardon, sir. I'll not use that term again."

"Very well, Sergeant. Carry on."

Harper was in charge whilst we were on the drill field or taking part in field exercises. He laughed at what we thought was proficient drill and held up a small manual, which had obviously been well used.

"The little book is called *Regulations for the Exercise of Riflemen and Light Infantry and Instructions for their Conduct in the Field*. It was written by a German, name of Lieutenant Colonel Rottenberg. All us training sergeants been given a copy and ordered to follow what it says. So from now on, this is your Bible. Those of you who can read are welcome to peruse it."

Rottenberg's drill routine was much more stringent than the one we'd been using. All movements were to be executed in quick time, 120 30-inch steps per minute. Sergeant Harper made sure that we marched at exactly that rate. The Regulations were similarly demanding on the firing range. Except for a few of the new recruits, the members of the First Company could quickly load and fire their rifles from a standing position and hit a target at up to two hundred paces. Rottenberg added four more positions—sitting cross-legged, kneeling, and lying on both our backs and stomachs. We were supposed to be able to load and accurately fire from all of these positions.

"Do you want to stand up and be an easy target for a crapaud?" Harper shouted at Private Hardwick, who seemed unable to fire his rifle from a sitting position.

"No, I'd rather be relaxing on me back," Hardwick muttered under his breath, but loud enough for me to hear. I could understand why kneeling and laying on our stomachs to fire our rifles made sense— the Virginians had used those positions in Venezuela—but sitting or lying on my back made no sense.

"Sergeant, you fought the French. You ever fire your rifle laying on your back?" Private Dawkins asked.

"No, but I've seen other men do it. Some say they can see more that way. But it's in the Regulations, so you're going to learn it. Come back and tell me when the war is over whether it was of any use."

There was no come back to that statement.

After six weeks we'd achieved proficiency with both quick-time drill and firing our rifles from all five of the Regulation's positions. Harper's next lessons were in the rifleman's main roles as the army's vanguard and as its skirmishers. As the vanguard, we were supposed to protect the army from being surprised by the enemy. In this formation each company split into seven squads arrayed in a square eight hundred paces on each side. From above, it must have been beautiful to behold, but only birds could get that view. Those of us on the ground couldn't see this beauty. We just cursed the generals who had decided to use this formation.

We practised establishing the vanguard formations for two days until we could do so smoothly. Then came the real challenge—maintaining the formation whilst moving forward, as the army would be doing. If we could all keep our places as we marched, we would create a web that would catch any enemy trying to sneak up on our army. However, if we didn't keep our places, the web would have holes through which the enemy could pass. We drilled for two weeks and attained some level of order, but it was nothing like the beautiful movements the Regulations envisioned.

The First Company had only four of the seven corporals needed to fill all of the positions the Regulations envisioned—three of the squads from each company were commanded by veteran privates. None of the Virginians' companies had a sufficient number of corporals. This resulted in much speculation as to whether more men would be promoted to corporal to fill the positions called for by the Regulations, but additional promotions were not forthcoming. When I asked Captain Jackson about this, he said that the colonel had made it clear that promotions were to be based on merit, not because there were positions to be filled. I didn't think it wise to share this intelligence with the rest of the company—no need to dash hopes.

The vanguard formation was used when the army didn't think we'd make contact with the enemy. It provided a useful screen for the army, but it was rare that the hills of Portugal and Spain allowed us to spread out the way the Regulations instructed. More often than not, we were squeezed closer to the line of march, or unable to keep a full eight hundred paces in front of the forward element of the march.

If the enemy was known to be in the vicinity, we arrayed in a skirmish line. Half the company formed two lines in extended order—six feet apart. The remainder of the company stayed fifty paces back in close order—six inches apart—as a reserve. We all moved forward at quick time until we got close enough to the enemy for accurate marksmanship. When the order was given, the men in the front rank would aim and fire. Whilst the front line reloaded, the men in the back line ran six paces past them and waited for those who were reloading to call "Ready." Then the men now in front would aim and fire. The drill would then be repeated, with the men who were now in back running forward, waiting to hear "Ready," then aiming and firing.

The drill for a skirmish line was simple compared to the vanguard formation we'd struggled to learn. But in battle we were rarely able to maintain the straight lines the Regulations envisioned. Trees, buildings, and walls conspired against that. More typically we worked in much smaller groups than a company—as few as two, or perhaps four, riflemen acting to protect each other in the face of the enemy.

The vanguard and skirmish formations assumed that the army was moving forward, but in the field we often were withdrawing—sometimes in good order, other times not. There were no established formations for withdrawal. We soon learned that to survive we had to stay together in small groups whenever we could and to aim carefully before firing.

Since its formation, the King's Own Virginians had depended on shouted orders. It never had the drummers or fifers that were part of older regiments. But Rottenberg's Regulations said that riflemen were to be guided by signals from whistles or bugles. Whistles were issued to all officers. Since a whistle can sound only one note, whistle calls were used for only three movements: advance, halt, and retreat.

Bugles were a different matter. A few of the men in the regiment claimed to be able to blow a bugle, but when tested could only produce a few hideous sounds. The call went out for buglers to transfer to the Virginians, but few British Army buglers wanted anything to do with a regiment of colonials, especially one that carried the unofficial title of Conquerors of Venezuela. Only three men volunteered, all of whom had run afoul of the officers in their former regiments. This hardly boded well for the Virginians, but "beggars can't be choosers."

"How many bugle calls are there?" I asked Bugler Daniels after listening to a bewildering array.

He thought for a moment and counted on his fingers a few times, before answering, "I know fifty-seven, and I think there may be more."

"That's an impossible number to learn," I said heatedly.

"I didn't make them up," he replied.

"Of course you didn't," I said, bringing my temper under control.

After some consultation, Colonel Lancaster decided that the Virginians would concentration on a dozen calls: forward, halt, retreat, and similar simple commands. Our three buglers played these over and over again as our regiment drilled. In addition to teaching the Virginians these calls, the buglers trained a dozen men in their skill. The colonel wanted each company to have at least two buglers.

At Shorncliffe, the Virginians formed a sergeants' mess, as required by the Regulations. This brought me into daily contact with Sergeant Pew. We'd been in the same mess together in Antigua, but that group had been so large that I could easily avoid contact with him. I'd been more interested in talking to the regular army sergeants. In the Virginians' smaller mess, there was no avoiding him. Pew had been my first introduction to the British Army. I wondered how he would treat me. Would an old *swad* like him accept me as an equal, or would he remember the days when I truly was a Johnny Newcombe and he was the source of knowledge for all things military?

"So Watson, what does it feel like to be in the real army, not playing at soldiers like the Virginians have been doing?" Pew asked after we'd spent a few days sizing each other up. We were sitting at a table in the sergeants' mess, eating our noonday meal.

"I don't know. None of the new drill we've had to learn would've been useful in New Orleans or Venezuela. Perhaps things will be different in Spain," I replied.

"Perhaps," he said, turning to his food.

Since Pew seemed to accept my implied criticism of the drill without rancour, I decided to press forward. "Do you remember Randolph Culpepper, one of the recruits from Davidson's Fort?"

"Of course I do, the red-headed troublemaker. The Virginians were well rid of him when he decided to desert."

"Do you also remember the time he said we should be fighting Indian-style, rather than firing our rifles in a volley?"

"Yes," Pew said with a small smile to show that he still believed that he was right. "Some of you new recruits agreed with him until I told you that the crapauds could load and fire their muskets twice as fast as you could load and fire your rifles."

"That you did, and we had no choice but to agree with you. But that meant we were using our rifles as if they were muskets that could hit a target farther way. What Harper's teaching us is more like fighting Indian-style." I was treading on dangerous ground here, since I was all but saying that the way that Pew had trained us was wrong.

"What Culpepper wanted was every man for himself, load and fire at will," Pew said, an edge to his voice. He'd put down his knife and fork, and was now looking directly at me. I put down my utensils and looked at him. "That's not what Harper's drill is about," Pew continued. "It's more elaborate than what I taught you, but it still has you firing in a volley."

"But aiming first, not just firing in the direction of the French." I felt this was my only chance to make Pew see things differently.

"I never said 'don't aim.'"

"But we never fired at targets, or did anything to practice aiming," I said.

"It wasn't part of the manual I was told to follow. I never saw a copy of Rottenberg's Regulations until I got here." He clearly understood my point, and appeared to agree with it, at least in a small way, but didn't seem very happy about having to do so.

"Not faulting you, Pew," I said, trying to smooth his ruffled feathers.

"We'll see if any of this works in Spain," he said, and our conversation was at an end.

A few weeks later, Captain Jackson passed a copy of *The Times of London* to me. "You might be interested in the letter on page four," he said with a broad smile. "It's from an old friend of ours."

The letter was from de Miranda. He laid out his familiar arguments against Spain and called upon the men of Britain to join the volunteer force he was assembling to free Venezuela. He made no mention of the British Army or of the Virginians' expedition.

Many years later I learned that de Miranda did, in fact, assemble about a hundred men and found a ship to transport then to Venezuela. The Spanish easily captured and imprisoned them. De Miranda was executed by firing squad. Venezuela eventually became free as part of the wave of revolution that swept through Spanish America in the early 1820s. By 1825, all of South and Central America were independent. Spain still controlled Cuba and Mexico, but there were many who believed that these colonies would also soon be free. I sometimes wonder how the people of Venezuela viewed de Miranda. Was he a hero, who was too early to be successful, or was he a misguided romantic, the most generous characterization I could make?

New Year's Day 1810 was a double celebration: the beginning of a new year and the completion of our training two days earlier. None of us who'd been on Antigua a year earlier had guessed that we'd be spending this day on the bleak Kentish coast. Only the few men who were assigned picquet duty had to endure the cold winds off the Channel. The rest of us had enough rum and brandy to keep us warm.

Notwithstanding his victory at Talavera, Viscount Wellington had to withdraw. The French brought up more reinforcements and defeated the Spanish force that was supposed to be defending the British flank. He retreated to central Portugal, near Lisbon, where the Royal Navy could provide any supplies his army needed that couldn't be obtained locally. The French now controlled northern Portugal and all of Spain except a small enclave around Cadiz.

Despite Wellington's retreat, we all thought that British prospects were good. He'd defeated the French in the two major battles he'd fought against them. All that was needed was to give him an army large enough to meet the French on equal terms. We assumed that we would soon be on our way to Portugal to be part of that army, but for the moment we had no orders to leave Shorncliffe.

CHAPTER 22

Having completed our training, the Virginians were anxious to join the rest of the army in Portugal, if for no other reason, to escape the cold and damp of the Channel coast. But we were destined to spend nearly the whole winter at Shorncliffe.

I would've liked to have spent some time in London, seeing the House of Parliament and the other landmarks that I'd heard about all my life, but the Virginians were kept on a tight leash, allowed to go no further than Folkestone, the nearest village, and then only when given leave. When I asked Captain Jackson about this treatment, he laughed and said that the army was afraid we'd desert.

John Sevier, one of the new recruits who joined the First Company before our expedition to Venezuela, was the oldest of the Virginians, over sixty when he enlisted, though he looked at least ten years younger. The fact that the recruiting sergeant accepted him was testament to the difficulty the Virginians had recruiting men in 1808.

A large man, Sevier several times demonstrated great strength, despite his age. He had a broad forehead and wide-spaced eyes, which made him look rather homely. His solemn demeanour—he rarely, if ever smiled—did nothing to improve his appearance. He was taciturn, not joining the banter of the other recruits, some of whom were young enough to be his grandsons. They seemed intimidated by him. As a result he wasn't the victim of practical jokes or similar mischief. He didn't distinguish himself for good or ill during the expedition to Venezuela or during our stay in Antigua.

"Sergeant Watson, may I ask you a personal question?" he enquired one evening as we sat in Shorncliffe Barracks, trying to stay warm by the fireplace.

"What is it, Sevier?"

"Were you in the rebel army?"

"Why do you ask?"

"I couldn't help notice that you winced when Hardwick made a disparaging remark about George Washington."

I paused for a moment before replying, trying to cypher out why he was asking. Since I was his sergeant, he'd always been formal with me, more so than some of the other recruits who'd made rather clumsy attempts to befriend me. From the first, Sevier showed a knowledge of drill that indicated he'd been a soldier. Since he didn't seem like the type who would've deserted from the British Army, I'd assumed that he'd been in the rebel army, but I didn't ask. His former military service was irrelevant. All that counted was his performance in the Virginians.

"Yes, Sevier, I was in the rebel army," I said, after concluding there was no harm in admitting this. "I was an orderly for General Washington, and knew him better than most. And yourself? Were you in the rebel army?"

"I was in the Virginia Militia, but my company never saw any fighting. We were assigned to guard Hampton Roads against a British invasion that never occurred."

This shared bond of both having served in the rebel army was the beginning of our friendship, which, whilst never as close as the one I had with Samuel Smith, helped me survive the rigours of the war.

Finally, in mid-March, we were given orders to march to Southampton, then board ship for Lisbon. I was to spend the next four years fighting the French. I can tell you what I experienced, and a little about the general course of the war, but as I've learned from reading histories of the events I took part in, my view was very limited.

Bigger battles took place elsewhere in Europe, and the machinations of governments in London, Paris, Vienna, Berlin, and Moscow, were often just as important as what armies were doing in the field. I again commend Sir Owen Madden's *A History of Spain and Portugal, 1760 – 1814* to anyone who wishes to know more about the war than I can possibly tell, especially about how events elsewhere in Europe affected the war on the Iberian Peninsula.

"Why do you think it took the army so long to send our orders?" I asked Sevier as we relaxed outside the barn we were to sleep in after our first day's march.

"Because it was cheaper to keep us at Shorncliffe than in Portugal," he answered.

"Weren't we needed in Portugal?"

"No, we weren't. Dumouriez had to be more worried about the Austrians than about our little army in Portugal."

"I don't understand."

"Haven't you been following the news from Europe?" Sevier asked incredulously. From anyone other than a friend, I would have taken that question as an affront, but I knew that John was not being malicious. I knew that he made a great effort to obtain newspapers from officers, once they had read them. Some thought this was John's way of toadying up to them, but I knew better. He was hungry for any scrap of information he could get about the wider world. I wish I knew what created this hunger, but, other than admitting he'd been in the rebel army, never said a word about his former life or why he enlisted.

"No, I haven't," I said.

"Then let me tell you what's been happening over the past year. February, a year ago, seeing that the French Army was tied up in Spain, Austria revoked the peace treaty Dumouriez forced on them in 1805, after defeating their army. Leopold, their Emperor, had been biding his time until he could renew the fight. The French revolutionaries executed his sister, Marie Antoinette, and he wanted vengeance. The Austrian Army is many times the size of the British Army, so Dumouriez had to move most of his forces from Spain to Germany to counter them. Viscount Wellington won at Talavera because the French could only put forty thousand men in the field."

"Now I remember—the French defeated the Austrians in July."

"Right, and Dumouriez forced them to accept a new peace treaty. Once he no longer had to worry about the Austrians, he could move the soldiers he needed to invade Portugal. But it's almost two thousand miles from Vienna to Lisbon, and Dumouriez wasn't going to be able to get his army in place before winter, or be able to attack before spring. So Horse Guards could keep us in England."

I was amazed at how Sevier was able to see the reasons behind what to me seemed like incomprehensible actions. He apparently had a good education, because he was able to identify the men and locations mentioned in news reports, and seemed to have a grasp of the ebb and flow of the war with France as well as any of the officers; better in some cases. I vowed to pay more attention to the war news, a vow I didn't keep.

We arrived in Portugal on 31st March 1810, on a balmy day with nary a cloud in the sky. I could feel my body soaking up the sun's heat. Like the other Virginians, I gawked at the Tower of Belém, a four-story, hundred-foot-high fortress that defended the entrance to Lisbon Harbour. It was made of a tan-coloured stone that shown in the bright sunlight.

"You can almost see Prince Henry the Navigator standing atop that tower, waiting for the ships he sent to explore Africa to return," one of the navy officers said, almost reverently.

I knew of Prince Henry the Navigator because Mr Anderson, my boyhood schoolteacher, mentioned him as commissioning the exploration that found the route around Africa that we British later used to sail to India. I'd always thought his ships left from the southernmost port in Portugal, not from Lisbon. I later found that I was right and the naval officer wrong. But having Prince Henry standing on this tower did make for a memorable image.

John Sevier was standing nearby, and mention of Portugal's illustrious history set him musing about the fate of nations.

"William," he said, "do you know that 250 years ago Portugal was one of the most powerful countries in the world? It had an empire that stretched from Brazil, to Africa, and India, whilst Great Britain had yet to come into existence. England and Wales had combined into a single nation, but Scotland was still an independent kingdom."

I told him that I vaguely remembered that from my schooldays.

"Now Portugal is so weak that it has to be protected by Britain. We're the one with the huge empire in India and the Americas, and strong enough to fight the French single-handedly. Will we suffer the fate of all empires from the ancient Babylonians onward? 250 years from now will we be so weak that we'll have to depend on another, stronger country to defend us?"

"I don't know John. I'm no philosopher," I replied, but the thought was frightening.

We were allowed to disembark and given three days' leave to visit the city. We were warned to be on best behaviour. Wellington needed the cooperation of the Portuguese and didn't want his soldiers causing any discord with the local populous. And to ensure that we would act with decorum, squads of Provost Marshal's men, easily identified by the red scarfs tied around their right shoulders, patrolled the city.

Samuel Smith and I headed for a tavern—Sevier had declined to join us. We didn't stop at the first few we saw, which were already overflowing with Virginians, but chose one a few blocks inland from the port. It looked like any harbourside drinking establishment: dark, with a long bar, and a scattering of tables filling the room. Even though it was midday, it was crowded with men in ragged uniforms. They were *Ordenanza,* the Portuguese militia. One of them shouted something in his native tongue.

"The man over there would like to buy you a glass of wine in honour of your army's victory over the French," the bartender said in heavily accented English.

We'd already heard that on the night of 19th – 20th March, the Light Brigade had won a victory over a much larger French force at a place called Barba del Puerco, at a bridge over the Agueda River. Riflemen had shown that they could load and fire almost as fast as musketeers, and could fight at close quarters. General Craufurd was being hailed as a hero.

Wary after O'Malley's experience in Antigua, Samuel and I looked at each other. The bartender must have sensed our discomfort and quickly added, "You have nothing to fear. These men are celebrating because they have just been paid for a month's work on the fortifications your general is building north of the city. And I will pour your wine from a bottle that I will unseal in front of you."

"In that case we accept his kind offer."

"This is *vinho verde* from the far north of Portugal," the barman said. "It is a specialty of our country, unlike any wine you have ever tasted." True to his word, he selected an unopened wine bottle from a rack behind him, uncorked it, and poured two glasses of a frothy white wine.

I knew enough Portuguese to translate "vinho verde" as green wine, but the wine the barman set before us was white and bubbly—what I thought champagne, which I'd heard about but never seen, would look like. It frothed gently, like the water from a soda spring. I took a small sip. The wine tasted bitter. I put my glass down, and mumbled something about it being different.

"Few Englishmen enjoy vinho verde," the barman said, an amused look on his face. "Let me give you some wine from Oporto, which I know you will like." He emptied my glass. Then he took another unopened bottle from the rack, uncorked it, and refilled my glass with a dark red wine. I took a sip and smiled. The wine had a rich, silky texture and slid easily down my throat.

"Tell me about the fortifications you say are being built," Samuel said after sampling his wine.

The barman called to one of the workmen, then after a quick discussion in Portuguese said, "Your General Wellington is building two chains of forts across the land north of Lisbon, from the River Tagus to the sea. João is uncertain, but he thinks there must be a hundred of them. They would prevent the French from marching into Lisbon."

We thanked the bartender, raised our glasses to salute the workmen, then retired to one of the tables in the room.

"If Wellington is depending on fortifications to defend Lisbon, then the Virginians will become marksmen," I said. "All that drill we learned at Shorncliffe will be for nought."

"You don't win a war by sitting in a fortification," Samuel replied. "At some point, you have to pursue the enemy. That's when the Virginians will get a chance to show their mettle."

At morning parade on our fourth day in Portugal, Colonel Lancaster proudly announced our orders.

"Virginians, the Light Brigade is being expanded into the Light Division. We march at dawn tomorrow morning to become part of this new division. We will be defending Portugal's northeast border with Spain, and will be accompanied by two battalions of Portuguese *caçadores*. Major Salazar of the Portuguese Army," the colonel said, nodding to an officer at his right, "Commander of the Portuguese First Battalion, will accompany us to act as guide and translator. Three cheers for the Virginians!"

I dutifully gave three cheers, but I was more concerned about our orders. The Light Division couldn't be expected to halt the French Army if it chose to attack. Would we be a tripwire to alert Viscount Wellington that the French were on their way, then allowed to retreat, or would we be ordered to stand and fight?

Once we'd learned that we were to be under General Craufurd's command, the British Army regulars at Shorncliffe told us many stories about him. He was known as "Black Bob" and had the reputation of being a harsh disciplinarian. Supposedly, he was under a cloud, having been part of Sir Home Popham's ill-fated expedition to Buenos Aires. In 1807, he'd been forced to surrender his brigade. The Spanish returned Craufurd and his men in 1808, when they became our allies in the fight against France.

Craufurd hadn't yet had a chance to recover from that humiliation. He'd driven the Light Brigade harshly in an attempt to reach Talavera in time to take part in that battle, but arrived a day late. Now his command could face the full brunt of an invading French Army. The combination of an ambitious general and a division that could easily be outnumbered by the enemy did not bode well.

Back at Shorncliffe we'd also heard many disparaging remarks about the Portuguese Army. Major Salazar did nothing to dispel them. He wore the brown uniform of a caçadore, which looked sensible enough, except for the red sash with white tassels tied around his waist. His only weapon was a sword, which looked more ceremonial than useful. I'm sure he cut a dashing figure with the ladies.

The caçadores were Portuguese light infantry, and supposed to serve the same purpose in the Portuguese Army that the Virginians served in the British Army. But as we soon found out, few had Baker rifles. The rest were armed with muskets, which would be much less useful for skirmishing.

It was easy to distinguish the Virginians' new recruits from its veterans as we marched north from Lisbon. The new recruits were light-hearted, boasting about the valour they'd show in the battle we all knew we'd soon experience. We veterans were sombre, eyeing the new recruits and the caçadores, both of whom we'd have to depend on, with a mixture of disdain and foreboding. The caçadores must have sensed our mistrust. They stared back at us with black expressions, as if trying to impress us with their fierceness.

Except for a few weeks in 1806, whilst we were building the pack trail from Fort Roanoke to French Lick, when there was disgruntlement amongst the ranks about not receiving meat rations, the Virginians had been a happy regiment. The quartermaster at Fort Roanoke had treated us unfairly—fifty men deserted as a result—but most of the regiment took it in stride. The teasing we received both aboard ship and in Antigua about being the "Conquerors of Venezuela" actually served to bring us closer together. But now nearly half the regiment hadn't shared those experiences and had yet to form bonds with those of us who had. Forming any sort of tie with the caçadores, with whom we couldn't even talk, seemed hopeless.

We ate well on our march north. The French had occupied northern Portugal during the first part of 1809, but Viscount Wellington had driven them out quickly enough for the Portuguese farmers to plant their crops and bring in a good harvest. We supplemented our rations with wine and fruit, which we bought for a pittance from the villages we passed through, and found dry places to sleep every evening. We posted picquets each night, more to keep away thieves than for concern about the French. It was the calm before the storm, but none of us thought about it in those terms. We just enjoyed the peaceful interlude.

We joined the Light Division a few miles east of the Coa River. We were in Spain, but just across the border from Portugal. The French, only a half dozen miles away, were busy besieging the Spanish trapped inside their fortress at Ciudad Rodrigo. General Herrasti, the Spanish commander, appealed to Viscount Wellington for help, but Wellington ordered the Light Division to maintain its position and didn't send any additional soldiers to the front.

The Virginians knew of these developments and were mystified by Wellington's orders, since we thought that attacking the besieging French from the rear should have been simple. It was only recently, when I read Madden's history, that I learned that the viscount was worried that if he moved his army onto the plain around Ciudad Rodrigo, it would be an easy target for the French, who could put many more men into a battle than he could. Wellington's primary concern was the protection of his army. He was only willing to risk a battle if he thought he had a good chance of winning and he had clear line of retreat if he lost.

The Spanish held out valiantly until 10th July, when Herrasti was forced to surrender. He loudly condemned Wellington for not coming to his aid. The incident did nothing to endear us to the Spaniards.

The fall of Ciudad Rodrigo allowed the French to attack the Light Division, which was still in Spain, east of the Coa River. The river had cut a deep gorge into the tableland, which extended for miles on either side. The Light Division, which consisted of the Virginians, the 95th Rifles, and two regiments of Portuguese caçadores, held a two-mile-long line, from the fortress at Almeida to the top of the river's gorge. The Virginians' position was in the centre of that line, close to the only road in the vicinity that crossed the river. We'd entered Spain along that road. On the Portuguese side, it twisted and turned down a rocky slope into the gorge, crossed a stone bridge, then climbed out via an equally difficult path on the Spanish side. It was our only route for retreat.

The French attacked on the morning of 24th July. The First Company was on picquet duty, in front of a regiment of Portuguese caçadores. It'd rained the night before and dawn brought a heavy fog, which hid the movements of the French Army.

"Will you look at that? The whole French Army is out there," Manfred Zellenbach said as the fog burnt off. Zellenbach was the youngest of the four other recruits who'd joined the Army with me at Davidson's Fort. He'd survived the attack on New Orleans and the expedition to Venezuela, and was now one of the veteran Virginians, though he was barely twenty. With the reorganisation of the regiment, he and Trotter, another of the recruits with whom I'd joined the Virginians, ended up in the First Company. I was pleased—they were dependable soldiers.

"You're exaggerating, Zellenbach," I said. "There are only a few hundred crapauds, and they only have muskets. With our Bakers, we can pick them off before they get close enough to do us any harm."

Colonel Lancaster came up to survey the scene and quickly sounded the alarm. He knew that the *voltigeurs*—as French skirmishers were called—in front of us were the vanguard of the French Army, which was rumoured to be twenty-five thousand strong. The Light Division totalled only four thousand men. Had we retreated then, we all could probably have made it safely over the Coa Bridge, but our orders were to hold our ground whilst wagons removed some of the supplies that Wellington had stockpiled at Almeida.

We exchanged fire with the voltigeurs. My nostrils were assailed by the now familiar acrid smell of burnt black powder, but there was enough of a breeze to keep the smoke from obscuring our view. My confident prediction that we could hold the French at bay was wrong. They were skilled soldiers, taking advantage of whatever cover they could find to get close enough for their muskets to be effective.

The Virginians suffered their first losses of the campaign that morning. I saw Trotter fall and thought him dead. I later learned that he survived, but lost a leg and was invalided out of the army. I heard others scream in pain, but couldn't tell who they were. If a soldier had to contemplate what was happening during a battle, he'd surely go mad, but battle doesn't give you time to think. It's load, aim, fire, then do it again, hoping that your shot struck one of the enemy and in some small way reduced the risk you faced.

After an hour the main French column marched into view east of us and began forming up in line position. When this manoeuvre was complete, they charged. We beat back their first charge, but they immediately formed up for a second charge. This charge forced many of the Light Division's companies to fall back. They didn't do this evenly, which left gaps in our line. Seeing these gaps, the French commander ordered a cavalry charge. We weren't able form squares to repulse the cavalry—as we had done in Venezuela—and the result was deadly. The French hussars were soon on top of us, slashing and stabbing many of our men. We were only about a hundred yards in front of the Portuguese battalion commanded by Major Salazar, who ordered his men to carefully aim and fire. Their bullets struck a few of our men, but forced the hussars to retreat. We were able to make it safely to the Portuguese line. I regretted my ill thoughts about Salazar and his men. A British battalion couldn't have done better.

"Form up the company," Captain Jackson ordered.

"First Company, form two lines, close order," I shouted.

"Stand easy," I ordered, once the lines were formed. A quick count showed that we were missing seven men. I assumed Trotter was dead, but there was no time to enquire about the others.

The Light Division's line was crumbling and men were beginning to run towards the bridge over the Coa, hoping to cross it and put some distance between themselves and the French.

"Have the company fall back to the gorge," Captain Jackson instructed me, after we'd been in formation for ten minutes.

"First line, withdraw fifty paces," I ordered. When they were in their new position, I told the second line to follow. It was the reverse of a skirmish line. We continued our withdrawal by lines until we reached the top of the gorge, where Colonel Lancaster waited.

"First Company, form up with Third and Fifth Companies, 95th Rifles. Take defensive positions and protect the men crossing the bridge," the colonel ordered. A grizzled old captain named O'Hare took charge and, without even a nod towards Captain Jackson, distributed us in the rocks on either side of the road. Captain Jackson didn't protest. O'Hare knew what he was doing.

The French continued their attack and pushed the remaining elements of the Light Division off the plateau and down the slope of the gorge. They streamed past us, hell-bent for the bridge. We were left in a truly precarious position, with French skirmishers firing down at us from above. O'Malley was hit—a musket ball creasing his left thigh. I quickly wrapped a bandage around his wound.

"O'Malley, can you walk?" Jackson asked.

O'Malley took a few steps on the steep, uneven ground, then fell.

"Watson, take him to the surgeons, then return as quickly as you can," Jackson ordered. I was surprised that he chose me, his sergeant, to help O'Malley—any private could've done the job—but I was happy to escape the fire from the voltigeurs above us.

As I helped O'Malley down to the bridge, Major MacLeod rode past me, up the slope. "Men, fix bayonets and follow me," I heard him shout a few moments later. He was trying to drive the voltigeurs back. About two hundred men responded and cleared the top of the ridge. It saved the riflemen, who were then able to retreat across the bridge. The First Company reached O'Malley and me just as we reached the eastern side of the bridge. Hardwick grabbed O'Malley's other arm and the two of us hustled him to safety.

Several companies from the 95th Rifles had set up a defensive line on the western side of the river, ready to repulse any Frenchmen who followed us too closely. As soon as we crossed, the French formed a column, ready to charge across the bridge. The men of the 95th carefully picked their targets and waited until they were closer before firing. As the first Frenchman set foot on the span, they fired and kept firing until the French retreated.

The battle was over. We'd lost and been driven from the field. The First Company suffered ten casualties, two dead, six wounded, and two missing, presumably taken prisoner. I was weary and black with powder from the many times I'd fired my rifle, but otherwise unharmed.

The fight at the Coa was my seventh time in combat. I no longer had the feeling of either fear or elation that I'd had the first times. I was a soldier. Soldiers fight. It was our duty, and I felt I'd acquitted myself well. I don't know if I'd killed or wounded any of the French. I saw a voltigeur fall after I'd fired at him, but a rifleman to my right shouted "Got the bastard," as soon as the Frenchman fell.

I was angry—as were many others in the Light Division—after the fighting ceased for the night. Why had we been left in such an exposed position and told to stand our ground when it was obvious that we were about to be attacked by a far superior force? Were the supplies rescued from Almeida more valuable than the lives of the riflemen lost? Craufurd went from being a hero to being a villain. We were surprised and disappointed when Wellington left him in command.

Reading Madden's history, I was amazed to find that Craufurd had disobeyed Wellington's orders not to risk a battle with the French. Had he followed those orders, and retreated back to Portugal, many lives would have been spared. This made Wellington's decision to leave him in command even more mystifying.

The Portuguese still held the fortress at Almeida and now that the Light Division had been driven away, the French besieged it. Even though Craufurd had removed some supplies, its defenders still had enough food and ammunition to withstand a long siege. But a lucky French artillery shot blew up the fortress' magazine and killed many of the defenders. Almeida surrendered on 27ᵗʰ August. Marshal Masséna, who Dumouriez had installed as dictator of Spain, had assumed personal command of the army invading Portugal. He was now free to concentrate all his forces against our army.

Viscount Wellington knew that the French Army lived off the land and was determined to make their advance as difficult as possible. Earlier that year he had issued a proclamation calling on the Portuguese people to make preparations to resist the French. All men capable of bearing arms were to learn to use them. He followed with a more explicit proclamation that made it a crime to refuse to supply carts, boats, or beasts of burden to the British or Portuguese Armies; or to refuse to remove or destroy food or other valuables when the French approached. The Portuguese militia was only too happy to enforce these orders.

As a result of Wellington's orders, and the diligence with which they were carried out, the French found their advance into Portugal hampered at every step. They didn't have good maps of the country and often chose poor quality roads. Their foraging parties, which had to be well defended against the Ordenanza, found little food. And they were constantly harassed by guerrilla groups, some well-disciplined, others little better than brigands.

During August and September the Virginians slowly withdrew southward into central Portugal, where, with the rest of Wellington's Army, we took up positions atop the Sierra de Bussaco to await the French Army.

CHAPTER 23

The Sierra de Bussaco, which quickly became known simply as Bussaco, is an imposing ridge about eighty miles southeast of the bridge over the River Coa and a hundred twenty-five miles north of Lisbon. Most of Bussaco rises steeply a thousand feet from the valley below to form a defensive bulwark athwart the route to Lisbon. Bussaco runs northwest from the River Mondego for almost four miles, before dipping slightly to the village of Sula. Past Sula, it regains its former height, runs a short distance, then drops sharply into the gorge of a small stream called the Milijoso Torrent. After the gorge it continues for another four miles before ending. The only road over Bussaco passes through the village of Sula. A cart track crosses it midway between Sula and the Mondego. Another cart track circles around the ridge's southern end, close to the river, and several roads pass north of it.

Viscount Wellington arrayed his fifty thousand men atop Bussaco, between the River Mondego and the top of the Milijoso Gorge. The Virginians were on the front slope, facing the French, along both sides of the middle track. Most of the rest of our army was hidden in positions on the reverse slope, the side of the ridge away from the French.

The French could bypass Bussaco, but if they did, we could attack them from the rear. Masséna had little option but to storm the ridge and displace us, but his choices for where to attack were limited to the road through Sula and the two tracks. The roads to the north didn't provide access. A few skirmishers might be able to climb the ridge, but the terrain was too difficult for coordinated assault by a large number of troops.

Bussaco was an excellent example of Wellington's genius at picking ideal conditions before committing to battle. We controlled the high ground. But if the French were to dislodge us, we could easily retreat to the defences under construction at Torres Vedras. They were incomplete, but sufficiently developed to offer us protection.

All was quiet on the evening of the 26th September. I was sitting with Samuel Smith and John Sevier outside a stone shepherd's hut, the only building atop the ridge near our positions, when news came that French officers, possibly even Masséna himself, had been seen reconnoitring our positions near Sula.

"I guess this means the French are ready to attack," Samuel said. John and I grunted in agreement.

"Think they'll attack up the road?" I asked. "That's the easiest way for them to get the bulk of their army into the battle."

"True," Sevier answered, "but they'll want to keep us off balance. There will be at least diversionary attacks along this track and the one to the south. Who knows, they may even try to send a large force of skirmishers up the ridge between the tracks."

"I don't think so," Samuel said. "Even a Cherokee would have trouble climbing this ridge fast enough to avoid us killing him."

"I think John is right," I said. "The French are likely to attack along all three paths simultaneously. They'll reinforce whichever attack works. It'll create a competition amongst their generals. Dumouriez likes to do that."

"My question is not how, but when?" Samuel said.

"If their generals are scouting our positions, it has to be soon," John replied.

"How soon?" I wondered.

"Maybe as early as tomorrow morning." John said.

"In that case, we better get some sleep." I said. The other two agreed and we called it a night.

As John had predicted, the French attacked at dawn the next morning, but to our surprise, the initial attack came up only the middle track, the position we were defending. The Virginians, along with six other rifle companies, were well hidden behind rocks and trees almost all the way down the slope. The Third Infantry Division waited on the reverse slope behind us. The French columns formed up in the valley below, turned, and to the beat of their drums, began their slow plod up the track. As soon as the French came into range, our riflemen started picking them off, taking every opportunity they could to aim at officers. The French didn't return our fire. To do so would have further slowed their advance. They had their bayonets fixed and obviously had been ordered to displace us with that weapon.

Scores of crapauds fell, but their loss did nothing to slow the advance of the French column. As each Virginian fired, he reloaded and scampered upslope to find a position from which to take his next shot. We weren't operating in the formations we'd been taught at Shorncliffe, but rather "Indian-style," with each man thinking and acting for himself.

The discipline that the French showed that day amazed me, particularly because, as was well known, French soldiers weren't flogged. They were encouraged with patriotic slogans and the opportunity for advancement if they showed valour in battle. Officers couldn't buy commissions. They had to be promoted from the ranks. Dumouriez was claimed to have said, "Each private carries a marshal's baton in his knapsack." That may have been an exaggeration, but the crapauds had to believe at least part of it or they wouldn't have shown such determination in battles like Bussaco.

The Virginians leapfrogged to the crest and quickly withdrew behind the advancing Third Division. We'd done our job. Now it was time for the infantry to do theirs. I fired four shots that day and I saw one Frenchman fall as a result. I cannot say whether I killed or wounded him.

The Virginians were now safe on the reverse slope a dozen yards below the crest. We didn't see the climax of the battle, but we heard about it in great detail from the redcoats.

Despite their casualties, the French reached the top of the ridge. The Third was there to meet them and delivered a devastating volley.

Several guns of the Royal Horse Artillery fired grapeshot into the advancing French. The French commander shouted *"En avant! En avant!"* to encourage his exhausted troops. They managed to capture the guns, but their victory was short-lived. The 43rd and 52nd Regiments of light infantry, which had been held in reserve, advanced up the reverse slope and, with a bayonet charge, dislodged the few Frenchmen still holding their position.

The French attack had been broken, and the surviving crapauds retreated as best they could. The 43rd and 52nd followed, using their bayonets to great effect, but in eerie silence. Unlike the French, who were always shouting and cheering, British infantrymen often went about their work without uttering a sound. Some say this inspired even greater terror, making a British bayonet charge seem like some impersonal killing machine.

The Virginians came back over the top of the ridge, swords—as we called our bayonets—fixed, and joined the fray. By this time the French were in full retreat and we didn't get close enough to any of them to use our swords. Since the French were out of reach, we began searching the bodies of the dead and wounded for anything of value. We didn't harm the wounded, nor did we offer them any succour. I found my first plunder. The pocket of a dead French lieutenant yielded a small gold coin with the head of a man I assumed was Dumouriez. I later sold it for a British pound.

The Virginians lost only two men at Bussaco, one killed and one wounded. Neither was from the First Company. It was impossible to tell how many French we killed or wounded that day, but I'm sure that it was a large number. The Virginians took a dozen prisoners, a small portion of the number collected by our army.

As we were resting after the battle, we learned that an hour after assaulting our position, the French had attacked along the road to Sula and had been beaten just as soundly. The French may have hoped that by delaying this attack they could draw off Wellington's reserves and prevail. But the viscount was either smart enough or lucky enough to avoid that trap. There was some light skirmishing along the southern track, near the River Mondego, but not enough to consider it a real battle.

Madden speculates that had the French attacked simultaneously at all three points, they might've prevailed. I doubt that. Our army was equal both in size and courage to the French, and we had by far the stronger position. No stratagem could have overcome our advantage.

One of the French prisoners, a private named Gerard Rettien, spoke passable English. We didn't question him, but the next day he seemed almost driven to tell us how his commander had poorly served the French Army.

"Marshal Masséna is an old man who cares only about his mistress," Rettien began, his eyes downcast and his shoulders slumped. "She is truly beautiful, but young enough to be his granddaughter. They say she was a dancer in the Paris Opera. That I can believe."

"So the marshal has a mistress. He's hardly the first officer to have one," I said.

"That is true, sergeant. I am a man of the world. I know that officers have mistresses . . . the younger and more beautiful the better . . . when they can afford them. But an officer must care about his men first."

"And Masséna didn't?"

"No, he did not. We stayed in Viseu for two days because Mademoiselle was tired after the long journey from Almeida. That gave you British even more time to prepare your defences. We had little food. You British turned Portugal into a desert. We saw no one on our march. All we could find to eat were some potatoes and turnips. Had we moved faster, our rations would have lasted until the battle."

"Bravo for Nosey," Samuel Smith, who'd been listening, said. "His strategy worked." When no officers were around, we often referred to Wellington as Nosey, in reference to his large Roman nose.

"Did he also plant all those rocks in the road?" Rettien asked.

"I don't think so. You French picked the wrong road," I said, smiling and hoping that Rettien would take it as a jest. He was disheartened enough without my adding to his misery.

"So our great marshal could not even get that right."

Bussaco was an overwhelming victory, the first for the Virginians. We'd prevailed at New Orleans, but only because Spanish soldiers had thrown the city's gates open for us. We'd defeated the Spanish in Venezuela, but had to evacuate the country. There were no such qualifications about Bussaco. We'd played our role as skirmishers flawlessly, then re-joined the infantry to take part in the battle's finale. General Craufurd's report, which he had read at morning parade three days after the battle, listed the Virginians as one of the units that had served meritoriously.

Whilst Bussaco was a victory, Wellington did not pursue the French. Rather, he fell back to the defensive lines at Torres Vedras, a hundred miles to the south, to give his army a chance to rest and resupply.

The withdrawal was the most difficult march Virginians had yet endured. Until now, the Commissary Corps had been able to feed us, but the normal arrangements broke down and on many days we didn't receive our rations. We were able to scavenge a bit of food from the deserted villages we passed, but far too little to fill our bellies. I was soon weak from hunger and appreciated Rettien's complaint about Portugal having been turned into a desert. In most places we couldn't even find a good supply of firewood. To add to our misery, we were drenched by a heavy downpour almost every afternoon, which soaked us to the skin and turned the road into a slough of mud. It was as bad as what I'd experienced more than thirty years earlier when I was General Washington's orderly during the rebel army's retreat across New Jersey. Neither the Virginians nor the rest of Wellington's soldiers were receiving the reward I would've expected for a victorious army.

It took us almost two weeks to reach our new position, a ridge above a town called Arruda. We overlooked the fortifications, which were manned by Portuguese Ordenanza. We were to be a reserve to support them in case of a French attack.

The defensive lines of Torres Vedras weren't a continuous fortification, which the French would be able to breach if they attacked in sufficient strength. Rather they were a series of earthworks bastions, most in the shape of a six-pointed star, placed to control every point between the River Tagus and the ocean where the enemy might try to move towards Lisbon. Each bastion contained two or three cannon and a few hundred men. Most were close enough to the next that they could create overlapping fields of fire. They were meant to slow the enemy long enough for Wellington to move a sufficient number of the troops he held in reserve to counter a French thrust. The lines were impressive, both in concept and when viewed on the ground. But I've no way of knowing whether these bastions would've protected Lisbon, especially since they were manned by poorer quality troops. The French never attacked them.

Arruda was deserted, but unlike the villages we'd passed earlier, it hadn't been stripped bare. There was food in some of the larders and good wine in many of the cellars. Given Wellington's orders that nothing be left that might aid the French, we had no difficulty justifying eating and drinking our fill. The hunger of our march was soon forgotten. The houses also yielded good quality furniture, some of which was commandeered and used for its intended purpose; the rest chopped up for firewood. After a few days Colonel Lancaster allowed us to sleep in the houses, my first night under a roof since leaving Shorncliffe.

I searched the house carefully, both out of a desire to discern as much about its former inhabitants as I could, and in hope of finding something of value. I can't say that I learned much about the people who lived there, but I did find a cache of jewellery that I sold for nearly four pounds. Custom dictated that having found this windfall, I spend some of it on a feast for my housemates. Food and wine were so cheap that I could do this for a crown, leaving me with over three pounds to add to my savings.

Having filled our bellies, patched our clothes, and been resupplied with powder and shot, I expected us to march north again. But it was now late fall. It didn't get very cold, but the rain that'd plagued us on the retreat from Bussaco continued, making even good quality road impassable and turning small streams into raging rivers. We had a long stay in Arruda.

Masséna also withdrew—all the way back to Spain, where he could feed his army. He left a few regiments of voltigeurs to keep contact with our army, but both they and we knew that these French infantry were too weak to threaten us. The result was a void in northern Portugal. Most of the inhabitants had fled and neither we, nor the French, were in control. But as Aristotle said, nature abhors a vacuum. The land was soon filled with a lawless mix of deserters from four armies—ours, the French, Spanish, and Portuguese— and brigands. When they were not busy fighting each other, they organised raids into Spain, and occasionally past our lines into the parts of Portugal that were still inhabited.

The viscount needed information about the French and he also needed to appear to be trying to suppress the deserters and brigands. I doubt he cared much about their activities. He could always clear them out in the spring, when he moved against the French. But if he allowed the deserters to go unpunished, he might encourage more desertion. And if he did nothing about the brigands, he would incur the wrath of both the Portuguese and those "high-minded" citizens in Britain, who seemed to think that war could be conducted according to the rules of good sportsmanship. Evildoers were to be punished, not allowed to run unfettered.

Towards the end of November, Wellington let it be known that he planned to send patrols north to search for the French, and suppress the deserters and brigands. He appeared to be looking for volunteers for what could either be a very dangerous mission— if the French were on the move or the brigands decided to attack—or a very boring one—if neither of these situations developed.

"Watson," Captain Jackson exclaimed when he heard the news. "This is wonderful. At last the Virginians will have a chance to show these British milords what we can do if given the chance."

"Isn't patrolling like that a task for the cavalry?" I asked.

"It is, but it's no secret that the viscount doesn't trust his cavalry . . . says they're undisciplined, always charging after something. He obviously trusts us more, even if he does call us the scum of the Earth." He rushed off to find Colonel Lancaster to volunteer the First Company.

I was less excited by the news. I was comfortable in the house in Arruda that we'd commandeered and would've been happy to spend the rest of the winter there. We were close enough to Lisbon to ensure that we got our rations every day. The likelihood of a French assault seemed low. Masséna had surely learned that attacking us when we held the high ground was pure folly. Why should I seek danger looking for deserters and brigands?

Jackson returned an hour later saying that the colonel had agreed to volunteer the First Company for patrol duty. He ordered me not to inform the rest of the company. There was only a small chance that the viscount would accept the Virginians for this mission. He was more likely to choose the 95th Rifles, or some other regiment with a longer string of achievements.

At morning parade two days later, the First Company was held in formation after the rest of the regiment had been dismissed. We waited only a few minutes before the colonel appeared.

Captain Jackson saluted the colonel, and ordered "Attention."

"Stand easy," the colonel said, returning the salute.

"Men of the First Company, you are indeed honoured," the colonel began. "Viscount Wellington has chosen you to be one of three patrols sent north to provide intelligence about French intentions and the location of any groups of brigands you encounter. You are not to engage the enemy nor do battle with brigands unless you have no choice. Your goal is to return safely with the information you gather." He turned to the captain, said "Captain Jackson, here are your orders," then turning back to us, closed with, "Three cheers for the Virginians!"

We snapped to attention and shouted three huzzahs. The colonel left without dismissing us.

Jackson tore open the orders he'd been given, read them quickly, then turned to the company.

"Stand easy. Our orders are to draw two weeks rations and supplies. We leave at dawn the day after tomorrow and are to patrol the road to Coimbra, then north of the village if we can. As the colonel said, we are not to engage in battle if we can avoid it. We are to be back in Arruda two days before the New Year.

"Watson, attend me in my office. Company dismissed."

"This is monstrous," Jackson snarled when I entered his office. "We are to run away if we see the French and not even try to punish those marauding lawbreakers who control the country north of us."

"Won't we be honoured if we bring back useful information?"

"We might be, but what chance is there of that? It's mid-December. The French aren't going to start a campaign now. The mud that's keeping us from marching north will prevent them from marching south. And if we find any brigands, they'll be miles away before the army can send anyone after them." He grumbled a bit more before signing the necessary requisitions for rations and other supplies.

"Make sure the men have blankets and warm clothing," were his final instructions as I left his office.

We left at dawn two days later—seventy-two men and three two-wheeled donkey carts full of rations. The carts were light. They could be drawn by two men if need be. Given how bare the countryside was, our rations would have made an attractive prize for any band of deserters or brigands strong enough to take them from us. Lieutenant Cabral of the Portuguese Army accompanied us as a translator.

The weather was miserable, grey and drizzly, with enough breeze to chill any exposed body parts. We were able to spend each night in some sort of shelter, and build fires to heat our food and provide at least a little warmth.

Our route was along the main road to Coimbra, about a hundred miles to the north. We reached the village in five days without seeing any deserters or brigands. It was still inhabited by a few score hearty souls, who had barricaded the road and the spaces between buildings to create a defensive perimeter. They kept picquets on duty both day and night, and each man—and some women—kept a musket close for defence.

When we approached, the village priest, a Padre Afonso, came out for a parley. Through our translator, Captain Jackson assured him that we meant the village no harm and that we'd brought our own food. With these assurances the priest pointed us to several barns outside their defences, and said that we could use them for bivouacs. Captain Jackson was not pleased at this treatment. He wanted to be in the village and under a more substantial roof than a barn could provide, but it was easy to see why we were being kept at a distance. The Portuguese had no assurance that we wouldn't plunder what little they had. Jackson held his temper. We headed for the barns and spent an uneventful night before again heading north.

Mid-afternoon the next day, as our column marched along the road to Bussaco, we approached a grove of trees along a stream bank. I was in front commanding six flankers, who served as the company's advanced guard. O'Malley, who'd again been promoted to corporal after his demotion to private in Antigua, commanded another party of flankers to the right. A steep hillside made it impossible to position flankers to the left. I was confident that Sergeant Harper back in Shorncliffe would have approved of our formation.

"That grove looks like a good place for the company to take fifteen minutes' rest," Captain Jackson, who had just come forward, said. "Let's make sure that it's safe."

With Jackson in the lead, my party of flankers advanced. We were completely unprepared for the volley of shots that erupted from the trees. Three men fell. I felt a sharp pain in my left thigh. I looked down and saw blood flowing from a bullet wound. It all seemed unreal. I dropped my rifle and grabbed at my leg with both hands to try to stop the bleeding. Then I collapsed.

I heard Captain Jackson shouting orders for the First Company to rush the trees and kill whoever had attacked us. I heard the sound of running feet and rifle shots. No one paid any attention to me or to the men who'd fallen. They were intent upon finding and killing our adversaries.

"Cease fire," the captain ordered after a short while.

My efforts to stop my bleeding were doing little good and I was becoming light-headed.

"Watson," Jackson called. Then a few seconds later, "Where's Watson? Anyone seen him?" It was only then that John Sevier looked back towards the road and saw me laying there.

"Watson's wounded," Sevier said.

"Take three men and tend to him," Jackson ordered.

Sevier, Samuel Smith, Nick Ogle, and Elias Parton trotted fifty feet back to me. John took a quick look at my wound, then pulled off his belt to make a tourniquet.

"Anyone got a clean strip of cloth for a bandage?" Samuel asked.

"Will these do?" Ogle replied, pulling a pair of stockings from his pack.

"They're not clean, but they'll have to do," Sevier said, tying the stocking around my wound as tightly as he could.

"Give me some water," I said, whilst John was working on my leg. Parton pulled out his canteen and held it to my mouth. I took a long draught.

"I have some rum, too," Parton offered. "It'll dull the pain."

Parton pulled a flask from his pack, opened it, took a sip himself, wiped its opening, and put it between my lips. I took a small sip and began coughing, which caused my leg to ache. I pushed the flask back to him.

"Can you stand, William?" Sevier asked.

I was light-headed and couldn't focus my eyes, but said, "I'll try."

"Lean on me," John replied.

I pulled myself up using John's arm for support. Even though I was leaning on him, I felt sharp pains running through my leg. Then I again collapsed. Purple blood flowed through my bandage. I can remember thinking that it was a good thing it wasn't bright red. If it had been, I'd have bled out and died.

"Better not try that again," Samuel said.

"Sergeant Watson's wounded in the left leg. He's unable to stand," Sevier said, as he saw Captain Jackson approach.

"He's lucky. Northrup, Fitzgerald, and Cunningham are dead," Jackson said, "but so are the seven deserters who fired on us. I hope those bastards roast in hell." He bent over and looked at my wound. "No broken bones. I'll do my best to get you to a surgeon who can sew you up. You'll keep that leg. I swear you will." He smiled at me, something he rarely did. It lifted my spirits.

"Smith, get the empty cart," Jackson ordered. "We need to get back to our lines before Watson's wound starts festering."

"Yes, sir," Smith said. Ogle and Parton went to help Samuel. John Sevier stayed with me.

Ogle and Parton had joined the Virginians the previous year, and other than the fact that they seemed inseparable, I knew little about them. They seemed like dependable men. Their helping me that day was the beginning of a bond that would last for the rest of my life.

I was later told that when Jackson asked for a dozen volunteers to bury our three dead every man in the company raised his hand. Jackson chose the dozen closest to him and left Samuel Smith in charge of the burial detail. They did their work and caught up with us at nightfall.

I was loaded onto the donkey cart, which was not made for carrying people. It had a simple axle between its two wheels and no springs. I felt every jolt as we headed south as fast as the donkey could be urged forward. The bouncing caused more bleeding. We stopped in Coimbra only long enough for Sevier, who was acting as my nurse, to get a clean linen sheet to use for bandaging. Captain Jackson offered to pay for it, but Padre Afonso, perhaps repenting his previous poor treatment of us, wouldn't accept any money. He said he'd pray for the men we'd lost and for my leg to be saved.

Whilst we were travelling, Captain Jackson visited me daily and had words of encouragement each time. I was honoured by his interest in me. He told me that our column had surprised the deserters who must have thought it better to die fighting than to be executed for desertion. One had lived long enough to say that he only regretted that they hadn't killed our officer.

"That bullet you're carrying in your leg was probably meant for me. I owe you a debt of gratitude," Jackson said wryly.

"They weren't very good shots," I responded. "I was five yards from you when I was hit."

"I can't do anything for the three the deserters killed, but I'll find a way to repay you," he said as he left.

We took only four days to reach Arruda. Mr Slaughter, an unfortunate name for a surgeon, took a look at my leg and removed the bullet, which was still lodged there, then sewed up the wound. He assured me that at worst, I'd have a slight limp.

I was given two mouthfuls of rum to deaden the pain, then strapped to a table. The last thing I remember was Slaughter advancing on me holding a large probe, then the most excruciating pain I've ever felt. When I awoke I was in a bed with a large, blood-stained bandage covering my thigh.

"I'm sending you to the hospital at Belém," Slaughter said. "All wounded who can't walk are supposed to be cared for there."

"Wouldn't it be easier for me to recover here?"

"Yes, but if you die on me or that wound festers and I have to hack off your leg, I'll be guilty of disobeying orders. There's no reason for me to do that."

Mr Slaughter had not mentioned dying or losing my leg as risks I still faced, but I was in no position to argue. The next morning I was loaded on a cart—a four wheeled one with springs—for the two-day trip to Belém, which had already gained a reputation throughout the army as a charnel house and a haven for skulkers.

CHAPTER 24

I spent New Year's Day 1811 lying on a none-too-clean pallet at Belém Barracks, as the hospital was officially known. On my arrival the previous day, Mr Ennis, the surgeon on duty, had looked at my wound and declared that there was nothing further to be done, that time would heal me. His assistant directed me to my pallet, which apparently had just been vacated. I was in a room with perhaps a score of other wounded—there was so much coming and going that I never got an accurate count. Out the window I could see the Belém Tower that I'd admired when we sailed into Lisbon Harbour nine months earlier.

On 4th January, I was carried into my interview with the Medical Board, a panel of three senior surgeons. They could make one of three decisions about me. The first was that I was so seriously injured that I needed to be sent back to England and pensioned off as an invalid. The second was that I be given blood money—a one-off payment for my wound—and extended leave to recuperate; the third that I stay at Belém until I was sufficiently recovered to return to duty. I wasn't surprised when the board chose the last option for me.

Mr Slaughter had done a good job of sewing me up. The Portuguese nuns who took care of us changed my bandage often enough that the wound didn't fester or become covered with maggots.

No one seemed interested in whether I stood up or not, but after a week I decided that I needed to get back onto my feet. I was strong enough to roll over and push myself into a crouch, but when I tried to stand, I collapsed in pain. I tried again the next day with the same result, but this time one of the nuns saw my efforts. She said something in Portuguese I didn't understand, then brought me a crutch, and motioned for me to try again. Despite my pain, I did. Once I was crouching, she slipped the crutch under my left arm and I was able, with her help, to get to a standing position. As soon as I was vertical, I put all my weight on my right leg and the crutch to relieve the pain. Even though it was a cool day, this effort left me covered in sweat. I carefully lowered myself down into a crouch, then rolled onto my pallet. I thanked the nun, who simply smiled and laid the crutch next to me. I was exhausted, but I'd made an important step in my recovery.

The next day I used the crutch to stand and take a few hops around the barracks room. I gingerly lowered my left leg to the floor and tested putting weight on it. The pain was still too great for that.

I grew stronger each day and after a week was able to hop out of the room, through the building, and into the fresh air and pale winter sunlight of the courtyard. My left leg could bear a little weight, but not enough for me to walk on it—that would take another two weeks. By the end of January, I traded my crutch for a cane. I could walk without difficulty on the flat, but stairs, where I had to put all my weight on my injured leg for a moment, required help from either the cane or a bannister.

During my recovery I talked to many of the others at the barracks. They fell into two categories. Some, about half, were eager to return to regiments and the camaraderie of their messmates. The others seemed content to stretch out their recuperation for as long as possible. They did what they could to delay their recoveries, but the more creative skulkers didn't want to be lying about on pallets. After they were discharged from hospital, they found ways to stay at Belém. A few made themselves useful around the barracks and found officers who were willing to tolerate their not returning to their regiments. The rest simply lingered there, hoping that their regiments wouldn't know that they were supposed to report for duty. Life on the outskirts of Lisbon was far more attractive than in the field. These creative skulkers became known throughout the army

as Belém Rangers. There were so many of them that they attracted Viscount Wellington's attention. He recognised the problem,
but seemed unable to do anything about it. He issued orders for all
able-bodied men to return to their units as quickly as possible, but
the orders had no effect.

In early February, Billy McNabb, one of the most skilful of the
Belém Rangers, presented what can only be described as a university
lecture on the fine art of skulking at a clandestine meeting at the
barracks. It had to be secret; Billy was absent without leave. A dozen
of us crowded into an unused storeroom to hear his story. We were
a mix of admirers and the curious—I was one of the latter. I judged
that I was in little danger attending the meeting. I could always claim
that I didn't know who Billy was and joined the group to find out.

McNabb had landed in Lisbon with 1st Battalion, 95th Rifles a
year and a half earlier.

"When I got here the army was just setting up this hospital," he
said. "They didn't have enough surgeons, assistant surgeons, orderlies,
or anyone, and there were hundreds of wounded arriving from Spain
every day. This place was a charnel house."

"How'd you get a job here?" one of the crowd asked.

"I met Mr Ennis, one of the surgeons. He asked me if I could read
and write. I said I could. Didn't hurt that we was both Methodists,
and I could quote Scripture as easily as he could." I smiled when I
heard the name Ennis. He was the surgeon who'd admitted me to
the hospital.

"Is quoting Scripture one of the requirements?" a man next to me
asked to a round of laughter.

"No, it isn't, but if you happen to meet a Methodist, it's helpful. Mr Ennis was impressed and hired me as his orderly. Not only
was I safe from 'Black Bob' Craufurd's forced marches and from the
French, I was earning six pence a day more."

"Sounds too good to be true," I said, but McNabb continued to
relate the events that led to his being absent without leave.

"The viscount issued orders that all trained soldiers should report
to their units as soon as they were fit for duty, and that Portuguese
should be hired as medical orderlies. Still I thought I was safe. Mr
Ennis and several of the other surgeons thought so highly of me that

they were happy to ignore Wellington's orders. But what we hadn't counted on was Captain Samuel Mitchell."

Billy told us that Mitchell had been wounded in the arm during the fighting at Coa Bridge and sent to Belém to recover, which he quickly did. As soon as he could, the captain organised a party to return to the 95th Rifles and insisted that Billy join them. Billy, supported by several of the surgeons, argued that his services were indispensable at the hospital, but this had no effect on Mitchell. Seeing that Billy would not come voluntarily, Mitchell had him tied to an ox-cart and paraded through Lisbon on the way back to Torres Vedras.

"It was like being in the stocks," he said. "I was taunted and jeered through the streets of Lisbon. Portuguese boys threw rotten vegetables and even more noxious things at me. I did the only thing any self-respecting old soldier could do under the circumstances . . . I deserted."

He was in hiding in Lisbon, trying to find a way back to England.

Despite his precarious status, McNabb had no qualms about what he'd done.

"There's different ways to stay out of the fighting," he said. "Some make their wounds worse by rubbing dirt in them. But that's dangerous. You may do too good a job and end up with the wound festering and you losing an arm or a leg. Some act like they have the fits or are insane, but that's also dangerous. They may send you to an asylum, which is not where you want to spend your time. The best way . . . if you can read and write . . . is to find a surgeon who's short an orderly and offer yourself for the position," he advised.

I had the necessary skills and thought briefly about taking Billy's advice. Even if I was eventually sent back to the Virginians, every additional day I could spend in Belém was a day out of danger. But there was a difference between not wishing to face danger and skulking. I'd been with the Virginians since they first mustered at Fort Roanoke, over five years earlier. I'd faced every danger they had, and more on my own, when Captain Pettit and I carried news of the Virginians' capture of New Orleans back to Fort Roanoke. This created a bond between me, Captain Jackson, Samuel Smith, John Sevier, and all of the Virginians who'd faced the same dangers. If I stayed at Belém longer than necessary, I'd be breaking that bond. I couldn't do that and still think myself a man.

The Virginians, and all other soldiers who faced the French, abhorred skulkers. Whilst they might secretly envy a man who legitimately got an assignment that took him out of danger, actively courting such assignments was seen as an act of cowardice. Even attempted skulkers were ostracised. And with good reason. You needed to be able to depend on the man standing next to you in battle to protect you, as you protected him. If he was a skulker, he'd likely run away, leaving you unprotected. The unwritten code we soldiers lived by was very clear about such matters.

By the end of February, I felt strong enough to return to the Virginians. My left leg still hurt if I put all my weight on it or turned it too sharply, but I was able to walk more than five miles through the hills above Lisbon carrying a pack full of rocks that weighed as much as my kit. I still couldn't run, especially with a pack, but I felt I'd at least be able to trot before too much longer.

"I'm ready to return to duty," I told Mr Ennis.

"Let me look at that wound. "

I dropped my trousers to expose the area, which was still bandaged. He stripped away the bandage and, after looking at the wound, poked it with a probe. That caused me to wince, but I willed myself not to utter a sound.

"The wound's clean, but it's still not fully healed," Ennis said. "You can stay here for a few more weeks until it is."

"Thank you, sir, but I'd rather return to the Virginians."

"As you wish, Sergeant . . .?"

"Watson, sir."

"Stand there for a minute whilst I write out your discharge orders. My recommendation is that you be placed on limited duty, but that will be your regimental surgeon's decision."

Finding transport back to the Virginians was more difficult than I'd anticipated. Since there was no fighting at that moment, no wagonloads of wounded were making their way from our lines to Belém. I finally found the Commissary Stores and, a week after seeing Mr Ennis, was riding one of their carts to Arruda.

"Why you go Arruda?" the Portuguese driver, who spoke very limited English, asked after seeing my cane and the difficulty I had climbing aboard the wagon.

"My mates are there," I answered and got a blank look in return.

"*Mis amigos en Arruda*," I tried in Spanish, figuring that he was more likely to understand this. He smiled broadly. Having satisfied his curiosity, he turned back to his donkeys and made no further attempt at conversation.

I was greeted warmly when I reappeared at the house I'd shared with Samuel, John, and the others. Two days of bouncing around on a donkey cart had left my wounded leg in agony and I was far less mobile than I'd been in Lisbon. After the mandatory jokes about the return of the prodigal, I was subjected to serious questioning about the condition of my leg.

"You came back too soon," Samuel said, after watching me struggle around some of the obstacles in the house.

"It was the cart ride," I said, grimacing a bit. "I'll be much better in a day or two."

"You can't go on full duty yet," John Sevier said, clearly not believing me. "You need to get to the surgeon and have him write you a ticket for limited duty."

"Give me two days," I pleaded.

"No," Samuel and John said, almost in unison.

"Where's Mr Slaughter's surgery?" I asked after looking at their determined faces.

"Not too far," Samuel replied. "I'll take you there."

"Couldn't it wait till tomorrow? A night's sleep will do wonders for me."

"No, let's do it now."

Faced with his intransigence, I complied. We walked the short distance to the house Slaughter had commandeered. He saw me immediately. With no fighting, he had few patients.

"Leg's healing well," was his judgement after examining my wound. "I promised you you'd have nothing worse than a limp."

"But Sergeant Watson isn't ready to resume full duties, is he?" Samuel asked.

"Walk across the room, turn about, and walk back," Slaughter instructed me.

I did that in good form, leaning rather heavily on my cane.

"Now do it without the cane," Slaughter said.

I managed to make the circuit, but winced in pain and almost collapsed when I turned about.

"You're not ready for full duty. I'll write you a ticket for limited duty. I'm certain that Captain Jackson and Colonel Lancaster will have no objections."

"How long will I be on limited duty?"

"Until you're fully recovered. Most men would jump at this opportunity."

"I know, sir," I said, "but I made the acquaintance of some of the Belém Rangers and I don't want to be counted as one of them."

"You won't be, Sergeant. Anyone looking at the way you're walking will know that you aren't shirking."

I reported to Captain Jackson the next morning. He had taken the sitting room of the only two-story house in Arruda as his office. It should have been a pleasant room, with a large window that faced the morning sun. But the glass had been smashed and the window was covered with slats of wood. A candle lantern provided light.

"Sergeant Watson, reporting for duty," I said, saluting.

"Good to see you back, Watson," Jackson said, returning the salute. "How's the leg?" A smile crossed his usually austere face.

"Healing, sir. I should be completely fit in a few more days," I answered.

"I told you you'd keep your leg."

"That you did, sir."

"And what instructions have you been given?"

"I'm to be on light duty," I said, handing him the notes from both Ennis and Slaughter.

"O'Malley's a corporal again and my clerk," Jackson said. "I'm sure he wouldn't appreciate your looking over his shoulder, and I don't have any other light duty. Take the time to build your leg's strength."

"I'd rather be doing something. I don't want anyone thinking I'm a skulker."

"You, a skulker? Send anyone who thinks that my way. I'll blister his ears."

"Thank you, sir," I said.

"That will be all, Watson."

I saluted, turned on my good right heel, and left Jackson's office.

I resumed my routine of walking with a fully loaded pack. It took a week to get back to the level of strength I'd achieved in Lisbon. I made an effort to use my cane as little as possible. By the end of the second week, I was carrying it most times, putting it down only when I had to climb. Running, even trotting, was still more than my leg would bear. I tried trotting without my pack and was able to make about a hundred yards before the pain became too intense. I was recovering, but slower than I wished.

CHAPTER 25

On 3rd April, Corporal O'Malley sought me out and told me to report to Captain Jackson.

"Watson," Jackson began, after I presented myself, "after our losses the Virginians can muster fewer than 500 men . . . 482 to be exact . . . and that includes the men captured at La Vela de Coro, who the Spanish finally released, and last year's recruits. General Craufurd wants our regiment to be brought up to full strength. He's authorised four recruiting parties to be sent back to America. Colonel Lancaster has approved your leading one of them."

I was speechless, but my mind was churning at a rapid rate. Recruiters had a well-deserved evil reputation. They got unsuspecting men drunk and lied to them about the realities of Army service to get them to take the King's shilling. I could never do that.

"I'd rather not do this, sir," I said, hoping that I wouldn't be treated to one of Jackson's famous eruptions of temper.

"Why not?" Jackson asked in a mild tone of voice. "You'll be out of harm's way and the pay is better than normal duty. You get a bonus for each recruit you bring in."

"The army would probably expect me to lie about how easy life is, how quickly you can get promoted, and how much plunder there will be."

"But is it all a lie?" Jackson asked. "You were promoted to sergeant in just over two years, and if what I've been told is correct, you've managed to collect a nice stash of plunder. And as for how hard life in the army is, most of the men you'll be talking to already have a hard life. At least they won't starve to death in the army."

I was silent whilst I considered what Jackson had said. I had been promoted rapidly, but I was still embarrassed by the way I'd been made a sergeant. And none of the other Virginians could match my record. Would it be fair to promise recruits they could? And as for plunder, I'd been lucky to find the cache of jewellery in the house we'd commandeered. Other than that, my takings had been meagre. Jackson was probably right about not starving to death in the army, but after our lack of rations on the retreat from Bussaco, how could I be certain?

"Do I have a choice in the matter?" I asked.

"No, these are your orders," Jackson replied, handing me a sealed packet. "But I'd hoped you'd go happily. A recruiting party is supposed to be composed of an officer, a sergeant, a corporal, a drummer, and two privates. The colonel assigned lieutenants to the other parties, but the Virginians can't spare any more officers, so you'll be in command of your party. Take O'Malley as your corporal, Jenkins as your drummer, and Tyson and Hollings as your privates."

Jackson had picked these men carefully. All were veterans. None was likely to cause any upset, and all would look like model soldiers in clean uniforms. My limp, which I hoped would be greatly diminished by the time I got to America, would be the only flaw.

"But that will leave the First Company without a sergeant or a clerk," I protested.

"That's my problem, Watson, not yours," Jackson said, the annoyance in his voice unmistakable. Once again, I'd overstepped my bounds and offered advice when it wasn't wanted.

"Yes, sir. Is there anything else, sir?"

"No, Watson, you may go."

Our orders were to report to the officer in charge of transport at Lisbon docks, take the first available ship for Southampton and, after getting new uniforms and kit, the first available ship for Hampton, Virginia. Since we had four days before we were to report, and the trip only took two days on one of the carts that left our lines daily, my housemates decided to use my new posting as an excuse for a feast. They invited the rest of my recruiting party. A whole pig was procured and roasted, then served with generous quantities of wine. The highlight of the evening was supposed to be an entertainment concocted by Samuel Smith. Tyson played the role of a naive recruit, beguiled into signing up by a silver-tongued recruiting sergeant, played by O'Malley. I'd not been recruited in this fashion and could laugh at the excesses O'Malley and Tyson portrayed, but their satire struck too close to home for Jenkins and Hollings, who'd been seduced by the blandishments of recruiters. The evening, which should have been pure fun, ended earlier than usual and on a sour note. I again vowed to be honest in what I told recruits.

Before I left, Samuel gave me the name and address of Jacques Defoe, a friend in Williamsburg, and asked me to see him if I could. I promised I would.

In Lisbon we joined the other three recruiting parties from the Virginians. We'd met in Arruda, but travelled to Lisbon separately. I knew a few of the men, but the majority had been drawn from the ranks of recruits who'd joined the regiment less than a year ago— men I was still getting to know. I wondered whether other company commanders were using the recruiting parties to get rid of men they didn't want. That hadn't been Jackson's approach.

Lieutenant Conroy, the gormless officer who'd led the reconnaissance of Nuevo Madrid, senior amongst the lieutenants in charge of the other three parties, was in overall command. He'd been given command of a company after the Virginians' losses in the attack on New Orleans left a vacancy, but lost that position when the regiment consolidated into six companies. Since then he'd been an aide to Colonel Lancaster. I was uncharitable enough to believe that the colonel had assigned Conroy to the recruiting mission to be free of him for at least nine months.

On the voyage to Southampton, our ship's captain spotted what he believed to be a French raider from the port of Bordeaux approaching our stern. He ordered maximum sail, even though the wind was brisk enough to make this a dangerous manoeuvre, and had the master-at-arms distribute cutlasses and pistols to the sailors. We members of the recruiting teams had our rifles, but they'd be useless on the wildly pitching deck.

It was a tense two hours as we slowly pulled away from the unknown ship, which finally disappeared beneath the horizon. The extra sail was furled and the weapons collected and stowed in their compartment.

"The captain sees every unknown ship as a French raider," I heard the first mate mutter. "All that extra sail could've capsized us. We'd all be dead."

"True, but you can't be too careful in these waters," one of the seamen responded. "There are French raiders about, and you'll be just as dead if one of them catches us." I remembered what Jack Nastyface had told me when I first met him on board the *Calcutta* . . . there are so many ways the sea can kill you.

In Southampton we were issued new uniforms and kit. A recruiting party was expected to be all spit-and-polish. Of course, we would have to pay the stoppages for everything. I didn't mind the new uniform—mine was more than a bit threadbare—but much of my kit, especially my rifle, was perfectly usable.

"The wood on your Baker is all chewed up, and the brass has scratches on it," the quartermaster said. He was exaggerating, but not by much. My Baker had been used hard over the years, but I kept it clean and well-oiled, and it worked as well as the day it was issued.

"But if you give me a shiny new one, how will anyone know I've been in combat?" I protested.

"My orders are to issue new kit to all members of recruiting parties. You'll make so much money from the bonus you get for each new recruit, you'll laugh at these stoppages."

We were housed in private residences in Southampton. Normally, the owners of these houses were reluctant to host British soldiers, but as colonials, we were the objects of curiosity. Mr and Mrs Ardmore, whose home I was staying in, questioned me at length about every aspect of life on the frontier. They pictured Davidson's Fort as under constant attack by howling mobs of savage Indians, and couldn't believe that there'd been peace for forty years. They were equally amazed that before joining the army, I ate and dressed much as they did.

I was equally curious about their lives. The house they lived in was over a hundred years old, and their church, nearly two hundred. Both were stone and looked as if they could last for centuries more. The stockade that gave Davidson's Fort its name was thirty years old and Henderson's Trading Post only two years younger, but both were wood and unlikely to last more than a few decades longer. Even in New York and Philadelphia, there were few stone or brick buildings that could hope to attain the age of many of the structures in Southampton.

The day we arrived in Southampton was cloudy, as was the next, but on the third day the sun came out and all was bright and shiny. I was surprised at the effect the weather had on the Ardmores. Their daily routine was forgotten. They sat in their small rear garden trying to soak up as much of the sun as they could.

"This is the first day of sunshine since October," Mr Ardmore told me. "Who knows when we'll see the next?"

"Now that's one thing that better in Davidson's Fort," I told him. "Even in mid-winter, we get sunny days."

"Yes, but you get feet of snow to trudge through," he replied, seeming to think it was necessary to defend his home's weather.

My short stay in Southampton was the only time I got a chance to see any of England, the "home" country I'd heard about all my life. I felt as if the visit should've given me some great revelation, but truth be told, I left England with no better understanding than I had before. I could list dozens of differences, many of which favoured the colonies, but I would be hard-pressed to decide whether life in Southampton was better or poorer than in Davidson's Fort. I also knew, from talking to the many Englishmen I'd met in the army, that life in other parts of England was as different from life in Southampton as it was from life on the North Carolina frontier.

After ten days in Southampton we boarded the *Bombay* for the ocean crossing. By now I was an old hand at sea voyages and knew to walk as much as possible to keep my bowels in working order. The walking also strengthened my leg and by the time we reached Hampton, I no longer needed the cane and could climb the ship's ladders without feeling pain. My limp was slight, but noticeable. I mused that it made me an old soldier like Sergeant Pew.

Once we landed, Lieutenant Conroy mustered the recruiting parties and marched us to the post the army had established adjacent to the sprawling naval base. We waited whilst he presented himself to the officer of the day and was escorted to see Major Williston, who commanded the Second Battalion.

"We've been expected," Conroy reported, when he returned. "Space will be found in the barracks. We have no duties tomorrow, but on the next day we are to begin two days' training on our mission."

"Is the Second Battalion training any men?" I asked.

Conroy smiled. "Yes, 153 men have volunteered in the year and a half since we last picked up recruits. That'll make our task easier."

"Not by much," Lieutenant Gibson said sourly. "That's less than a third the number we're supposed to bring back with us."

"But it's more than I expected to be here." Conroy was optimistic about everything.

Gibson was not to be placated. "I would've thought that in eighteen months the army could have enticed five hundred men to join, and that we'd simply have to escort them to Portugal."

Conroy did not respond to this jibe. He asked whether there were any questions. When no one spoke, he dismissed us.

The next morning I watched for an hour as Sergeant O'Mara bullied and harassed a squad of recruits. Given how little they knew about drill, they must have only recently enlisted. He called them filth and vermin, and wondered how men as witless as they were had survived this long on Earth. O'Mara was one of the cadre of sergeants and corporals assigned to the Virginians' Second Battalion to convert new enlistees into soldiers. The battalion also had quartermasters to kit out the new soldiers, cooks and their helpers to feed them, and two squads of riflemen to guard the barracks each night to ensure that none of the new recruits skipped.

I thought that Sergeant Pew had been a hard taskmaster when I was a Johnny Newcombe, but watching O'Mara made me realise that Pew had been gentle as a nanny with us. The only saving grace was that O'Mara would have these recruits for only a few weeks. Any man too weak to withstand his abuse was unlikely to survive in battle. I didn't need to warn recruits about drill sergeants. They'd probably heard stories about the likes of Sergeant O'Mara.

What bothered me more than O'Mara's invective and his frequent caning of the recruits was the guard mounted each night. It gave the barracks the feel of a prison. I was under guard when I was a new recruit at Fort Roanoke, but because the fort was at the edge of the wilderness, and an attack by Indians was always a possibility, the guards served as sentries. Their presence was comforting, rather than threatening. I doubt any of the recruits at Hampton Barracks worried about the guard. After a day under Sergeant O'Mara or one of his ilk, they seemed only too happy to fall onto their pallets and get what sleep they could.

Our training was about the procedures needed to ensure that a recruit was suitable to be a soldier, then to see that he was properly enlisted. To join the Virginians, a man had to be at least fifteen years old but no more than fifty. He had to be at least sixty-five inches tall, but an allowance was made for "growing lads" who could be expected to attain this height. To be properly enlisted, a recruit had to take the King's shilling. A surgeon had to examine him to ensure that he was fit to be a soldier—not suffering from fits, broken bones, or hernia, and didn't have running sores, or any obvious infirmity of body or limbs. Once he had the doctor's approval, he had to appear before a magistrate to swear that he was suitable for enlistment—that he didn't have hidden illnesses—that he wasn't an apprentice or serving a term of indenture—and that he wasn't a deserter from another Army or militia unit. If he attested to these particulars, he then had to swear an oath of allegiance to the King and his officers.

These procedures hadn't been followed when I enlisted. I took the shilling and swore the oath, but no doctor examined me, nor was I brought before a magistrate. Whilst a doctor was available, the nearest magistrate was in Salisbury, a hundred miles away. I wondered whether I was actually a soldier, but decided not to raise the question. The lieutenant who had been instructing us didn't seem to have a sense of humour.

We also learned about recruiting bonuses. The enlistment bonus paid to recruits had been raised since I'd joined the Virginians and now stood at ten guineas, less stoppages, of course. The only money the recruit saw immediately was the King's shilling—the rest would be paid after he was fully in the army. Paying the money all at once was an invitation for the recruit to flee or for it to be stolen from him—often by the members of the recruiting party.

More interesting was the one pound, eleven shillings, six pence bonus paid to the commander of the recruiting party for each new recruit. How the army came up with this precise sum was a mystery I was certain I'd never solve. Part of the money had to be spent for entertaining potential recruits, and I was obligated to give a gratuity of five shillings to any man, civilian or army, who brought a new recruit. I could keep the rest, but even the dour lieutenant who was instructing us said that this would be unwise, that the money should be divided amongst the members of the party, with its commander keeping the lion's share. He didn't indicate what a fair split should be.

CHAPTER 26

O nce our training was complete, my party was ordered to begin recruiting in the huge area between the James and Patomack Rivers as far west as the Proclamation Line, the western limit of settlement. Lieutenant Conroy's party was given Virginia south of the James River; Lieutenant Gibson's party, North Carolina; and the remaining party, South Carolina and Georgia. I was happy my party hadn't been sent to North Carolina, even though it was unlikely we'd have travelled west of Salisbury. I wasn't yet ready to face any of my former neighbours in Davidson's Fort, and a trip to Guilford Courthouse, where Mr Henderson had his office, would've been painful.

There seemed little sense in starting our recruiting in Hampton. Any man wishing to join the army could've simply presented himself at the post. We'd been advanced ten pounds for expenses to be repaid from the recruiting bonuses we were expected to earn. I decided that we could afford the luxury of a coach to Williamsburg.

Williamsburg had been Virginia's capital before and during the Great Rebellion, but after the war, lost that honour to Richmond. The coach stopped in front of The King's Arms, which seemed like a propitious name. I booked a room with three beds for us. Rank had its privileges. I'd occupy one and the rest of the party would share the other two. The tavern-keeper was happy to recommend a doctor and a magistrate who'd served past recruiting parties.

I led the party as we marched through the town's streets. Jenkins was behind me beating a steady tattoo. We'd been given flyers announcing that the Virginians were recruiting and promising a ten-guinea enlistment bonus. The rest of the party handed these to any likely looking man and invited them to join us that night at eight p.m. at The King's Arms, and that we'd be buying drinks for men who were willing to take the shilling.

A half dozen men were waiting for us when the recruiting party entered The King's Arms that night. I motioned everyone to a large table against the room's back wall. Two candle lanterns provided better light than anywhere else except the bar. I wanted to be able to see the men I was talking to and gauge their reaction to what I said.

After introducing myself—I'd been advised not to ask them their names, since some might not want it known that they were interested in joining the army—I began telling them about the Virginians. I had to be careful. I'd told the first part of my tale to Mr Cooper, who'd published it in *The Philadelphia Chronicle*. Other newspapers—I'd no way of knowing how many—had reprinted the story. It was possible that one or more of the men had read Cooper's account. Also, even when I started my speech, I was unsure how I could balance my resolve to tell the truth with my mission to recruit soldiers for our regiment.

I told no lies about the Virginians that night, but neither did I tell the whole truth. I minimised the hardships we endured building the packhorse trail to French Lick. I said that we'd lost many men in the assault on New Orleans, but didn't give the actual number. Instead I talked about the heroic feat of conquering a huge territory for the King. I blamed our failure in Venezuela on the generalissimo, which was true. I lauded the Virginians' courage in facing the Spanish cavalry on the road from Coro, their discipline at the Coa Bridge, and their success at Bussaco, then ended with the question: "Are you worthy of joining such an illustrious regiment?"

After I finished, O'Malley whispered, "I don't think I am," which brought a smile to my face.

The potential recruits were a mixed lot. Two were boys, no more than sixteen or seventeen years old. They were big lads, taller than the required sixty-five inches. A third had a doleful face and looked to be about twenty. I wondered whether he'd suffered some personal tragedy, as had Harry Judkins, who joined the Virginians at the same time I did after losing his wife in childbirth. Two others were older, perhaps thirty. They seemed to be friends and looked as if it had been a while since they'd eaten a good meal. This left the sixth man, who looked to be about forty. He was well fed and well dressed. I wondered whether he had a story similar to mine, forced to join the army or be unmasked as a criminal. No use speculating.

"Barman, pints of ale for my friends," I shouted.

One of the hungry-looking men took a deep draught from the drink he'd been served before saying, "I hear a man can get rich on plunder."

"If you're lucky," I said. "There's plunder to be had, but it's every man for himself."

"If it depends on luck, then I'll not get rich. I haven't had any good luck for so long, I've forgotten what it feels like."

"Buck up, Joshua," the other hungry-looking man said. "At least we'll know where our next meal is coming from."

"Aye, that you will," I said. "I'm not going to tell you that army food is wonderful. Many times it's salt pork and hardtack, but you won't go hungry. And you get your rum ration every day."

"How long did it take you to become a sergeant?" one of the boys asked.

"A little more than two years."

"Could I be promoted that fast?"

"If you're good enough."

"Sergeant, were you in another regiment before the Virginians?" the well-fed man asked.

"No, the Kings' Own Virginians is the only regiment I've ever served in."

"Weren't you a little old to be joining the army?"

"I was, but I had no family and after eighteen years I was bored with being a shopkeeper. I wanted a little adventure in my life."

"Sounds like you got it. How'd you get the limp?"

I gave him a brief version of the encounter with the deserters. When I'd finished, he said, "A word with you in private," pointing to a dark corner across the room.

"O'Malley, keep these men's mugs full. I'll be back in a few moments," I said as I followed the well-fed man across the room.

"Sergeant, I'm Victor Ashe. John Ashe is my uncle." He held out his hand. I had a twinge of fear that my past was about to catch up to me, and that I was about to be exposed as an embezzler. I quickly decided I had no choice but to put up a brave front.

I shook his hand, then said, "You're obviously not interested in joining the army, and you don't need a free beer. Why'd you come tonight?"

"I was curious to see you. My uncle writes regularly to my father, who always shares the letters with the rest of the family. When he replaced you in Davidson's Fort, he told us that neither he nor anyone else in town believed your story about wanting to be part of the Virginians when they conquered Louisiana, but that no one knew your real reason." I breathed a silent sigh of relief. My secret was still safe. "When I heard your name, I thought I'd meet you and see if I could tell Uncle John anything more. But you're still telling the same story, so it's safe to say that he'll have to wait a bit longer to learn the real story."

"I'm sorry to disappoint you, but I did tell the truth," I lied. "The Virginians were given the mission of capturing St Louis and New Orleans, and I'm proud of the part I was able to play." I wasn't going to tell a man I'd just met that I'd gotten into debt gambling, embezzled money from Leonard Henderson and had no choice but to join the army when my crime was discovered.

"You should be proud. You're a hero. The whole of British North America knows how you risked death to carry the message of the Virginians' victory back to Fort Roanoke," Ashe said.

"Thank you for those kind words."

"Is there anything you'd like me to tell Uncle John?"

"Please tell him that I'm alive and well, and extend my apologies for not being able to visit."

"Shall I tell him about your wound?"

"If you must, but there's no need to."

"As you wish, Sergeant. I'll write to my uncle and convey your message," Ashe said. "A pleasure meeting you." We shook hands again, and he left.

"Who was that?" O'Malley asked when I returned.

"Someone who knew of me before I joined the Virginians."

"Did you know him?"

"No, this is the first time I've laid eyes on him."

At about ten o'clock, the mother of one of the boys, a red-faced harridan wearing a soiled dress and a mobcap, stormed into the bar.

"Thaddeus Martin, you come home this minute, or big as you are, I'll pull your britches down and thrash you within an inch of your life. I didn't raise you to go off and be a soldier. Your father must be rolling over in his grave that you even thought about enlisting. Get away from this sergeant before he gets you drunk and in the army. You too, Warren Oakes, or do I have to get your father after you?"

Thaddeus stood up, shamefaced, and to hoots of derision from the others in the tavern, followed his mother out to the street. Warren followed them a few seconds later.

"Well, gentlemen, shall we have another round?" I asked the three remaining men, trying to put the best face I could on the last few minutes.

"I think not," the sad-faced man said. "Thank you for the pint." He also took his leave. This left the two hungry-looking men, Joshua and his friend.

"I'm ready to take the shilling," Joshua said. "I'm a weaver, but now that they've started bringing in power looms, there's no work to be had." He turned to look at his friend. "What about you, Noah?"

"Doesn't look like I've much choice. Almost starved last winter."

"Barman, can you serve up some supper for my friends?"

"All I have is some cheese and day-old bread."

"That will be fine," Joshua and Noah said, almost in unison. Their food appeared a few minutes later, and they attacked it with gusto. I felt sorry for them, but men rarely joined the army without something pushing them. Hunger was one of the better reasons.

Noah's surname was McClellan, and like Joshua—whose surname was Emerson—he was an unemployed weaver. Both seemed like law-abiding members of the colony, and I found it sad that they were driven to join the army and face the hardships of a soldier's life because they couldn't find work. But if I turned them away, or convinced them not to enlist, I could be driving them to become criminals or face death by starvation. In this light, accepting them as recruits was an act of kindness, or so I convinced myself.

"You'll spend the night here at the pub," I told the two recruits. "Tomorrow morning you'll be examined by a doctor and swear before a magistrate. Then you'll be part of the army," I explained as they ate. I handed each of them a shilling. Joshua immediately ordered more food.

I pulled Tyson and Hollings, the two privates in my recruiting party, aside and told them to keep close watch on Noah and Joshua, that their bonus for the trip would be forfeit if either of these two jumped. I didn't think this likely, but didn't want to risk being wrong.

I'd been told to have the recruits examined by a physician named Oglesby, then taken before a magistrate named Jones. First thing the next morning O'Malley and I marched McClellan and Emerson to Mr Oglesby's house. I knocked at the door and was told to enter, but to leave the rest of the party on the porch. This seemed strange, but I complied.

"What's your name, Sergeant?" Oglesby asked. He was red-eyed either from drink or lack of sleep, and was still in a nightgown, covered by a robe for decency.

"Watson, sir."

"Sergeant Watson, those imbeciles at Hampton Barracks obviously didn't tell you about the procedure I use for new recruits."

"I don't understand."

"In the future, don't bring recruits to my door." Oglesby said. "If you do, I have to examine them, and there's no telling what I'll find. If you tell me that the recruits are healthy, and pay me the examination fee, I'll be happy to sign the papers saying they're healthy."

"But what if they aren't?"

"The army will find that out soon enough, but I'll have helped you fill your recruiting quota. Now bring in those two men and don't make the same mistake next time."

Oglesby did little more than look at McClellan and Emerson before declaring them fit to serve the King. I paid him two shillings for the service and left even more troubled by my mission. The recruits were not bothered by this treatment. They had no reason to want to be found unfit for the army.

Our next stop was the magistrate, who took his role more seriously. He had forms, which he filled out with each man's name, age, place of birth, and occupation. These bits were followed by an oath in which the recruit swore he did not belong to any other part of the British military and would serve in the Virginians until legally discharged. It pleased me to see that both men were able to sign their names. The magistrate then filled out and signed his portion of the document, which described the man who had signed the oath, stated that he was physically fit for service, that the man had voluntarily enlisted, and would be paid a bounty of ten guineas. The process took less than five minutes and I paid the magistrate two shillings for his services. McClellan and Emerson were now members of the Virginians.

We stayed in Williamsburg two more days, but were unable to add to our tally. With only two enlistees, and having spent much of the bonus I would receive for recruiting them, I decided that we'd walk back to Hampton Barracks.

I reported to Major Williston in his office as soon as we arrived at the barracks. He was far from happy when he heard that our trip had generated only two men.

"You need some lessons on how to entice men to take the shilling," the major said. "See Sergeant Thompson. He'll teach you a trick or two."

"Yes, sir," I said, before saluting and leaving the office.

After a few enquiries, I found Thompson in the barracks' common room, shining an already gleaming pair of boots.

"Major told me to talk to you, said you knew some ways to get men to join the army."

"You mean other than getting them drunk?" the sergeant said with a laugh.

"Yes."

"How'd you tell them about the enlistment bonus?"

"I just said that it was ten guineas and would be paid with their regular pay."

"That won't work. They've got to see the money and you've got to make a show if it."

"I don't understand."

Thompson looked around and saw a stack of draughts. He scooped up ten. "Pretend these are guinea coins."

"Acton, come over here." A tall, thin corporal joined us. "Cup your hands and hold them out."

"Now if I were talking to a bunch of men about taking the shilling, this is what I'd say. Ten guineas enlistment bounty. More money than you've ever seen in your life. Then I'd drop the coins slowly into my corporal's hands. 'One . . . two . . . three . . . think about how you'll be able to charm the ladies with all this money . . . four . . . five . . . six . . . or maybe you want to take care of your old mum . . . seven . . . eight . . . nine . . . or throw a party for all your friends . . . including yours truly, Sergeant Thompson . . . ten. Yes, gentlemen, ten gold guineas, more money than you'll ever again see in your life."

"Not enough of an inducement? How many of you been hungry? In the army each day you'll get a pound of meat and a pound of bread, and you'll wash it down with a quarter pint of rum. You'll eat better than you've ever eaten before. And that's as a private. Lads as bright and eager as you will make sergeant in no time. The food and pay's better." Thompson stopped to pat his ample paunch.

"Look at those clothes you're wearing. Never attract a pretty lass dressed that way. But in a uniform with bright shining boots and a fine shako, the girls will flock to you." Thompson's patter went on in the same vein for at least another five minutes.

"Do the recruits believe you?" I asked, since some of what he said was more than a little fanciful.

"Probably not," he replied. "But it gives them time to think about the money they've seen. That's what gets the ones who aren't running away from something—and the ones who are running away will enlist, no matter what you say. You won't have to look for them. They hunt you up."

Thompson's patter was beguiling, but I didn't see how I could emulate it. I could drop ten gold guineas into O'Malley's hands, but other than counting them out, what could I say that would be convincing? "Any other suggestions?" I asked.

"Only that you have to size each man up," Thompson replied. "They're all interested in the money. If they're running away, you need to find a way to tell them that they'll be safe in the army. If they're looking to be housed and fed, you need to talk about the Army providing food and shelter. And if they're looking for adventure, you need to tell them a few more war stories. You can't do this when you're talking to a group, but you can do it when you're talking individually to one or two men. You need to craft your spiel accordingly. It's something that comes with practice."

"I hope I don't have much time to practice. I'd rather be back in Portugal with the Virginians."

Thompson looked at me as if he couldn't believe his ears. "Recruiting is the easiest duty you'll ever have in the army, and with bonuses, pays the most money you're ever likely to make. Why would you want to be facing French muskets instead?"

"Daft, I suppose," I said. I wasn't about to tell him that I didn't want to lie the way he seemed happy to do.

Our next foray was to the village of Belhaven, on the banks of the Patomack River. I'd never heard of the place, which I soon learned was also called Alexandria. It was on the post road to Philadelphia and New York, and a thriving port, as far upstream as ocean-going vessels could travel. We stopped at a tavern named The Loyalist, and repeated our march through the town and entertainment in the evening. I counted coins into O'Malley's hands to emphasize the enlistment bonus. I could see men's eyes focused on me as I did this and could almost sense their greed. I wanted to shout that it was a bargain with the devil, and not to sell themselves so cheaply, but couldn't. Our trip netted six recruits, better than we'd done in Williamsburg, but still far too few to fill the Virginians' needs. I hoped the other recruiting parties were doing better.

We made four more trips to Virginia towns and improved our results each time. By mid-August, we'd enlisted seventy-two men. After deductions, we had a pool of £48 recruiting bonus to share. I took a third, and gave a sixth to each of the other four men. Everyone seemed happy. £8 was a windfall for a corporal or private, as was £16 to me.

The other recruiting parties had done slightly better and we had a group of nearly five hundred recruits to take back across the Atlantic with us. I was relieved. Our mission was a success. The only thing that would come of my encounter with Victor Ashe was that his Uncle John, the rest of Davidson's Fort, and Mr Henderson would know that I was still alive. I couldn't see how this could cause me any problems.

Lieutenant Conroy would take the new men to Shorncliffe to be turned into riflemen. The rest of us would return to the Virginians, who by this time had advanced to the Portuguese border with Spain, some of the very positions we'd occupied the previous year. With luck, I'd spend New Year Day's 1812 with the regiment.

CHAPTER 27

I re-joined the Virginians on 20th December after an arduous journey across the Atlantic to Southampton. Our ship was buffeted by storms for most of the six-week crossing. At one point the winds were so strong the sailors swore we were in a hurricane. I wasn't going to argue, but, bad as they were, these gales weren't as hard as the ones I'd experienced in New Orleans, and Herr Hauser had called that only a small hurricane.

I had no rest in Southampton. A convoy of ships laden with supplies for our army was scheduled to sail for Lisbon the day after we arrived. It behoved those of us in the recruiting mission who were returning to the regiment to be on board. From Lisbon it was a two-week march through northern Portugal to Gallegos, a small Spanish village just east of the border, where the Virginians were taking a brief respite from months of almost continuous skirmishing or battle.

Viscount Wellington, having concluded that there would be no more campaigning in 1811, had ordered our army into winter quarters nearly two months earlier. For most regiments that meant a chance to rest and recuperate after the summer's fighting. Men who couldn't find bivouacs in houses or barns built shanties from tree branches and whatever other material was at hand to provide

shelter. Not so for the Virginians, who, as part of the army's vanguard, were almost constantly on the move responding to French
probes of Wellington's positions. They spent many nights sleeping
rough, exposed to the cold, wet, fall weather that is common in León,
as this part of Spain is known. More than a year of campaigning had
hardened the Virginians, but this routine exhausted them.

My first duty after arriving at Gallegos was to report to Captain
Jackson. I was shocked when I saw him. Jackson's fortitude was well
known amongst the Virginians. In the past he'd shrugged off long
marches and short rations as few others could. But now he looked
grey-faced and haggard.

"I trust your mission was successful," he said after we'd exchanged
salutes and he'd allowed me to stand easy.

"It was. Lieutenant Conroy took 473 recruits to Shorncliffe. They
should join us in the spring in time for next year's campaign."

"That's good. Between the summer's fighting and Guadiana fever,
the Virginians have lost almost a hundred men this year." My face
must have shown the dismay I felt at hearing this news because Jackson immediately moved to reassure me. "Don't worry. Your mates
Smith and Sevier are still amongst the living. Smith had a bout of the
fever, but seems recovered now. Why don't you find him and Sevier
and catch up with what's been happening?"

"Thank you, sir. I'll do that." Jackson had said nothing about
himself. I guessed that he, too, had been ill with the fever. I knew
I couldn't ask him about his health, but resolved to find out from
others.

It took only a few minutes to find Samuel Smith. He looked emaciated and must have lost at least two stone since I'd last seen him.

"My God, Samuel, what happened to you?" I blurted out when I
saw him.

"Fever, short rations . . . it's been a hard few months."

"And John, is he fit?"

"Yes, he seems indestructible."

Samuel proceeded to tell me how a week after the recruiting
parties left in April the viscount had begun his summer campaign.

There was no fighting for the first three weeks as the army advanced to the River Coa, just west of the Spanish border. It was familiar territory, and there were abundant signs of the previous year's battle—the skulls of horses killed in the conflict, broken wagon parts, and the like. Samuel was thankful that there were no unburied dead. They passed several mounds topped with crosses, which they assumed contained the bodies of those killed in the fighting. Of course there was no plunder. Anything of value had long since been scavenged. Despite the poor quality of the roads, commissary wagons arrived on time and the army had adequate rations.

"We fought our only battle of the year at a village called Fuentes d'Onoro, about five miles southwest from where we are now," Samuel said.

"I heard about it whilst I was in Virginia. They said it was French cavalry against our rifles and infantry . . . that the redcoats suffered greatly, but that the rifles won the day."

"That's a pretty good summary. We riflemen were free to skirmish and protect ourselves. We didn't lose a man killed that day and had only five wounded. The Camerons, a Scottish infantry regiment, lost hundreds. They were trying to defend the village itself, but didn't have space to form squares to protect themselves against the French *chasseurs*. They stood out in the open instead of taking cover behind buildings, the way riflemen would've. The French rode them down. I was part of the patrol that went through the village after the battle. It was a slaughterhouse."

"If the French took the village, how'd we win the battle?" I asked.

"'Twas simple. The French cavalry couldn't break the Light Division's skirmish line and had to withdraw. We were left in control of the battlefield and the viscount counted it as a victory."

"Then what happened?"

"We'd been besieging the French in the fortress at Almeida, which I'm sure you remember from last year. Someone must have been asleep on watch, because one night, about a week after Fuentes, the crapauds all escaped."

"I guess that's better than having to storm the place."

"True," Samuel responded. "For the rest of the summer we just skirmished with the French. Our real enemies were lack of rations and the fever. I caught it two months ago. It's worse than the illness I had in New Orleans, and there's no medicine to cure it. I had chills and fever . . . I was too weak to stand . . . I couldn't eat . . . but I was lucky. I had a mild case and I didn't become delirious. Some men become violent and have to be tied down. Last I heard sixty men from our regiment alone have died in hospital . . . more than we lost to the French. Jackson had it too, but he didn't go to hospital or turn over his command. He's too tough for that."

I told Samuel that I'd found Jacques Defoe, his friend in Williamsburg, and spent an enjoyable evening with him. Defoe had given me a letter for Samuel, which I proudly presented. Samuel excused himself and read it, chuckling as he turned the pages. Then he told me the long story of how he'd met Defoe and why they'd remained friends, even when he faced debtors' prison and his other friends had abandoned him.

"Did you see anyone you knew?" Samuel asked, after he finished his story.

"No, and I'm happy I didn't." I felt a pang of guilt when I said this, even if it was true —I hadn't known Victor Ashe before meeting him in Williamsburg.

I hadn't told Samuel about my gambling debts and embezzling money from Leonard Henderson. When we first met at Fort Roanoke, I didn't know whether I could trust him. As our friendship grew, and my trust in him developed, there never seemed to be an appropriate time to tell him my sad story. I'm sure that Samuel didn't believe that I'd joined the Virginians to be part of the conquest of Louisiana anymore than John Ashe did, but he never questioned me. After six years, how could I suddenly confess that I'd been keeping this secret from him?

John Sevier joined us and told me about his year. "I was lucky not to catch the fever," he said. "I think it comes from the water. I've been extra careful about what I drink. But enough about us. How'd the recruiting go?"

I spent the next few minutes telling them about my experiences.

"Good. You didn't lie to any of the recruits," John said.

"No, but I didn't tell them the whole truth."

"It's only in court that you have to tell the whole truth."

"Next you're going to start philosophising about the nature of truth," I said.

"I will not," he protested, before smiling and saying, "Welcome back, William."

Over the next few days, I learned that the summer campaign had been so hard that some of the old swads from the 95th had deserted to the French. They knew that the crapauds weren't flogged and that everyone believed that French officers took better care of their men than our officers did.

For the past week, a man with an Irish brogue had been taunting our picquets. We didn't know whether he was a deserter or an Irishman who'd joined the French Army under the theory that the enemy of my enemy is my friend. He said that the French would welcome with open arms any rifleman who crossed over to their side. None of the Virginians seemed tempted, but it was hardly something you'd reveal to others.

As usual, John Sevier had analysed the military situation. He wasn't happy with his conclusion.

"There are two main roads from Lisbon into Spain. Wellington hasn't paid much attention to the southern route that heads towards Madrid. It's protected by a fortress at Badajoz. General Beresford and his Portuguese Army attacked it earlier this year, but had to withdraw because they lacked the siege guns necessary to breach its walls.

"For the past two years, we've been fighting along the northern route that goes to Burgos and the French border. It's protected by two large fortresses, Almeida and Ciudad Rodrigo. We now control Almeida, but we have to take Ciudad Rodrigo before we can advance towards France. The viscount can't head for France with that strong a fortress behind our lines. The French know this and will fight hard to hold it. It won't be like Almeida, where they decamped in the dark of night. We'll have to lay siege and storm the ramparts. But before we can do that, the viscount has to find some guns big enough to breach the walls."

"And if he can't find the guns?" I asked.

"Then we sit here until we're killed by some crapaud or die of the fever."

"What other cheerful thoughts do you have?"

"We'll also have to storm Badajoz. It's further away, but even stronger than Ciudad Rodrigo."

We didn't celebrate New Year's Day 1812 with any enthusiasm. We got an extra tot of rum in honour of the holiday and there were some toasts, but to a man the Virginians knew that as soon as the weather warmed, we'd be called upon to attack the two fortresses that controlled the roads into Spain. No one doubted that the butcher bill would be high.

We were surprised when, only a week into 1812, Wellington decided to begin his assault on Ciudad Rodrigo. The fortress had one weakness—a flat-topped hill known as the Greater Teson was about seven hundred yards from, and a dozen feet higher than, the top of the fortification. It was an obvious place to mount siege guns to batter the fortress. The French realised this weakness, as well they should. They'd used the hill when they attacked Ciudad Rodrigo in 1810. To prevent us from doing the same, they built a redoubt atop the hill and mounted three guns there to defend it.

A daylight attack on the hill would have been suicidal, so four companies of the 95th and four of the Virginians, including Jackson's First Company, were ordered to make a night assault. That should've been eight hundred men, but our ranks were so depleted that we mustered merely four hundred. The weather was bitterly cold, with snow on the ground and a piercing wind. We had to wait, shivering in the dark, for several hours whilst officers of the 95th positioned themselves along our route up the hill to act as guides. Without this careful preparation our attack could easily have headed off in the wrong direction and failed.

We reached the top of the hill without being detected and could see the redoubt. It had an earthen wall, but no ditch. We were able to get within fifty yards of the glacis before a French sentry saw us and sounded the alarm. As soon as he called out, we ran as fast as we could and threw ourselves against the wall. The Virginians' Third Company had been charged with carrying scaling ladders and hurried forward to place them. We threw grenades with lit fuses over the wall to cower the defenders, then climbed to the top of the glacis. The French, who numbered fewer than a hundred, quickly realised they were outmanned. Most threw up their hands and surrendered.

The few who resisted were shot or bayonetted. The storming of the redoubt had been a complete success. Wellington was now in position to begin the siege of Ciudad Rodrigo. Even General Craufurd, Commander of the Light Division, who was usually sparse with his praise, was jubilant.

The prisoners were stripped of anything of value, in some cases even their clothes, and a frantic search started for other plunder. Pickings were slim—I found nothing of value. After about ten minutes our officers took control. We were formed back into companies. Two companies were left in control of the hilltop, and the rest of us marched back to our bivouacs. The Virginians lost no men that night and suffered only one injury. One of the men of the Second Company broke his leg when he fell from a scaling ladder.

Wellington wasted no time in beginning the siege. Ciudad Rodrigo's main defence was its walls, which varied from twenty to thirty feet high. A ditch in front of them added to the climb to the top. Scaling the fortification would be impossible. The French could pick off our men at their leisure as they made the long climb. We needed to breach the wall to reduce the ascent and give our attackers a ramp over which they could climb. Wellington now had twenty-four-pounders—bigger guns than he'd previously had. They were capable of destroying the wall if they could get close enough to accurately aim their fire.

A trench, known as a parallel, was dug atop the Grand Teson and more than two dozen guns mounted in it. They began blasting away at the northwest corner of the fortress. Once the parallel was completed, digging began on a perpendicular, or communication, trench to move closer to the wall. The perpendicular proceeded downslope from the Grand Teson and across that flat between the hill and Ciudad Rodrigo's walls. When it was finished, a second parallel, known as the attack trench, was dug, a mere two hundred yards from Ciudad Rodrigo's wall. The digging had to take place at night, and even then French cannon and mortars, which had been aimed in daylight, made the work dangerous. Our cannon fired back, but hearing cannon balls flying through the air over our heads was hardly comforting.

Once the attack trench was completed, our guns were moved up and began an around the clock bombardment. After a week, the cannon had created two breaches considered suitable for attack.

Leading such an attack was as dangerous as anything the army could ask of an officer, so deadly that it was known as the Forlorn Hope. But if an officer was successful, and survived, he was assured of immediate promotion. The men who followed the officer were assured of praise from their mates and would have first access to plunder, again assuming they survived. With these inducements there was no shortage of volunteers for the Forlorn Hope.

Many expected Captain Jackson to volunteer for the Forlorn Hope, but he didn't. The fire that he'd once felt to fight the French and win glory had been extinguished. Those who didn't know him well chalked up his new demeanour to his bout of Guadiana fever, but the change started long before he became ill. I'd first noticed it more than a year earlier when I was wounded. I would've expected him to detach a man or two to take me back to our lines. Instead he had the whole company return, even though they could've continued on patrol for another day. Some might've classified this as skulking, but that seemed too harsh a judgement. Jackson wanted the war to be over and to return home—feelings he shared with many of the Virginians. He'd do his duty, but would no longer look for opportunities to do more.

I couldn't say anything to him, but I was happy about Jackson's change of heart. He was a good man, who'd been kind to me. Whilst it might be too much to say that he'd been like a father to me, there were many times when that would have described our relationship. I wanted him to survive the war and to return home. He'd served long and honourably. He didn't have to risk death by volunteering for the Forlorn Hope.

The French knew that the attack was coming and prepared for it by stacking loaded muskets and grenades at key points so that their soldiers could fire several times without stopping to reload. They also placed mines with long fuses in the rubble of the breaches. When our attack came, the French could light those fuses so the mines exploded as our soldiers passed over them. The French had every incentive to fight to the death. They knew that to work themselves into the frenzy necessary for the Forlorn Hope, our men would either be drunk or half crazed. Men in these states often do not stop to take prisoners.

The assault began in the early evening. Volunteers from the Light

Division, including many of the Virginians, attacked one breach, red-coats from the Third Division the other. The lead companies carried bales of hay, which they threw into the ditch to break their fall when they jumped in. They scrambled up the breach and enough managed to survive to push aside the French and enter the town. The rest of the Light and Third Divisions quickly followed. Ciudad Rodrigo was ours.

The butcher bill for the assault was lighter than expected. The Virginians lost a dozen men killed and two dozen wounded, most in the initial charge of the Forlorn Hope. The most significant casualty that night was our commander, Black Bob Craufurd. He'd been standing on a high point in front of Ciudad Rodrigo's wall at the beginning of the battle, shouting orders to the members of the Forlorn Hope, when he was mortally wounded by canister shot from a French gun. He died a few hours later. He was buried with full military honours in a niche cut in the rubble of the breach in Ciudad Rodrigo's wall. This burial place may seem strange, but we thought it was a fitting resting place for the man who'd conquered the fortress.

Craufurd had been a harsh taskmaster, who used the lash freely. But his constant driving had proven the worth of riflemen and brought praise and fame to the Light Division. He was both respected and hated by his soldiers and his officers. He obviously had Wellington's support else he would've been sacked after any one of his several serious blunders. I suspect the viscount championed Craufurd because he was bold, sometimes to the extent of being foolhardy, when so many of the other generals were timid. Wellington, himself, was bold—though with more sense than Craufurd—and obviously admired that trait in others. I looked forward to the naming of Crau-furd's replacement with a mixture of hope and dread.

Under the accepted rules of war, a besieged town or fortress had to be offered the opportunity to surrender. If the offer was accept-ed, the town would be spared. If it was refused, and the besieging army prevailed, they were permitted to sack the place. I was not privy to Viscount Wellington's communication with the French, but I'm certain that at the beginning of the siege he called upon them to surrender. The French refused, and we were free to sack Ciudad Rod-rigo. Residents were stripped half-naked, despite the freezing weath-er. Their houses were searched with great care and locked drawers or cupboards smashed open.

For a while the pillaging was done in a systematic way, with monetary gain the only objective, but as the night progressed careful plundering degenerated into general mayhem. Some of our men broke into taverns and grog shops and quickly became drunk. They started firing their weapons wildly, killing not only Spanish and French but also a number of our own soldiers. As events roiled out of control some of Ciudad Rodrigo's less desirable inhabitants took advantage of the chaos and helped themselves to whatever they could. Some women were raped, but there were sufficient officers and sergeants patrolling the town to protect most of the town's females.

Our officers regained full control in the morning and marched us back to our bivouacs. Some of the Virginians were wearing finery that they'd looted from the town and were hardly recognizable as soldiers. I stayed in uniform. I'd been in the rear of the assault and in little danger. I got to the town well after the first wave and didn't expect to find much plunder left. But I stayed sober that night and came away with about five pounds' worth of coins and valuables. Over the next few months, I spent some of it on food and drink, but my savings, which were being held by the paymaster, were growing at a rapid rate. I had no plans for this money, but the war would not last forever. If I survived, having some funds available would make lifer easier, no matter what came next.

Wellington took nearly two thousand French prisoners at Ciudad Rodrigo, about a quarter of whom were wounded. Amongst the prisoners we found ten deserters, half from the 95th Rifles. At their courts martial, the deserters pleaded not guilty, claiming that they'd been driven to desert by the harsh conditions they'd been forced to endure the previous summer. These arguments were rejected by the officers who composed the court, and by their former mates, who'd suffered the same hardships. The deserters were executed by firing squad and buried in unmarked graves. Afterward, some of their mates found good things to say about them, but all agreed that they deserved to be put to death.

CHAPTER 28

The capture of Ciudad Rodrigo resulted in promotions or reward for many, from Wellington to your humble servant. The viscount was promoted to Earl of Wellington. Brigadier Barnard, who'd commanded the First Brigade, was appointed brevet, or acting, major general and given command of the Light Division, replacing General Craufurd. Colonel Lancaster was appointed brevet brigadier in command of the First Brigade. Captain Jackson was appointed brevet colonel in command of the Virginians, and I was appointed brevet captain, in command of the First Company. These ranks were temporary. Whilst there was a chance that one or more of us would be permanently promoted to his brevet rank, it was far more likely that we'd revert back to our former ranks when other officers were chosen for command.

It was a heady time for me—I'd never before had such authority. The First Company treated me with respect and I had no difficulty having my orders followed. They all knew me and were happy that I was in command rather than some stranger they'd have to cypher out. I'd expected to be teased, especially by Samuel and John, but my officer's rank protected me. Of course, I had no way of knowing what was being said behind my back.

Most of the decisions I made as a brevet captain were easy. Our routine in bivouac was well established. Once we started marching towards Badajoz, three weeks after the capture of Ciudad Rodrigo, officers above me made the choices about the route, when to start and stop, and which companies would have guard duty. My role was to make certain that the First Company carried out its duties completely and promptly. I had to chide several of the men, but didn't have to discipline any of them.

Stanley Jamison, who had a well-deserved reputation as a bully and a barracks-room barrister caused my only problem during my time in command. Sergeant O'Conner, the quartermaster, came to me complaining that Jamison was protesting a stoppage for a new knapsack. He claimed that the pack had been damaged during the assault on Ciudad Rodrigo, and that he shouldn't have to pay for it. Sergeant O'Conner and several others said that it had been damaged in the sack of the town, and that Jamison was responsible for its replacement. After listening to both sides, I decided that Jamison should be assessed the stoppage. I'm certain that this earned me his eternal enmity.

My fellow officers in the Virginians treated me as an equal, but regular army officers, particularly those who had purchased their commissions, ignored me to the extent possible. I knew this was the usual treatment accorded officers promoted from the ranks, but still their slights caused pain. I wasn't sad when, after two months, Earl Wellington appointed Major General Charles Alten commander of the Light Division and we all reverted to our former positions. Captain Jackson was again in command of the First Company and I was again his sergeant.

But I was perplexed as to why Captain Jackson hadn't been promoted to major, second-in-command of the Virginians. That position had been vacant for five years, since Major Seabury had collapsed in a fit of apoplexy. At first I thought the army was waiting for someone to buy Seabury's commission. Then, when Colonel Lancaster took command of the regiment, I thought he would arrange for a regular army officer to transfer to the Virginians as its major. Perhaps he tried, but was unable, to find a qualified officer who'd transfer to a regiment of colonials that would be disbanded at the end of the war. Next, I thought, perhaps the colonel doesn't think well of Captain Jackson, but if that were true, Jackson wouldn't have received his brevet appointment. Then I realised that none of the Virginians' captains had been promoted. I could only conclude that the British Army didn't think a colonial officer was worthy of the rank of major, and that none would be promoted to that level—and none were.

"You did a good job, William," Jackson said, after reviewing my order books and the company records. I was pleased with his compliment. It was one more sign of the change that had come over him. The Jackson I'd first met would've expected flawless performance and not seen the need to acknowledge it.

After the capture of Ciudad Rodrigo, Wellington turned south to invest Badajoz. As John Sevier had deduced, His Lordship was unwilling to leave this strong a fortification behind our lines. The historians I've read have accepted the earl's decision without question, but the price we paid for Badajoz has left me wondering whether this fortress could not have been surrounded and left to wither away.

By mid-March we'd surrounded Badajoz and begun our siege. Wellington divided his army into three parts. Fourteen thousand men were sent north and nineteen thousand sent south to block any attempt by the French to relieve the fortress. The remaining twenty-seven thousand, including the Light Division under the command of General Alten, stayed at Badajoz to carry out the assault.

Badajoz was a huge fortification, about a thousand by twelve hundred yards. It dwarfed Ciudad Rodrigo, which was only five hundred by seven hundred yards. Badajoz's northern side was protected by the River Guadiana; part of its east side, by the Rivallas Brook, which the French had dammed to create a six-hundred-yard-long moat. The remainder of the east side was protected by Badajoz's Castle, a huge fort at the northeast corner. This left the south and west sides of the fortress open to attack. The French protected the south side with two small forts, Pieurina and Pardeleras, and planted mines to protect the west side. Inside Badajoz and its outlying forts, five thousand French soldiers awaited our attack, more than twice the number who'd defended Ciudad Rodrigo.

The earl's plan of attack became obvious in late March, when five hundred men of the Third Division stormed Fort Pieurina. They succeeded, but fully half of them were killed or wounded. Once this

obstacle had been removed, more than three dozen heavy guns began bombarding Badajoz's southeast corner to create a breach, and
we started digging trenches for the final assault. It was dangerous
work. French observers on the walls could see us working and aim
the cannon fire that killed many of our men. Our sharpshooters
silenced some of those guns by killing or wounding their gunners,
but they never succeeded in suppressing the French artillery. Each
night, companies of French soldiers made sallies out of the fortress
to disrupt our work. We fought them hand-to-hand, shovels against
bayonets. The ferocity of these attacks was an early sign of the difficulty we'd face in storming the fortress. This battle would be very
different from Ciudad Rodrigo.

In one of the French attacks, I hit a crapaud over the head,
knocking him senseless. He survived and was taken prisoner. He
was young—twenty-one or twenty-two I guessed—probably part of
the latest *levee en masse*, the annual draft of men into the French
Army. Since everyone had to serve, the French Army was far more
democratic than ours, but was that a good thing?

I saw joining the Virginians as the only thing I could do once I was
exposed as an embezzler, but at least I had the opportunity to consider other choices. Many of the other men in the Virginians faced
similar unenviable choices. But most men avoided life's vicissitudes
and never had to face becoming a soldier. The young Frenchman I
fought had no choice. Had he not reported for the levee en masse,
soldiers would have shown up at his door and hauled him away to
the nearest army post.

It took two weeks to create the breach and prepare for the
attack. The main thrust would be over the breach by two divisions.
Three other attacks, each by a division, were supposed to create
diversions and keep the French from concentrating their forces,
but Wellington's meticulous plans went awry. The diversionary
attacks did not commence on time. One was too early, the others
too late.

Two Forlorn Hope assaults were planned, the first by five hundred
men of the Light Division, the second by an equal number from the
Fourth Division. Both were repelled with the loss of nearly all their
men. After these attacks failed, companies and smaller groups from

both divisions continued assaulting the breach. After the battle we were told that there had been forty separate attacks. All failed.

The breach could not be repaired, but the French made it impassable with barriers of sword blades and planks with nails sticking out to impale our advancing men. Barrels of gunpowder were planted, to be exploded as our men passed. Each French soldier had three muskets. About the only device the French didn't use was the medieval one of pouring cauldrons of burning oil onto our men as they climbed the scaling ladders. I think they would have done this had sufficient oil been available.

Wellington was ready to admit defeat when, miraculously, two of the diversionary attacks succeeded. The Fifth Division penetrated the northwest corner of the fortress and quickly moved to attack the French defending the closest breach from the rear. The crapauds who survived either surrendered or fled, allowing those of our men still assaulting that breach to enter Badajoz. Whilst this was happening, the Third Division was successful in its assault of Badajoz's Castle, preventing the French soldiers there from moving against the Fifth Division. This two-pronged attack was too much for the French. Those who could escaped across the Guadiana to a fort named San Cristobal. They surrendered the next morning.

The cost of the assault on Badajoz was horrific—nearly five thousand dead or wounded, almost a fifth of the men involved. An even larger fraction of officers, sergeants, and corporals leading the attacks were lost. The butcher bill alone would have been sufficient to make Badajoz one of the worst events of the war, but what happened after the battle marked it in ignominy.

Even before the fighting ended, the army, including, I'm sad to say, many of the Virginians, went on an uncontrolled rampage that lasted for two full days. Our soldiers sought drink first, then whatever valuables they could lay their hands on. When there was nothing more of value to be had, furniture and other goods were destroyed for the sake of destruction. No woman's virtue was safe, and many were violated numerous times. Some survived physically but with their minds impaired. Prisoners were abused and more than a few beaten to death. Officers who tried to stop this riotous behaviour were shot. Some histories of the war have tried to excuse these events by pointing to the difficulty of the assault, but I cannot accept their arguments. Sir Owen Madden, whose *A History of Spain and Portugal, 1760–1814*, I've already recommended, is more honest. He bluntly states that the British Army disgraced itself at Badajoz.

Jackson's First Company was not part of the Light Division's Forlorn Hope, but once that attack failed, we tried assaulting the breach. As with all similar efforts, we failed. Once the Third and Fifth Divisions had been successful, we joined the rest of the Light Division and scrambled up the breach and into Badajoz. A few hundred French soldiers were still fighting, but the looting had already started.

With five other men, I went in search of plunder. A dozen more Virginians quickly joined us. It was not a place where one wanted to be alone or in a small group. We came on the house of Señor Bañez, a Spanish surgeon, who quickly gave us a bag of coins, hoping that this would convince us to leave. It didn't. We searched the house and soon found his wife and two daughters, who appeared to be about thirteen and fifteen, hiding in the attic. In Spanish I told the doctor that we would protect him and his family if he gave us the rest of his valuables. There was grumbling from a few of the men, who looked lustily at the girls. I was lucky to have O'Malley and a handful of other men willing to follow my direction. The doctor complied, and led us to various points in the house where he had secreted more coins and some jewellery. It was quite a find, even after being divided by nearly twenty men. I suspect he had other caches around the house, but we didn't search further. We kept our part of the bargain and stood guard over the family for the rest of the night. The next morning we escorted them out of Badajoz to a church a few miles away.

Wellington visited Badajoz the morning after the assault and ordered the looting to stop. He sent the Provost Marshal and some Portuguese soldiers to enforce this order, but they were unable to. The Portuguese soon joined our men in their drunkenness and pillage. On the second day after the assault, surviving officers and some trustworthy soldiers slowly began to restore order. Gallows were erected. A few men who'd been seen to commit the worst atrocities were hung. Others were flogged. But it would've been impossible for the earl to punish all who deserved it. It would've decimated his army.

Events like Badajoz created an image of the British soldier in Spain as the "scum of the Earth." It was an unfair characterisation. Most of the men who served in that war were honourable. They were sometimes driven to theft of food and drink as the only way to survive. Plundering was recognised as a right, but molesting civilians was not. I think I acted honourably at Badajoz. I shall find out soon enough whether the Good Lord thinks differently.

The horror of Badajoz marked all who participated in the battle for the rest of their lives. Some men fell into melancholia and could drag themselves through their duties only by dint of will. A few committed suicide. Others drank themselves into oblivion whenever they could. Visions of the assault I took part in came to me unbidden for months after the battle, much the same as the visions I'd had of killing the thief in New Jersey more than thirty years earlier. I also wondered what would've happened if the Virginians who were guarding Señor Bañez and his family had been confronted by another group of soldiers bent on ravishing the women. Would we have fought them, stood aside, or joined them? Thankfully that question never arose.

I didn't discuss Badajoz with Samuel and John the way we'd discussed previous battles. We didn't have the words to describe what had happened or how we felt about it. Instead we focused on the future.

"Where do you think we'll be marching next?" I asked, when the three of us were together on the third day after the battle.

"I haven't a clue," Samuel said quickly. "All Spain is before us, but the French will be waiting, whichever direction the earl chooses."

Samuel was right. We could march south to destroy the French army that was still besieging Cadiz, or east to liberate Madrid and restore the Spanish government to its capital, or north towards the French border.

"John, you usually cypher these things out," I said. "What's your guess?"

"There's no obvious choice, but my guess is we'll head north. Wellington has to worry about feeding us. The roads are better in that direction, so there's at least a chance that the commissary wagons can keep up with us."

After Badajoz, only 267 Virginians were fit for duty. Fewer than a hundred of the thousand men who'd mustered at Fort Roanoke in November 1805 were still with the regiment. Some had deserted in 1806, or stayed in New Orleans in 1808, but most had either been killed in battle, died of illness, or been invalided out of the army because of their wounds. Of the group of seven that had travelled from Davidson's Fort after I enlisted, only three remained: Sergeant Pew, Manfred Zellenbach, and me. Randolph Cunningham had deserted, Harry Judkins and Gideon Long had died in our failed assault on New Orleans, and Morgan Trotter had been invalided out of the army after he lost a leg at the Battle of Coa Bridge.

The loss of officers in the battle led to brevet appointments for many, but not for Captain Jackson, and thus, not for me. Jackson's malaise was now obvious to many and he was no longer seen as a candidate for advancement. It didn't appear to bother him, and it certainly didn't bother me. I was happy to be his sergeant.

Wellington wanted his army away from Badajoz and the evil it represented as quickly as possible. He marched us back to Ciudad Rodrigo, where we were put to work repairing the fortress walls. This work had a salutary effect on me, and on many others. Slowly the army returned to its normal state. After a week or so, some men were able to banter, though their jests often had a macabre tone.

We still had no hint as to what lay in store for us.

CHAPTER 29

A week after we arrived at Ciudad Rodrigo, Lieutenant Conroy brought 457 recruits to join the regiment, 16 fewer than we'd sent to Shorncliffe. A few had deserted, the others had died or been wounded in training. Still Conroy brought more new additions to the regiments than expected. He was rewarded with promotion to captain, and given command of a new Seventh Company, made up of half new recruits, half veterans transferred from the six existing companies, including, to my disappointment, Manfred Zellenbach. I thought I'd broken all links with Davidson's Fort, but meeting Victor Ashe had re-established a connexion. Zellenbach embodied that connexion and I regretted that he'd be more distant. Sergeant Pew was assigned to whip the new company into shape. The rest of the recruits were assigned to the old companies, some of which were over strength. When I pointed this out to Captain Jackson, he said that the situation would not last for long, that battle and disease would soon reduce our numbers.

As I've previously written, Conroy was a gormless officer, held in low regard by the regiment and often the victim of practical jokes. He seemed to accept his treatment and laughed along with the rest of us.

Conroy needed to choose a second sergeant for his company, but didn't do so immediately. I hoped that he might choose Samuel

Smith, who deserved the promotion as much as any man in the regiment. After three days, Conroy chose Corporal Ford of the Fifth Company as his sergeant. He let it be known that he'd made this choice because Ford had never demeaned him.

"I'm sorry that Conroy didn't choose you to be his sergeant," I told Samuel the next time I saw him.

"I didn't deserve the position," he replied.

"What do you mean? You're as good a corporal as any in the Virginians."

"I hope that's true. But I've made as many jokes at Conroy's expense as any one. They must've hurt him deeply, even if he laughed along with us."

"So he chose Ford to get revenge?"

"I don't think that's fair," Samuel said. "Ford's a good man and will be a competent sergeant."

I didn't reply, but I knew that Samuel was right. Ford was a deeply religious man, one of the few in the Virginians, who always tried to do the right thing. That's why he didn't join in taking advantage of Conroy, and now he was being rewarded for his conduct.

The French Army in Spain, whilst more numerous than Wellington's, was a small fraction of what France could muster. I'd always wondered why, and finally decided to ask John Sevier for his opinion.

"'Tis simple. Dumouriez has to worry far more about the Austrians and Russians than about us. He can't conquer either of them. Their empires are too big. But he has to keep most of his army in the east to prevent them from combining and marching west towards France. We wouldn't last a month if Dumouriez was free to mass the full weight of the French Army against us."

"So should I be praying for the health of Emperor Leopold and Tsar Alexander?"

"I wouldn't go that far. They're despots who make our rulers look like saints. Pray for the strength of their armies and the wisdom of their generals."

In June our army began marching towards Salamanca, a city fifty miles east and a little north of Ciudad Rodrigo. We took the city without a fight a week later, but we didn't stay long — the earl was far more interested in destroying the French Army. We manoeuvred for a month before he found the opportunity he sought.

On 22nd July, the French tried to circle around our army and cut our supply line from Portugal. In doing so, they extended their flank, and opened a mile-long gap between their forward division and the main part of their army. They also didn't know that the Third Division was in position to defend the road to Portugal. Wellington ordered the Third to attack the forward French division whilst three other divisions attacked the main part of the French Army. The French were caught completely by surprise and vanquished in short order. The Light Division, which was at the far end of Wellington's line, played only a minor role in this battle. I didn't even fire my rifle. The battle became known as the Battle of Salamanca, even though it was fought some ten miles from the city.

The French lost fifteen thousand men at Salamanca, half of them taken as prisoners. Those who survived fled eastward, abandoning their wounded comrades, many of whom burnt to death when the dried grass that covered much of the battlefield caught fire. It was an unqualified victory and raised the earl's stature even higher. He'd long been known as a brilliant defensive general, but now his ability to be aggressive when given favourable circumstances was also recognised.

Regiments in most armies, including the British, have colours—unique flags that they carry on parade and into battle. Because the colours are the symbol of the regiment, protecting them is given highest priority. Capturing the enemy's colours enhances a victory, whilst losing one's own colours is a disgrace. But the French went further. Emulating Roman legions, each French division had an eagle, a gold-covered statue of the bird, which they carried into battle atop a long pole. French soldiers revered their eagles as much as their regimental colours.

At Salamanca, the French lost two eagles and six regimental colours, which devastated their morale. Their army had lost battles before, but never so decisively. Our earlier victories had convinced us that the French were not invincible, but encouraged by their revolutionary slogans, the French acted as if they couldn't be beaten. After Salamanca even the most ardent revolutionaries had to accept that their army was no longer the all-conquering force it once was.

Our victory at Salamanca left Madrid, a hundred miles to the southeast, open to attack. Marshal Masséna, his entourage—

presumably including his beautiful young mistress—and the French government of Spain, abandoned the city and retreated to Valencia, on the Mediterranean. Our army entered Madrid on 12th August and was greeted by crowds of Spanish happy to be free after four years of French rule. For days we were offered bread, fruit, and wine by the celebrating citizens. Even though our pay was six months behind, after plundering Ciudad Rodrigo and Badajoz, most of the Virginians had enough money to buy all the food, brandy, and women they wanted. I ate better those first few days than I had since returning from Virginia.

Wellington's conquest of Madrid brought him another promotion, his second of the year. He was now to be known as the Marquess of Wellington.

The French had invaded Spain in 1808, and by early 1810 controlled the whole country except for a small enclave at Cadiz, the southernmost port on Spain's Atlantic coast. What remained of the Spanish government took refuge there. The French laid siege to the city, but without a navy to shut off resupply from the sea, were unable to prevail. When General Soult, commander of the French forces in southern Spain, learned that Masséna had abandoned Madrid, and that he faced attack from the rear, he abandoned the siege and withdrew northeast towards Valencia. All of southern Spain was now free of the French. The Spanish government quickly made its way to Madrid and, with great ceremony, re-established itself in its capital.

"Watson, care for a little entertainment?" Corporal O'Malley asked on our third night in Madrid.

"What do you have in mind?" I asked. I'd drunk enough brandy to be willing to try almost anything.

"I've learned of an establishment a short distance from here where a man might purchase a little female company," he replied. The lecherous look on his face left no question as to the nature of that female company.

"I'm game. Lead on."

We walked about a quarter mile into a shabby part of the city to a house with two red lanterns outside its entrance. We weren't the only ones who wanted to make use of its services. There was a noisy queue outside the door. That was enough to sober me up. I bade O'Malley goodnight and returned to our bivouac. O'Malley appeared the next morning, his mission accomplished.

The marquess rested our army in Madrid for a month before marching north first to Valladolid, then to Burgos, which he would have to besiege and storm. He couldn't expect the Fourth and Light Divisions, which had paid such a high price at Badajoz, to lead yet another Forlorn Hope. Our two divisions were left to garrison Madrid. I wasn't sorry when the rest of the army marched off. Madrid offered comforts that wouldn't be available elsewhere in Spain.

The night after the marquess marched off, O'Malley suggested another visit to the brothel. Even though I'd walked away before entering on our first visit, the experience had awakened feelings of lust that'd long been dormant. Had O'Malley not suggested the visit, I might've gone by myself.

With far fewer soldiers in the city, and many of those who remained out of funds, there was no queue. The woman who serviced me was attractive enough in a dark-skinned way, but I found the experience demeaning. I remembered my nights with Awinita and with Judy Slater, and was ashamed to have sunk this low. I'd had the same feeling more than a decade earlier after several visits to Betty, the Cherokee whore who lived outside of Davidson's Fort. I decided to stop visiting her and hadn't been with a whore since. I renewed my resolve and when O'Malley next suggested a visit, I told him I wasn't interested. He gave me quizzical look, but didn't say anything. I'm certain that I gained a reputation as a prude, but that wasn't something I was going to worry about.

The marquess' attack on Burgos failed and he was forced to retreat to Ciudad Rodrigo. This left the two divisions in Madrid at great risk. At the end of October we quit the city. The crowds, which had so enthusiastically greeted us two-and-a-half months earlier, shouted curses and vile imprecations at us. They were justified in doing so. We were leaving them to the mercy of the French, who would reappear as soon as we were safely gone.

The Light Division's march back to the Portuguese border was the most difficult I experienced during my time as a soldier. The weather was foul. We were continually drenched with cold rain. The Commissary Corps hadn't anticipated our march and on most days couldn't supply us with either rum or rations. We bought or stole what wine and food we could, adding to the reputation we'd earned at Badajoz as the scum of the Earth.

One noon we were issued a ration of biscuits, but told to put them in our knapsacks and continue our march. At mid-afternoon we came upon three cows, which we commandeered and slaughtered. The animals were quickly butchered and slabs of meat handed out. It had been raining all day, and lighting a fire was almost impossible. Before we had time to cook any of the meat, we were ordered to march. A few of the Virginians threw their portions of meat away, but I, as most of the regiment, stuffed the still bloody meat into my knapsack with my bread ration. At sunset, when we were allowed to stop, the blood from the meat had soaked my biscuits, turning them into a soggy mess with an extremely unpleasant taste. I was so hungry that I ate the blood-soaked bread, whilst trying to cook my slab of beef over an inadequate fire. Before I could finish cooking the meat, I was racked with severe stomach pains, which caused me to wretch up the bread I'd eaten. As soon as my stomach settled a bit, I ate the beef, which was now cooked. Sick as I was, I had to eat whatever food was available.

The soles of our shoes wore out—there were no replacements. Many of us walked barefooted and couldn't keep up with the pace of the march. Stragglers were listed as missing. Some of them fought the French vanguard, which was not far behind us, and were either killed or taken prisoner. A few deserted to the French, whilst others eventually returned to our lines.

The Virginians had scores of men listed as missing on the march, mostly from the ranks of the new recruits. I was certain that none of the handful of veterans who went missing joined the French, but I was far less sure about the new recruits. These men may have become friends with each other, but they were still outsiders as far as the rest of us were concerned.

The French, who'd been harassing the Light Division, finally caught up with us only thirty miles from Ciudad Rodrigo. We had to cross the fast-flowing River Huebra, which caused confusion and slowed our march. We were still a mile from the ford when a messenger came running up to Colonel Lancaster with orders to defend the ridge above the river. The colonel called a quick conference with his company commanders. Five companies, including the First, were assigned positions facing the French in the oak forest atop the ridge. The remaining two companies were held in reserve, and positioned just below the ridgeline on the river side.

We didn't have long to wait. A troop of French dragoons started making its way up the slope towards us.

"Hold your fire," Jackson ordered in little more than a whisper. When the first of the dragoons was within a hundred yards, he shouted, "First rank, fire."

Fifty rifles fired almost in unison. Five dragoons fell. The rest beat a hasty retreat. We lost no casualties in that attack.

It didn't take long for the dragoons to reform, and to be joined by several companies of voltigeurs. The second French attack was more cautious. The dragoons let the voltigeurs lead the attack. They were skilful and used the trees for cover, but their muskets were no match for our rifles. We must have killed or wounded several dozen Frenchmen before they broke off their attack.

More French appeared and it looked like there might be a full division, supported by several pieces of artillery, available for the next attack.

"Prepare to withdraw," Colonel Lancaster shouted as soon as it was obvious that the French were forming up for their third attack. "Form a column."

I was perplexed by this order. A column would give French gunners, who were rolling their cannon into place on the ridgeline we'd just vacated, a much easier target. The colonel must have judged that the dragoons we'd seen earlier posed a greater threat to our safety than the cannon. We could repel a cavalry charge in column formation better than in loose files.

We paid a high price for the colonel's decision. We moved as quickly as we could, but lost more than a score dead or wounded that day, most to cannon fire.

The regiments that crossed the river before us had set up a strong defensive position to prevent the French from following. We quickly retreated behind that position and were granted a much-needed rest.

We'd lost most of our baggage train. No rations were issued, but we did commandeer a few cattle and had meat, which we managed to cook despite the wet weather.

We still had more than a day's march to Ciudad Rodrigo. We marched the first day on empty stomachs, then got a bread ration— no meat or rum—that evening. We arrived outside the fortress the following day. We were told that we'd be issued three days' rations, but were so hungry and so distrustful of the commissary that we charged their wagons. When the commissary staff saw a horde of Virginians running towards them, they mounted their wagons and beat a hasty retreat. We were left without food and in an ugly mood. Finally, with two companies of redcoats to protect them, the commissary wagons returned. With infantry muskets pointed at us, we were issued the bread and rum rations we'd been promised. I ate and drank these greedily, after which I was overcome by a wave of exhaustion. I found a tree to lean on, pulled my blanket around me, and was asleep in a few seconds.

When I awoke the next morning, the enormity of what the Virginians had done struck me. I'd never seen a whole regiment punished and could only guess at what lay in store for us. But someone must have taken mercy on us because, other than a stern lecture from Colonel Lancaster, there was no further mention of our insurrection.

The year that had begun so hopefully with the capture of Ciudad Rodrigo had turned to ashes. We ended in almost the same place as we'd started with very little to show for our efforts. By now I knew better than to worry about the course of the war. Wellington had ordered his army into winter quarters, and I hoped that winter would last longer this year than it had the last.

Captain Jackson and the First Company were assigned to a set of houses inside Ciudad Rodrigo's wall and we began making them as comfortable as we could. We received regular rations, which we supplemented with food and wine purchased from the village. The difficulties of the march from Madrid and our behaviour at the commissary wagons became unpleasant memories.

The woods around Ciudad Rodrigo had pheasant and a few deer. After seeing some officers return from hunting with fresh meat, I asked Captain Jackson whether I could take a few men to do the same. He thought it was a good idea, but when he asked permission from Colonel Lancaster, he was rejected. This caused great unhappiness in the regiment, as it showed once again that enlisted men couldn't hope to enjoy any of the privileges of officers.

Our unhappiness was compounded in early December when Colonel Lancaster read Wellington's latest general order at morning parade. The marquess had expressed his displeasure at his army's proclivity for plundering on many previous occasions and threatened dire consequences for those caught stealing from the local population. He'd also complained about stragglers. But in this general order, he went a step further. He stated that the number of soldiers straggling from their regiments for no reason other than plunder was a disgrace to the army, and strong proof of lack of discipline. He ordered the Provost Marshal to arrest officers who allowed straggling. No concession was made for mud, lack of shoes and rations, or any of the other difficulties of our march to Ciudad Rodrigo. If we straggled, it must have been because we were off searching for plunder.

The colonel, who at least in theory faced arrest if any of the Virginians straggled, was as unhappy as we were:

"Virginians," he began, once he'd finished reading Wellington's order, "I know that you acted with great fortitude on our recent march and did the best you could in trying circumstances. However, I won't expose myself to possible arrest by allowing straggling in the future. Captains will be responsible for seeing that their companies maintain the pace of the march. If any men are having legitimate difficulties keeping up, their needs must be reported and attended to. Any attempt at looting will be punished with the utmost severity." He paused for a few moments to allow his message to be absorbed, then dismissed us.

The marquess' order was the main topic of discussion for a few days after we heard it read. To a man, the Virginians were dismayed that Wellington had so little concern about the difficulties we faced. We thought he worried at least a little about our welfare, if for no other reason than to keep us fit enough to continue fighting. A few men thought that since he'd not been on the march from Madrid to Ciudad Rodrigo, he might not have known of the difficulties we faced. But we soon learned that the men who'd retreated from Burgos to Ciudad Rodrigo had experienced the same trying conditions as the Virginians.

Since the army was in winter quarters and not marching anywhere, we didn't have a chance to see if or how the marquess' order would be enforced. That would have to wait for spring.

As usual, we celebrated New Year's Day 1813 with a double ration of rum. Some of the other sergeants had concocted a panto. It starred Corporal O'Malley, who played Messéna as a decrepit old man with a huge stomach. O'Malley hobbled on stage aided by a cane, and what was supposed to be a beautiful young woman, to report to Sergeant Sommerville, who played Dumouriez. Sommerville was sitting on a throne, surrounded by more beautiful women. Since beautiful women were in short supply in the Virginians' ranks, the youngest privates in the regiment filled these roles. Masséna said his soldiers had won every battle they had fought. Sergeant Pew dressed as a Virginian snuck up behind O'Malley and kicked him in the backside as punishment for this lie. O'Malley went sprawling, but, aided by his beautiful consort, struggled to his feet and continued his report, only to lie and be kicked in the backside again. This went on several more times until Sommerville asked why the British were still in Spain. O'Malley answered "To give my soldiers the chance to win more victories," for which he received a final boot in the arse. It was the crudest type of humour, but all in attendance laughed heartily and congratulated the players.

A few days into the new year, I asked John Sevier where he though we'd be marching once the winter was over.

"Since the French haven't retaken control of Spain south of Madrid, there are only two choices, east to Madrid or north towards the French border. After last year's debacle, I don't think the marquess will want to return to Madrid any time soon, so I guess we'll be heading north."

During the winter our army was reinforced and now totalled more than eighty thousand men. Most of the new troops were Johnny Newcombes and looked much like the recruits we'd received in the past. But we were also joined by two regiments of Household Cavalry, parade ground soldiers who hadn't seen combat in many years. They were dressed in fine uniforms—not the ragged attire we wore—and were mounted on large strong horses—not the Portuguese or Spanish nags that the rest of the army used.

"I wonder how they'll survive against the French," I mused the next time Samuel, John, and I were together.

"They might do better than you think," Samuel replied. "Their horses are stronger than the ones the French ride, and their parade ground training means they'll stay in formation."

"Someone at Horse Guards must think this war is nearly over to be sending them here," John added. "They want the Household Cavalry to be in at final victory to add to their laurels."

"How can anyone think that we're close to victory after we were forced to retreat last fall and ended up with little to show for the year?" I asked incredulously.

"We may've ended up in the same place as we started, but half of Spain is now free of the French," John replied. "Their army retreated from southern Spain when we took Madrid, but didn't go back when we left. They aren't strong enough to fight both us and the Spanish."

"But it's a long way from freeing half of Spain to defeating the French."

"True, but you're not paying attention to what's happening in Russia and Germany. That's where the real war is. We're just a side-show. The Russians have stopped the French and are pushing them back—the first time they've been able to do that. When they think the time is right, the Prussians and Austrians will join them. Together they have more than enough soldiers to overwhelm the French."

"If that's the case, why doesn't Wellington sit tight and let those other countries do the fighting?"

"An interesting thought, but I think the marquess and the Prince Regent want as much glory for Britain as we can earn for them. We, and the Portuguese, are the only countries that never made peace with France. How could we give up the fight before we can claim victory?"

Samuel and I had no answer for that question.

It was only many years later, after I'd read several histories of the war with France, that I realised how perceptive John Sevier had been; 1812 was indeed the turning point in that long war. Early that year, Dumouriez had decided to strike a blow against the Russians. He massed a huge army on the Russian-Polish border and in late June, when the spring mud had dried enough to allow his army to move, he attacked. The Russians gave ground grudgingly and in September fought the French to a standstill at the village of Borodino. The carnage of that battle was unprecedented. Over seventy thousand men, more than thirty thousand French and forty thousand Russians, were killed or wounded in a single day. The French licked their wounds for a few days, then began a slow retreat back to Poland.

The French had expected to spend the winter in Moscow, not in bivouacs in the Polish swamps. By November, there was hard frost every night. By early December the temperature never rose above freezing. Afterward, many claimed that it was the coldest winter in memory. The crapauds had only summer uniforms and canvas tents to protect them against the cold. Thousands froze to death and thousands more lost limbs to frostbite. The Russians joked that General Winter was their best ally. It wasn't a joke. General Winter probably killed more Frenchmen than the Russian Army.

Russian guerrillas savaged the retreating French, torturing and killing any crapaud they could lay their hands on. The French retaliated by shooting or hanging hundreds of Russians, most of whom had nothing to do with the attacks on their army. It was a repeat of the brutality that had been practised in Spain in the four years since they invaded.

French vulnerability was not lost on the Germans or Italians who had suffered under French rule for a decade or more. They, too, formed guerrilla groups to attack the French, and suffered French reprisals. By the end of 1812, there was no place outside of France where a French soldier was safe.

French vulnerability also was not lost on the rulers of Prussia and Austria. In Fall 1812, Prussia, which had been under French domination for many years, and was a reluctant partner in the invasion of Russia, switched sides to become Russia's ally. In Spring 1813, the Austrians judged the time right and again declared war against France. The armies of these three countries totalled nearly a half-million men, six times the number Wellington commanded. Sevier had been right when he called our war in Spain a sideshow.

Through Spring 1813 the sergeants' mess was abuzz with reports about Dumouriez's efforts to rebuild his army. We had bits of information gleaned from the London newspapers and from our conversations with officers, but I didn't know how much of it to trust. Captain Jackson had become easier to approach, now that his main concern seemed to be surviving the war, not winning glory. One morning in late March, after making my morning report, I decided that the time was as good as any to question him about developments in France.

"Captain Jackson, sir. What do you think about the reports that Dumouriez is raising a new army?"

"I'm sure they're true. What else can he do?"

"I've read he's conscripting men who'd avoided the levee en masse in the past."

An article in *The Times* said that Frenchmen who'd avoided the levee by faking marriages or injuring themselves slightly were now being conscripted. The levee, which was supposed to take twenty-one-year-old men, was now enlisting boys as young as seventeen. According to the newspaper, between the new conscription, the grief caused by the loss of so many of their sons, and the higher taxes they had to pay, the French peasantry was angry to the point of rebellion.

"I've read the same reports," Jackson said. "They say the French could rebel against Dumouriez, but I wonder if that's not wishful thinking."

"Why wouldn't the French rebel?" I asked. "They've suffered enough."

"True, but a rebellion needs a leader, and nothing I've read says that leader has appeared."

"The French didn't have a leader when they rebelled in 1789. The leaders appeared after the rebellion started."

"It's not as simple as that. The French Revolution didn't start in the organised way our Great Rebellion did. It started as independent bread riots and only grew into a revolution later."

"So you don't think any of what's happening in France will affect the war."

"I didn't say that," Jackson replied testily. "The boys and men being conscripted into the French Army won't make good soldiers. They're either too young or don't want to be fighting. We probably won't see any of them here in Spain, but it should make it easier for the Russians and Prussians."

I didn't have any more questions to ask and Jackson was silent, so I took my leave. I told the other sergeants what Jackson had said. All agreed when Sergeant Pew summed it up, "No easy road for us. We get to fight the best France has to offer."

The French Army might not be what it had been, but it was still powerful. During the early summer, we learned that Dumouriez had gone on the attack in Germany and that our allies manoeuvred rather than fight him. That didn't sound like good news, but by that time the demands of our own war took precedence over any worries about developments in Germany.

CHAPTER 30

On 22nd May, our army broke winter quarters and began marching along the road to Salamanca, on the way to Madrid. My first thought was that John had been wrong in saying we'd head north, but he cautioned against coming to a conclusion too quickly. Wellington was well known for misdirection, and this could be only a feint. As usual, Sevier was correct. After three days, long before we reached Salamanca, we turned towards the French border.

Our advance was up a series of valleys with seemingly impassable mountains on either side. The French tried to block our army's advance by setting up defensive lines across the valleys. Each time they did, the marquess sent the Light Division through the mountains to turn their flank, forcing them to retreat again.

On 18th June, the Virginians and 95th Rifles, who were at the vanguard of our army, surprised several battalions of French troops in a village called San Millan. They must not have realised we were anywhere close, because they hadn't set out picquets or any other defence. We charged and drove them from the village, then chased them for a short distance down the road before returning to see what plunder we could find in the wagons they'd abandoned.

After six years of fighting, the rules for plunder were well established. Food, drink and anything light enough to carry belonged to the first man who found them. He was expected to share some of his find with his messmates, usually by converting it into wine or brandy. Wagons, draft animals, and items too large to carry belonged to the regiment. The army took what it could use. The rest was auctioned off, with the proceeds shared amongst all members of the regiment. With so many dividing the takings, each man usually got only a shilling or two.

I'd become selective in my choice of plunder. I was no longer interested in souvenirs, and only took cash or things that could quickly be turned into cash, or food and drink that could be consumed in a few days. I watched with amusement as some of the new recruits picked up items of women's clothing and similar useless items from the luggage the French had left behind.

Three days later we marched through a mountain pass into the valley of the River Zadorra. The French Army was arrayed on the north side of the river, waiting for our attack. We had no opportunity to turn their flank and force them to again retreat. Wellington planned for several regiments to attack simultaneously at different points along the river. The Virginians would be one of those regiments. We were ordered to capture one of the bridges over the Zadorra. We arrayed ourselves on the ridge above the river, but then were ordered to wait whilst the other regiments got in place to make their attacks. The French quickly noted our presence and started firing at us. They were too far away to do any harm, but we'd lost any element of surprise we might've had.

We were finally given the order to attack and started down the ridge, when an old Spanish peasant came running up, waving his arms frantically to get Colonel Lancaster's attention. The colonel halted our advance and signalled to me to come along to translate.

"*Commandante*," the peasant began, "there is a bridge less than two of your miles from here that is unprotected."

"How would we get there?" the colonel asked.

"Follow that path," the peasant answered, pointing to a narrow rocky track on the side of the hill.

"You will lead," the colonel said, "and you will pay with your life if you have lied."

"I am not lying," the peasant responded. "The French killed my son. All I want is to see them dead."

The peasant, whose name was Miguel, wasn't lying, and at noon, little more than a half hour later, we crossed an unprotected bridge into a village called Tres Puentes. We moved forward cautiously along the road out of the village. We had no difficulty pushing aside the few voltigeurs guarding that road and soon found ourselves athwart the French right flank, but we weren't strong enough to exploit that advantage. We had to wait until we were reinforced.

Our manoeuvre was so unexpected that the British gunners on the heights above the river mistook us for French soldiers and treated us to a barrage that killed several of our men before they could be told that we were on the same side. One of the dead was Sergeant Pew. I immediately remembered him telling me and the five other recruits he marched from Davidson's Fort to Fort Roanoke that he'd rather be killed by a French musket ball than face the indignity of living out his life as a pensioner at Chelsea Hospital. He'd gotten his wish. He'd died in battle, though from a British cannon ball. He'd probably never considered this possibility, but then again, cynical old soldier that he was, perhaps he had.

I didn't mourn Pew. As my first introduction to the army, he'd taught me much I needed to know, but he wasn't my friend, nor was I his. I added his name to the long list of men I'd known and seen die. We left his body to be buried after the battle.

The Third and Seventh Divisions advanced across the Zadorra at numerous points. We soon had a sufficient force on the north side of the river to attack the Hill of Arinez, which dominated this part of the battlefield. By this time the French resistance had begun to crumble and we took the hill with few casualties. Once it was in our hands, the French gave up the fight. The Battle of Vitoria, named after the main town in the area, was over. It'd been a clear victory for the marquess. The French abandoned all but one of their cannon, and fled in disarray. Wellington probably could've destroyed the French army had he pursued them vigorously, but he couldn't because his army was more interested in plunder.

The French left hundreds of wagons loaded with loot, and what loot it was. Masséna and his entourage had evacuated Madrid and were fleeing back to France with the booty they'd stolen in the four years they'd ruled Spain. Their route took them through Vitoria, which they must've believed was well protected by their army. When that army was defeated, they abandoned their belongings and fled however they could. The centre of Vitoria was impassable as men scrambled over the wagons breaking open crates and various other containers stuffed with coins, jewellery, and other valuables.

O'Malley was the most fortunate of the Virginians. He came upon a Spanish mule driver leading a very heavily laden animal away from town. O'Malley confronted the man, who tried to put up a fight, but was soon subdued. The mule was carrying Spanish coins worth nearly a thousand pounds. O'Malley realised that he would have to protect this trove and assembled his messmates and a few others, including me. We each were rewarded with a hundred Spanish dollars, almost twenty pounds. O'Malley put most of the rest of his windfall on account with the paymaster, who was more than happy to take the coins. It would allow him to pay at least some of our back pay. O'Malley was the first to be paid. I don't know whether anyone other than John Sevier appreciated the irony of O'Malley paying himself.

Had Wellington enforced his order about arresting officers who allowed their men to straggle in search of plunder, he would've had to gaol most of his senior officers. The men who looted Vitoria were straggling in search of plunder rather than pursuing the French. Their officers did nothing to stop them, and in many cases joined the search for swag. The marquess said nothing in the days that followed the battle and looting, and we thought he'd forgotten the issue. We were wrong. When, only a week after the battle, some of the 95th Rifles were too complete in stripping a farm of its produce and firewood, he had one of his staff write an angry letter to General Alten, Commander of the Light Division, again saying that such looting was a sign of poor discipline. This time Wellington did not threaten to arrest officers, but such action couldn't have been far from his mind.

Two weeks after the Battle of Vitoria, prisoners told us that Messéna had been relieved of his command and ordered to return to France, presumably to face the French equivalent of a court of enquiry about his many defeats at our hands. Marshal Soult was now commander of the French forces in Spain. This seemed a strange choice, since Soult had been unable to capture Cadiz, despite besieging it for two years. He'd not had much more success against the

Spanish guerrillas, who now controlled all of southern Spain. But as we soon found out, Soult was a better general than we guessed.

The Pyrenees are the mountains, some of which are more than ten thousand feet high, that separate Spain from France. They are a formidable barrier, which can be crossed only through a limited number of passes. Spies told us that Soult had been very busy fortifying these passes. By mid-July we were at the base of the mountains, expecting to have to attack Soult's fortifications in the next few days. Our army had marched four hundred miles in forty days and fought a major battle. It was now strung out over a fifty-mile front from San Sebastian on the coast to Pamplona. The French still held both of these towns, and fully a quarter of our army had been diverted to besieging them. But we were confident. We had every reason to be. We'd driven the French back and were now poised to enter France itself.

Soult didn't wait for us to attack. On 25th July he launched simultaneous assaults on the towns of Maya and Roncesvalles on the Spanish side of the mountains with forces that greatly outnumbered ours. The Light Division was not involved in either battle, but we were forced to retreat when the divisions defending the towns retreated. Our army regrouped ten miles north of Pamplona and on 28th July withstood a determined French attack. The battle was a stalemate. Both sides held their positions. Two days later, Wellington was able to bring up sufficient reinforcements to drive the French back to their fortifications in the Pyrenees.

The Virginians and most of the Light Division were deployed to hold the southern side of the River Bidossa, which followed the western part of the Spanish-French border. Our positions were near the town of Vera, a few miles inside Spain and about twenty miles from the river's mouth. We hadn't yet had the pleasure of walking on French soil. We spent a quiet August—the focus of the fighting had moved westward to the siege at San Sebastian. At night we could hear the siege guns.

On 31st August, Soult launched a two-pronged attack to relieve San Sebastian. The first prong advanced along the coast road. The three Spanish divisions defending the road fought well and were able to defeat the French without any help, the first time they'd done so in a large battle.

The second prong was through the pass north of Vera. Four French divisions marched through the pass, crossed the Bidossa, and advanced cautiously towards the Light Division's positions. By afternoon, Soult realised that the other prong of his attack had failed and ordered his men to withdraw. However, it had been raining hard, and the Bidossa had risen to a height of six feet, making the French retreat difficult. Thousands were trapped on the south side of the river. One French division found a narrow bridge that was defended by the Virginians' Fourth Company. Captain Squire's men held off the French for nearly two hours before being overwhelmed. The captain was killed and only a handful of his men escaped death, injury or capture.

During the battle, the Virginians appealed to General Skerrett, who was now in command of the Light Division's First Brigade, for help in holding the bridge, but none was forthcoming. This caused much anger. Skerrett was relieved of his command, more likely because he had missed an opportunity to destroy a large French force than because of any animosity his troops felt for him.

The survivors of the Fourth Company were distributed amongst the other companies. The Fourth Company no longer existed, but its valiant fight would be remembered by all who served with them in the Virginians.

Immediately after Soult's attack Colonel Lancaster asked for volunteers for the Forlorn Hope that would soon be leading the attack on San Sebastian. A few of the new recruits volunteered, but none of the older soldiers who'd survived the assault on Ciudad Rodrigo and Badajoz wanted to repeat the experience. San Sebastian fell to a combined British-Portuguese assault a week after Soult's attacks failed. Pamplona, which wasn't assaulted, surrendered at the end of October, by which time our army was already in France.

I realise, looking back over some of the pages I've written, that I've spent an inordinate amount of time describing the battles I fought in. Vitoria was a turning point. There was still nearly a year of hard fighting ahead, and we did suffer minor setbacks, but there was no question that we would prevail and defeat the French. The French did not yield easily, and many good men died prising them out of the defensive positions they took. I'll tell the story of that last year more succinctly lest the details become overwhelming.

CHAPTER 31

Those of us wise enough not to volunteer for the Forlorn Hope spent the month of September contemplating the fortifications the French had built to defend a massive ridge known as La Grande Rhune, about three miles north-east of the town of Vera. We knew we would have to assault them, and feared that the butcher bill would be just as high as if we were assaulting a fortress like Ciudad Rodrigo or Badajoz. But Wellington was too wise to plan a direct assault. The Spanish would mount a diversionary attack at La Grande Rhune. The Light Division would make the main attack over a smaller mountain on the French flank called La Petite Rhune.

On the morning of 7th October, we were awakened at two a.m., had breakfast, and began marching towards our objective. We were told to maintain strict silence, not to alert the French that we were on the way. By dawn we were in position and waiting for the three cannon shots from our artillery that would signal the assault, which was to be a bayonet charge.

All worked as planned. Once we started our charge, the French fired a volley, then fled. When the crapauds on La Grande Rhune realised that we were on their flank, they too retired. By mid-afternoon, we were in control of the heights, taking our comfort in the huts they'd built and eating the food they'd left. We were in France.

Our arrival in France created a new set of problems with our allies, the Portuguese and Spanish. We were now far from the borders of Portugal. The caçadores, the Portuguese infantrymen whose valour we'd come to respect, no longer fought with the same zeal they had when they were protecting their homeland. Wellington could not afford to lose them and made the best of it. The Spanish were a greater problem. They'd not been gentle with civilians in their own country, and once we crossed into France, any restraint they'd shown disappeared. In November, they violently plundered the town of Ascain, saying that it was retribution for by the way the French had treated Spain. The marquess couldn't risk the French countryside rebelling against our army, and issued orders that there be no retribution against the French or plundering of their towns. All supplies were to be paid for. In an attempt to enforce these orders, Wellington sent the Spanish back across the border, provoking the fury of both the Spanish government and their generals.

One would've thought that every member of Wellington's Army would joyously greet the realisation that the war would soon be over, but many junior officers, and even some enlisted men, began worrying about how to stay in the army. Everyone knew that once the French were beaten, the army would shrink. Fencible regiments, such as the Virginians, would be discharged. Some permanent regiments would see one or more of their battalions disbanded. Others would cease to exist. Officers who couldn't retain their positions would be put on half-pay; enlisted men would simply be sent packing.

I had no idea what I'd do after the war, but realised that the army would have no use for a fifty-year-old sergeant. I resolved not to think about my future and to concentrate on surviving the rest of the war. I wasn't always successful in this resolve. When I did think about my future, I couldn't come up with any attractive alternatives.

Whilst it was normal practice for junior officers and enlisted men to stay with their regiments for the duration of their service, exceptions could be made if another regiment had unfilled positions. The year's fighting had left many such vacancies in the Light Division's other regiments, and Colonel Lancaster was willing to provide good characters for those Virginians who wished to transfer. In short order, Captains Craig and Hopewell, the British captains who commanded the Fifth and Sixth Companies, transferred to the 43rd and 52nd respectively, both regular army infantry regiments.

Lieutenants Sheridan and Moss, who were promoted to captains, filled these vacancies. This left the regiment with only two lieutenants, both of whom requested and were granted transfers. The Virginians were back in the same situation they'd been in when the regiment was first formed. Each company had a captain, but not the two lieutenants that would normally be on its roster. Sergeants and corporals assumed their duties.

"Why do you think the colonel is allowing so many officers to transfer?" Samuel asked me.

"He's British Army, and that's his first loyalty. The officers he's transferred are better than most who buy their commissions."

"But he's leaving the Virginians in a precarious position."

"I don't think so. You as a corporal and I as a sergeant know more about how to do things than most of the officers who are leaving."

"You're right about that."

Seeing the success that officers were having transferring out of the regiment, some of the younger men applied for transfer. Manfred Zellenbach was one of them. He came to me on the day he was to leave to join the 43rd.

"I wanted to say goodbye, Sergeant Watson."

"Manfred, we've know each other long enough for you to call me William."

"I know, William, but the 43rd is regular army and I won't be able to address a sergeant by his Christian name."

"Why are you doing this?" I asked. "The war is almost over. You could go back to North Carolina."

"There's nothing there for me. My parents are dead and I haven't had a letter from my brother in five years. The army's been good to me. I might as well stay on."

"Once the war is over, the army will be different."

"I know that. But I think it'll be better . . . no battles, regular rations, and a roof over you head every night . . . that's what I've heard some of the old swads say."

"I hope you're right. I wish you well."

I was sorry to see Zellenbach go. He was my last connexion in the Virginians with Davidson's Fort.

With the war ending, some officers sought opportunities to distinguish themselves with heroic acts so that they'd have preference when the selection was made between those who stayed on active duty and those who went on half-pay. Captain Newsome was one of these officers. Two weeks after Zellenbach transferred, he was in command of two companies of the 43rd skirmishing with the French at the base of Bassussarry Ridge in the foothills north of the Pyrenees. The redcoats were in a good position behind trees in a grove. The French were also in a good position in trenches on the other side of an open field. Despite orders not to proceed beyond the protection of the woods, Captain Newsome ordered his men to charge the French. Had the charge succeeded, it would have called attention to Newsome's fighting spirit, but it was a suicidal tactic. The redcoats were cut down by French musket fire. A third of them were killed, wounded, or taken prisoner, with few, if any, French casualties. Zellenbach, who'd survived eight years in the Virginians, was one of the dead. Newsome was captured, which probably saved his life. Had he returned alive, I'm sure that one of the other survivors of the battle would have found a way to take vengeance for his criminal act.

By the end of November, the Light Division had driven the French from Bassussarry Ridge and established a fortified position at Arcangues, a village in the valley on the southern side. In hindsight, this was a foolish move, since the village would be vulnerable if the French could retake the high ground. Marshal Soult hadn't given up the fight and in early December launched an attack that drove our forces from the ridge top. The French then positioned a dozen cannon only 350 yards from Arcangues, almost point blank range. Whenever French gunners were close enough, our marksmen fired on them, and sometimes disabled a gun by killing its gunners. But 350 yards was considered too far for accurate fire. That didn't stop the Virginians and 95th Rifles from filling the air with a hailstorm of lead. We killed enough of the French to discourage the rest. They withdrew, leaving us in control of the village. We retook ridge the next day.

Whilst we were engaged around Arcangues, west of us, the bulk of our army attempted to cross the River Nive to attack the French defending the city of Bayonne. Our forces met little resistance on the first day, but on the second, Soult attacked with superior numbers and forced us to retreat. There was fierce fighting for the next four days. In the end we drove the French back to Bayonne with heavy casualties. Soult also lost nearly five thousand German soldiers to the changing political scene. Three battalions deserted to our side under instructions from their ruler, the Duke of Nassau, who'd switched sides after Dumouriez's defeat at Leipzig. No longer trusting the remaining Germans, Soult sent another three thousand of them home.

We didn't formally go into winter quarters that year. Heavy rains through December and January made it impossible for either army to mount a major attack, but skirmishing continued. Half of Soult's men defended the city of Bayonne, the other half faced our troops along the River Nive.

On the morning of 30th January, the First Company was on patrol in the vicinity of Cambo-les-Bains, a town on the Nive about twenty miles upstream of Bayonne, when we came upon a company of voltigeurs in a wooded area. I was leading the most advanced squad when musket fire forced us to take cover behind trees. We returned fire and the crapauds withdrew. We thought all of them had retreated, but a few remained hidden behind trees of their own. We remained protected for a few minutes. When there was no further musket fire, we moved forward. Captain Jackson came up to survey the scene, advancing cautiously until he was about twenty yards to my right.

Suddenly a musket shot rang out and Jackson fell. That shot was followed by about a half dozen more, none of which hit our men. The crapauds who'd fired them ran off as quickly as they could. Our men felled four of them with well-placed rifle shots.

I rushed to the captain and saw the voltigeur who'd shot him only ten yards away frantically trying to reload his musket. He was poorly trained and taking far more time at the task than he should have. I ran over, knocked him senseless with the butt of my rifle, then returned to Jackson. It was too late. He was dead, his coat stained with bright red blood from a large wound in his chest. The musket ball must have penetrated his heart.

Most of the company gathered around Jackson's body, but a few, including O'Malley, pointed their rifles at the voltigeur, who looked to be no more than seventeen. I heard O'Malley shout, "I'm going to kill this bastard."

Nick Ogle and Elias Parton grabbed him. "Don't do that, Shaun. He's only a boy," Nick said in a calm voice. O'Malley wrestled with them for a few moments, then calmed down. Parton took his canteen and splashed some water on the boy's face, which woke him. He rubbed his head, then seeing a crowd of British soldiers around him started whimpering and gesturing that he was surrendering. Ogle and Parton turned loose of O'Malley and pulled the crapaud to his feet. O'Malley, now free of restraint, punched the boy savagely in the face, causing his nose to bleed, then turned away, and walked to where Jackson's body lay on the ground. Ogle gave the voltigeur a cloth to hold to his nose, searched him for anything of value—finding only a few coins—then bound the boy's hands behind him so he could be led off as a prisoner.

We used Jackson's greatcoat to form a litter and carried his body back to our lines. We buried him that afternoon. Colonel Lancaster read the funeral service. I remained dry-eyed, but more than one man turned away coughing to hide his weeping. Jackson was stern, but always fair, and, to a man, the Virginians respected him. He'd been like a father to me, especially over the past two years when he'd stopped thinking about gaining glory and began worrying about how he and the rest of the Virginians could survive the war. Every 30th January, on the anniversary of Jackson's death, I remember his kindness to me when I was wounded.

I was summoned to Colonel Lancaster's office as soon as Jackson's funeral was over. "Watson," he began, "you've been a brevet captain before and performed admirably. I'm appointing you brevet captain of the First Company. You realise that any officer who joins the regiment can replace you."

"Yes, sir, and thank you. I'll do my best."

"I'm sure you will. Dismissed."

I was surprized that the colonel didn't say more, but not in a position to question him, I saluted and left his office.

My previous stint as a brevet captain had lasted two months. I was far from certain that I could discharge all the duties of a company commander, and resolved that whenever I had a question about what to do, I'd consider how Captain Jackson would've acted. The men of the First Company were less surprised than I was about my appointment. As Samuel told me later, they expected it since I'd held the rank before.

Had I been appointed captain in another regiment, I would have immediately faced expenses for a dress uniform, a horse, and my share of the cost of the officers' mess. Luckily, the Virginians were less formal. I had to pay for my meals, but no one seemed concerned about my uniform or my having a horse. The increase in pay I received was much larger than the cost of the officers' mess. After a few months, I found a French tailor to make a captain's uniform for me. O'Malley gave me Captain Jackson's sword and shako, saying that the men of the First Company felt I should have them. The shako was not much different from the one I'd worn as a rifleman, but I always felt like an imposter when I wore the sword. I never did buy a horse.

Being the company commander again put a distance between me, Samuel, and John. I missed discussing the course of the war with John, but his insights were replaced by those of my fellow officers, who had much more information. After my first night in the officer's mess, which was devoted to memories of Captain Jackson, developments in France and the fate of the French Army in Germany seemed to be the main topics of conversation.

"I wouldn't want to be a French tax collector these days," Captain McIntyre said as we were sipping brandy after my second supper in the mess. "According to *The Times*, anyone trying to collect taxes from a French farmer is likely to be tarred and feathered, if not worse."

"That's probably why the crapaud we took prisoner the other day said that he'd not been paid in three months," Captain Dey added. "I had to laugh a bit. Most of my men haven't been paid in six months. If it weren't for the plunder from Vitoria, and the brandy they can get in trade with the French, we'd probably have a mutiny on our hands."

"Will those French farmers welcome us as we advance?" I asked.

"I think that depends on how we treat them," Colonel Lancaster said. "Thus far His Lordship has been able to enforce his orders to respect the French and pay for any supplies we take from them. Some of the French say that they prefer us to their own army, which commandeers what it wants."

"With respect, Colonel," Captain Sheridan said. "His Lordship's orders haven't been put to the test. What will happen when we capture a town? The men have gotten used to plundering after a battle. How do we keep them from treating the French the way they've treated the Spanish?"

"My understanding is that when New Orleans surrendered the regiment understood that they couldn't plunder the city," the colonel replied.

"That's true," said Captain McIntyre, the only other man in the mess who'd been present at New Orleans' surrender. "But it took flogging two men to convince the others that Colonel Whiteside really meant no looting."

"He only had to flog two men?" Colonel Lancaster asked, as if he didn't believe what he was hearing.

"Yes, sir," Captain McIntyre continued, "but you have to realise that in the two years between the regiment's formation and our capture of New Orleans, only two men had been flogged and that they'd each received only twenty-five lashes."

"How'd Whiteside enforce discipline?" Captain Sheridan asked.

"In those days the Virginians were all enthusiastic volunteers," McIntyre replied. "We maintained discipline the way the French Army does, with promotions and encouragement rather than punishment. Watson here was one of the men promoted first to corporal, then to sergeant."

"Watson, do you agree with Captain McIntyre's version of events?" the colonel asked.

"Yes, sir," I responded. "The regiment had very high morale in those days, and our victory at New Orleans, even though it cost us dearly, was vindication of our abilities."

"And the men we have now don't live up to that standard?"

I didn't know how to answer that question. I didn't think the recruits that joined the regiment in the past few years had the same spirit as the thousand who first mustered at Fort Roanoke, but I knew that wasn't what the colonel wanted to hear. Captain McIntyre came to my rescue.

"With respect, Colonel, a comparison is not possible. The mission the Virginians were given in 1806 involved them marching off on their own into a thousand miles of wilderness. Now the regiment is part of the Light Division, which is part of Lord Wellington's Army."

"I don't understand what you're trying to tell me, Mr McIntyre, but I'll not push you on the subject," the colonel said in a friendly manner. I breathed a silent sigh of relief.

A few nights later, the topic switched to the fate of the French Army. In August and September 1813, the French had fought a series of great battles in Germany against the alliance of nations opposing them. Besides Russia, Prussia, and Austria, the alliance now included Sweden and Sardinia, though the latter only fought the French in Italy. The allies manoeuvred Dumouriez into a defensive position around the city of Leipzig, then crushed his army with a series of attacks. The French lost seventy thousand killed, wounded, or taken prisoner. Dumouriez lost another ninety thousand men when his garrisons at Dresden and Danzig were forced to surrender. These numbers were so large as to be incomprehensible. French losses were twice the size of the British-Portuguese army Wellington commanded.

Our allies followed up their victory at Leipzig by driving the French Army back to the Rhine, the border of France. Then the politicians took over. Russia and Prussia wanted to invade France immediately, but Austria worried that this would leave Russia in control of Europe. As I found out much later, Britain also worried about Russian power, and was willing to make peace with France provided that it gave Flanders and the Netherlands their freedom. I'm glad I didn't know at the time how cynical our government could be. How could I live with the deaths of Jackson and so many other good men if Dumouriez was allowed to retain power?

The political manoeuvring came to nought. Dumouriez rejected compromise and set about to rebuild his army yet again. He'd been elected President-for-Life in 1804. The vote was more than a thousand to one in Dumouriez's favour, so lopsided that none of us in Davidson's Fort could believe that it had been a fair election. That ballot gave Dumouriez the powers of a dictator, but until now he'd been careful to pay lip service to the revolutionaries' concept of democracy. He submitted his proposals and actions for approval by the Senate, which unfailingly supported him. But in November the Senate had the temerity to criticise him for his conduct of the war. He responded in a fury, abolishing the Senate and saying that he alone represented the best interests of the French people.

Dumouriez could do as he pleased because Fouché, his Minister of Police, had built an elaborate network of spies that had infiltrated every village and town in France. Anyone speaking out openly against Dumouriez would either be publically tried as an anti-revolutionary, subject to a death sentence, or killed without the formality of a trial. Fouché's spies did not see apprehending men who avoided the levee en masse, or farmers who refused to pay their taxes as part of their role. Their only function was to protect Dumouriez. Other crimes were the province of the national police, who also reported to Fouché, but received much less of his attention.

French prisoners and deserters told us that the French countryside was slowly deteriorating into anarchy, as had occurred after the 1789 Revolution. I didn't know how much of these tales to believe. The French could've been saying that just to curry favour with us.

Whatever the truth about the situation in the French countryside, the French Army hadn't given up. In mid-February, Wellington launched an attack that split the French forces in two. Half retreated behind Bayonne's walls, where they were besieged. The rest retreated east until Soult established a defensive position on a five-hundred-foot high ridge above the town of Orthez. The ridge had three spurs, separated by marshy areas, which were impassable due to the recent rains. The French repulsed the marquess' first attack, on the rightmost ridge. His Lordship then sent the Light Division up the middle spur, the site of remains of a Roman fortification. We were successful, splitting the French line. The Second Division was then able to attack the French flank, and the Third Division what remained of the French centre. Soult, seeing his lines crumble, ordered his men to withdraw. This would have been the perfect time for the cavalrymen of the Household Guard to ride down the retreating French and inflict a coup de grâce, but because of the wet, uneven terrain, only the Seventh Hussars were able to mount an effective charge. They took two hundred prisoners. Those of us who'd been sceptical of the value of these picture book soldiers saw no reason to change our opinion.

Wellington was slightly injured in the battle. A canister shot hit his sword hilt, bruising him so badly that he was unable to ride for a week. One can only wonder how history might have been changed had that shot inflicted a more serious wound. After an almost unbroken string of victories, the marquess had developed an aura of invincibility. Our army had other capable generals—Hill and Beresford come to mind—but they couldn't command the respect

Wellington did. Would our army follow either of them the way it was willing to follow Wellington?

After Orthez, Soult fell back to Toulouse, the site of Wellington's final battle. The city is on a peninsula formed by the River Garonne and its tributary, the River Ers. Within this peninsula, east of the city itself, Calvinet Ridge—two-and-a-half-miles long and six-hundred-feet high—forms a natural redoubt. Half of the French Army was arrayed atop this ridge and would have to be dislodged by brute force. The rest of the French Army was in defensive positions north and south of the city. The narrowness of the peninsula left little room to manoeuvre around them. To add to the marquess' problems, the Garonne was five-hundred-feet wide and in spring flood.

On 4th April, our army began crossing the Garonne, north of Toulouse, using a temporary bridge built by our sappers. The bridge swept away after twenty thousand men —half our army, including the Light Division—had crossed. Had the French attacked, they could have overwhelmed us, but they didn't. It took the sappers three days to get the bridge back in place, and for the rest of our army to cross.

On Easter Sunday, 10th April 1814, Wellington attacked. His plan was for the Third Division to make a diversionary attack north of the city, but Picton, their general, disobeyed orders and attacked in full strength. The Third was beaten back with heavy casualties.

The rest of our army marched around to the east to attack Calvinet Ridge. Two divisions took position to attack the north end of the ridge, then waited until the rest of the army could get in place. As they marched our gunners exchanged fire with the French. The two divisions left behind thought the battle had begun and attacked. They, too, were beaten back with heavy casualties. Eventually, the rest of our army got into position. They attacked and after a long afternoon of fighting, drove the French from the ridge. The rest of the French Army abandoned its defensive potions and retreated north.

The Light Division played no part in the Battle of Toulouse. We were held in reserve north of the city, then, in the late afternoon, ordered to march east and south to support the attack on Calvinet Ridge. The fighting was over before we arrived. By now, no member of the regiment was sorry that we hadn't take part in the battle, even if it meant we didn't share in what little plunder there was. We'd fought enough, bled enough, to be spared this final ordeal.

Toulouse was a victory, but a very costly one. Wellington lost over four thousand men, more than the French and nearly a tenth of his army. Soult had withdrawn on good order and we worried that he might counter-attack. The Light Division was ordered to establish a ring of picquets around the army.

What made Toulouse most painful was that it was unnecessary. Earlier that year, whilst we were fighting our way through southern France, the Russians and their allies fought a series of battles against Dumouriez in eastern France. Their sheer numbers overwhelmed the French Army. On 30th March, they entered Paris. The city surrendered on 1st April. Dumouriez and what remained of his army were in Fontainebleau, thirty miles to the south. At first he issued a defiant statement promising to retake Paris, but he soon realised the hopelessness of his situation. On 6th April he surrendered to a delegation of high-ranking Russian, Prussian, and Austrian officers.

News of Dumouriez's surrender didn't reach Wellington until the night of 12th April, after the Battle of Toulouse. He informed Soult, who refused to believe that his commander had capitulated, but agreed to a truce. Some time over the next few days, Soult learned that Wellington had told him the truth. He surrendered on 17th April. My war was over.

CHAPTER 32

The war against France came to an end on 26th April, when Bayonne surrendered. Dumouriez, Brissot, Carnot, and the other surviving members of the Revolutionary Council were prisoners of our allies. The Paris mob beat Fouché, the hated Minister of Police, to death, fitting justice for the many times he'd stirred them to violence.

The Virginians had enlisted for the duration of the war. When the French surrendered, we wanted to return home. But our orders were to stay in Toulouse to suppress the bandits terrorising the countryside. Most were former French soldiers who had no alternative to theft as a way to survive. We marched through the countryside, but our movements were so obvious that we had no success in capturing any of the brigands. Had we been allowed to use our backwoods skills, I'm sure we would've done a better job.

Whilst we were fighting the French, I'd made an effort not to worry about my future, but to concentrate on surviving. With the war over, I could no longer avoid thinking about what lay ahead for me. I couldn't see going to a place where I didn't know anyone. This left me two choices. The first was to return to Davidson's Fort, the nearest thing I had to a home. I felt I'd redeemed myself from the crime I'd committed by embezzling money from Mr Henderson, my employer for eighteen years, to pay my gambling debts. I'd repaid with interest the money I'd stolen from him. I knew from my conversation with Victor Ashe that no one in Davidson's Fort believed the story I'd told, that I'd joined the Virginians because I wanted some adventure in my life, but I was confident that the real reason was still a secret. I believed that if I returned to Davidson's Fort as a sergeant, I'd be unable to avoid questions about why I joined the army. But, if somehow, I returned as an officer, I'd be able to deflect them. I thought that I'd never be promoted to captain, but I harboured a hope that I might be promoted to lieutenant.

My other choice was New York City, where my sister Charlotte, brother-in-law Phillip, their children, and grandchildren lived. I'd also had a brother, Richard, but as I learned from one of the few letters I received from Charlotte, he died shortly after my last visit in 1808. Richard and his wife, Amanda, had seemed wealthy. They lived in a fine house in the best part of the city, but when Richard died, the truth came out. His house and trappings of wealth were funded by borrowed money. His creditors wanted immediate repayment. Amanda appealed to her family for help, but they spurned her. She was left penniless, living on the charity Charlotte and Phillip provided.

After visiting New York in 1796, I'd decided that I could never live with the crowds, stink, and rush of the city. I felt so strongly about this that as much as I wanted to marry Judy Slater, I could not accept her condition that we live in New York or some other big city. My visit with Charlotte and her family in 1808 confirmed that opinion. But if I returned to America as a sergeant, living in New York seemed the lesser of two evils.

In late May, we learned that Wellington had been awarded one final honour—he was now to be known as the Duke of Wellington. We celebrated in the officers' mess by breaking out a bottle of brandy we'd been saving to celebrate our orders to return to North America.

On 15th July, Colonel Lancaster called a meeting of his officers.

"Gentlemen, I have very good news. Our orders are to march to Bordeaux, then embark on the first available transport to America." Though it wasn't correct behaviour for a meeting with our superior officer, we cheered long and loud.

"That's not all," the colonel continued when proper decorum had been re-established. "In recognition for their dedication, the King will grant land in the vicinity of Fort Tennessee to all members of the regiment who have served for two years or longer. Captains will receive four hundred acres; lieutenants, two hundred; sergeants, one hundred; corporals, fifty; and privates, twenty-five. All brevet ranks will be made permanent. However, the King does not want this land to be used for speculation. You will be required to build a house and farm the land for at least two years to receive title to your freehold. There will be no quit rents until you own the land, and ha'penny an acre for the first five years after that."

This news was greeted with stunned silence. Every captain in the room—there were still no lieutenants—could be wealthy, provided he was willing to endure the hardships and dangers of frontier life for at least two years. I could see from the looks on my fellow officers' faces that each was engaged in his own calculation of whether the grant was of sufficient value to be worth accepting.

"Colonel, sir," Captain McIntyre said at last, "I've never heard of Fort Tennessee. Where is it?"

"At a meeting of Indian trails, a place that used to be called French Lick. My understanding is that older members of the regiment are familiar with that locale."

"That we are, sir," Captain McIntyre said. "We built a packhorse path to it from Fort Roanoke, and it was our jumping-off point for our raft trip down the Cumberland, Ohio, and Mississippi Rivers to New Orleans. It's rich land for farming. When do we have to make our decision?"

"You'll have a year from the time you are discharged from the army to appear at Fort Tennessee to claim your land. The land will be distributed on a first-come, first-served basis, so if you choose to accept the King's generosity, it behoves you to do so quickly."

The colonel's references to the King were a polite fiction. We all knew that George III was mad and no longer in control of Britain's affairs. The change in policy had been made by the Prince Regent, or perhaps by some parliamentary official, but it was a curious decision. The Proclamation Line, which encompassed the watersheds of rivers flowing into the Atlantic Ocean, had been the western limit of settlement for the past fifty years. White men were free to cross the line to hunt or to trade with the natives, but only men living with their Indian families in established villages could build houses west of it. The tribes were only too happy to help the British Army destroy any illegal settlement.

Whilst the reason for removing the restriction on settlement was unclear, the choice of the Virginians to be the first settlers was obvious. It was a practice going back to the Romans, who settled old legionnaires in frontier areas to assist their army in retaining control.

"Sir," I said, "Fort Tennessee is across the Proclamation Line, on land promised to the Cherokee. They won't take kindly to our settling on it and will probably attack us. Are there sufficient soldiers to defend us?"

"My understanding, Watson, is that the fort normally houses a company of light infantry and two squadrons of cavalry. The Virginians will be expected to help defend their property. When you take up your land grant, you'll be issued a Baker rifle and will be able to draw ammunition from the fort for this purpose. If needed, you could withdraw to the fort for safety. I am assured that there is now a good road from Fort Roanoke to Fort Tennessee, and that reinforcements could be provided within two months. Fort Tennessee should be able to hold out against the Cherokee for much longer than that."

The detail with which the colonel answered my question made it clear that the army had been involved in planning this change. That was some comfort, but still didn't indicate why the decision had been made to settle Tennessee and, I assumed, other areas west of the Proclamation Line. Were the Virginians to be pawns in some global chess game? If so, who was our opponent?

Captain McIntyre was quick to pick up on the colonel's use of *you* rather than *we*. "I take it from your last statement that you will not be accompanying us to Tennessee."

"Correct, McIntyre. You and the rest of the regiment are fencibles, committed to serve only for the duration of the war. My commission is in the British Army. I serve at the King's pleasure, until I sell my commission, or am allowed to retire. I'll march with you to Bordeaux, then return to England for my next posting. It has been my pleasure to be your commander for the past five years, but I have no desire to return to North America."

The land we would be settling was part of Louisiana, the vast watershed of the Mississippi River. The French claimed this area in 1682, but in 1762, as they were about to lose a war to Britain, the French gave Louisiana to Spain in hopes that this would keep the land out of British hands. Their ploy was only partially successful. Britain took the part of Louisiana east of the Mississippi, but left the western part and New Orleans, the only town of any size in the sprawling colony, under Spanish control. Pitt the Elder, who was Prime Minister at the time, argued that ruling western Louisiana, which was full of hostile Indians, would cost more than it was worth.

In 1800 a much stronger France took back what remained of its gift to Spain. Britain could not allow the French to use Louisiana as a base from which to threaten its North American colonies. The Virginians were formed and given orders to eject the French from New Orleans and St Louis, their other foothold on the Mississippi.

As I have already related, the Virginians successfully carried out this mission, but at a cost of two in five of our number, over four hundred men, dead either in battle or from disease. After our victory at New Orleans, the Virginians were assured that the land we'd conquered for King George III would remain British forever. But as they had done for the past fifty years, the King and Parliament prohibited white men from settling in Louisiana, leaving the land to the Indian tribes. The only exception made was for French and Spanish settlers who'd established themselves before we took control.

Now the rules were about to change. Those of us in the Virginians who took our land grants would be the first legal British settlers west of the Proclamation Line. I had no doubt that more would follow, but how many and how quickly? Would these later settlers be given land grants as we had, or would they have to purchase their land from the Crown?

I had no difficulty deciding to accept the land grant. It would save me from having to live in New York City. I'd been frugal and amassed over a hundred pounds from my pay, the money I'd taken from Captain Pettit's body, the recruiting bonuses I'd earned, the plunder I'd collected, and the nearly twenty ponds that O'Malley had given me for helping guard the treasure in Spanish coins he'd been able to plunder. It was more than enough to begin a new life in Tennessee with all the tools I'd need to start a farm. Before I could claim my four hundred acres, I'd have to find a wife. A man couldn't start a successful farm without a woman's help. As usual when faced with such a problem, I consulted Samuel Smith.

"Are you going to take your land grant?" I asked him a week after the colonel's announcement.

"I think not. I'm only a corporal and fifty acres is not a big induce-ment. I'll be fifty-nine by the time we get back to America, too old to be starting anew on the frontier. I've enough money to repay my debts and invest in a business venture. I'll go back to Williamsburg and do what I can to re-establish my old life."

Samuel had joined the Virginians to avoid debtor's prison after his business partner absconded with the proceeds from a trad-ing expedition, leaving him to face their creditors. He was only seven years my senior and it was difficult for me to think of him as old. But what he said about his age was equally true for me. I was probably too old to start over again on the frontier, and I had enough money to try something other than shopkeeping. But try as I might, nothing else came to mind. Fur trading, my other skill, was no longer practised as I'd learned it. The Indians in Tennessee and Kentucky had no reason to hunt. To keep the peace the army gave them all they needed to survive. Fur trading was still pursued west of the Mississippi from depots in St Louis and New Orleans, but the hostility of the Indian tribes and the long distances involved made it a difficult and dangerous occupation. Farming in Tennessee would be easier and far safer.

We were silent for a few moments, then Samuel asked, "Will you take the grant?"

"I'd like to, but I need to find a wife."

"Yes, you do. A man can't survive on the frontier alone."

"But how am I going to find one?"

"That's simple. Place an ad in a newspaper. Say you're a returning soldier with a four-hundred-acre land grant. There'll be so many women at your doorstep you'll have to chase them away with a stick."

Samuel was right. Men seeking wives placed ads in newspapers all the time, but I was revolted by the idea. I'd loved two women in my life, Jenny and Awinita, and asked a third, Judy Slater, to marry me. In each situation I'd known the woman well and could envision what life with her would be like. Having some woman I'd never met respond to an ad and say she was willing to marry me was not something I could comprehend. I thanked Samuel and said that I would give his suggestion serious thought. It was a lie, but a small one, and well justified for the sake of friendship.

To my surprise, most of my fellow officers decided against taking the land grant. As Captain Moss put it, "Now that the war is over, there should be many opportunities for a returning hero. Why spend two years in the wilderness for only four hundred acres of land?" I didn't know what kind of opportunities he was referring to. I wondered whether he would use his officer status for something unethical.

Captain McIntyre was the only officer who seemed uncertain about the land grant. He refused to say whether or not he'd take it, and didn't want to discuss the subject. He'd been a company commander in the Virginians for as long as the regiment had existed. He'd bought his commission a few weeks after Jackson had, and with Jackson dead, he was the longest serving member of the regiment. I knew him to be a fair, thoughtful man.

The Virginians spent two weeks preparing to march. The paymasters wanted an accounting for every piece of equipment that had been issued to us to tally against their records. Stoppages were assessed against men who had lost any of their personal kit, but accounting for the regiment's equipment was much more difficult. Some of it had been lost in battle and some had been misplaced. Once we had satisfied the paymasters we took another two weeks to march the nearly two hundred miles from Toulouse to Bordeaux. Had we travelled that slowly whilst fighting the French, we probably would've never made it out of Portugal.

Colonel Lancaster left us in Bordeaux. He turned the regiment over to Captain McIntyre, who now was senior captain.

Ships to transport us across the Atlantic arrived three weeks later. We sailed for Hampton Roads on Friday, 9th September and arrived there after a six-week voyage. Travelling as an officer was a great improvement. I shared a small cabin on deck with Captain Sheridan, not a hold below deck with hundreds of unwashed soldiers. I had wine and brandy to drink, not grog. But officer or not, some things didn't change. After a few days, when the fresh food ran out, we ate salt meat and biscuit, much the same fare as our men, and I had to spend several hours doing the missionary walk to keep my bowels working.

France had been first England's then Britain's traditional enemy for centuries. We'd prevailed over them many times, only to have them rise up a few years later to challenge us once more. I couldn't help feeling that this would happen again, but the France we left was a country with an uncertain future.

When Dumouriez and the Revolutionary Council were deposed, few called for the reinstatement of the King. Louis XVIII, the heir to the throne, was an uninspiring figure. He only seemed interested in eating and regularly over-indulged, such as the time he was reported to have eaten a hundred oysters at a single sitting. He was a corpulent man, who waddled rather than walked. Also, twenty-five years of revolutionary rule had left the French with little taste for a monarchy. The leaders of the revolution had amassed great wealth and lived as lavishly as any royal court, but they'd been careful to avoid taking noble titles. They still referred to themselves as *citoyens*, and could be addressed as such by any man.

The man chosen to lead the new French Republic was Marie-Joseph Paul Yves Roch Gilbert du Motier, Marquis de LaFayette, who now called himself *Citoyen* du Motier. He was a member of the nobility, but had established his revolutionary credentials in 1775, when as a young officer in the French Army, he first heard about the Great Rebellion. At the time he wrote, "My heart was enlisted and I thought only of joining the colours." He made contact with rebel agents in Paris, but the rebellion ended before he could join it.

Du Motier was elected to represent the nobility from his district in the Estates General that Louis XVI was forced to convene in 1789 when the French treasury ran out of credit and could no longer borrow. He quickly aligned himself with the assembly's revolutionary bloc, and in July was named commander-in-chief of the National Guard, the revolutionary army that controlled Paris and its environs. He attempted to maintain order, even to the extent of firing on an unruly mob of *sans-culottes*. This angered the Jacobins, who controlled the government at that time, and in August 1791, they forced du Motier to resign. The timing was propitious, since it avoided a confrontation with Dumouriez, who, in 1792, led the French Army in its suppression of the National Guard.

Dumouriez didn't trust du Motier and never allowed him to play a significant role in the revolutionary hierarchy. He was appointed military commander for Auvergne, his home province in south-central France, where his main responsibility was to ensure that it supplied its quota of men to the army. Du Motier did this fairly and, unlike so many of his peers, did not accept bribes to keep men out of the army. The citoyens of Auvergne complained bitterly about the military draft, but they respected their marquis.

After Dumouriez's fall, the French looked for a man who had strong revolutionary credentials as well as a commitment to maintaining order. Du Motier was the obvious choice. Even though he was not a member, the Senate elected him its president, which effectively made him ruler of France. He promised to restore order and to convene a convention to write a new constitution. Neither event occurred during the first months of his reign. The Senate, which had been unanimous in their support for him, was growing restive, and there was open talk of yet another rebellion. No one had emerged as a leader for such a rebellion, but it seemed only a matter of time before that happened. Would a new leader of France seek revenge for the defeat we had just inflicted on his country? If he did, how would it affect me? We discussed these questions in the officers' mess, but couldn't answer them.

We had only one more duty after landing in Virginia, a triumphal parade through Williamsburg on 29th October. After that we were all eager to be on our separate ways, but there was the inevitable delay whilst discharge orders were written for us. We were housed in a small barracks on the outskirts of town.

Captain McIntyre approached me the day after our parade. "Do you still plan to accept the land grant?" he asked.

"I do, sir."

"William, you don't have to address me as sir any longer. You're now my equal."

"Old habits are hard to break," I said, embarrassed by my gaffe. "And your plans?"

"I've decided to take up my land grant, but I have to find a wife first."

"I have the same problem."

"Perhaps we could travel to Tennessee together?" McIntyre asked. "We could meet at Ingles Tavern outside Fort Roanoke."

"That makes sense. It would be safer than travelling alone. When shall we meet?"

"Would the first of April be agreeable? Any later and we might get to Tennessee too late for planting."

"The first of April it is," I said.

Meeting McIntyre that early wouldn't leave me much time to find a wife, but I'd already decided to begin my search at Davidson's Fort. It wouldn't take long. There couldn't be too many choices in the village. I was painfully aware that I had no second plan if I was unsuccessful there.

It took nearly a month for the Virginians to be disbanded. We had already accounted for all of our equipment, but now we had to clean and package it for storage. Each man's accounts had to be brought up to date and he had to be given his back pay, less accumulated stoppages. It was a frustrating time, but our complaints seemed only to further slow the process.

Whilst we were winding down the Virginians' affairs, nearly forty men, including John Sevier, asked either Captain McIntyre or me whether they could travel with us to Tennessee. We welcomed all, even the two men we knew to be potential troublemakers. The first, Stanley Jamison, was a bully and a barracks-room barrister, who was always looking for ways to twist situations to his benefit. During my stint as brevet commander of the First Company after Ciudad Rodrigo, I had to adjudicate Jamison's protest over a stoppage for a damaged knapsack. I judged that he should pay the stoppage. I was certain he still remembered the incident and harboured ill feelings against me. The second, Thomas Stimson, didn't seem inherently malevolent, but he was in Jamison's thrall and followed him like a faithful dog. McIntyre and I discussed these two and concluded that since all that was involved was the trip to Tennessee, we could keep them under control. We didn't think about what would happen once we got there. Neither of us had any sense of what would be involved in establishing a new settlement.

I was discharged from the army on 19th December 1814, having served for nine years and two months. I was given two pieces of paper, the first attesting that I'd served honourably and attained the rank of captain; the second stating that I was entitled to claim four hundred acres of Crown land in the vicinity of Fort Tennessee at any time during the next twelve months.

A new phase of my life was starting, and even though I was nearly fifty-two years old, I was as uncertain as a boy. Would I be able to find a wife, and if I did, would I be able to start a farm in the wilderness? If I couldn't, would I be condemned to spend the rest of my life as a shopkeeper? But, like a boy, I thought I could overcome any challenge. I'd survived the war that killed or invalided more than nine out of ten of the Virginians who first mustered at Fort Roanoke. I'd risen from private to captain, an achievement unmatched by any other Virginian. I faced the future with hope and confidence.

TRANSCRIBER'S POSTSCRIPT

Britain's war against Revolutionary France, our nation's longest in modern times, lasted from 1793 to 1814. In many respects the first fourteen years of this war were a stalemate. The French controlled a growing portion of the European continent, but Britain controlled the seas around that continent. Britain was unwilling to raise a large enough army to challenge the French on land, and the French could not build a fleet strong enough to break the Royal Navy's dominance.

The strategic situation began to change in 1807, when Britain dispatched an army to help the Portuguese, who at that time were our country's only European ally. For the first time in the war, Britain committed to maintaining an army on the European continent. It took many years for that army to prevail. The Duke of Wellington—arguably Britain's greatest general—won battle after battle, but he could not convert those victories into a decisive defeat of France. Feeding his army was the duke's constant challenge, and he often had to retreat back to Portugal, where he could be supplied by the Royal Navy.

Historians now argue that it was the loss of revolutionary fervour—not Wellington's military genius—that led to France's ultimate defeat. There is more than a little truth in that assertion, which can be demonstrated in two ways. The first was in resistance to the levee en masse, which required all unmarried men to serve in the army. Until 1813, men reported on schedule. Not all were needed and some were sent back to their farms and villages. After his 1812 defeat in Russia, Dumouriez needed to quickly rebuild his army. Men who'd previously been excused from the levee were now conscripted, along with those who turned twenty-one that year. But with service in the French Army looking more like a death sentence than an opportunity for glory, men began doing everything they could to avoid becoming soldiers. Some hid; others injured themselves. Dumouriez was able to raise the numbers of soldiers he needed, but they were a sullen, poorly trained mass, not the enthusiastic, well-trained army that had carried the revolutionaries' banner across Europe. The best measure of an army's morale is its rate of desertion, and far more French soldiers deserted in late 1813 and early 1814 than had earlier in the war

The second indicator of loss of revolution fervour was the unwillingness of the French to pay the higher taxes that Dumouriez had to levy. As long as the French Army was adding new territories to the revolutionaries' domain—territories that could be systematically plundered to enrich France—French taxes could be kept low. But in 1809, when the French Army could no longer conquer new lands, the revolutionaries had to begin raising taxes. By the end of 1813, French taxes were as high as they had been before the revolution, and the French people reacted the same way as they had in 1789—they refused to pay. Only Dumouriez's defeat at the hands of the Russians and their allies prevented another revolution.

Whilst loss of revolutionary fervour may have contributed to France's defeat, a far more reasonable explanation is that the French lost because they had to fight on two fronts, facing armies whose combined size was larger than theirs. You've already read Watson's account of the Duke of Wellington's advance from Portugal, through Spain, into southern France. He tells in passing how the Russians, Prussians, and Austrians attacked France from the east and captured Paris, forcing Dumouriez to surrender. The Russians and their allies may not have had a general as brilliant as Wellington, but they had numbers. In their final battles in 1814, they were able to field twice as many soldiers as the French. No amount of revolutionary fervour or good leadership can overcome such odds.

A widely accepted myth has grown up over the past two centuries that the soldiers in Wellington's Army were idlers and petty criminals, who only joined the army for drink or to escape gaol. The duke, and many after him, characterised them as the scum of the Earth. But, as modern historians have shown, most British Army recruits were driven to enlist by economic hardship. No doubt a few were given the choice that Sergeant Pew faced, enlist or be transported as a prisoner to North America, or in later times to Australia, but they were a minority. Even Watson's enlistment could be chalked up to economic necessity. He'd embezzled money from his employer, Leonard Henderson, who fired him, but stopped short of reporting the crime to the authorities. Watson was left unemployed and nearly penniless. His situation wasn't much different from that of Noah McClellan and Joshua Emerson, the two unemployed weavers he recruited in Williamsburg.

The British Army in Spain earned a well-deserved reputation for drunkenness, looting, and thievery. Much of this behaviour was driven by the harsh conditions British soldiers faced. If they drank themselves into oblivion whenever they could, it was to ease the pain they felt. If they stole food, or money for food, it was because Wellington's Commissary Corps could not reliably provide them with rations. And, as modern scholarship has shown, when they did get their rations, they were insufficient to provide the calories needed to march and fight. One study showed that Venetian galley slaves were fed better than British soldiers in Spain.

By the standards of the times, British soldiers were restrained. They had some hope of getting rations, whilst the French had to live off the land. Their behaviour towards women, whilst not always exemplary, was far better than the French. I don't wish to be seen as an apologist for Wellington's soldiers, but it isn't reasonable to judge them by the standards applied to today's soldiers.

That said, not all of the British Army's behaviour in Spain can be explained. As Watson documents, the rape and pillage after the fall of Badajoz was unprecedented and inexcusable. Many blame Wellington for not bringing the situation under control more quickly, as he did after the capture of Ciudad Rodrigo. But blaming Wellington does not address a fundamental question: Why did his army go on such a violent rampage? The conventional answer is the horror of the battle. I am unwilling to accept this answer. Badajoz was horrible, but not that different from the assault on Ciudad Rodrigo or the failed assault on Burgos—a battle Watson doesn't describe because he didn't take part in it. It will take a far more astute student of human behaviour than I to explain why Badajoz was in a class by itself.

When I first read Watson's manuscript, I couldn't believe the story he told about Generalissimo Francisco de Miranda. I thought: at last, Watson is embellishing the truth. But I was wrong. Francisco de Miranda was a real person, who travelled the world promoting Venezuelan independence. Joaquin Segovia's biography, *La Vida de Francisco de Miranda*, published in English translation in 1998, recounts all the incidents in de Miranda's life that Watson mentioned and documents the Virginians' expedition to Venezuela. Other histories of Venezuela also tell about de Miranda and the Virginians expedition, but in less detail than Segovia does.

In the mid-nineteenth century, when William Watson wrote his autobiography, spelling was still more of an art than a science. His manuscript contains many words that look misspelled, but probably were acceptable when he wrote them. I've changed these words to modern North American English spelling. However, I made an exception for the name Bussaco, the Virginians' most complete victory during their four years as part of the Duke of Wellington's Army. The modern spelling of this name is Busaco, but this is often mispronounced as if it had only two syllables—Bus-aco. Watson's spelling, with two s's, encourages the proper three syllable pronunciation—Bu-sah-co.

At the end of this book, Watson tells the reader that he has a four-hundred-acre land grant in Tennessee, but has to find a wife before he can take advantage of it. To find out how he found a wife and became the leader of the first legal British settlement west of the Appalachian Mountains, read *Settling Tennessee: Book Three of The Autobiography of William Watson*.

READ ON FOR AN EXCERPT FROM

Settling Tennessee

BOOK THREE OF
THE AUTOBIOGRAPHY
OF WILLIAM WATSON

LENNY BERNSTEIN

KIMBERLY CREST BOOKS • ASHEVILLE, NC

CHAPTER 1

The war against the French revolutionaries ended on 26th April 1814, but I wasn't discharged from the army until 19th December. I'd been a soldier for nine years and two months. I was given my back pay, less accumulated stoppages, and two documents. The first attested that I'd served honourably in the King's Own Virginians and attained the rank of captain. The second stated that, as a captain, I had the right to claim four hundred acres of crown land in the vicinity of Fort Tennessee any time during the next year.

The Virginians, as our regiment was usually called, were American rifleman who'd volunteered to fight the French revolutionaries. For the past four years we'd been part of the Duke of Wellington's Light Division, fighting in Portugal, Spain, and France. We were used mostly as skirmishers and long-range marksmen. Our skill drew grudging respect from the rest of the army, even if we were only colonials. As a reward for our service, all Virginians who'd served honourably for at least two years were given land grants. Captains got four hundred acres; lieutenants, two hundred; sergeants, a hundred; corporals, fifty; and privates, twenty-five. We'd pay nothing for the land and no quit rents until we owned it, then only a ha'penny an acre for the first five years afterwards. But we had to live on our land for two years and build a house before we would get title to it. This meant I had to find a wife before setting out for Tennessee. A man couldn't build a farm on the frontier alone.

For fifty years Britain had prohibited white settlement on land west the Appalachian Mountains. Why change such a long-standing policy? Two theories have been advanced. First, that Parliament needed to raise money to pay the debt Britain had incurred in its war with the French revolutionaries, and that the Virginians would be followed by settlers who had to pay for their land and would be assessed higher taxes. Second, that since there were thousands of French and Spanish already living west of the mountains, Britain needed to people that land with settlers whose loyalty could be trusted. Whatever the reason for the change, choosing the Virginians to be the first settlers was no surprise. It was a practice going back to the Romans, who colonised their frontier areas with retired legionnaires.

Even thought I was fifty-one, I was excited as a boy about starting this new phase of my life. But first I had the melancholy duty of saying goodbye to Samuel Smith. On the day we were discharged, I found him in our temporary barracks in Williamsburg, packing his belongings into a small trunk.

"Where will you go?" I asked.

"I'll stay with my friend Jacques Defoe here in Williamsburg until I can get settled. Why don't you join us until you're ready to leave? You've met Jacques and I'm certain he'll put you up."

"I wouldn't want to impose . . . there's no hope of convincing you to come to Tennessee?" I asked, in what I thought was a jovial tone.

"I'm afraid not," Samuel replied. "I've saved enough money to pay my debts and be able to invest in a trading venture. I'll be much more careful in choosing a partner this time. Besides, I'm too old for life on the frontier."

Samuel looked old. What little hair he had was white and his years of service in the army had left him stooped. He didn't look strong enough to carve a farm out of the wilderness.

"You're only seven years older than me," I said.

"Yes, but I can hear my joints creak when I get out of bed in the morning."

"Can we write to each other?"

"I'd like that. Let me give you Jacques Defoe's address. If you write to him, your letters will get to me." Samuel found a piece of paper and a pencil and wrote out the address.

"I'll write when I'm settled in Tennessee. Good luck to you Samuel."

"And good luck to you, William. Find a pretty young wife."

We shook hands and parted company.

I'd first met Samuel nearly forty years earlier when he was captain of the company my father and I joined during the Great Rebellion. I served as his messenger. He was taken prisoner at the Battle of Brooklyn, the battle in which my father was killed. I lost track of him for the next thirty years until I saw him at Fort Roanoke, shortly after I joined the Virginians. Samuel had joined the Virginians to avoid debtor's prison after his business partner absconded with the proceeds from a trading expedition, leaving him to face their creditors. Our duties brought us together and he became a close friend, the first I'd had since I was a boy.

Saying goodbye to John Sevier who'd also become my friend, was much easier, since he'd decided to take his land grant and we expected to see each other in a few months. John had joined the Virginians in 1809. By that time I was a sergeant and it wouldn't have been proper for me to enquire about a recruit's background. I was supposed to judge the men in my company on the way they performed their duties and nothing else. Other than saying he'd been in the Virginia Militia during the Great Rebellion, but hadn't seen any combat, John never provided the slightest hint about his former life. It was almost as if he'd been born the day he joined the Virginians. But I soon came to appreciate his sharp insights about the war we were fighting. He could usually deduce what Wellington's strategy would be and why. John was obviously educated—he may even have been to university—and well read.

John was a large man, who several times demonstrated great strength, despite his age. He had a broad forehead and wide-spaced eyes, which made him look rather homely. His solemn demeanour—he rarely, if ever, smiled—did nothing to improve his appearance. He was sixty-three, older than Samuel, but his years in the Virginians hadn't aged him. He'd decided to take his land grant, and seemed to have no concerns about finding a wife.

John and I said our farewells, shook hands, and promised to meet at Ingles Tavern at Fort Roanoke. The forty Virginians who planned to take their land grants had agreed to meet there by 1st April and travel together to Tennessee. Captain McIntyre would be the only other officer in the group.

I'd decided to start my search for a wife at Davidson's Fort, the westernmost settlement in North Carolina. I'd lived there for eighteen years before being forced to join the army, when my employer, Leonard Henderson, discovered that I'd been embezzling money from him to pay my gambling debts. I had no second plan if I failed to find a wife in the town.

I spent the remaining two weeks of the year in Williamsburg, purchasing a horse, saddle, rifle, and the supplies I would need for my trip to Davidson's Fort. I left on Monday, 2nd January, a cold, clear day. There had been a light snow three days earlier, traces of which were still visible. I wore my uniform, though there was no need to. I told myself that it would save wear on the one set of clothes I had from the days before I joined the army, but looking back, I think it was vanity. I wanted everyone to know that I'd been a captain in the British Army and to be accorded the deference and respect my position deserved.

My first destination was Salisbury. I'd lived in the town for two years as a young man, earning my keep first as a fur trader, then as a clerk in Amos Cartwright's general store. I fell in love with Amos' daughter, Jenny. We'd planned to marry. Instead, only four months before our wedding, I stupidly went off with Josiah Terrill on one last fur-trading expedition. I was gone for six years—four years as a prisoner of the Spanish, then another two whilst I lived with the Cherokee. With the fecklessness of youth, I reasoned that Jenny must have given me up for dead and that I was free to marry Awinita, a beautiful Cherokee woman I'd become besotted with. She died giving birth to our son, a child I couldn't raise. When he was three days old, I turned the boy over to his grandmother. I returned to Salisbury and a confrontation with Amos Cartwright.

Amos told me that I'd left Jenny with child, and that she'd given birth to a son. Despite my disappearance, she kept her promise and named him David after my father. Jenny had assumed that I was dead, married Adam Stahlworth, and was living in Charleston. Amos made me promise not to bother either her or my son, a promise I kept even when David, as an adult, joined the Virginians. He was killed in the assault on New Orleans. I never spoke to him, but I feel his loss to this day.

I no longer had to fear an encounter with Amos or any of the Cartwrights. None of them still lived in Salisbury. Amos had died almost twenty years earlier. Eleanor, Jenny's mother, died shortly afterward. Billy, her brother, inherited the family shop, but was an indifferent merchant who went bankrupt three years later. He moved away, but I didn't know where.

I revelled in the winter beauty of the Virginia countryside. Compared with the jungles of Venezuela or the harsh plains of Spain, it was a rich, gentle land. I enjoyed hearing the familiar cadences of American speech after being surrounded for so many years by French, Spanish, Portuguese, and unfamiliar English accents. I was home, even if I didn't have a house or family to return to. I'd been called an American for many years, but for the first time, I felt it was my proper designation.

There was now a good quality post road from Williamsburg to Salisbury and for about fifty miles west towards Davidson's Fort. The last fifty miles to the village were still only a path full of mud and potholes. A wagon could traverse it, but it would be slow going. The road from Salisbury was still the only one connecting Davidson's Fort to the rest of the world. Before I joined the army, Viscount Haversham, the royal governor of North Carolina, had promised to improve the road, but like many such promises, it was still waiting to be fulfilled.

Davidson's Fort had prospered during my absence. It was larger and could correctly be called a town. More of the houses were painted and there were now clearly defined streets radiating from the fort and green. The trading post that I'd run for eighteen years had been renamed

Henderson's General Store, which more correctly identified its function. It was no longer the only shop in town. I noted a bakery, a butchery, and a combination saddle-and-cobbler's shop around the town green, and soon learned that other businesses were present on the side streets.

John Ashe still presided over Henderson's shop. He was alone when I entered at mid-afternoon. The shop was spotless and the goods displayed in better order than they'd been when I'd been in charge. Ashe was truly the meticulous man I judged him to be when I'd first met him.

"How may I help you, Captain?" he asked when I entered.

"I thought I'd check up on how well you're running my shop," I said jovially.

Ashe was confused for a few moments, then the light dawned. "Is that you, William?"

"It is, despite this disguise."

"Captain . . . that's pretty impressive. How'd you accomplish it?"

"It's too long a story to tell now. It needs at least a pint of ale for even the first chapter."

"The tavern is still in business, and I'm sure your friends from years ago will be happy to see you. You'll be quite the celebrity. May I tell them that you'll be there tonight?"

"You may, but I have a few questions first. Does Mr Henderson still own this shop?"

"Yes, he does. Strange about how he refers to you. For the first few years he didn't mention your name. Then about four years ago he started talking about you as if you were a long-lost son. Do you know why that might be?"

I knew what had prompted the change. Mr Henderson had received the money I'd sent and considered my debt to him paid. I couldn't say anything about this to Ashe, but it was a great relief.

"I can't answer that question, but I'm happy to hear that he holds me in high regard. I'll have to pay him a visit some day. Is his office still in Guilford Courthouse?"

"It is."

"And what about Sergeant Ames? Is he still stationed at the fort?"

"No, he left three or four years ago—I'm not certain about the date."

Another relief. I wouldn't have to face that nemesis.

"What's the business like these days? I see that it's no longer called a trading post."

"Mr Henderson changed the name three years ago, when he put up the new sign. I still do a little trading for ginseng and deerskin, but mostly it's selling goods to the fort and to farm wives. The shop is very profitable."

Then it was Ashe's turn to ask questions. "Is what we've heard about the Virginians getting land grants in Tennessee true?"

"It's true. I have a grant of four hundred acres, but I have to build a house and farm the land for two years before I can receive title to it."

"Are you going to do that?"

"If I can find a wife. I can't do it alone."

"So that's why you've returned to Davidson's Fort."

"Yes, but don't announce it to the town. I'd rather be a little more discrete than posting an ad on the tavern wall."

"I may have a solution to your problem," Ashe said, after stroking his well-trimmed beard for a few moments. "Anne Christian lives on a farm about two miles east of here. Her husband went off to sell whisky to the Indians over a year ago and hasn't returned. There've been rumours that he's living with a Cherokee woman, but most people think he's dead. Anne's a good woman and would make any man a fine wife. I'll be happy to introduce you to her."

"Let me think on that for a while. It's been a long time since I've courted a woman. I need to remember how it's done." Actually, I wanted to find out more about Anne Christian and the story that Ashe had told.

I took a room above the tavern for a week. Mr Soames was now the innkeeper. He'd moved to town after I left. When I went down for supper, I saw that John Ashe had spread the word of my return. Many of my old acquaintances, David Vance and Geoffrey Turner to name two, were already there, and more were entering by the minute. The barroom was soon filled to capacity, and a cluster of men stood in the doorway. I greeted as many of them as I could.

"William," David Vance said at last, in a voice loud enough to silence other conversations, "we've heard about your exploits carrying the message of the Virginians' victory at New Orleans back to Philadelphia, but we want to hear about your other adventures and how you ended up a captain. Soames, give the man a pint and don't let his mug go empty."

"Friends, it's a long story, so I'll not be angry if some of you decide to leave before I'm finished."

A wave of laughter filled the room. I knew from long experience that travellers' tales, especially from people they knew, were the town's main form of entertainment. Even if I talked till dawn, no one would leave. I spoke for nearly two hours, recounting the Virginians' road-building, our trip down the Mississippi, our unsuccessful attack on New Orleans, the town's capitulation, our expedition to Venezuela, and finally our exploits in Portugal, Spain, and France. I left out some of the gruesome details—Captain Bates' treatment of the prisoners building the road to Tennessee and the rape and plunder of Badajoz. I also left out the story of how I was wounded, though I'm certain that everyone present had noted that I walked with a limp, and assumed that it was the result of a wound.

When I finished there was a long round of applause, then a barrage of questions. The first was the same one Ashe had asked—whether it was true that soldiers were being given land grants west of the mountains. I assured them that it was true and that I planned to settle in Tennessee. I left out my search for a wife, but from the looks I received, I suspected that some of the men in the room had surmised that was the reason for my returning to Davidson's Fort.

ACKNOWLEDGMENTS

This book would never have come to be without the help of many people. My thanks to: Tommy Hays and Elizabeth Lutyens and the members of their classes in the Great Smokies Writing Program for teaching me how to write fiction; the members of the Appalachian Roundtable for their critiques of my drafts; Dave Wetmore for sharing his expertise on Revolutionary War era woodcraft and weaponry; Rob Swart for teaching me a bit of Dutch; and my son Neil for teaching me a bit of Latin. I am also indebted to all the historians I read to absorb the details of the first years of the American Revolution and of that era's Cherokee life and customs.

My thanks to my beta readers: Joe Burchfield, Michael Cornn, Marie Hefley, and Kathy Kyle for helping put this story in its final form, and to my production team: Nicole Ayers, copyeditor; Doug Gibson, layout designer; and Elizabeth Hunt, cover artist; for the expertise and effort they contributed to creating this book.

My special thanks to my wife Danny (Danielle), who encouraged me for the seven years it took to bring William Watson's story to life. Danny was the first to read every word of Watson's story. Her comments were invaluable.

ABOUT THE AUTHOR

Lenny Bernstein started writing fiction in 2008. *The Autobiography of William Watson* is his first project. It started as a single book but rapidly grew into a trilogy. Book One, *The Great Rebellion*, was published in 2015.

Lenny earned a Ph.D. in chemical engineering from Purdue University in 1969, then pursued a forty-year industrial career that focused on environmental issues, most notably climate change. He was an author on the UN Intergovernmental Panel on Climate Change's Third and Fourth Assessment Reports, and was recognized as contributing to that organization's winning half the 2007 Nobel Peace Prize—Al Gore won the other half.

Lenny and his wife Danny (Danielle) have lived in Asheville, North Carolina, since 2001. They are avid hikers, who have hiked the full length of the Appalachian Trail, most of the high mountains east of the Mississippi, and trails in Australia, Canada, Europe, and New Zealand. Lenny was President of Carolina Mountain Club, the oldest and largest hiking and trail-maintaining club in Western North Carolina, and held a variety of volunteer leadership positions in the Appalachian Trail Conservancy. Lenny passed away in 2016 after a courageous battle with cancer.

HOW THIS STORY CAME TO BE

I learned about the Revolutionary War in elementary school. I was taught that, while difficult, an American victory over the British was inevitable. It took a visit to Washington's Crossing State Park, Pennsylvania, in the early 1980s, to learn how desperate the Americans were at the end of 1776, and how close the revolution was to collapsing. This raised an obvious question: what if Americans had lost? I conceived of telling this story as the autobiography of an old man named William Watson, who, as a young boy, lived through the failed revolution and its aftermath.

My idea lay dormant for over two decades until I retired in 2008 and had time to develop William Watson's story. I enrolled in the Great Smokies Writing Program (GSWP) where I discovered that before I could interest readers in my story, I had to learn how to write fiction – a very different skill from writing the hundreds of technical reports I'd authored during my career. With the help of GSWP and my fellow authors in the Appalachian Roundtable, I learned enough to write this book, but I'm still learning.

Lenny Bernstein
April 2015

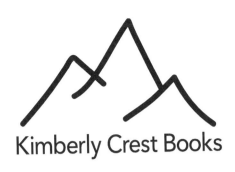

Kimberly Crest Books

AVAILABLE FROM KIMBERLY CREST BOOKS

The Great Rebellion: Book One of The Autobiography of William Watson

Lenny Bernstein

Forests, Alligators, Battlefields: My Journey through the National Parks of the South

Danny Bernstein

COMING SOON

Settling Tennessee: Book Three of The Autobiography of William Watson

Lenny Bernstein

Made in the USA
Columbia, SC
07 October 2017